Writing With A View Books

Tea with *Isabel*

JULIE SNEED WOMACK

Cover design by Deranged Doctor Design
Formatting by Polgarus Studio

For Grandma.

Prologue

I have a soft spot for old Mexican women. In them, I always find a feature that reminds me of Grandma Isabel. The soothing melody of their Spanish tongue sounds so nurturing and maternal, it brings me both comfort and painful longing. Grandma was that one person who was so special to me that I just long for her. We all have one.

My emotional triggers don't totally discriminate. There aren't many Hispanic women in this town, so my subconscious has become very inclusive. I've noticed the fair and freckled hands of the red-headed woman who works the counter at the post office as she handed me my stamps. They were akin to Grandma's tender hands that were wrinkled with years of housework. An elderly Native American smiled at me at the pharmacy, and the deep creases around her eyes crinkled with her sweet disposition and yanked at my heartstrings.

But yesterday when I got out of my car in front of the dry cleaner's, the sense of familiarity in a complete stranger was so uncanny and powerful that I just leaned against my car and watched her. She power-walked by me, a vision in pink, from her visor to her tennis shoes. She clutched her rosary, mumbling a prayer, and her gray curls bounced along as she walked. I should have said hello and enjoyed a moment of conversation with her, but I was too awestruck to act. It transported me back to Grandma's green Formica kitchen table where I was little Nina in pink rosebud jammies.

I often spent the night at Grandma's house. We would sit at that kitchen table with two steaming cups of fragrant chamomile tea, sweet with honey. She would tell me stories about when she was a little girl in Obregón, and I would share my secrets as I grew from a little girl into a young woman— my uncertainty about Santa Claus, the woes of puberty, and who I hoped would ask me to prom. No matter what was going on at the time, sitting at that table made it seem like everything in the world was going to be all right.

Chapter 1

We drive east along Highway 20 as we head towards town. We pass cows grazing in lush green pastures, some taking a morning drink from a misty pond. Luminous rays of sun rise into the rainbow sherbet sky.

Rolled bales of hay are scattered across the flat expanse of land reminiscent of a Van Gogh painting. "The Siesta". "Haystacks". "Haystacks in Provence". Vincent really did appreciate a good tableau of fresh-cut golden hay under a swirling sky. He'd love this.

I pop a Rolaids into my mouth and rub my chest.

Under my bucolic moment of appreciating nature lies a tightness of impending doom. It's always there when I think about Brandon. And underneath everything, I'm always thinking about Brandon.

Not cool, really, when this is my day.

It is silent as we drive. We are observing our peaceful morning ritual in which nobody talks until we get to the first stoplight in town. Otherwise, I would not be granted a quiet moment for deep thoughts about hay… and Brandon.

One morning when Roma had a biology test, she asked that Jane and I stay completely quiet on the drive into school while she reviewed her flashcards on meiosis and mitosis. After that, it stuck. It gives us a chance to get our thoughts together for the day.

I reverently grip my travel mug of strong coffee, another necessary morning rite. I believe I developed a taste for it around age four. With a lifetime of caffeine, it's amazing that I ended up being five nine. When I spent the night at Grandma and Grandpa's house as a kid, they would pour me a few drops of coffee and dilute it with milk and sugar until it was a light beige. Grandma used to call her morning cup of coffee "el primer placer del dia," the first pleasure of the day. I'm with her.

I take a generous swig. I'm exhausted from a night of restless sleep and watching the clock.

As we continue down Highway 20, we enter the city limits of Skiatook, Oklahoma. Just about every restaurant, shop, and church (and there are a lot of churches) has a weathered marquee advertising the daily specials or events in tattered plastic letters. Today, the old-fashioned butcher shop promotes a whole hog dinner. Fern's Frozen Custard and Coneys is advertising pineapple whip frozen custard. I glance in the rearview mirror as Jane's eyes widen with excitement. The marquee in front of the Church of Christ announces the wedding of Belinda Wright and Darryl Farnsley on Saturday at two pm. I guess we're all invited.

The first light turns yellow and we slow to a stop.

"Mommy, can I wear diamonds tonight?" Jane blurts out.

"What?"

"At your party. I want to be extra fancy for you."

Roma rolls her eyes from the passenger seat.

"We'll see," I say.

At six years old, Jane is curious and constantly instigating fun. She's got a cute little dark brown bob with bangs and dark chocolate-brown eyes. Jane's everything country— playing with bugs, riding horses, rescuing injured birds, and digging in the dirt. She's rough-and-tumble like her daddy.

Roma is the opposite. While Jane lives in the moment, Roma is ahead of her time, in a rush to pass up all of this juvenile stuff and become an adult already. With long dark brown wavy locks and Brandon's hazel eyes, she's mature and sophisticated, introverted and creative. Brandon calls her his artsy-fartsy girl. Roma goes after what she wants. She skipped the second grade, and at sixteen, she's the youngest high-school junior at Skiatook High. She's a big fish in a little pond, and she makes it no secret that she's ready to dive into a bigger one.

Roma is my cosmopolitan girl. Jane is my country bumpkin. My city mouse and my country mouse. Brandon and I took turns naming our babies. I picked Roma, elegant and ethnic. Brandon chose the most plain-Jane name he could think of. Literally.

"How do your days look?" I ask.

"Mrs. Hawthorne is going to change our desks," Jane answers excitedly.

"If she sits you by Delilah, don't be a chatterbox."

"I'm hoping she'll put me next to Teddy Lambly. He's a hottie."

I almost spit out my coffee. "Okay… well, behave if you sit next to him, too."

"Yes, Mama." Her tone turns conspiratorial. "Teddy says that Mrs. Hawthorne has a wooden leg and that's why she only wears long skirts."

A belly laugh escapes my lips. I recover. "I'm sure that's not true. And if I were you, I wouldn't spread that around. It's not nice to spread rumors."

"Okay, Mama."

I turn to Roma, who's putting on lip gloss. "How about you, my love? What's on the agenda for today?"

"The usual. Get good grades so I can get out of here."

I frown.

Should I take it personally, or is she just being a hormonal teenager? Comments like that are reserved only for me. She would never say anything like that to Brandon. She wouldn't want to hurt his feelings. Roma always seems to be irritated with me these days, but I suppose it's just the age.

We pass a large banner that says "Generosity." The city council started putting them up as a way to foster positive character traits.

"It's October first, guys. They put up the new sign," Jane observes excitedly. "I'm not sure what it said, though."

"Generosity," I answer.

"Wow, what does that mean?" Jane asks.

Jane takes the character signs very seriously. She feels like it's everyone's civic duty to uphold the monthly character trait.

"It means to give freely. To be unselfish," Roma says.

I smile at her and receive a partial smile in return.

"Mama, will you buy me some pineapple whip on the way home?" Jane asks.

"I think I can do that," I answer, feigning seriousness. I knew it was only a matter of time.

"Thank you. That would be very generous of you," she says grandly.

"Oh, you are so smart," I tease.

"Nicely done," Roma compliments her sister.

Jane beams.

I turn right onto Osage Avenue and pull quickly into the parking lot. As I enter the school zone, Mr. Frizzly, the crossing guard, waves his arms at me.

"Slow down, Mama!" Jane insists.

"Sorry." I ease on the brakes.

"You always do that," Roma says, annoyed.

"I know. I'm sorry."

I pull our Range Rover into the drop-off line at the elementary school. I drop Roma here, as well, so she can walk across the street to the high school. I guess it's better than being seen with me.

"Bye, my loves. Have a great day!"

"I have play rehearsal after school. I'll be done at six-thirty." Roma grabs her backpack and opens the passenger door. The balmy humidity invades us. "Bye."

"I love you," I say quietly, like it's a secret. I get it out of my mouth just before the door closes.

"Mama," Jane announces, "I have a surprise for you."

She pulls out a silver plastic tiara encrusted with colorful plastic jewels. Brandon gave it to her when she got her tonsils out.

My face brightens. "For me?"

She nods. "Wear it like the queen you are."

I adjust the tiara on my head with a smile. "If I'm a queen, that makes you a princess."

Jane leans over the front seat and I kiss her on the nose. "I know," she says as she puts on her backpack. "And that's why we're both wearing diamonds tonight."

I laugh. "All right. Maybe."

Jane opens her door and points to my head. "Don't take it off!"

I draw a cross over my heart using my fingers.

"Happy birthday!" she shouts. She slams the car door and runs off.

Chapter 2

The city of Skiatook is basically one straight line. Highway 20 runs right through the whole thing. If you head north out of Tulsa for about forty minutes up Highway 75 and turn left onto Highway 20, you will drive through flat open plains until you approach a sign that says, "Skiatook, Gateway to Skiatook Lake".

You'll cross over Bird Creek and pass Worley's Nursery and the Tastee Freeze. So begins our downtown, a humble strip of weathered, yet lovely old brick buildings which house antique stores, a pharmacy with windows that boast "We Support Our Troops" in red, white and blue paint, a stately brick post office, and a small library. There is a two-story mural of an American flag waving in the wind on the side of the police station that demonstrates that we are proud to be Americans. There are many vacant, neglected store fronts on the strip patiently waiting for a buyer to breathe new life into them.

Skiatook consists of older homes clustered on the north and south sides of downtown and pristine new subdivisions that stretch a little farther west down Highway 20. There are also farmhouses on large plots of land that families have handed down for generations. We have a grand total of three intersections, two with stoplights and one with a flashing light.

Skiatook Lake is on the opposite end of town, and it is our gem.

It has one hundred and sixty-eight miles of shoreline and eleven thousand acres of water. Our town is flat as a pancake, but the lake is surrounded by glorious hills that give the terrain beautiful variation. It's like an oasis in the middle of the Sahara, especially for a girl who grew up in the hills of Malibu.

Smack dab in the middle of town is the hub of Skiatook- the Walmart Supercenter.

* * *

I glide through the automatic sliding doors of Walmart and grab a shopping cart.

"Good morning, princess," says Bob, the sweet, white-haired Walmart greeter. I adore Bob. His darling smile just makes my day.

"Hi, Bob! How are you?"

"Oh, I'm wonderful," he says cheerfully. "I'm living on borrowed time."

"No. You're as vivacious as I am!"

He shoos away the crazy notion with his tan, wrinkled hand. "You're a sweetheart. Have a good one, dear."

"You, too, Bob."

I head towards the soda aisle and remember that I'm wearing the crown. Princess. Haha. I'm tempted to take it off, but I'm a woman of my word.

I need to pick up some sodas and paper goods here and head to the liquor store for beer and libations. Later, Mac's BBQ will be delivering their famous barbecued beef brisket, pulled pork, potato salad, corn on the cob and fried okra. The Skiatook Bakery is delivering a humongous chocolate cake with raspberry filling and chocolate buttercream frosting— my favorite.

Last night as I lay in bed, I actually watched as the clock changed from eleven fifty-nine to midnight. I felt my youth slip away as

Brandon snored with his back to me. It felt very anticlimactic, yet significant at the same time. I'm no longer in my thirties. They're gone. I am a forty-year-old woman.

I guess I'm being a little dramatic. I'm not really freaking out about it, but how did this happen already? It's all gone so fast. It doesn't even feel like it's been that long since I left L.A.

Up until seventeen years ago, I was a city girl. I lived in an apartment in Marina del Rey and I had a dream job. After interning at the *Santa Monica Chronicle* in college, I landed the position of writing a travel column in the *Los Angeles Times*. Who wouldn't want that job?

I got lucky. The travel columnist at the *Times* retired and my boss at the *Chronicle* was friends with the head of human resources at the *Times*. He convinced her to take a chance on a venturesome new journalist. The job gave me wings, and allowed me to experience adventures all over the world.

I soon realized that with those wings, serious relationships weren't feasible for me. I was okay with that. While some of my girlfriends were looking for guys to settle down with, I was having first dates with men all over the world. Until that fateful Friday night.

As per our routine, I waited in front of my apartment building until Kenny, our taxi driver, barreled down the street. I climbed into the back seat, where Alison, Kate and Christina greeted me boisterously. So many nights had started the same way. How was I to know that this one would change the entire path of my life forever?

I'd known these girls since kindergarten at St. Bede's of Malibu. We'd gone our separate ways in college, but we all ended up back in L.A. and were inseparable. Alison, with curly, tawny shoulder-length hair with sun-kissed highlights and amber eyes, is the sweet and comforting one. She's the friend I go to when I need a hug. Kate, with straight, chestnut-brown hair down her back, chocolate eyes, and a spray of girlish freckles across her cheeks, is the even-tempered one I go to for sensible advice. And Christina, with wavy, sunny locks and sky-blue eyes, is the feisty one I go to when I need someone to have my back or for a crazy good time. All so different, but all my sisters.

Like most Friday nights, we headed to Harry O's in Manhattan Beach. There was a mechanical bull that drunk guys got thrown off and drunk girls provocatively rode while said drunk guys encouraged them.

We sipped our habitual gin and tonics and got down to Def Leppard's *Pour Some Sugar On Me* on the dance floor. Suddenly, the crowd surrounding the mechanical bull-riding pen started to go crazy.

I turned around and found myself watching a sexy, rugged man with dark brown hair and laughing hazel eyes who was, for once, putting that mechanical bull in its place. He wore a blue and brown plaid button-down shirt tucked into his Levis, a belt with a sizeable silver buckle and cowboy boots. Really.

"Holy cow," Alison said in awe.

"That's why God invented saddles," Kate remarked.

"That's why God invented jeans," Christina countered.

We headed over to the mechanical bull-riding ring for a closer look.

A group of rowdy guys cheered their buddy on. The cowboy's sleeves were rolled up and his forearm bulged as his hand grasped the rope around the bull. His free hand waved in the air for balance like a pro. His strong thigh muscles gripped the bull with ease as it swung around. As the bull dove forward, he leaned back. His weight shifted rhythmically as the bull bucked back and forth, back and forth, back and forth. Oh, boy. This specimen of manhood was dripping with confidence and virility. Girls were screaming and jumping up and down all over the place.

The four of us stared motionless with our mouths hanging open.

"He knows what he's doing," Christina said with admiration.

"Clearly not from around here," added Alison.

I kept my eyes glued on the man. "I did a rodeo piece in Omak, Washington, and I observed cowboys flipping calves onto their backs and tying their ankles together in two seconds flat."

I gave a nod and took a swig of my drink. Alison's eyes widened innocently as she visualized the image.

"Mooooooo!" Christina bellowed at our cowboy.

Surprised, I sprayed out my mouthful of gin and tonic. Alison, Kate and Christina burst into hysterical laughter.

The rodeo cowboy's eyes locked onto mine and he smirked.

When his ride was over, he dismounted the bull, sauntered over to us gals, and introduced himself as Brandon McCoy of Skiatook, Oklahoma. He bought us a round of drinks and explained that he was in town for his college roommate's bachelor party.

I'll never forget that first moment of being in the presence of Brandon McCoy. My heartbeat quickened immediately. As he spoke, his eyes crinkled and his southern accent made my knees buckle. He was polite and gentlemanly, yet at the same time so hunky and masculine. As cute as he looked in his plaid shirt, I wanted to rip it right off of him.

Brandon and I engaged in competitive yet flirtatious banter. Every time I opened my mouth with a snarky remark, he grinned. When my girlfriends realized they'd been beat, they left us in search of new prospects and headed in the direction of the rambunctious bachelors.

Brandon and I chatted, and as I got lost in his hazel eyes, I noticed the flecks of gold in them. After a while, he asked if I'd like some air. I nodded.

He placed his hand on the small of my back and led me out of the bar. We walked the two blocks down to the beach and took our shoes off for a walk in the sand. We came across a swing set, sat on the swings, our feet dangling in the sand, and talked until three in the morning.

There's a word for men like Brandon McCoy. Chivalrous. Like Cary Grant in an old film. Well, maybe a combination of Cary Grant and John Wayne. Nevertheless, I'd left bars plenty of times with guys, and not one ever took me to a swing set.

Now I wheel the shopping cart into the checkout lane and load my items on the conveyor belt. The cashier eyes me as she scans the items.

"I've got ten of those two-liter sodas in the cart," I tell her. She nods.

She continues to scrutinize me. I assume she's wondering why a grown woman is wearing a plastic tiara while she's grocery-shopping.

"I promised my daughter that I wouldn't take it off. It's my birthday," I explain.

"Happy birthday." She scans packages of paper plates. "I'm so sorry, Ms. Blake," she blurts out. "I just have to ask. I think my Merv is having an affair. At the very least, I think he's flirtin' with the idea. What do I do?"

"It's no trouble." I take a thoughtful breath. It often comes to this. Everyone thinks I have the answers for their relationships. I glance at her name tag. I've seen her around, but I don't know her by name. "Pearl, it's easy to get comfortable after a while when we've settled into a relationship. How long have you been with Merv?"

"We've been married for four years," she replies.

I nod. "Remind him why he fell for you in the first place. Sometimes we let those beginning qualities slip a little. How did you dress then? How did you smell? I know it sounds shallow, but men use their senses. Their sight, sense of smell, touch, and most of all that sixth sense."

"The sixth one?"

"Yes. The one they reason with more than their brain. The sixth sense," I tell her. "And I'm not talking about seeing dead people."

Pearl laughs. "Gracious. I'll keep that in mind."

Chapter 3

I turn left off Highway 20 onto Lake Road. After I cross over the dam and head up into the emerald wooded hills, I make a right into the Beverly Hills Community. That's right. Beverly Hills. The developer who built these gorgeous homes on the bluffs overlooking Skiatook Lake decided that it would be very swanky to compare Skiatook's most elite neighborhood to the posh lifestyle of L.A.'s most elite neighborhood. The streets are named Giorgio Boulevard, Tiffany Place and Rodeo Drive. However, the latter is often mispronounced. The developer either had a very good sense of humor or thought this stretch of Oklahoma real estate was the absolute cream of the crop.

We live at the very end of Versace Drive. I moved all the way to Oklahoma to live in Beverly Hills. What can I say? It's the best.

Our home is a two-story five-thousand-square-foot cabin-style house that Brandon and I designed. It's the color of cafe mocha with dark espresso trim, log pillars, and several stone chimneys, and is surrounded by abundant blackjack and post oak trees. When you pull into our driveway, it looks like you have arrived at a lakeside lodge. It was my husband's dream to live in a log cabin. I was okay with that as long as it was a really big one.

The exterior of the house is everything Brandon ever imagined. We have a front porch with a swing for sipping lemonade and talking about the weather. A massive wooden deck overlooks the lake on the lower end of the backyard, and our outdoor kitchen is Brandon's happy place, boasting the grand-daddy of grills. The land surrounding the lake is scattered with large red rocks. These have been incorporated into the landscaping as steps leading down to the deck and stacked to build retaining walls.

Brandon planted a long row of hydrangea bushes below the front porch as an anniversary gift to me since I adore them so much. I love that on any given bush there can be a variety of colors on the spherical bunches of blooms—lime green, sky blue, periwinkle, green morphing into blue, and every shade in between. They thrive from the humidity.

We have two horses, Silver Heart and Valentine (Roma named them when she was six), that reside in a stable and corral on the north side of the house. There are many hilly trails surrounding the bluffs and shoreline of the lake which make for beautiful horseback rides.

The interior of our home was mine to create, with each room representing a different adventure from my travels. The guest bathroom is beach-themed with framed photographs of Bali that I myself shot and an apothecary vase full of shells and sand dollars that the girls collected from our various trips to Malibu. My office is decorated with Aboriginal art and framed photos of the Australian outback. Our French dining room is opulent with gold and beige jacquard wallpaper, a bronze sunburst mirror, an eighteen-arm bronze and crystal chandelier, and a nineteenth-century carved sideboard and long dining table. Louis XVI would feel at home in my dining room. I admit it's a little over the top, but I love it.

My absolute favorite room in the house is our sprawling kitchen complete with two ovens, an industrial-size range, and a massive Italian marble island. A wine rack in the wall showcases bottles like art, and oversized ceramic bowls painted with lemons and birds and a tile back-splash showcasing bunches of grapes flavor the room with delicious Italian authenticity. An enormous painting of the Spanish Steps in Rome hangs over a stone fireplace, sending us back to a place that changed our lives.

When it came to the living room Brandon put his foot down. He said he didn't want an elaborate international experience when he was watching TV, so I made some concessions. Its style is modern farmhouse with a rugged leather L-shaped couch, a coffee table and shelves of galvanized pipe and distressed wood to bring out the exposed beams in the high-ceiling. I added a few shabby chic elements with a colorful paisley armchair that had belonged to Brandon's grandmother and a floral area rug. He looked the other way on those two "girly" items.

For the master bedroom I went "House in the Hamptons" with walls a light robin's-egg blue and light gray furniture. The rustic four-poster bed is covered in a sumptuous white duvet and lavish pillows and has a gray upholstered tufted headboard. The windows that showcase Skiatook Lake are framed with gauzy sheer white curtains. It's very clean and simple, yet indulgent.

With us living out here in the middle of nowhere, my decorating is my way of bringing the rest of the world to us.

* * *

When I finish unloading the groceries, I fill a tumbler with crushed ice and sweet tea. I set it on a tray along with my laptop and head out the kitchen door to the side yard where there is a small brick patio. Two red wooden Adirondack chairs face the lake with a small matching table nestled in between. A chiminea fireplace sits in the corner for roasting marshmallows on chilly nights.

It's warm for early October, and the cicadas are melodiously buzzing. I settle into a chair and grab a can of mosquito repellent off the ground. It rattles as I shake it, and I spray down my arms and legs. The mosquitoes will eat me alive if I don't, but the solitude of this view makes it worth the trouble.

Lush green foliage surrounds the brilliant blue waters of Skiatook Lake. The water is perfectly calm and a few lone boats float atop like toy boats in a bathtub. Probably retired old men delighted to fish away a Friday afternoon. A myriad of ancient oak and maple trees sway and whisper from the sultry breeze.

I flip open my laptop and open the document entitled "Down and Dirty Down Under". I write romance novels. In the summertime, this little deck is my office. In the winter, I move to the massive oak desk in our cozy study and light a roaring fire.

Book tours allow me to move around when I get antsy. And sometimes I do start to feel a little claustrophobic in the beautiful, yet landlocked state of Oklahoma. I can't help it. I love my life here, but sometimes I need to feel the buzz of a big city.

Brandon is always my leading man. His strong and strapping physique has inspired many sexy, hunky characters. His sweet, playful, noble and bold traits have sculpted those characters into realistic and irresistible men that my readers can't get enough of. However, when I write, I long for the words that I type to transcend into real life.

Brandon and I have drifted apart. I love him, but things between us are strained. Our easy conversations have regressed into annoyed, staccato statements. We aren't connected anymore, and our physical relationship is non-existent. God, it's been forever since we've made love.

I don't write Brandon as he is now. I write about the Brandon I used to know. The one who used to say offbeat things in an attempt to make me laugh. The one who smirked at my dry humor. The man who used to hug me so hard and kiss me so tenderly.

This little laptop holds all of my fantasies and wishes for my own relationship. The truth is, I've made a living off of the unfulfilled fantasies that I have about my own husband. It's totally ironic— the romance novelist whose marriage is devoid of romance. It's my deep, dark secret.

Everyone assumes that I have a perfect marriage and desirable sex life. My friends ask for advice. Strangers on the street and in line at the post office ask me for input into their relationships. It's ridiculous because I'm not a marriage counselor or sex therapist. But people think the titillating scenes in my books reflect my real life. They translate, "Wow, this book is steamy. Nina really knows about passion. Lucky her."

I play along because I don't want to blow my cover. To them, to the outside world, to the naked eye, I am a romantic professional. It's pretty pathetic.

Chapter 4

What a lovely night. The grass is freshly cut and smells damp and clean. The humidity in the air is still very present, but not intolerable like it was a few weeks ago. It gives your skin a moist, dewy feeling. Moisturizing is simply not necessary during the humid months.

Tiki torches are lit around the perimeter of the yard. Down on the deck a three-man band plays *The Devil Went Down to Georgia* and the fiddler is kicking butt. The reflection of the moon blazes a buttery yellow trail through the still, dark surface of the lake.

I stand in our outdoor kitchen where the food buffet and drinks are set up. I pull two chilled mason jars out of the mini-fridge and ladle some cowboy lemonade into them. It's pink lemonade spiked with a multitude of liquors and boy, is it good, but it'll getcha if you're not careful.

I walk over to the back porch and sit down on the patio loveseat next to my best friend, Becky Jameson. I set the two frosty jars on the table in front of us.

"Mmm. Thanks, pal," she says with her mouth full.

Becky is tall and trim with chestnut-colored hair cut in a short pixie and friendly brown eyes. She is the most easy-going person I know and I just love her.

I grab my own plate off the table, balance it on my lap and take a juicy bite of brisket dripping with tangy sauce.

"Any dinner you need a bib for is my kind of meal," Becky says. She and many others are wearing thin plastic bibs adorned with Mac's logo.

I laugh and nod, my mouth too full to respond.

"So," she asks, "what did Brandon get you for your birthday?"

"Oh." I swallow. He didn't get me anything. "Well, he planned the party. I guess that's my gift."

Even though I was out today buying supplies for my own birthday party.

"Great party," she says as she takes another bite.

I nod.

Becky shakes her head. "Look at our husbands."

Down on the deck, Brandon and RJ dance around, slapping their knees and stamping their feet. As buddies since childhood, they are straight-up silly together. Brandon throws his arm around RJ.

RJ is tall and lanky with a cute, boyish face. He looks like a wet noodle flopping around on the deck. My husband looks so good in his plaid button-down shirt and jeans. He's six one and has strong broad shoulders from hauling bales of hay in his youth. Some other friends laugh and join in.

"They're such rednecks," I observe. "My poor mother. She would've been delighted if I married a metropolitan architect or financial planner. Instead, I married a bona fide redneck."

"Yeah, I'm from here. A redneck husband was my destiny. You chose this."

We laugh.

Brandon cracks up as he dances. As always, he is the life of the party. He has that twinkle in his eye that is so endearing and sexy. Why doesn't he have that twinkle in his eye when he's just with me?

Jane runs by and breaks my thoughts. "Mama, let's cut the cake!"

As planned, she is decked out in lots and lots of jewels. She is covered in costume jewelry from the top of her head to her shoulders.

"Wow! Look at you sparkle!" Becky tells her. "You look so fancy!"

"Thank you, Miss Becky," Jane answers proudly. "They're diamonds."

Becky raises her eyebrows. This pleases Jane. "Mama, the cake!"

"Okay. Tell Daddy," I say. "He's running the show."

"All right," Jane says, but she veers in the opposite direction of Brandon when she sees Roma handing out empty mason jars and lids to the kids for catching fireflies.

"They're rhinestones," I explain to Becky. "I let her ransack my costume jewelry for the sake of celebrating the demise of her mother's youth." I fan my fingers at my ears. "I get to wear the real thing, though."

"As you should, my dear," Becky says. She searches my face. "You're not letting this birthday get to you, are you?"

I roll my eyes.

"You know, they say forty is the new thirty," she says.

I chuckle. "Yay, I loved thirty."

I take a deep breath and sink deeper into my chair and assess the scene in front of me. I glance at the man I love so much but just can't seem to reach anymore.

"It's fine. Forty is... whatever." I shoo away the thought of aging with my hand. "Sheesh. It's not like it's old. It's just... a milestone."

"I feel like these milestone birthdays aren't a big deal if you're happy with where you are in your life," Becky says. "And you have an awesome life. This is a celebration of that."

"Yeah. It has just caused me to pause and reflect. My thirties were the sweet years of raising small children. My writing career. What will this next phase bring?"

In a moment of weakness, I'm about to confess my sad, shameful secret to my best friend. I'm about to admit that my marriage is on the rocks. But the music stops and Brandon grabs the microphone.

"It's time for my middle-aged wife to get down here and join the party."

I shake my head at Becky. "Middle-aged? It's worse than I thought," I joke. "Well, I guess I'm halfway to eighty!"

"Yikes! Come on," she says as she rises from her chair. "If this is your demise, you're going down with a bang."

We head down to the deck.

"Hey, somebody get Nina a drink," Brandon says into the microphone.

I step onto the deck, and suddenly, it's too quiet. All I can hear are the cicadas chirping and my jeweled sandals clicking as I walk across the long oak planks towards Brandon. I start to get anxious for no good reason.

My good friend, Carrie Ann, squeezes my arm warmly as I walk by. I'm surrounded by the smiles of all of the friends who embraced me in this town as one of their own so long ago.

Roy, my father-in-law, winks at me and hands me a fresh mason jar of cowboy lemonade. This is my fortieth birthday party. This *is* a milestone moment in my life. My husband is about to make a toast on my behalf. This is a scenario in which a husband announces to family and close friends beautiful words about how much he loves his wife and that she should be celebrated. The ball is in Brandon's court. Am I worried that what he says won't be good enough or that it won't be sincere?

As I stand next to Brandon, his amplified voice beckons through the thick air and out over the water. The lake stretches farther than I can see and makes me feel small.

"Thank you all for coming out and celebrating Nina's fortieth birthday. I can't believe I'm saying that. When we met, she was twenty-three and I was twenty-seven. Where the hell did the time go?"

Everyone laughs.

"She's just as pretty now as the day I met her."

My heart sinks. It seems he chose the safe, noncommittal route.

"Hear, hear!" RJ shouts.

Our friends and family begin to clap and I smile gratefully for their love.

"And now, Janie would like to lead us in singing 'Happy Birthday' to her mama."

Jane takes the mic and wholeheartedly belts out in song. I laugh at her gusto and smile as everyone joins in.

A rogue tear runs down my cheek and I wipe it away. I'm not quite sure of its origin— the intensity of this significant moment, the love that I feel from my loved ones or my disappointment in my husband. Maybe a mixture of all three.

* * *

I dot wrinkle cream around my eyes as I swish my mouth with Listerine. I've used eye cream since I was in college, however tonight it seems a little more significant.

I take a moment and evaluate myself in the mirror. My hair is so dark brown it's almost black and still not a single gray. That is a trait I can thank my grandpa Julio for. He had a full head of mostly black hair clear into his eighties. I wear mine in a sleek straight bob. I come from a long line of child-bearing Mexican women, hence my curvaceous hips and ample bust. I run and power-walk regularly to keep those curves under control. My dad's Irish genes gave me a light complexion and vivid green eyes.

I turn off the bedroom light, walk to my side of the bed and slide under the covers next to Brandon. "Tonight was fun. Thank you."

"You're welcome," Brandon says, stretched out on his back. "The band was really good. We should have them again."

"Definitely."

My foot finds his and I rub it up and down his leg. I nuzzle my head into his neck and give him a few kisses right under his chin. He smells faintly and deliciously of the aftershave he pulls out for special occasions.

He groans. "Too much barbeque." The words stop my kisses in their tracks.

He gives me a light kiss on the lips and rolls over. "Love you," he mumbles.

I lie on my back in the dark. A few hot tears trickle down my face. This is not the first time I have cried after being rejected by my husband. I am quiet, though, and he's oblivious to my tears. I breathe carefully as I wouldn't dare have him hear a sniffle.

Happy damn birthday to me.

Chapter 5

The luscious smell of maple bacon and the muffled sound of music slowly seep into my consciousness as I stretch. Sunshine glints through the gauzy white curtains and casts rainbows onto the walls. I emerge from my bed wearing a tank top and pajama shorts. As soon as I open my bedroom door into the hallway, the comforting voice of John Denver fills the air. This is a familiar scenario. John Denver's greatest hits are our Saturday morning soundtrack. "Country road, take me home to the place I belong..."

I pad downstairs, glance through the floor-to-ceiling windows in the living room, and am greeted by the glistening waters of Skiatook Lake.

I peek into the kitchen. Jane stands on a stool in front of the stove wearing an apron that my grandma Isabel made for me when I was a little girl. It's blue and green plaid cotton with shiny red and gold thread running through it. Grandma had a matching apron and we used to wear them when we made pancakes together.

Despite the fact that we make pancakes every weekend, I cannot for the life of me perfectly duplicate Grandma's recipe. It was a basic pancake recipe and we would add Mexican vanilla extract as our secret ingredient, but I still can't get it exactly right.

Brandon joins Jane at the stove with a bowl full of batter. He hands her a ladle and leans in close to observe her work as she spoons batter onto the griddle. It's a sight that melts me every time—my buff and brawny man being so tender and playful with our children. However, my heart clenches at the memory of how he so casually brushed me off last night.

"Ooh, that's a beauty. That one should be yours," Brandon says.

"Okay, Daddy," Jane says excitedly.

"Now pour out the rest of the batter to make one giant pancake for me."

"No!" Jane laughs.

"Why not? I'm the biggest, I should get the biggest pancake."

"But we have to make some for Roma and Mama."

"Well, they're being lazy daisies. You snooze, you lose."

"Daddy," she simultaneously scolds and giggles.

"You'll never get away with it," I say as I breeze into the kitchen. "I awoke from the smell of bacon."

"Mama, I was going to save you some." Jane throws her hands up in the air innocently.

"I won't take it personally. I know how much you and Daddy love pancakes." I give Brandon a peck on the cheek. "Good morning."

"Good morning," he returns.

I walk over to the stove and give Jane a kiss. "Hi, sweet pea." I inspect her pancake-making. "Nice work."

Her chest puffs out proudly. "Thank you, Mama." She hops down from her stool and begins to set the table.

I pour a splash of hazelnut creamer into a mug and top it off with strong, fragrant French roast and a dash of cinnamon on top. Brandon is an early riser and the coffee is always made when I appear in the kitchen. It's a nice husbandly attribute.

He flips a few pancakes. "I was thinking of taking you girls fishing this morning."

"Yay!" cheers Jane.

"We can drop anchor in a quiet cove and catch some dinner."

"That sounds great, Daddy." Jane fist bumps her dad. "I'll dig up some worms after breakfast!"

"Great idea." I turn to Brandon. "I wish I could go, but I should pump a few chapters out for Stan since I'll see him this week at the Marshall Books party."

Brandon purses his lips and nods. I know what it means. He thinks I should join them since I'll be leaving tomorrow morning.

"I need to have pages to show him and today's really my last chance to write. Tomorrow's a travel day and I have three book signings before the party. The party's Friday night."

Why am I explaining my entire itinerary?

"No big deal, Nina."

"I'll pack a cooler for you," I offer.

"Okay," he says with an edge.

Jane returns to Brandon's side.

"Are they ready?" Brandon smiles at Jane.

"They are. Grab the syrup."

Roma slowly saunters into the kitchen.

"Good morning, my love," I say cheerfully.

She grunts in return.

Brandon kisses the top of her head as she passes. She grabs a carton of orange juice from the fridge and pours herself a glass.

We sit down at the table and I start distributing pancakes to each plate.

"So, Roma," Brandon starts, "Jane and I are planning on going fishing this morning. You up for it?"

"I need to study," Roma says as she drizzles syrup on her short stack.

"You can study later," he tells her.

"I have an AP chemistry test this week. It's really hard."

"Maybe you could study on the boat," I offer.

Brandon shoots me a look of disapproval.

"What? Can't scold the girl for wanting to get a good grade." I shrug.

Brandon turns his attention to Roma. "Roma, when you're eighty, you're not going to wish you had studied more for a chemistry test. You're going to wish you had spent more time fishing with your dad."

Roma looks at me, annoyed, asking for help.

"She said it's really hard," I counter.

Brandon's face turns red.

"I believe her." I go on. "I really struggled in chemistry."

"Nina, can I talk to you, please?"

Roma and Jane look at me.

"Of course." Brandon and I step out of the kitchen.

"Will you please not challenge me in front of the girls?" he says in a loud whisper.

My eyebrows furrow. "Oh, am I supposed to just go along with everything you say even when our daughter is trying to do the right thing?"

Brandon purses his lips and shakes his head. "I was just trying to instigate some family time. Dammit."

I scoff, angry.

We walk back into the kitchen and join Roma and Jane at the table.

We all eat our pancakes in silence.

* * *

I can't sleep. I have too much anticipation about my trip to L.A. The purpose of the trip is to attend the fiftieth anniversary party of my publishing house. However my publicist jumped at the opportunity to squeeze in a small book tour while I'm in the area.

I love book tours. I feel like I get to be "the old me". I just feel so in my element when I'm in a big city promoting my work.

I snuggle up to Brandon. "I love you," I tell him.

There is a pause. "I love you, too." And then another pause.

I sigh.

"What?" he asks.

"Professing our love for each other should not leave such a heavy feeling in the air."

It's his turn to sigh.

"What's wrong with us?" I finally ask.

Silence hangs between us in the dark.

"I think we need some time apart."

"Well, you're about to have eight days without me."

"I think we need more than that, Nina. I think…" He stops. "I think we should consider separating."

I sit straight up in bed. "What?" I fumble for the switch on the lamp on my nightstand. "Separate? You can't be serious."

"I think we need to evaluate why we're married to each other."

"What?" I repeat in disbelief. "Here are two reasons, Roma and Jane."

"Don't you dare presume that I haven't thought about my daughters in all of this."

"Okay, have you thought about me?" I ask. "Have you thought about what I want?"

"I don't know what you want, Nina."

"Then why don't you ever ask?"

Silence.

"I want us to have a conversation that actually has some substance to it. I want you to hold my hand. I want you to laugh with me when no one else is around. I want you to look at me how you used to. I want *you* to kiss *me.* "

I didn't realize that I had this speech prepared. A tear rolls down my face.

Brandon's face softens and he wipes it away. And with that, I feel a solitary moment of hope. It's the only genuine gesture of love and sensitivity that I've received from Brandon for a very long time.

"I want that, too," he says honestly.

I let out a breath. Thank God, he wants it, too.

"I just don't know how to get there again."

And just like that, the gesture has been snatched away. I feel like the wind has been knocked out of me.

"I think we need to sit down and talk to someone," he says. "If we're going to get through this, we need counseling."

"We are going to get through this. We have to. But we can figure this out on our own."

Brandon's face hardens. "And why is that?"

"Look, we've just admitted that we need to work on things. We've taken the first step. I think we should just try to talk things out together."

"I get it. You don't want this to affect your career," he says coldly.

"That's not fair, Brandon."

"But it's true."

"You don't understand. I know it's hard to believe, but people think we have a perfect marriage."

"I know what people believe."

"Defacing that reputation damages my credibility."

Brandon scoffs.

My sadness blooms into anger. "You always do that," I sneer. "You make me feel like my career is a selfish hobby. That it does nothing for our family."

He exhales angrily. "I'm not having this conversation now. The point is that we need a break. We need to do some major thinking while we're apart."

"Fine, Brandon. Fine. I don't know how it's going to do any good. I think about us all the time."

Chapter 6

I sit at Gate A13 and watch the planes take off through a window of the Tulsa Airport.

A man loads luggage from a cart and transfers it to the plane that I will be boarding in fifteen minutes for my afternoon flight. A child behind me throws a tantrum screaming for a bag of Skittles. In the end, he gets them.

Life bustles around me in the terminal. It baffles me that things continue full speed ahead while my marriage is screeching to a halt. What the hell is Brandon thinking? How could he so recklessly ponder the idea of ending a life? Regardless of what happens between us, we will go on living and breathing. But this relationship that Brandon and I have breathed life into for seventeen years could potentially flatline. I can't fathom the thought of Brandon and I not being married to each other.

He's the only man containing that special something that could tame me when I was young. I was a wild thing, and after a matter of days he managed to marry me and settle me in a town whose population equated my high school's student body. How would I exist in Skiatook without him? I love Skiatook, but I would feel completely irrelevant there without him as my husband. I would be stranded. The thought of it constricts my throat.

Okay, calm down, Nina. He didn't say that he wants a divorce.

He said that perhaps we need to separate, have some time apart. But isn't that the same thing? Does anybody actually get back together after they separate?

I hate that I have to leave town at a time like this. Before our conversation last night, I couldn't wait for this trip, but now it seems like the worst possible time to go. Clearly though, this is what Brandon wants— some time apart to decide on this.

What if he already knows what he wants to do? What if his mind is made up and he just wants to add some more space between us until there's no turning back? How can I leave for an entire week when my marriage is hanging by a thread? When did my relationship with my husband become so fragile that one mere week apart could make or break us? These questions are firing at me out of nowhere. I feel like I could crack, just like the kid before he got his Skittles.

I grab my cell phone out of my purse and dial his cell. I get his voicemail. I have the urge to say that I love him and plead for him to forget this crazy talk about us potentially being over. I hear the beep and take a breath, ready to get into it.

The words don't come. I hang up. The man asked for space and that's what I'm going to give him.

* * *

I usually love flying. I don't mind being crammed into a tiny space on a plane or even waiting around at the airport beforehand. I relish in buying a cappuccino and a novel or magazine. It's all part of the journey. Each trip is an adventure.

But today I just couldn't relax on the flight. I felt like I was symbolically flying away from Brandon. I had been looking forward to getting immersed in my favorite author's newest book. But even Adriana Trigiani's exquisite imagery couldn't distract me from my restless thoughts.

Unexpectedly, the moment we touched down on the tarmac, I felt a sense of comfort. I was home. I was in Los Angeles and I could already feel the pulse of action and activity.

After I picked up my rental car, I stopped by my favorite Westside coffee shop for a frosty ice-blended mocha. It would be safe to say that the only espresso machine in all of Skiatook resides at my house. It's surprising that there isn't a line outside my door, but apparently the drip coffee down at the Daylight Donuts is sufficient for the rest of the town.

After cruising up the Pacific Coast Highway along the shimmering shoreline, I wind my way up a twisty Malibu road dotted with olive trees. The road plateaus and I drive by grand picturesque houses.

A man pulls a stack of envelopes out of his mailbox in front of his French-country style home. I wave.

The man looks confused, like, *Do I know you?*

Embarrassed, I put my hand back on the steering wheel and look away. I momentarily forgot that I'm not in Oklahoma where everybody waves to everybody.

I pull into the circular driveway of Mom and Dad's hacienda— a two-story Spanish house with terracotta shingles and cobalt-blue awnings. Fuchsia bougainvillea clings to sections of the alabaster walls. The grounds are covered with native California plants such as poppies, succulents, fragrant lavender and rosemary bushes. I step out of the car and my senses are overloaded with the trickle of the fountain, the smell of the rosemary, and the feeling of being home again. It's a complicated feeling to express. The nostalgia of childhood memories, the sadness that I don't live here anymore, and the love that waits for me inside. There's no place like home.

Moments later, I'm standing on the doorstep where I received my first kiss. I fumble with my keys, find the one that I so rarely use anymore, and let myself in.

"Mom! Dad!" I call through the marble foyer.

The house is completely still.

Through the sliding glass doors I let myself out into the backyard, take in the deep blue immensity of the Pacific Ocean and breathe in the briny air. Skiatook Lake may be beautiful, but there is nothing like the ocean. Infinite, dangerous, mysterious and resplendent. When I look at the ocean, I am free.

I take a sip of my almost empty ice-blended mocha. It's magic. It won't be my last one this week. I lie down on a lounge chair by the pond as an assortment of orange and white koi fish swim under floating lily pads. It's a gorgeous Southern California day and I drink in the hot, golden sun. White tubular blossoms of night-blooming jasmine meander across a plaster wall, and its sweet floral perfume snakes its way to my nostrils.

I blissfully stretch my toes and my fingers as far as they'll reach. And yet there is a dark cloud hanging over my sunny desire to enjoy my setting. I hear Brandon's voice in my head.

"I think we need to evaluate why we're married to each other."

My heart wrenches. How can he ask me that and not remember Rome?

I think back to our spontaneous first date on the sand of Manhattan Beach. At three in the morning, I said I had to go. Brandon asked me if he could take me out to dinner that evening, and I replied that I would have loved to, but I had a plane to catch. I was leaving for Rome in a matter of hours to do a travel piece for the *L.A. Times*, but I would be back in five days. Brandon looked crushed. He would be back in Oklahoma by the time I returned.

Brandon grabbed me and kissed me passionately, our first kiss. My stomach did somersaults. The kiss was intense and urgent, especially since we thought it might be our last. It was absolutely perfect with our feet in the sand, the waves crashing, and the moon above us.

He told me that he never wanted to say goodbye to me. I impulsively said, "Then don't. Come with me to Rome." And he did.

We had the most marvelous time together. I had to research the city, the very best spots to see and dine, and together we found those places.

We found a ristorante at the base of the Spanish Steps where we ate alfresco, as the Roman nightlife pulsed around us. We feasted on spaghetti alla carbonara, moist veal sautéed with fresh baby artichokes, and delicate zucchini flowers filled with mozzarella cheese, battered and fried.

Brandon cracked up as we moaned our way through our amazing feast. "This is your job?" he laughed. "What am I doing with my life?"

I raised my hand and feigned seriousness. "I graciously accept my mission to bring this experience to the masses."

We ended the meal with ricotta cheesecake flavored with oranges and Marsala wine, and strong espresso to awaken us for the rest of the night.

We drank carafes of red wine and danced in each other's arms at a crowded discoteca late into the night. Then we retreated back to our hotel and made the most passionate love as the moon, round and full as a wheel of fresh mozzarella, poured into our luxurious suite. Thank you, *L.A. Times*.

Brandon told me that he had never met anyone like me and knew that he never would ever again. And then he told me that he loved me.

The next morning we walked to a café down the street and ordered cappuccinos and biscotti. We held hands across the table and shared stories about our childhoods. From our table, we noticed a beautiful little church at the top of the hill.

That evening, we got married there. And nine months after we returned to Skiatook, we welcomed our Roma into the world.

Some might believe that I jumped into things with Brandon. The relationships that I'd had in high school and college were not very serious. But in those first few days with Brandon I knew in my heart that what I felt was really *it*.

Brandon and I had such an intense whirlwind romance. I can't believe the topic I'm being forced to contemplate at this moment. How can love that powerful just disintegrate?

Chapter 7

I wake up with my dad patting my shoulder. I look up at his smiling face and then around me to find that I am still lying on the chaise longue by the pond.

"Hi, Dad." I smile and sit up.

My dad leans down and hugs me. He grins as he surveys the familiar scene–me on a lounge chair with an ice-blended mocha.

"Still a California girl, I see."

"Damn right, I am."

The screen door opens and I see my mom's smiling face. I stand up to greet her.

"My baby is here!" she says excitedly. She runs over and envelops me. "Your plane arrived early. How's my favorite novelist?"

"Fine, Mom," I reply as we hug. "But I'm dying for some chicken panang."

My mom pulls away, with a shocked expression. "They still don't have Thai food in Skiatook?"

"No, Mom. Not yet."

* * *

The kitchen table is cluttered with containers of pineapple fried rice, green curry, tom kha gai soup (a rich coconut broth with chicken and lemongrass), and Thai iced teas.

We decided to have a cozy meal without making the trek back down the hill. Oh, the luxury and convenience of delivery. Most establishments in Skiatook only deliver within the city limits, which leaves us McCoys and many others out of luck.

It feels so good to be sitting at this table, in this warm and loving home. I gaze at the faces across from me. I am so much like my dad, both physically and personality-wise. Charlie Blake has bright green Irish eyes and a bald head that you just want to kiss. He is very easy-going and has a fantastic sense of humor.

My mother, Pilar, is petite and feisty with dark brown eyes and black hair that she wears in a French twist. Both of her parents were born and raised in Mexico and she is a first-generation American. She is very Americanized and always dresses elegantly.

After cleaning up our takeout containers, we lounge in the den and chat with the TV on in the background. It's been a long emotional day of travel and reflection. So I kiss my parents goodnight, take a hot shower and retire to my childhood bedroom for a night of restful sleep.

* * *

In a quest to clear my head before my first book signing of the week, I secure my faded navy-blue LMU baseball cap onto my head and put in a few miles on the beach at Leo Carillo State Park. Running has been a gift in my life. It's the time when I converse with myself without even trying. As long as my feet are moving, my subconscious can flow a running dialogue and oftentimes devise a plan of action to work out an issue.

Now, as my feet strike the wet sand, my mind goes to the beginning of my marriage.

When I spontaneously got hitched and moved to Skiatook, I hadn't thought through how that would affect my job. I was so swept up with

Brandon, I didn't think about logistics at all. The *L.A. Times* graciously allowed me to do a piece on the restaurant scene in Tulsa, then Dallas, then New Orleans. All were doable drives from Skiatook.

I gave birth to my beautiful Roma Grace and took a three-month maternity leave. So far, I had done an excellent job of skirting around the issue that I lived nowhere near the *L.A. Times*.

I was then assigned to do a piece in Tahiti, which Brandon, Roma and I turned into a family vacation. But the next two assignments took me to London and Dublin. Brandon couldn't come along. He had his own business to run. So I strapped baby Roma to the front of me and off we went. It took Brandon way out of his comfort zone to put his wife and baby on an international flight without him, but he did it to appease his bride. When Roma and I returned, Brandon and I had a huge fight. He said he didn't like his wife gallivanting around the world with his child. I countered that I gave up my life for him and that it wasn't fair that I had to sacrifice so much. This would be a thorn in our marriage. Geography.

But, as much as I tried to fight it, I saw Brandon's point. In the end, I decided to tuck my passport in a drawer and settle down with my family. The *L.A. Times* and I begrudgingly parted ways, but we knew it was for the best.

I'm an all-or-nothing girl. So I embraced our simple family life in the country. When Roma was around three, Brandon and I tried to get pregnant with another child. But it didn't come as easily as the first pregnancy. We decided that a baby would eventually come in its own time, and we stopped focusing on the effort to expand our family.

However, when Roma was four I started to get restless and needed a creative outlet. I set out writing a novel. It was fun for me to think about my last international adventure in Ireland, so I started imagining a love story that took place in the mystical fog and romantic rolling hills of the Emerald Isle. I jotted down character and story notes here and there between housecleaning and visits to the park, and I would input those notes into the computer after I tucked Roma in at night. The writing process restored me.

With a curious child in tow, it took me about two years to write a solid first draft. I used some of my *L.A. Times* contacts to get in touch with possible publishers, and at age thirty-one, I sold my first book! It was absolutely exhilarating.

My traveling for work started up again slowly. It worked out okay, since we had Brandon's mom and dad around to help out with Roma. After we had pretty much written off the idea of being blessed with another child, I became pregnant with Jane. We were surprised and ecstatic.

As I plod along the beach, I think about how Brandon and I have made it all work. We really have compromised for each other. I relocated for him, he humored me as I traveled and transitioned out of the *L.A. Times* job. I quit and became a stay-at-home mom, and he was supportive as I started my book-writing career. There has been a lot of give and take. But we've hit a huge bump in the road. Whose turn is it to compromise now? When do we get to stop compromising and just be happy together?

Chapter 8

There is a large turnout at Book Soup on Sunset Boulevard, and they eagerly listen as I read a snippet of my upcoming novel.

"For a moment, Veronica pushes aside the fact that Clive is a scruffy, smug and egotistical beast with absolutely no social graces. For the first time, she notices that her savage guide looks and sounds a lot like Hugh Jackman. They may have fought and disagreed since the moment they met two days ago at the beginning of her tour of the outback, but he just saved her life and the adrenaline coursing through her veins momentarily cancels out her judgement and disdain for him.

"She grabs his face hard and pulls him to her lips. His unshaven face is rough, but his lips are soft. She doesn't care if she'll regret this tomorrow. She yanks Clive's shirt over his head and runs her hands over his chiseled arms and shoulders as he kisses her hungrily. How can such a brute be such a skilled and tender kisser? This is such a bad decision. But who will know anyway? There isn't another soul out here as the sun sets on the rugged, unforgiving and magnificent landscape."

I smile and lower my iPad. "And that is just a sample of something I've been working on called *Down and Dirty Down Under*."

The audience erupts into applause and cheers enthusiastically.

Now comes the part I really love. I sit at a table displaying several of my hottest novels. A long line of women (and a few men) wait to chat with me and have me sign their books, some brought from home, some bought today.

Here I am connecting with real people whom my stories reach out to and entertain. It gives me such a sense of validation and satisfaction. However, it's ironic that complete strangers think my ideas are sexy and erotic. My own husband could care less.

A young man with a snug t-shirt and skinny jeans hands me his copy of *Two-Night Stand*. "Your books should come with a pack of cigarettes."

I laugh. "Now, there's a marketing idea. What's your name?"

"Xavier."

I scribble a note in his book.

"Would you mind a picture, Ms. Blake?"

"Please, call me Nina. Come on over here."

"Okay, Nina." Xavier giggles. He throws his arm around me, squishes his face up next to mine and takes a selfie. "Oh my God, thank you!"

"It was so nice to meet you, Xavier," I gleam.

He grabs his book and rushes off.

When the line dwindles down, Veronica Knight, my publicist, approaches me.

"That was great, Nina," she cheers. She was thrilled that I named my latest heroine after her. "There's something so rugged and sexy about Australia. I can't wait to read the entire book."

Veronica, a go-getter in her early thirties, has long flowing curly brown hair and lively blue eyes. My books always excite her, as she is always on the quest for romance herself.

"When did you go there?" she asks.

"Goodness, it's been almost twenty years. But when you go

somewhere that really captivates you, it stays with you forever."

Veronica shakes her head in disbelief. "Nina, you have the coolest life."

* * *

Once my three book signings in Hollywood, Orange County and Santa Barbara are behind me, I have a few days to cram in seeing friends and family. I will have lunch with a few of my old coworkers from the *Times*, hit a Dodgers game with my dad, have dinner with Alison, Kate and Christina, and do some much-needed shopping at Nordstrom and Anthropologie.

But today is mother-daughter day. Following an early lunch of macadamia nut-encrusted tilapia and lava flow cocktails at Dukes in Malibu, Mom and I trek over to Koreatown for some pampering at the Olympic Spa.

After stripping down completely and showering off all our cooties, we meet in the tea jacuzzi. They actually put tea in the water, it's great for the circulation. I lean my head back on the side of the Jacuzzi and my legs and feet float to the surface like a bag of English Breakfast bobbing around in a giant tea cup.

I exhale and close my eyes. "Aaah. This was a great idea, Mom."

"Yikes," she says as she dips a foot into the water. "This is hot." She gingerly steps down until she is seated across from me. "I feel like a chicken in a pot."

I smile.

"How good can this be for our internal organs? We're actually being poached."

Only my mom would complain at a spa. "I'm sure it's fine, Mom." She fans herself with her hand. "The Koreans have been poaching themselves for hundreds of years and they seem like a very healthy people."

"Okay," she responds, shortly.

I shake my head.

"You seem tense this trip, Nina. Were your book signings okay?"

"They were great," I reply.

I thought I was acting perfectly normal, but I can't hide anything from my mom. I really don't want to discuss my marital problems. Discussing it makes it real.

"Okay," she presses. "So what's *not* great?"

I hesitate. I'm reluctant to give my mom ammunition to use against me about Brandon. However, I've got to talk to someone about this and it's not like I want anyone back in Skiatook to know. As much as I can tell Alison, Kate and Christina anything, they adore Brandon and I don't want to taint their image of him. And Becky is my best friend in Skiatook, but RJ is Brandon's best friend. It's so complicated. Venting to my mom might actually be a good thing.

"Brandon and I"—*last chance to bail*—"are having some problems."

"Hmm… Okay…" Mom furrows her brows in concentration, the wheels in her head already spinning, finding a solution before she knows what the problem is.

"It's kind of serious, Mom. He thinks we should separate."

Mom's mouth opens in shock like when she heard that *All My Children* was coming to an end after forty-one years. But she pulls herself together in order to be constructive.

"You need to give him a son, Nina."

Just like that, my mom gives me the answer to saving my marriage.

I roll my eyes like a teenager.

"I've kept my mouth shut long enough," she continues.

"Mother. Really?" I only call my mom "mother" when I'm annoyed or mad at her.

"He needs someone to carry on the family name. Brandon's a traditional guy. When you chose not to take his name, that completely disrupted the natural order of things. And he doesn't even have a son to continue his legacy."

I make an imaginary gun out of my hand and point it at my head. I cock my thumb like a trigger. Bang.

"There's a lot of estrogen in that house. I'm just saying."

"Trust me, Mother. That has nothing to do with what's going on here. Besides, people would be laying flowers on my doorstep and naming a feast day after me if I was expecting a child."

"Nina, watch your mouth."

As Mom shakes her head at her sacrilegious daughter, she interprets my analogy.

"Ohhhh," she says loudly.

She gets shushed by a petite Korean masseuse at a nearby massage table who vigorously scrubs a woman's leg as she holds it straight up in the air.

"How long has it been?" my mom whispers.

I shake my head and shrug. "I don't know. A long time."

"Oy vey," she says dramatically.

We're Catholic, actually, but my mom says her favorite Yiddish phrase anytime she can.

The masseuse shushes her again.

"What about a new nightgown? Or making his favorite meal?"

I exhale. It's my own fault for admitting this. I knew better.

"Or roleplaying. Your father and I…"

"No, Mother. Definitely not another word."

"For goodness' sake, Nina. Don't be such a prude." We both close our eyes and lean against the edge of the spa. "Try something erotic from one of your books. You have such an elaborate imagination."

"I'm so sorry I mentioned it."

My mother rolls her eyes at me for a change. "Sheesh, Nina. Take a compliment."

Chapter 9

As I ride the elevator up to the top floor of the Standard Hotel, I can't help but feel a flutter of anticipation in my stomach. I'm about to enjoy a sparkling evening with my colleagues, people like me who love what we do. I smooth my hands over my emerald-green cocktail dress and momentarily relish in the fact that I'm wearing high heels and a plunging neckline. This outfit hasn't seen an outing since Carrie Ann and Todd hosted a "formal" Academy Awards party two years ago. It was an exciting opportunity for us all to be fancy.

For a moment, I wish that Brandon could be here to enjoy this with me. A much-needed date night. However, I immediately remember that he wouldn't enjoy it at all.

He doesn't appreciate the logistics of my career— my traveling the country to sign books for complete strangers when my family is at home. Or rubbing elbows with people Brandon thinks just need their egos fed. I, on the other hand, adore schmoozing. It's fun.

The elevator door opens to a bustling party. Waiters circulate the room, carrying silver trays offering tasty bites of bacon-wrapped scallops, chicken satay skewers and California rolls. I exit the elevator.

I catch my editor's eye and he excuses himself from a group of people. Stan Pasternak is fifty-three, short, bald, brilliant and loveable.

He embraces me warmly. "Nina! Welcome home, kiddo."

"Thank you, Stan. It's great to be home."

"It's so good to see you! Your last few chapters were smoldering, by the way."

"Yay!"

He squeezes my arm. "Let's get some champagne."

* * *

After catching up with all the necessary colleagues, I've located the cheese table, and I'm in heaven. They don't carry Gruyère or the likes of a good stinky Gorgonzola at the Skiatook Walmart, so I'm making my time at this cheese platter count.

Cotswold, aged Gouda and Brie. Oh my!

"Hey, beautiful."

It can't be. I quickly finish chewing my bite.

Without turning around, I know exactly who that sultry vocal register belongs to. Josh Decker. He covered sports for the *L.A. Times* and we used to date. Boy, did we date.

Josh and I didn't have a long relationship, more like a ton of tiny relationships when we both happened to be in town at the same time. He swept me off my feet, and I fell for him hard. One of his specialties was wining and dining. Tapas and sangria, sushi rolls and sake bombs, ravioli and wine: you name it, we ate it and drank it. A sexy and smart foodie is a deadly combination for me. Seduce me *and* feed me well? I'm yours.

Josh took me on quintessential Los Angeles dates. We watched the stars at the Griffith Observatory, rode the Ferris wheel at the Santa Monica pier, and walked the beautiful grounds and admired art at the Getty Museum. We ate dim sum in Chinatown, tacos on Olvera Street. We also took countless starlit walks on the beach, followed by endless makeout sessions on various lifeguard towers. It was like we were tourists in our own town. Dating Josh was an adventure.

We were away often, me internationally and he domestically for sporting events, so we didn't allow our relationship to become too serious. Unlike the other people we both dated, we understood that it was a short matter of time before the next business trip whisked one of us away. But when we were in the same place at the same time we would pick up right where we left off. It worked for us. We just clicked. We enjoyed being together. And then I met Brandon.

I turn around and see the familiar dark brown hair and eyes as intensely blue as the Mediterranean Sea. He flashes me his most mischievous grin. OMG, he's still as hot as ever. I know that underneath his cobalt-blue collared dress shirt is the body of a swimmer— a long, sleek back and sculpted six-pack abs. God help me. I force myself to snap out of my lusty thoughts.

"I was hoping you would be here," he says.

"Josh." I wrap my arms around his neck in a friendly hug. Whoa. He still wears the same cologne and it takes me back. I pray I don't smell like stinky cheese. "It's been ages, hasn't it?"

"Ages," he replies. "You've reached celebrity status. I'm surprised you're even talking to me," he jokes.

"Come on."

He grabs two glasses of champagne on a passing tray and hands me one. "Seriously. You've really done it, Nina." He lifts his glass to me in a toast. "Congratulations."

"Thank you." We clink glasses.

"Funny, isn't it? You gallivanted all over the world and found stardom in a little podunk town we've never heard of."

"Ha ha," I say dryly. I wonder if he's bitter. Josh basically returned from one of his work trips and I was gone and hitched. I decide to change the subject. "So, give me a glimpse into the life of Josh Decker. Are you married?"

"I am not married. I was for a short period of time, but it didn't take."

I frown. "I'm sorry."

He shrugs. "We were too different. She didn't like me traveling so much. She said that she could handle it, but in the end, she couldn't."

"Oh," I say awkwardly. I feel my cheeks flush a little, as if Josh was just talking about my marriage.

"It's okay. Work and volunteering are my passions. I volunteer at the Humane Society. I just love dogs, but I'm not home enough to have my own. I also head up beach clean-ups."

"Wow, that's wonderful. You still have a heart of gold."

"I remember we once shared a love of the ocean."

And lifeguard towers. "Yes, despite your failed attempts to teach me how to surf."

We laugh and it turns into a eye-contact-heavy smile that begins to feel too intense.

"So, what are you doing at a Marshall Books party?" I ask. "Are you doing books now?"

"No, I'm with *Sports Illustrated* now."

"Wow. Cool."

"I'm here with Kimberly Patterson."

"That's my name," a sing-songy voice calls out. A tall, beautiful redhead, probably in her late twenties, attaches herself to Josh's shoulder. Her eyes widen when she sees me. "Oh, my gosh! You're Nina Blake!"

"Kimberly, I would like you to meet a friend of mine, Nina Blake."

Kimberly shakes my hand vigorously. "It is soooo nice to meet you! I love your novels. When a girl doesn't have a boyfriend, your books are a great substitute."

I laugh. "It's my mission to help the greater good."

Kimberly throws back her head full of red locks and laughs. Josh smiles at me, amused, and for a moment I really miss him.

"Kimberly just signed with Marshall Books."

"Fantastic! Congratulations. They've been really good to me, so best of luck."

"Thank you so much!" she gushes.

Josh shakes his head, grinning.

"Joshy, are you ready to go?" Kimberly asks.

He looks at me, hesitant.

I don't really want to stop catching up either. But I am not his date. I smile at him.

"Well," I say, "there are still some people I need to catch up with. It was wonderful meeting you, Kimberly. I look forward to reading some of your books."

"Are you kidding me? Thanks! So nice to meet you!"

"Good night, Nina." Josh's blue eyes burn into mine. "It was really good to see you."

He leans in and gives me a kiss on the cheek. My lungs fill with his intoxicating scent and his soft lips brush against my skin. For the innocent gesture that it is, it feels very inappropriate.

Kimberly doesn't seem to notice.

Josh whispers in my ear, "Your husband is an extremely lucky man."

Little hairs have just stood up on the back of my neck. I'm not sure if it's being this close to Josh's lips again or what he has just said to me.

I force a smile, my cool completely gone. "Uh, goodnight."

I nod politely in Kimberly's direction, full well knowing that she's going to be walking like a cowgirl in the morning.

They leave me standing there and enter the elevator. As the doors close, Josh and I lock eyes and I hear his breathy words again muffled in my ear.

"Your husband is an extremely lucky man." And then it hits me. Damn right, he is.

* * *

As I drive back to my parents' house, it's hard not to fantasize about Josh a little. He's been out of sight, out of mind for so long. But it was kind of exhilarating being in his presence again. The way he looked at me tonight was the same way he looked at me when I was twenty-two years old.

I have many different feelings bubbling inside. Josh has stroked my ego a little. How crazy that our chemistry was still there. Our involvement with each other ended seventeen years ago and he's still interested in me. It's the same amount of time that Brandon and I have been married, and our chemistry has totally disintegrated. He's not interested in me in the least.

Which leads me to my next emotion. Anger. Brandon is totally taking me for granted. Josh is right. Brandon is lucky to have me, and he's on the verge of throwing me away!

I'm a beautiful, successful woman and he doesn't give me the slightest glance. I should tell him. I should call Brandon and wake him up right now. I'll tell him that I ran into Josh and he was flirting with me like crazy… okay, that phone call could very well backfire. Brandon met Josh before at a few *L.A. Times* parties. He knows that we dated and doesn't care for him one bit. That phone call would definitely fire Brandon up and cause him to resent the social events that my business requires of me even more than he already does.

The good thing about my run-in with Josh is that he reminded me that I am desirable and deserving. I have lain in bed so many nights with my husband's back to me and wondered what I'm missing. Maybe it's not me. Maybe Brandon's the one lacking something.

I turn onto my parents' street feeling a little better about myself, since I've decided that I'm not missing any vital characteristics that would make me a desirable wife. But then I start to wonder, what's going on with Brandon?

You know what they say. If he's not getting it at home, he's getting it somewhere else.

My mind racing, I pull into the driveway and turn off the ignition. The dark night is still and quiet. All I can hear is the muffled sound of my rapid heartbeat and the dreadful question— is Brandon having an affair?

I don't know how long I sit in the silence of the car pondering that question. Brandon wouldn't do that. I trust him. He's not that kind of man. Yet something is going on with him.

When I snap out of my hypnotized state I make a decision. Contemplation time is over. I'm not scheduled to fly home until Monday, but this just can't wait. I'm going home tomorrow to reclaim what is mine.

Chapter 10

I have one stop to make before I head to the airport. I drive through the huge iron gates of Forest Lawn Cemetery and cruise through the beautifully groomed grounds. A fountain bathes a flock of ducks that spread their wings out under the spray of water while others waddle around on the grass.

I continue up the hill past the Great Mausoleum that houses the radiant stained-glass recreation of *The Last Supper*, which I viewed on a field trip in the fifth grade of my Catholic education. After a few turns, I pull up to the curb and get those old feelings back. Though it's been eighteen years since her death, my throat still tightens up as I prepare to visit with my all-time favorite person.

I tuck two bouquets of flowers under my arm, grab two steaming cardboard cups of tea out of the cup holders and lock the car doors. You wouldn't believe it, but they say people will actually rob your car as you are visiting the deceased. Sounds like awfully bad karma to me.

I search the curb and find the headstone that says Colonel Arnold Nicholson, then walk straight for about twenty yards, respectfully trying not to step on anyone.

"There you are."

The bronze plaque says *Isabel Maria Apodaca— Devoted Wife,*

Mother, and Grandmother. Next to hers is a similar plaque for my grandpa Julio.

I nestle the hot cups of tea into the grass, squat down, dust the loose grass off the bronze plaques with my hands, and blow the dust away. I set the bouquets into the flower holders that are set into the earth below each plaque. I kiss my hand and touch Grandpa's plaque.

"Hi, Gramps. I love you."

After a few quiet moments of thought and prayer to my grandpa, I sit down between the two headstones. Grandma and Grandpa have a fantastic view overlooking the cityscape of downtown Los Angeles.

I pause for a few moments with my eyes closed. I always start with a few Hail Marys before I begin my monologue to Grandma.

Grandma loved to pray to Mary. I learned to play *Ave Maria* on the piano for her when I was a little girl. She would sit quietly in an armchair in my parents' living room and listen to me for as long as I would play.

"Hi, Grandmacita. I brought you a cup of tea. Chamomile, our favorite." I take a tentative sip of mine. "Sorry it's been a while. Roma and Jane are doing great. You know that. I know you watch us."

I always begin my monologue a little awkwardly.

"I have so much to tell you, but I don't know where to start. I dreamt about you the other night. I was in a parking structure, which is strange because there aren't any parking structures in Skiatook." I chuckle. "I was parking my car and I saw a group of older ladies power-walking up and down the levels of the structure. Again, strange. You were among them, and I kept driving up and down the levels until I could catch you. And when I finally did, I jumped out of the car and hugged you, and I just couldn't believe that you were there. The women you were with scolded me, saying, 'Why haven't you visited your grandma for all these years?' And I said, 'They told me you died!'" I get choked up when I say this.

"Isn't it funny that I still dream that you're alive, after all these years? In my dreams, I'm still looking for you." I wipe a tear from my cheek.

"Brandon and I are not doing well. We don't really fight. We just don't connect. I don't know what's wrong or when it happened. All I know is that something big is missing. We're supposed to be thinking about whether or not we even want to be married to each other. Can you believe that?" I laugh in disbelief. "I feel so naive. I thought we'd always just keep on going even though there have been some bumps. What have I done to make him question us? I feel like I'm a good wife. I'm a good mother. I help provide for our family. I'm all these things, yet Brandon rejects me. What is it? What's wrong with me?"

I wince that I would even ask that question. I have always been a confident woman. It's what has gotten me to take advantage of the amazing opportunities in my life. It's what got me an impressive job in journalism when I was twenty-two, and it's what got me Brandon.

I shake my head in frustration.

Talking this out to my grandma's grave is not helping. She's the only one I want to be honest with, but I can't get any feedback from her. I need her here. I need her to talk back to me and it's really frustrating.

"Grandma." I look up at the sky. "Give me a sign! I need your advice." My voice cracks. "I wish we could actually have a cup of tea and you could tell me what to do."

I burst into tears like a foolish little kid.

After a moment of a good indulgent cry, I wipe my face. I take a steadying breath and look at the view of downtown L.A. I sip my tea. This is reality. Grandma is still dead and I have a plane to catch.

I kiss my fingers and touch Grandma's headstone. If Grandma was here, she would touch my cheek and call me "*mi linda*". My pretty.

I take the lid off Grandma's cup of tea and pour the hot, fragrant liquid over her grave. The flowery aroma floats up to my nostrils as the steaming chamomile concoction seeps into the soil.

"I love you, Grandma."

The warm Santa Ana winds begin to blow as I rise to my feet. The long willowy branches of a nearby pepper tree sways. Strands of my hair waft across my face. I smile and close my eyes as the tranquil breeze comforts me.

A sudden gust sweeps one of the empty cups right out of my hand.

"Shit!"

Great, not only have I just littered in a cemetery, but now I've cussed in the presence of all of these souls who are just trying to rest in peace. I try to grab the cup but it continues to blow away, just inches out of reach. I run across about seven graves, hunched over, trying to snatch it.

"Sorry!" I apologize to everyone that I am trampling over.

I finally catch the damn cup and clutch it to my chest. I let out a deep exhale and blow the hair away from my face. I glance up to the heavens and smirk.

Grandma always had a great sense of humor.

Chapter 11

When I turn into the driveway of 13714 Versace Drive I can barely contain my mosaic of emotions. I can't wait to see my girls and I'm anxious to tell Brandon how much I love him. But I'm nervous about what I may discover. There is a sense of dread imposing on my chest, caused by anticipation of the worst possible outcome of this situation. The lump in my throat is ready to send a signal to my brain to unleash the tears. Yet in my heart I hold a glimmer of hope in getting back the love that Brandon and I once had. Under all of it is growing, bubbling desperation.

I announce my arrival as I walk through the foyer, but through the living room windows I see Jane, Roma and Brandon jumping on the trampoline. My heart swells.

I open the sliding glass door and walk out onto the porch. The late afternoon sun glistens on the lake so brightly that it is almost blinding. Unnoticed, I take a moment to observe the sweet scene before me.

Roma is curled into a tight ball, her arms clasped around her legs while Brandon and Jane jump around her trying to "crack the egg". Roma laughs hysterically. She can be so carefree and silly with Brandon. Jane jumps a circle around Roma, determined to crack her.

I jog over to the trampoline. "Hi, guys!"

"Mama!" Jane jumps off the trampoline into my arms.

"I missed you all so much," I say with a tear in my eye.

"Hi, Mama." Roma smiles.

"You're home two days early," Brandon says, perplexed.

"I couldn't stay away another minute."

"How did it go?" Brandon asks.

"Great. It went great." I smile at him. "And Grandma and Grandpa stuffed a few surprises in my suitcase."

"Yay!" Jane exclaims. She wriggles out of my arms. "Come on, Roma!" Roma hops down and I hug her. The girls run off towards the house.

"Let's talk," I say.

Brandon nods, his expression neutral. He jumps off the trampoline and I hug him.

"Let's go down here so we can be alone," he says.

He leads me by the hand down to the big deck. A tender gesture meaning one of two things: he loves me and wants to work things out or he's about to break my heart.

My stomach is in knots and I suddenly feel like I've had entirely too much coffee today as nervous energy courses through my veins. We take a seat on patio chairs and Brandon grabs my hand again.

Despite my melange of emotions, the lake remains calm and unchanging. I try to focus on that.

"I'll start," I attempt. "I missed you so much. I couldn't get you off my mind. I thought so much about our beginning and Rome and how intensely we were in love. I don't know what the answers are for us right now, but I know that we're supposed to be together."

Brandon nods slowly, digesting his thoughts. He massages the top of my hand with his thumb. His touch feels so good, so needed. He has the kindest eyes, and right now the sun is making the flecks of gold in them stand out. But they look troubled, and I can see in this moment that they don't hold love for me. My eyes plead with his.

"We need some time apart," he says. "It's just not working right now. It hasn't been."

I feel like I've been stabbed in the back. After a week of immersing myself in the riveting memories of our great love story, I've just divulged that I'm all in. Love conquers all. And Brandon has just squashed that.

"What are you suggesting?" I ask.

"I'm going to live in the room over RJ and Becky's garage for a while."

"You've already made arrangements?"

Brandon's poker face doesn't break.

"While I was two thousand miles away, pining over you, reaffirming that my heart is totally with you, you made sleeping arrangements?" A painful sigh escapes my lips. "Your mind was made up before I even left."

Brandon remains silent.

"It was, wasn't it? And you thought you'd take advantage of the distance between us."

"I don't want to fight, Nina. But yes. This is what I want to do. It's what I've wanted to do for a while."

I nod, angry. "Is there someone else?"

"Hell, no."

I exhale in relief. "Do you... want to divorce me?" I ask slowly. These unbelievable words leaving my mouth unleash the tears.

"Nina, let's not get ahead of ourselves. If we are going to survive this, I need some space. I need to be out of this situation for a while and come back with a clear head."

I want to sit on Brandon's lap and throw my arms around his neck. I want to remind him about that first night on the beach, how he couldn't bear the thought of not seeing me again. I want him to think back to our time in Italy when we couldn't keep our hands off each other, where Roma was conceived out of our overpowering love for each other. How we took our own separate lives and merged them into one.

But I'm pretty sure what I, the ever-so-wise love expert, would advise to fellow townspeople at the gas station or in the checkout line at Walmart. Do not beg.

So I wipe my face and ask the next dreaded question.

"What do we tell the kids?"

* * *

I escape to the downstairs guest bathroom for a few private moments. A few runaway tears escape down my cheeks. Oh, my gosh. Is this really happening? I'm dying to feel the release of bursting into tears, but I don't have the luxury of breaking down right now. I take some deep breaths and pull it together for the sake of my children. This is going to break their hearts.

The four of us sit on the couch in the living room. The kids know something's up. Family meetings like this are rare, unless there is something serious for us to discuss.

"Are we moving?" Jane blurts out.

I smile. Leave it to Jane for some comic relief.

"No, honey," I reply.

"Then why are there suitcases in the back of Daddy's truck?"

My smile disappears. Okay, not funny. Anger washes over me that Brandon's bags were packed days before he expected me home. I feel so betrayed. I file these emotions away for later when I can deal with them in private.

Brandon jumps in. "Sweetie, I'm going to have a sleepover at the Jamesons' house for a while."

"Cool. Can I come?" Jane asks excitedly.

"No, sweetie. I have to go by myself."

"Why?"

"Well"—he looks at me with pain in his eyes—"your mama and I are not getting along right now."

My eyes dart to his, but my poker face does not reveal my annoyance. Why is he involving me? This is not what *I* want. This is solely his doing.

"I knew it," Roma says angrily.

I glance at Roma, concerned. My poor baby.

"You know when you girls have a fight," I jump in, "and we tell you to go to your rooms to cool off and think about what you're fighting about?"

Jane nods. "Yep, and then we have to come out and hug." I glance at Brandon, but he's looking at the floor.

"Always gotta come out and hug," Jane adds for emphasis.

Roma ends her silence. "Are you guys getting a divorce?"

"No," Brandon and I both say at the same time.

Well, that was promising. Hopefully, that emphatic reply was not just for the girls' benefit.

"We just need to think about some things," Brandon tells them. "Sometimes it's easier to think about things when you're alone. And that's why I'm going to leave for a little while. But I love you both. You can call me any time you want to, and we're still going to spend a lot of time together."

Roma stands up. "This is"—she looks at Jane and hesitates—"B.S.!" She runs to the stairs and charges up them, two at a time.

Jane raises her eyebrows. "Whoa. Those are bad letters. I better go talk to her." Jane runs up the stairs. Brandon and I both exhale.

"I can't believe that just happened," I say, dismayed.

"It wasn't fun." Brandon looks down at the floor.

Thanks for the understatement of the year.

"Honestly. Do you want things to work out for us?" I ask.

"Of course."

"And you think separating is a solution? Like you're going to just leave for a while and come back refreshed with answers?"

Okay, I'm beating a dead horse now. It's a trait I get from my mother.

"It's a move, Nina. It gets us moving in a new direction. Otherwise, we're stagnant. We stay right here. And we've been here too long." He gets up off the couch and walks to the door.

"What if it's the wrong direction?" I persist.

Brandon doesn't answer. He shakes his head, out of answers.

"I would rather be unhappy with you, than happy without you," I say, my eyes swelling with hot, salty tears.

Brandon walks back to me. "I don't want you to be unhappy at all." He touches my face, turns, and lets himself out the front door.

I glance up the stairs to make sure the girls are out of sight.

Now, I can cry.

Chapter 12

I realize that it's six forty-five and I order a pizza. Since we're out of the delivery zone, I drive into town to pick it up.

I drive without the radio on. I'm in shock. It crosses my mind that Brandon and I went for a drive on my first Valentine's Day in Oklahoma. We ended up in a small town called Barnsdall. Okay, when I specify that it's a small town, that means it's even smaller than Skiatook. I'm talking about a town that has one flashing light.

We came across Big Heart Pizza, a pizza parlor that consisted of a Pac-Man arcade game and table tennis. The high-school kid who made our pizza decorated it with a huge heart made entirely out of bacon bits. That really cracked us up. Brandon didn't think twice about a lot of these small-town touches until I waltzed into town and laughed hysterically about everything. I wasn't laughing in a condescending way. I was amused because things were so cute and endearing, and drastically different from the westside of Los Angeles.

I think about that pizza with the heart on it as I drive to pick up my inaugural pizza as a separated woman. As a writer, the irony is not lost on me.

* * *

I toss the pizza box on the island.

"Dinner," I shout.

Jane sulks into the room and sits down at the kitchen table.

Roma doesn't come down.

I serve Jane a slice of pepperoni on a paper plate with an apple. It's the best I can do right now.

As I fill myself a glass of ice water, I glance at my daughter. She's crying. But she's doing it silently so I won't hear her.

I rush to her side. "Janie. Don't cry."

"Why shouldn't I?"

I'm at a loss. She's right. She should. "I'm sorry. This is only temporary. Daddy and I will figure this out."

"How do you know?" she asks.

I open my mouth and wait for the words to come. "I don't. But I believe that we will, and I'll do everything I can to patch us up."

Jane nods, but she's not convinced.

"No matter what, you are loved." I hug her with all my might. I pick up her apple and take a bite out of the top of it, right under the stem.

She looks at me funny. "Why'd you do that?

"Don't you see it?" I ask.

She looks at her apple, and at the top is a heart cut out of the white flesh of the fruit surrounded by red peel.

"My mom used to do that to my apples. I completely forgot about it until now."

She tries to smile. "Thanks. You're the best." She leans against me.

Chapter 13

I huff and roll over in bed for what must be the hundredth time. I glance over at the alarm clock. Four-fourteen. I'm so congested from crying that I can't breathe out of my nose. Sleep is not happening. I head downstairs through a dark, still house to prepare a cup of tea.

When the microwave beeps, I grab the mug, add an oozing spoonful of honey, and leave the tea bag in, as always. I plop down at the kitchen table and lean my face on my hands, propped up by my elbows. I hang my head over the steaming cup. Hot swirls of chamomile steam moisten my face and penetrate my nostrils. I inhale the vapor deeply through my sinuses even though it burns.

The sobbing resumes and it shakes my entire body. It rises from my toes and erupts into convulsing shoulders and climactic sobs.

"I don't know. I don't know what I did." I'm talking to myself now. I put my face in my hands and let out a long moaning cry.

"It's okay, *mi linda*. Let it out," says a familiar voice that I haven't heard in a very long time.

I look up. Sitting in the chair next to me, with her own cup of tea, is my grandma Isabel. My long-since-dead grandma Isabel.

I stand up, shake my head, rub my eyes, and all the other things that crazy people do when they're hallucinating.

She's still there, though.

"Hi, my baby." She sips her tea.

Okay, time for Plan B. I march over to the cabinet over the microwave where we keep the liquor and pull out a bottle of whatever. I hastily unscrew the lid and take a huge swig.

I shudder. It's tequila. There's a reason I stopped taking shots so many years ago. I eventually realized that just being Mexican didn't lessen the possibility of a Jose Cuervo hangover.

Grandma scrunches up her face as she watches me take my second swig. "Put down the bottle, *mi linda*. I know you're surprised, but come sit down." She nods encouragingly and pats my chair.

"I've lost it," I say. "What will happen to the girls?"

"They will be fine. Now come here."

I head to the kitchen sink and turn the faucet on high. I stick my face under the stream of cold water. Dripping, I turn around to face the kitchen table.

Still there. Again, Grandma pats the chair.

I grab a dish towel and wipe my face and neck.

I inch toward the woman I've loved so much and lost almost two decades ago. I bring the bottle of tequila. I sit down carefully like I'm sitting down next to a rabid pit bull.

"Don't be scared. I know you are a little surprised to see me."

"Surprised? Grandma, no offense"—I laugh hysterically—"but I'm not supposed to see you until I walk through the Pearly Gates. Have I arrived?"

Grandma chuckles. "No, my love."

"Am I crazy?"

"Of course not."

"Then how is this happening? This is not possible. It's completely illogical and out of the question."

"Nina, I am here because you need me. Clearly, you need me. I knew it was coming. But, when you came to me in the cemetery, I knew that I had to help you." She takes my hand, and I jump. Her soft, warm, wrinkled hand squeezes mine.

"It's really you," I say softly. "How is this?"

Grandma smiles. "It just is."

I search her eyes, needing an explanation. She replies with only a shrug.

"This is amazing!" I envelop her in a hug and inhale her sweet vanilla scent. "How's Grandpa?"

"Grandpa is wonderful. We are young, happy and in love."

"Wow. What's heaven like?" I ask, bursting with curiosity.

"Heaven is… there are no words for it. You have to see it to believe how beautiful and warm and happy it is. I can't ruin that surprise."

I shake my head in amazement. "Oh, Grandmacita. I've missed you."

She smiles and her eyes crinkle. Her silver curls surround her head like a halo. "I am with you all the time. But I, too, miss our talks. So let's get to it." She clinks my mug with hers.

I laugh at the impossibility of this. I'm so grateful. She's here and she's going to help. I feel an immense sense of relief. . I've been completely alone in my suffering marriage for years. Until my recent trip home, I hadn't confided in anyone. And though I mentioned it to my mom, I didn't really unleash my feelings. I've kept it all inside like bubbles in a pressurized bottle of champagne. I begin to sob.

"Grandma, Brandon left me."

"I know, my baby. I know all about it."

I put my head into her lap and allow myself to be consoled. I could just fall asleep as she plays with my hair, like she used to when I was a child.

"Oh." I sit up quickly, remembering that Grandma holds all the answers. "So, what do I do to get him back?"

"It's not that easy, Nina. I can't just tell you."

"Of course you can. Didn't you bring me a divine answer to fix my marriage?"

"No, *mi linda*. But you will figure it out. "

"Figure it out? I've been struggling with this mystery for a while now. I need your guidance."

"And you will have it. When you need me, we will talk over a cup of tea like old times."

"Really? I can just make a cup of tea, and you'll show up?"

"See the canister on the counter?" Grandma gestures with a tilt of her head.

I glance over at the kitchen counter. Right next to the flour and sugar jars is the old terracotta canister in the shape of a rooster. The same one that sat on Grandma's kitchen counter so many years ago. I took it from her house when she was moved into the nursing home as she began to deteriorate. It still had a handful of tea bags in it. That particular tea has since been discontinued. I never drank any of the tea. They only served as a special memento of our precious tea times together.

"Of course. I love that rooster."

"Just make a cup of tea. And I will come. But only when you really need me. You can't just run down to the market and buy some more. They're special." She winks.

"How many are there?" I ask hopefully.

"There are ten. Nine now."

My heart surges. "Wow. Nine more visits with you?" My eyes fill with happy tears. "I can't believe it!"

Grandma smiles warmly at me and squeezes my hand. I can feel that time is fleeting and this visit is about to come to an end.

"Okay. But Grandma, don't go. I need you now. I want to spend time with you, and I need answers."

"No, *mi linda*. You don't need answers yet. You just need to get settled in this new situation. You need to feel. And you need to sleep. *Buenas noches*."

Chapter 14

I wake up feeling like I have a hangover. The "something bad has happened and I've been crying all night" hangover. Oh, yeah, it did. My husband left me. And that's right, I was drinking tequila straight out of the bottle even though I'm forty.

I turn over to the reality of Brandon's empty side of the bed and my heart drops. And then I remember her.

I sit straight up in bed and my head sways from the sudden movement. Did I dream it? Yes, it was obviously just a dream. I did not sit at my kitchen table and chat over a good ol' cup of tea with my beloved yet deceased grandma.

But it was so vivid! I could actually feel her. My throat constricts as I feel a pang of sadness and longing over the thought of spending another moment with Grandma Isabel.

I walk into the bathroom, turn on the faucet, and splash icy water on my face. I look up and see a haggard face in the mirror with red, puffy eyelids and narrow slits for eyes.

Lovely.

* * *

I arrive at an empty coffee maker. In the grand scheme of things, it's low on the list of tragedies, but it's still a major disappointment. It's symbolic *and* I have to wait five minutes for my caffeine. As the coffee percolates, I decide to make French toast. I've just run my children's father out of the house. The least I can do is make them a good breakfast.

I crack eggs into a bowl and toss the shells into the trash can. As I rinse egg off my hands, I glance out the window.

Brandon, Roma and I used to live in a little house in town by the high school. When my writing career took off, we decided to buy a lot out here by the lake and build our dream home. When we moved in, my parents had a mature golden delicious apple tree planted on the side of our yard as a wish for a fruitful life. The tree has continued to bloom over the years and looms just past the small brick deck. Jane frequently takes our horses apples to snack on. Now that fall is arriving and it's bursting with fruit, I need to get some bags of apples to my mother-in-law and sister-in-law, the true bakers in the family. Years ago Brandon secured a wooden swing on the tree, which is now weathered with age. I should probably sand it so Jane doesn't get a splinter. Lost in thought, I stare out at the apple tree.

I snap out of my daze when I notice movement. Grandma Isabel uses a long pole with a hook to knock down apples. She bends down, holds up the hem of her apron, and lays a few golden delicious apples in its fabric. My eyes widen in disbelief and I lurch over the sink to get a closer look.

This is a familiar sight, actually. At my grandparents' house in Eagle Rock, California, a huge orange tree canopied the backyard and fragranced the air with its sweet blossoms. On sleepover mornings, we would make breakfast together in our matching aprons. We ran "Grandma and Nina's Restaurant" for our one and only esteemed customer, my grandpa Julio. Grandma and I would head out into the backyard, her in her housecoat and light blue slip-on open-toed slippers and I in my pajamas. We would knock oranges down with the pole and hook that Grandpa had rigged for her, and we would gather the oranges in the hem of her housecoat. I was always excited when Grandma let me operate the automatic orange juicer. I can practically smell the fresh, vibrant citrus.

Grandma looks at me and waves.

I jump. My heart skips a bit. It wasn't a dream! Grandma was really here! *Is* really here! I'm waving excitedly when Roma shuffles into the kitchen.

"Who are you waving at?" she asks groggily.

"You wouldn't believe it!" I exclaim, but I can't quite get the rest out of my mouth. I guess I need to think about how I'm going to break this to the girls before I blurt out that we'll be receiving regular visits from their dead great-grandma. "No one, sweetie."

Roma looks at me funny. She grabs a carton of orange juice out of the fridge and pours herself a glass. "French toast, yum." She gets a bottle of syrup out of the pantry. "Can we have sausage, too?"

I hastily look out the window at the apple tree. All that moves is the tree swing, swaying from an early fall breeze. My eyes scan the yard for Grandma.

"Mom," Roma repeats loudly.

I jump. "What, honey?"

"Sausage?" she asks.

"Oh, sure," I answer, distracted. She's here. Grandma really is here. Through my pain and shock, I feel hope.

"You're acting weird," Roma says as she takes sausage out of the refrigerator. She brings it over to the stove. "Mom." Her voice softens as she looks at me with concern. "Your face looks horrible."

The way she says it makes me laugh.

"Oh, Mom," she says, worried. She puts her arms around me and hugs me.

"I'm fine, sweetie. Everything's going to be fine."

Chapter 15

"Hi, honey."

As soon as I hear my mom's voice, I long for her. I'm dreading this conversation— the judgement, the disappointment. But I'm also yearning for my mom to console me and tell me it will be all right. "He moved out."

There is silence on the other end. "I'm sorry, Nina. I really am."

"Honestly, Mom, this is so hard."

"The girls will keep you busy," she coaxes.

"I know. It's just that I need to be strong for them, but I'm just so sad. And I don't want anyone else to know about our problems, but I'm lonely."

"Well, you decided to live there away from your family and friends. If you were home, I could be with you. You'd have Alison, Kate, and Christina to help you through this."

Seriously?

After all this time that I've lived in Oklahoma, my mom still takes a jab about my moving any chance she gets. She is still bitter that I left her. She never admired or related to the romantic side of me falling madly in love with a country boy and moving halfway across the country to have a life with him. She takes it personally that I'm not near her. I choose not to respond to her untimely comment.

"Mom, maybe you could come out for a visit."

"Well, I'm swamped with the upcoming Women's League's Fall Fundraiser. But after that I would love to come. Let's figure it out in a few weeks."

A few weeks. The thought of a few weeks on my own is agonizing.

"Okay, Mom," I reply, defeated.

"Stay strong, honey."

* * *

It's been four days since Brandon moved out and I haven't heard a word from him. Is this how we're supposed to make progress? No contact between us whatsoever? It just doesn't feel right to me.

I decide to drop in on Brandon at work. I just want to see him.

Brandon's family owns and operates a chain of stores called McCoy Feed and Farm Supply. They sell varieties of hay and grains, ointments, grooming supplies such as brushes, clippers, shampoos and conditioners, hoof picks, and tack such as saddles, stirrups, reins— anything you could possibly need for your horses and livestock. They have also branched out over the years to supply other farming supplies that are in demand in our area, including fencing and welding products. Tractors and four-wheelers can be special-ordered, and there is even an apparel section where you can buy boots and western wear.

McCoy Feed and Farm Supply is located in the heart of town, on the block next to Walmart. Brandon's office is in the very back of the store, where he fulfills his duties as vice president of the company. His father, the president, is transitioning into retirement. He has pretty much passed all duties onto Brandon, but is still consulted for major decisions.

I walk through the store, greeting several employees as I pass. I knock on Brandon's open office door and pop my head in. "Jane insisted on decorating the house for Halloween yesterday."

Brandon looks up from his work.

"Somehow, we got around to it so late this year. We made oatmeal cookies with candy corns in them. Don't break a tooth." I smile and hand him the tin of cookies.

"Thanks." He returns a neutral smile.

I nod, waiting for him to say more. "How are you?" I ask.

"I'm okay." He doesn't offer anything else. He just stares at me with an insipid expression.

I notice a heating pad plugged into the wall, sandwiched between him and the back of his chair. He took a lot of hits as a high-school and college linebacker and pain in his lower back flares up occasionally.

"Is your back bothering you?" I ask.

"It's not too bad."

"Would you like me to bring you some muscle relaxers from home?"

"I'll manage."

I immediately feel hurt and defensive. "Are we supposed to just ignore each other?"

"Of course not."

"I was trying to be nice," I say.

"I know." He shakes his head. "Thanks."

"Why it does it feel like we're strangers?" I ask.

"I don't know."

After another moment of silence, I sigh. "All right, goodbye. Take care. Whatever." I walk away, completely defeated. I walk out of his office and breeze through the store, careful not to make eye contact with anyone. I barely make it inside the car before I start to sob.

I drive straight home and climb into bed. I cry. I cry the whole afternoon. The old Brandon would have rushed after me if I was upset. But no one appeared at my car as I cried in the parking lot and no one has called or texted to see if I'm okay.

I slip off into a heavy, blurry sleep and I wake up and cry some more. Luckily, Jane has 4H after school, Roma has play rehearsal, and Becky will drop them off at home, so I've had a few hours to feel totally sorry for myself.

I don't know what to do. It feels like Brandon and I have a war to fight for our marriage and he's already waving the white flag, but not because he's surrendering to me— because he's done. I know I can't give up, but I already feel so defeated.

He doesn't want to try. He doesn't want to put in any effort.

And furthermore, he doesn't want me to.

I'm so sad. "Sad" seems like such a small, light word; a word for a child to use. But that's what I am. Sad. I miss Brandon. I've missed him for a long time, though now he is physically absent in addition to being emotionally absent. There's no more pretending to ourselves or the girls that everything is all right.

"Mama, why are you sleeping?" Jane asks as she enters the dark room.

I sit up fast and my head sways. How could it already be five o'clock? Have I really slept all day?

"Are you okay, Mama?" Jane sits down on the bed.

"I was just really tired this afternoon. I needed a nap."

Jane looks concerned. "Okay." She rubs my leg. "I'm hungry. Should I put some chicken nuggets in the microwave for dinner?"

"That's a great idea, sweet pea."

Jane walks out of the dark room, looking back a few times.

"I'm okay. I'll be down soon," I try to say strongly. "I'll be down soon," I repeat, willing it to happen.

Chapter 16

Oh, right. I'm a *New York Times*-bestselling author and I'm supposed to be writing my next bodice-ripper. I sit on the side porch, document open, poised, waiting for the words to come. I've always believed that the best way to work through writer's block is to just get something down, it doesn't even matter if it's good. There might be a glimmer of an idea that can take off. You can always edit. You can always delete. But the worst thing to do is to stare at a stagnant screen.

I sigh.

Not even a glimmer. The words blur together as I stare, uninspired and unproductive, at the unchanging screen.

* * *

Jane and I drive home from school. Roma is at play rehearsal so we're on our own for the evening. We're at a spot on Highway 20 where it goes up a slight hill towards the turn-off to Lake Road. Right when we get toward the top, I see a tortoise smack-dab in the middle of the road. Maybe he's trying to haul ass across the dangerous stretch of highway, but he's not making very good time.

"Oh, no, there's a tortoise," I say.

I hear Jane's sharp intake of breath from the back seat. "You have to go back!"

I look in the rear-view mirror and see the concern in Janie's eyes. I pull into the Handlebar Bar's dirt parking lot and turn around to go back east on Highway 20.

"Oh, thank you, Mama."

I pull over on the side of the road and park. "Stay in the car, Jane. I'll save the tortoise." I unbuckle my seat belt and open the car door.

"It's actually a turtle," Jane explains. "Tortoises aren't native to Oklahoma. Turtles live in water habitats and this turtle is probably looking for a stream or a pond."

I nod and hop out quickly because whichever species it is, and whatever it's looking for, it's about to be flat.

This is not a great spot to be running back and forth on the highway. Cars, pickups and the occasional big rig travel fast on this road, and I'm right on the angle of the hill where oncoming vehicles won't see me until they're practically right on me.

I listen for oncoming traffic down the hill. I wait until a red pick-up passes. And then I run into the middle of the highway, grab the tortoise—or turtle, rather—and run back to the side of the road. A charcoal-colored pick-up passes and I feel its gust of wind whoosh against me. My heartbeat quickens from the adrenaline. The pick-up pulls over.

I see that it's Brandon's truck. He opens the door and climbs out angrily. "What the hell are you doing?" He jogs across the highway to me.

"Hi!" I say. I'm so pleased that he's the one initiating this interaction. "I'm rescuing this turtle." I lift the prehistoric-looking creature to show Brandon.

Brandon looks at me like I'm crazy. "Are you trying to get yourself killed?"

"Oh, yeah, Brandon. I've decided that I just can't take it anymore."

He raises his eyebrows, surprised by my sarcasm.

"We have an animal lover in the back seat and there was no way she could go on with her evening if she had to wonder about the fate of this turtle. You know her."

"I know," he replies. He shakes his head. "Just be careful, okay?"

"Okay." I smile, pleased with his concern for me.

Brandon opens the back door of our S.U.V. and gives Jane a hug and a kiss. I watch him jog back to his truck and wonder what I'm going to have to do to get back into his heart.

I place the turtle in the dirt a few feet from the highway and point him in the right direction. He starts to crawl along.

"Safe travels, little guy. You've got a long journey ahead." Maybe this turtle and I have more in common than one would think.

I climb into the driver's seat.

"Thank you, Mama!"

"You're welcome."

"You know, I actually think the turtle might be looking for a place to hibernate. It is about that time of year. It's finally starting to cool down."

As Jane continues her theories about the intentions of the turtle, I make a careful u-turn back west on the highway and make the left onto Lake Road.

Brandon McCoy coming to my rescue. I'll replay it in my head for days.

Chapter 17

"How's my makeup?" Jane asks from the back seat.

She wears a royal blue sequin dress, a white feather boa, black full-length gloves, and half of my collection of costume jewelry. We also managed to find glittery silver knee-high boots at a garage sale a few weeks ago in the hunt for Halloween treasures. Why someone had silver go-go boots in their wardrobe in this town is beyond me.

Jane's makeup is very dramatic with blue lids to match her dress, rosy cheeks, bright red lips, and false eyelashes that stick out like fuzzy caterpillars on her little face. I gave her one of my formal clutch purses to hold a little pad of paper and pen for signing autographs.

"You look simply mahvelous, dahling," I say. "You're the most glamorous movie star I have ever seen."

Jane giggles. "Thanks! Roma did a really fantastic job with my hair. Thanks a lot, Roma."

Roma put Jane's hair in curlers to add flair to her normally pin-straight bob and hairsprayed the heck out of it. The result is quite poofy. She also pinned a white feather in Jane's hair to match her boa.

"No problem, Janie. You look great."

We pull into the Church of Christ's parking lot for their Annual Trunk or Treat. The parking lot is filled with cars, minivans and pick-up trucks. Trunks are open, tailgates are pulled down and they are filled with loads of candy. Little princesses, ninjas and monsters walk from car to car and fill their pillowcases.

When I first heard about this concept, I cracked up. I thought it was the most redneck Halloween idea I had ever heard of. But now, as a parent living in the country, I totally get it. The way some of the neighborhoods are with the houses so far apart, it would take children all night and a whole lot of legwork to get any candy. This way, they are all together, supervised, and have enough goodies by the end of the evening to happily gorge themselves as the holiday intended.

Roma stopped Trunk or Treating ages ago. However, the high school kids still come to hang out together in a corner of the parking lot.

I pull into a parking spot in the "non-participating trunk" section. We already donated our bag of candy at church on Sunday. We attend the Sacred Heart Catholic Church, but all of the local churches and businesses support and participate in the Church of Christ's Trunk or Treat so there's no competition. It's a very united event.

"See you guys later. I'll find you later to get your autograph!" Roma says.

"You got it," Jane says with sass.

As we climb out of our vehicle Alice Atwater waves from a few cars over. Her kids run off toward the hoopla but she hangs behind.

"Happy Halloween, Alice," I greet.

"Nina, do you have a moment? I need some pointers to spice things up with Carl," she shouts over three cars.

Nice, Alice. A little tact in front of my kids, please?

Roma rolls her eyes. "Seriously?" she mumbles.

"Sorry," I say to Roma.

She shakes her head and takes off.

"I'd be happy to chat with you later once I get my kids settled," I call over to Alice.

"Sure thing, honey," she answers.

"Have fun, Roma," I call.

She zigzags her way through cars in her inconspicuous jeans and hoodie as the sky swirls into the candy-corn colors of dusk.

"Come on, dahling! I can't keep my fans waiting." Jane grabs my hands and leads me toward the festivities.

* * *

Becky and I sit on the tailgate of her white pick-up. She is parked one row over from the Trunk or Treat vehicles so we can watch the action. Between the participating cars and pickups are bales of hay covered with pumpkins, scarecrows, witches and ghosts. *The Monster Mash* plays over speakers and competes with the shrill sound of excited children hopped up on sugar. We watch as Jane and Becky's daughter Delilah bounce from trunk to trunk saying "Trick or treat!" in sing-songy voices.

Outside of the trunk-or-treating loop is a section of festival booths selling Halloween treats and beverages. There is also a flatbed truck covered in bales of hay that gives hay rides in the empty field behind the church, which is covered in pumpkins of all sizes that can be purchased. The same field will be transformed into a Christmas tree lot in December.

Becky and I sip hot spiced cider and munch on the sticky popcorn balls that Belinda Farnsley makes every year. They are perfectly sweet and salty. I'll definitely have to floss later.

Becky gestures with her head toward a booth. "We'll have to rescue Carrie Ann at some point."

Carrie Ann stands at a folding table covered with festive baked goods such as pumpkin bars and brownies covered in Halloween sprinkles. She ladles hot chocolate into styrofoam cups and tops them with mini-marshmallows. A long line of children jump up and down impatiently.

"Nah. You know when she's at a church event, she's all in," I counter. "She's serving Jesus, one cup of cocoa at a time."

Despite being a mother of four, Carrie Ann has a petite little body. Her sandy-blonde hair is shoulder-length and she has kind, honey-brown eyes. We met at a Mommy and Me group when Roma and Carrie Ann's daughter Hailey were just nine months old. She was an experienced mother of two so far, and I was still a shell-shocked new mom. We immediately clicked. None of my other friends had kids yet, and she understood what I was going through like nobody else, and I found that so comforting. She and I are so different from each other, but she is a true friend. Roma and Hailey are still two peas in a pod, as well. Carrie Ann's kids run the gamut of ages. In addition to sixteen-year-old Hailey, Justin, twenty, is in college, Evelyn is nine and Robbie is four. It seems that every time she felt like her children were getting easier, she decided to have another one.

Becky, on the other hand, was one and done with Delilah.

"Delilah looks adorable in her unicorn costume," I tell Becky.

"Thanks. I procrastinated a little. I finished it last night."

"I don't know how you do it. I can't sew to save my life. Show me a loaded closet, though, and I can do wonders in creating a costume."

"Yes, you can."

A chilly Northerly wind blows a delicious whiff of sugary cotton candy our way from the Skiatook PTA booth and Becky catches her witch's hat before it blows off her head. I shiver and pull the hood of my black and orange Halloween sweatshirt over my head. I blink into the bright fluorescent lights of the church parking lot that glow in the now raven sky.

"I've got about thirty minutes before I need to put my time in at the Sacred Heart booth dipping caramel apples."

"Yep." Becky nods awkwardly after a pause in our small talk. "So, how are *things*?"

"I don't want to talk about it," I say without flinching.

"Nina, you can't pretend nothing is wrong. The man is living above my garage."

"I'm well aware. We're going to figure things out, and we don't need to involve anybody."

Becky exhales. "All right. When you're ready to talk, I'm here for you."

I feel bad about being so snippy. "I know you are. Thanks for taking him in."

Becky pats my hand. "Of course. How else would I spy on him and report back to you?"

I manage a smile. "You're a great friend." I watch as Jane signs autographs for her fellow first-graders.

She catches my eye and waves.

I smile and wave back.

I scan the group of high-school kids for Roma. A boy is clearly trying to flirt with her and it is obvious that she says something to blow him off. That girl doesn't make things easy for anyone, I'll give her that much. I think the boy's last name is Anderson. I don't know much about him. He transferred to Skiatook a few years ago when his family moved from another town in Osage County.

I continue to watch and something seems off. The boy walks back over to his group of boys and Roma watches him, a little sadly, I think.

"Marlena's here," Becky says.

I peruse the crowd.

Marlena was Brandon's high-school sweetheart. She has crystal-clear blue eyes and shiny blonde hair that she wears in long, layered waves. She's always dolled up with major makeup like a true Southern belle. She owns the Skiatook Bakery. She bugs the heck out of me, but the girl makes a damn good cake.

My eyes land on a group of women and Marlena is in the center of them. She speaks very animatedly with her hands flying all over the place. She's decked out in a very short, tight red and black Skiatook Bulldogs cheerleading uniform.

"Why is she wearing that?" Becky asks, appalled.

"She wants everyone to know that she still fits in her high-school cheerleading uniform."

"I can just picture her an hour ago, frantically stretching out the sweater so her boobs could fit in it. Because she didn't have *them* in high school." Becky wasn't a fan of Marlena's then or now.

I shake my head in disgust.

"What a skank," Becky adds.

I throw my head back and laugh. "I love you."

"Love you back," she answers with a wink.

"Hot apple cider and ex-girlfriend bashing on a blustery Halloween night. Just what I needed."

"Happy Halloween." Becky holds up her styrofoam cup and taps it against mine.

* * *

"Hi, sweet pea," I say as I approach Jane. "How'd you make out?"

"So good, Mama! I'm going to have to brush my teeth like ten times after I eat all of this!"

"Good planning, hon."

"Oh. My. Gosh. Is that really Jane McCoy?"

Jane giggles.

My heart sinks as Brandon walks up to us. He looks so cozy in his worn-in Levis, plaid flannel shirt, Carhartt jacket and baseball cap. I want to hug him.

"Oh, please, oh, please, can I have your autograph?" he gushes to Jane.

"Of course. Who should I make it out to?" Jane asks playfully.

"'Daddy' will work."

"'To: Daddy,'" Jane says as she writes, "'My biggest fan.'"

"You got that right," he says as he scoops her up. He turns to me. "How are you?"

I shrug. "Fine. And you?"

"I'm holding up."

High-school kids are having more complex conversations fifteen feet away from us.

"Wanna go for a hay ride?" he asks Jane.

"Yeah!" she screeches enthusiastically. "Mama, will you hold my candy?"

"Of course. But it will cost you an Almond Joy."

Jane hands me her pillowcase. "Help yourself. Generosity," she adds with a dramatic wink.

Brandon grabs Jane's hand and they head toward the hay ride.

"Hey, honey?" I say, louder and needier than I intended. I walk towards them.

Brandon stops walking and puts Jane down. "Janie, why don't you get us a spot in line?"

"Okay," she says, and runs off.

Brandon looks at me.

I lower my voice. "So, when are you coming home?" I ask.

"I don't know. I need some time."

My heart sinks. "But our anniversary is next week."

Brandon sighs. "I'm sorry, Nina. It just doesn't feel right to celebrate."

I actually feel a pain in my stomach like he just punched me in the gut. "Wow. Okay." I turn and walk away.

I hear Brandon say my name a few times, but if I turn around, I will burst into tears. I inhale some cleansing breaths of Halloween air, pull myself together, and head to the Sacred Heart Church booth to dip apples in caramel like there is no tomorrow.

Chapter 18

Our seventeenth wedding anniversary came and went. I didn't call Brandon, and he didn't call me. As a writer, I am well-versed in the art of foreshadowing. Ignoring the date we promised to love and cherish each other doesn't bode well for our happy ending.

I took the day off. Staring at my computer screen, uninspired and alone with my thoughts, would've been agony. So, after I dropped the girls off at school, I drove into Tulsa and took myself to the movies.

I went to my favorite little theater that shows classics. As luck would have it, *Casablanca*, one of my all-time favorites, was playing. But a torturous story about a man and a woman who had a previous whirlwind love affair, the man now cynical and bitterly angry with the woman, and in the end, even though they still love each other, he puts her on a plane and sends her away forever, turned out to be a bad choice.

After the movie, I treated myself to a lunch buffet at the one and only Indian restaurant in Tulsa. As usual, the restaurant was empty. (I must explain to the state of Oklahoma that Indian food is amazing.) Normally, I would relish having lunch by myself in the city, but on that day my table for one was depressing and I was unable to enjoy my chicken tikka masala.

With Brandon out of the house, I've had to make a real effort to keep my mind occupied. Keeping my calendar full has helped with that goal. I've been volunteering in Jane's classroom, answering fan mail, and attempting to write. However, my creativity is totally shot. It's hard to write about romance and love when I feel so much despair.

I've also been running and walking around the lake a lot. The endorphins are a welcome drug that elevate me out of my fog.

Becky, Carrie Ann and I now pump our arms as we hike the rocky trail that surrounds Skiatook Lake. I have kept my situation to myself. I just plain don't want people to know about it. However, keeping all of these feelings of despondency bottled up inside is killing me. It's been one month since Brandon moved out and I can't understand why he needs more time. I have to confide in my girlfriends. I need them. We trek up a steep hill, only moments away from the end of our workout, so I guess there's no time like the present.

"So… there's something I'd like to talk to you girls about," I start. "Just between the three of us."

Becky looks surprised.

"What's going on?" Carrie Ann asks.

I nod to Becky. I want to get things off my chest, but I can't even state the problem out loud.

"Um," Becky starts, caught off guard. "Nina and Brandon are experiencing some problems." She eyes me, unsure how much to divulge.

Carrie Ann looks at Becky, confused.

I nod to Becky to continue.

"They are not getting along."

Carrie Ann's gaze shifts to me.

I nod impatiently to Becky and she raises her eyebrows. "Brandon has temporarily moved out and is living over my garage?"

Carrie Ann comes to an abrupt halt. "You've separated? When did this happen?"

Becky and I stop walking.

"And why?" Carrie Ann continues.

I guess it's my turn. I take a breath.

"It's been about four weeks. And I'm not really sure why. There has been a lot of tension between us for quite a while now, a few years maybe. But I don't know what the root of the problem is."

"A few years?" Carrie Ann shrieks. She gapes at me, still dumbfounded. I can barely take it.

"Walk and talk, ladies," I demand. "If I'm going to discuss this, I need to keep moving." I take off and they follow me.

"How are you holding up?" Becky asks tentatively.

"Honestly, not so great. I try to put on a brave face for Roma and Jane. But once they're asleep I drink wine in the bathtub. And cry."

"Oh, sweetie." Becky puts her arm around me as we walk. I begin to tear up at the feeling of being comforted. I've been dying for someone to console me, but as it turns out my isolation is all that is holding me together.

"No, no," I say. "Don't hug me. I'll cry."

Becky removes her arm. "Sorry."

"So what are you going to *do*?" Carrie Ann asks dramatically.

"I don't know. Brandon says he wants space, so right now I'm not really doing anything."

Carrie Ann gawks at me. I can actually see a filling in one of her molars. "Not doing *anything*?"

"Will you please stop repeating everything I say?" I ask.

"No, no. This won't do. You are my relationship champion. You have to know what to do."

Becky and I make eye contact.

We round the last corner of the wooded, rocky trail and emerge into the parking lot adjacent to the boat ramps in the marina.

"I'm not a marriage therapist," I explain. "I don't have a degree in psychology or special training in marital counseling."

Carrie Ann looks at me like I'm a quack, but I continue.

"A woman I worked with at the *L.A. Times* gave me some very valuable advice almost twenty years ago, and I think it still applies today. It was my first week on the job and I was inexperienced, full of doubt, and totally shocked that I got the position. I was insecure about my first article that was about go to print. She told me, 'Nina, you're the professional. Your name will be at the top of that article, and if you don't know what you're doing, you better damn well fake it so people believe you know what you're doing.'"

"That's good advice," Becky says.

"So... what are you saying?" Carrie Ann asks.

"I'm saying I'm a phony!" I practically shout. "No one should ask me for marital advice! I just write trashy literature!"

Carrie Ann looks freaked out.

I breathe hard from my outburst. "Okay," Becky soothes. "Let's all relax."

"I'm sorry. I'm upset," I say.

"No problem," Carrie Ann says, quiet as a mouse.

We stop near our cars and begin to stretch. I pull my foot up behind me and hold it in a quadriceps stretch.

"Look, girls. I don't want people to know about Brandon and me, okay? I just need to be able to confide in you. I need your support."

"Okay," Carrie Ann says with her brows furrowed.

"Of course," Becky adds. "We're here for you."

Becky and I continue to stretch as Carrie Ann gets in her minivan and drives away.

"Are you kidding me?" I finally say. "I knew I would be judged by my readers, but even my own friends expect me to have a perfect marriage."

"She's just in shock. Besides, what *should* we expect? That's what you portray."

"Sheesh, venting was supposed to make me feel better. This is exactly why I've kept all of this to myself."

"Now, hold on a second," Becky says. "Don't sell us short. You need us now."

I exhale. "Okay. You're right."

"What can I do?" Becky asks.

"Wine donations are greatly appreciated."

She smiles. "You got it. You know I'm the charitable kind." Becky unlocks her pickup and opens the door. She turns back to me. "You know I'll do anything for you."

"I know."

* * *

I woke to rain this morning. It was a continuous rush of white noise, pouring buckets on the roof. It baffles me that so much precipitation can fall from the sky when I originated from a state continuously plagued with drought. Yet it has poured here all morning, for hours on end.

When I experienced my first storm out here, Brandon was in Oklahoma City for work. The thunder and lightning shook our little house in town so violently that I hid under the covers. There was nowhere else to go.

But Brandon loves a good storm. He sits out on the porch and watches it, reveling in the deep bass-like roar of thunder and taking in the luminous electricity from afar. He started including Roma, then Jane, in his ritual since they were babies, despite my initial protests. As a result, they love it, too.

I wonder where he is right now watching this storm. I can picture him standing underneath the awning of the feed store in awe of a force so much bigger than all of us.

The rain matches my mood. Not the precipitation, as I seem to be all cried out for now, but the white noise. It's like a numbness that you don't notice after a while. And the thunder and lightning gives me an underlying sense of uneasiness. Under my anesthetized detachedness, there are rumblings of more impending doom in my subconscious.

I dropped the girls at school an hour ago and I'm vacuuming the upstairs. White noise to drown out the white noise.

When I turn the vacuum off to pick up clothes off Jane's floor, I hear pounding on the front door. I run downstairs to see who's trying to break down my door.

I open the door to find Carrie Ann with a sheepish smile on her face, her hair wet and matted. Her arms are full with a pot and two Tupperware containers.

"Sheesh," I say. "Who knew little ol' you could pound that hard?"

"I saw your car so I knew you were here," she explains.

"Come in." I usher her in out of the rain and she follows me into the kitchen. "Let me pour you some coffee." I pull a fresh kitchen towel out of a drawer and hand it to her.

"Oh, thanks," she says as she dries her face. "I'm chilled to the bone! I love a good storm, though. Thank you, Lord Jesus, for this glorious rain!" she shouts to the heavens.

I smile at her as I set a mug of coffee in front of her on the island. "To what do I owe this surprise?" I ask.

She grabs my hand. "I came to apologize about my reaction yesterday. I was just caught off guard. You're our resident relationship professional."

"Well, I didn't run for that position. I just didn't see any other option than to go with it."

"I'm sure you're right. You're just always so upbeat and encouraging about relationships."

"Well, I am. I'm a hopeless romantic. Always have been." I shrug.

"The point is, no one is perfect. We all have our struggles. Yet I was upset at you and Brandon for not being perfect and I apologize. I'm here to support you, however that may be. I'm gonna pray for you both, and I'm gonna listen to you when you need a friend."

I smile. "I appreciate it. I'm going to need both." I glance at Carrie Ann's offerings. "It appears that you're also going to feed me. What did you bring?"

"Beef stew, corn bread and brownies."

"Wow! I haven't eaten yet today. Can we have some now?"

Carrie Ann smiles. "Absolutely."

Chapter 19

I haven't used another tea bag to summon my dead grandma's spirit. The day after she came to me, I tucked the terracotta rooster out of sight at the back of a cupboard so I wouldn't have to deal with it just yet.

I'm definitely sending myself mixed messages. I was amazed and thrilled to be with Grandma when I used that first tea bag. But I've needed time to wrap my head around how this is really happening. I mean, I think it is. I was there. I felt her. And I saw Grandma in my backyard the next morning. But how can I push logic aside and accept that I spent time with my dearly departed grandma when I know that it's just not possible?

That being said, even though I haven't summoned her, I have been seeing her. The other day she was standing next to the November character banner on Highway 20. It said "Patience." She waved her hand down it like she was Vanna White.

One morning while dropping the kids off at school, I breezed towards the crosswalk a little too swiftly, and Mr. Frizzly waved his arms at me to slow down. Grandma sat near him in his camping chair with her legs crossed and mouthed to me to "slow down." I quickly looked in the rearview mirror at the girls' reactions and they just stared out their windows.

I could simply be hallucinating. I'm exhausted. I've been staying up late trying to get some chapters down because I have pages due to Stan. And a few days ago I had a book signing in Tulsa that felt like an out-of-body experience. I felt like I was putting on a show. A forced and unconvincing show. I was drained by the time I got home.

I can also sense Grandma's presence. It's hard to explain. I can just tell that she's around. Grandma used to always wear a sweet vanilla powder from Mexico called Poudre de Riz—Demoiselle Polvo de Arroz. It came in a red and gold rounded square cardboard box which she kept on her bathroom counter. She used a big red powder puff to dust it all over herself after her baths and she always smelled like warm vanilla. That box of powder is one of the things of hers that I kept after she died. I used to open that box and sniff it often during those first few years of missing her so much. I haven't smelled it in ages, but I remember it exactly. And unless someone in Skiatook is wearing vanilla powder from Mexico and following me around, Grandma is not far.

* * *

Since Brandon left, I haven't been eating. I've been in such a fog I guess I've forgotten to. My jeans are definitely bigger in the waist. Normally, I'd be pumped about that.

But I seem to have come to a new phase in my grief. I lean against the kitchen counter and slather a hunk of crusty French bread with butter and orange marmalade. I was excited when I found an unopened jar in the pantry, made with love by my sister-in-law. *Thank you, Jolene.* The pathetic rush of delight when I saw the jar on the shelf will likely be the highlight of my day.

I have shifted into burying my sorrows in bread. Why not? I deserve some pleasure. If you want to come to my pity party, it's BYOC—bring your own carbohydrates. I've got the wine covered, but if you could bring some cinnamon rolls, that would be awesome.

Maybe I should actually throw a pity party. Invite some gals over, eat a lot of bread and cheese, watch chick flicks. Yes, I need to organize that.

The sound of the front door shutting interrupts my thoughts.

"Hi, Mama!" calls Jane's voice.

"Hi!" I call with my mouth full.

Jane and Brandon are suddenly in the kitchen. I straighten up and dust large crusty flakes of French bread off my shirt. How embarrassing.

Brandon is carrying a basket and Jane carries a plastic bag full of carrots from the feed store. She puts the carrots on the counter and hugs me around my middle.

"Hi, my love." I lean down and kiss her on the top of her head.

"Can I take some carrots to Silver Heart and Valentine?"

"Sure."

Jane grabs a few and exits the side door out of the kitchen to head to the stable.

"Hello, stranger," I say to Brandon. Instead of it sounding coy and friendly, it comes out harsh. I think he notices.

"How are you?" Brandon asks.

"I'm... I don't know how to answer that question, honestly."

Brandon nods. For once lately, he can relate to what I'm talking about.

"What's that?" I ask, gesturing to the basket.

"I was going to ask you the same thing," he replies.

I take it from him. It contains a bottle of bubble bath, a box of chocolates and a bottle of cabernet sauvignon. I chuckle.

"Who's it from?" Brandon asks.

"Becky. Who else would it be from?"

"I have no idea," he says sharply.

"Okay, well, it's from Becky. She's trying to cheer me up."

He nods.

I cock my head, confused. Is Brandon suggesting that I'm being unfaithful? That *I'm* disloyal? I'm the one who wanted to celebrate our anniversary, but he wasn't interested. I'm the one trying to put this broken marriage back together. An unexpected surge of anger surfaces.

"You know, I'm really busy," I say. I watch Brandon assess the situation— me wearing sweatpants, eating a messy snack. "I think you should leave."

His look of surprise morphs into animosity. "Sometimes I really don't get you. Good night."

Chapter 20

It's nearing Thanksgiving and the leaves are finally morphing into brilliant warm hues. At the peak of their color, the oak trees will look like an autumn wreath surrounding the dark waters of the lake.

This is my absolute favorite time of year. The air is just brisk enough to pull out the cozy sweaters and scarves. Spectators at the Friday night football games begin to sip hot chocolate and cover their laps with plaid wool blankets.

The girls and I spend weekends in the kitchen baking cookies together and fill the house with the irresistible aromas of melted butter, cinnamon, and vanilla.

Though just like many precious things, this magical part of the season doesn't last long. Soon a biting wind will blow down from Kansas, turning the vibrant leaves brown and sending them on their way, leaving stark and lonely trunks and boughs behind.

I'm at the brick patio with my laptop on my lap, hammering out a few unconvincing middle chapters in *Down and Dirty Down Under*. I always write the beginning and ending of a book first. When I have a story idea, I usually know where I want to start and end. I can never hold myself back from writing that dramatic and romantic ending. The journey in the middle is always the challenging part for me. The writing is starting to come again. It's not great, but it's coming. I'm still grasping onto my *L.A. Times* colleague's advice for this one—fake it 'til you make it.

I pull a chenille blanket tighter around my shoulders. The air is crisp. This is probably my last day of working out here before I move my office back into the house until springtime. I sip a pumpkin spice latte and rap my fingers on my laptop as I think.

Brandon laughed at me when I had the brilliant idea of creating my own home espresso bar. He said, "Only you." He used to use that phrase often when referring to things that I did, and it used to be a good thing.

I bought a coffeehouse-caliber espresso machine and set it up in the wet bar in the living room. I lined the counter with ten different kinds of flavored syrups and bought giant mugs to hold my caffeinated concoctions.

Sounds a little extravagant, I realize, but I used to walk across the street from my apartment in Marina del Rey to Starbucks or the Coffee Bean & Tea Leaf every morning before I headed to work. Now, the closest gourmet coffee establishment is a few towns away in Owasso. What's a girl to do? A writer needs her coffee.

When I decided to break my espresso machine in and make the inaugural latte, I twisted the knob to steam the milk, and the machine started to hiss. Steam started to spit and spray, and Brandon grabbed Roma and hit the living room floor. He said he thought the damn thing was going to explode! I doubled over laughing.

I haven't seen much of Brandon since I asked him to leave that afternoon. I realize that we both messed up an opportunity to delve into solving our marital issues, to begin chipping away at what we've built up over the years. Instead, we pushed each other away yet again.

On Tuesdays and Thursdays, Roma and Jane help at the feed store after school. Jane helps stock small items on the shelves and Roma runs the cash register. On those days as I "casually" rushed out to intercept the girls, I received a quick wave as he reversed in the driveway.

He has also taken them out to dinner on several occasions. However, an invitation has not been extended my way. I've been strong. I've granted Brandon the space he needs to think so he can come back with a clear head, hoping that he will, in fact, come back.

But I've been inactive long enough. I need to do something. I need to devise a plan.

What bullshit advice would I prescribe for someone else's troubled marriage? I need to get in the same room with him, alone. I could invite him over to dinner to talk things over. I could plan the perfect scenario.

He could show up and I could be waiting in a bathtub overflowing with bubbles like Rebecca did in *Irish Fog*. We could run down to the lake after dinner and skinny-dip under the stars like Anna and Jasper in *Moonlight Meadow*. Or maybe I don't have to wait until our dinner at all. I could just show up on his doorstep wearing a trench coat and heels like Emily in *Lovestruck*. Well, maybe I won't show up at Becky's garage wearing nothing but a trench coat.

I sigh.

These are stupid ideas. This is real life, not a paperback.

It's not lost on me that my mother suggested that I a) cook for Brandon, and b) try something erotic from one of my books. Here I am scheming to do both.

I call Brandon's cell phone and of course he doesn't answer. I leave a message that I need to talk to him and would like to have him over for dinner.

So, what are the phone rules for a separated married couple? Is he going to wait a certain number of days before he calls me? Am I not allowed to call again until then? I used to be so good at this kind of stuff, but this is uncharted territory for me. I used to be the girl who didn't call and I was never home when the guys did.

After several hours I decide to take the assertive route. I leave yet another message on Brandon's phone with the date (tomorrow), the time, and that Roma and Jane will be at a church youth group sleepover. I don't want him coming under false pretenses that he'll be spending time with them.

* * *

I received a very brief phone call from Brandon agreeing to join me for dinner tonight. I've decided to prepare his favorite— chicken-fried steak, mashed potatoes and gravy, and corn, straight out of the can. A homemade pecan pie for dessert, his mom's recipe.

They say the way to a man's heart is through his stomach. I guess that's assuming his arteries aren't blocked with fried southern food.

I set the coffee table with silverware, cloth napkins and tea lights to encourage a relaxed atmosphere. I dim the lights and put on David Gray's *Greatest Hits*, one of our very favorites. David Gray's emotional voice resonates throughout the downstairs.

I pour myself a glass of pinot noir to smooth my nerves. I catch a glimpse of my reflection in the oven door. I'm wearing jeans and a teal wrap top with a low neckline. Okay, it's definitely a boob shirt. I look desperate. I feel desperate. This feels so forced, but it shouldn't. How many times have Brandon and the girls and I sat on the floor and eaten pizza around the coffee table? How many times have Brandon and I made love listening to this music? Okay, not recently, but many a time, nevertheless. Yet somehow, it feels like a charade.

There's a knock on the door and I hear it open.

"I'm in the kitchen," I call.

Brandon walks in looking a little unsure of the situation. It can't be easy for him to feel like he has to knock on his own door.

I smile at him. "Hi."

"Hi," he answers with an uncertain smile. "It smells good in here."

I grab a beer for him out of the fridge. Without a second thought, I unscrew the lid, take a swig, and hand it to him.

Brandon smiles sadly. "Thanks."

Oops. It's what I've always done. I guess he doesn't want any reminders that we've been married for seventeen years.

"Help yourself," I say, handing Brandon a plate. "We'll eat in the living room."

"Thanks for making my favorite."

"My pleasure." I smile.

We fill our plates and I lead the way to the coffee table flickering with candlelight.

"It's dark in here," he comments and adjusts the dimmer to bring up the lights.

We sit down and awkwardly begin to eat our dinner in silence.

Except, of course, for David Gray serenading us with love songs, which now feels like an awkward choice.

"Did you tell Roma she could go to California for Thanksgiving break?" Brandon asks.

"Oh," I say, caught off guard. "Yes and no. I told her I thought it sounded like a good idea, but that you and I needed to talk about it. She wants to see some of the colleges out there, and I know my parents would be thrilled to show her around." I cut a piece of chicken-fried steak and swirl it around in ketchup.

"She's sixteen. It's not necessary for her to be looking at colleges right now."

"It actually is. She's got to research them this year so she can start applying next fall. She wants to see what's out there. I think it's great that she's so motivated to explore this."

"Of course you do," he remarks, annoyed.

Okay, this is not a good start.

"So, what did you want to talk to me about?" Brandon asks.

"Oh…" I fumble. That's right. I said that I wanted to talk to him about *something*. It was really just an excuse to get him here. "I wanted to discuss how things are coming along with your… time away. What have your thoughts been?"

"I don't know, Nina."

"Well, you've been out of here for over a month. When are you going to be ready to come home?"

"It's not a vacation. I'm not going to wake up tomorrow and decide that I'm refreshed and ready to come home to you."

"Well, what's it going to take? We miss you. I miss you."

"What have *you* thought about since I've been gone?" he asks.

I look at him funny. "I haven't thought… I'm not the one who needs to think about stuff."

"There are issues we need to deal with," Brandon says.

"Okay, then. Let's deal with them. Let's finally do this."

Brandon exhales. "I don't want to do this right now."

"So we need to deal with things, but not right now. What do you want, Brandon? To just live over our friends' garage indefinitely?"

"Oh, yeah, Nina. It's been really fun for me. Being away from my kids for a month."

"Then come home. It sucks for all of us."

Brandon shakes his head. "It's just not time yet."

"Help me understand, Brandon. Because it seems like you just don't want to be married right now. Are you seeing someone?"

"No. I already told you that."

It is silent for a long time. Except, again, for David Gray still singing our intended makeout music.

"This is not how tonight was supposed to go," I say sadly.

"I'm sorry, Nina," Brandon says. "But it's going to take a lot more than chicken-fried steak and candlelight to get us back together."

My face crinkles. "Now, you're just being rude."

"I know you, remember? I know exactly what you thought was going to happen tonight. You thought you'd throw together a romantic evening that would fix everything, just like you would prescribe to one of your readers in a fan letter. We have major problems. You can't just use your generic romance crap on me."

My jaw drops, offended. "At least I'm trying. I don't know what the hell you want. I know we have problems. I just don't know what the hell they are!"

I hadn't planned on yelling "hell" repeatedly at this man tonight.

"That's amazing. Because I can't stop thinking about them," Brandon says curtly.

"Enlighten me, please."

"I don't want to do this. Not yet," he says.

"You're impossible! I'm not even sure if you want to fix this."

"I'm tired," Brandon says. "I just want a break from all of this. I need a break from you."

"I've given you plenty of space. I'm trying to talk to you and reconcile. I don't know what else I can do. What are the other options?"

Brandon purses his lips and shakes his head. "I don't know."

I growl with frustration. "Okay, then. Call me whenever you are ready. I will be here waiting for you because you have all of the power and I have none!"

Brandon stands up. He shakes his head angrily. "Thanks for the chicken fried steak." He storms out the front door.

Chapter 21

Since the girls are gone for the night, I lay on the couch and drink a bottomless glass of pinot noir. I catch a glimpse of myself on a silver coaster and my teeth are stained purple. I'm buzzed, but it doesn't feel good. I feel lethargic and very sorry for myself.

The flirty and flickering tea lights mock me and I've decided that I hate David Gray. He's singing my very favorite song, *Please Forgive Me*. "'Please forgive me if I act a little strange for I know not what I do. Feels like lightning's running through my veins, every time I look at you...'" Brandon used to feel that way about me. This music sucks.

Brandon is being such a jerk. This isn't the real Brandon. He's a good guy. The type of guy who sees a moving van in front of a house in the neighborhood and knocks on the door and offers to help perfect strangers carry their furniture in. The type of guy my girlfriends call if they hear a strange sound in the middle of the night when their husbands are away on a business trip. The Brandon I know would do anything to avoid hurting someone's feelings. Especially mine.

I reach for the bottle of wine on the coffee table and pour myself another glass. At least I'm still drinking out of a glass. See? I'm a lady. I haven't yet resorted to swigging out of the bottle, so I suppose I haven't hit rock bottom quite yet. I won't mention the half-eaten pecan pie that sits on the coffee table with a fork resting among its remains. I have to admit I made a damn good pie. Brandon's loss.

He's not going to make this easy for me. It doesn't even seem like he wants to work things out. What am I going to do? What *can* I do? It's going to take sheer magic to fix our relationship.

Magic. I sit up.

"Magic!" I shriek out loud and laugh maniacally. I stand up too fast and stumble on the coffee table.

I teeter into the kitchen. It's a mess, as I still haven't cleaned up from dinner. I grabbed the bottle of pinot and the pecan pie and have been on the couch ever since.

I open the cabinet and rummage through boxes of tea and foil packages of coffee. There it is. The terracotta rooster! I fish out a tea bag, stick it in a mug of water and shove it into the microwave.

When the microwave beeps I open the door and pull out the mug. Piping-hot tea sloshes over the top of the mug and burns my hand. "Ouch!" I cry as I grab a towel.

One should not deal with scalding-hot liquids when they are under the influence. I swirl a spoon around in the mug to help the tea percolate and rush over to the kitchen table. No time for honey.

I close my eyes and inhale the hot steam. It burns my nostrils.

I open my eyes to reveal that nobody has joined me at the table. I exhale, disappointed. I really am losing it. I have made a cup of tea expecting it to magically conjure up my grandma from the dead. I am a separated, middle-aged lunatic.

I put my feet up on another chair, take a sip of tea and cradle the mug in my lap. I close my eyes and moan. I suppose this is rock bottom.

"*Mi linda*, you are drinking too much," a voice says.

I jump, spilling the tea on my lap. "Ouch!" I cry.

"Sorry, my love." Grandma cringes as she sits across from me. She looks around. "This place is a mess."

I sit up in my chair. "Grandma," I breathe. "You came."

"I told you I would," she answers. "You need to stop doubting me."

"Forgive me, Grandma, but it's not you that I'm doubting. It's my sanity."

"Trust me. I am really here."

"Well then, this is incredible! I wish the girls were here tonight to see you. I tell them so much about you."

"I see them every day. But this situation would only scare them, I'm afraid."

I nod. "That's true. This whole thing freaks me out. But you've got to visit Mom. She misses you so much."

"No, Nina. This would be hard on her, too. But you can handle this. And you need me now."

"Grandma, you said that I would figure this out, but I haven't and I don't know if I can. Brandon wants nothing to do with me. You've got to tell me what to do," I plead.

"You need to pay attention, Nina. Look for the *signs*," Grandma says.

"Signs? Oh, I saw you standing next to the 'Patience' sign. You mean signs, literally?"

"Focus. If you want your husband, you're going to have to work for him."

"I'm trying to work for him. I want him desperately."

"Okay then. Think."

"Patience." I shake my head. "I've been more than patient. I've allowed Brandon to live apart from us and have his space while he does nothing to mend our marriage."

"And what have you done in the meantime?" Grandma questions.

I shake my head, at a loss. "I don't know, Grandma. I'm just trying to get through it."

"Exactly," Grandma says. "You've been trying to numb yourself and do anything possible to avoid your thoughts."

"Of course I have! I don't want to think about the possibility that the love of my life isn't in love with me anymore. I don't want to even consider that the father of my children is contemplating breaking up our family." I cradle my head in my hands.

"I'm sorry, *mi linda*. Give me your hand."

I reach across the table and her soft, gentle hand takes mine. It's absolutely amazing to be holding it again.

"I know this is the hardest thing you've ever gone through. But you're going to have to be strong. You need to stop passing the time and be present. What is that little crossing guard man always telling you to do?"

I chuckle. "Mr. Frizzly? He's always flapping his arms at me to slow down."

"Hmmm…" Grandma raises her eyebrows knowingly. "The first thing you need to do is take care of yourself. You need to slow down and get some sleep. You are running yourself ragged. Did it ever occur to you that space away from your husband might be good for you, too?"

"No," I answer, dumbfounded.

"Think about what you want from your marriage. Think about why things were good with Brandon back when your marriage was really good."

"Okay…"

"Brandon isn't going to wake up one day and decide that he feels better and is ready to come home to the same marriage," Grandma says.

"That's exactly what he said," I interject. I shake my head, thinking that there might have been some validity to that statement when it made me so mad at the time.

"You two will need to start communicating your feelings and thoughts when you're ready," Grandma continues. "So when he's ready, you need to have your thoughts ready. Clearly, neither one of you was ready tonight."

I groan, seeing the truth to that statement.

"It's not going to happen overnight. The issues between the two of you have many layers. And for goodness' sake," Grandma says, "focus on your entire marriage, not just the romance and sex."

"Grandma!" I say, shocked.

"Oh, don't act so innocent. You make a living off the stuff."

"I've just never heard you talk about it before," I say, still dumbfounded.

"Come on, *mi linda*. I wasn't always dead."

I laugh. "Oh, Grandma. It's so good to talk to you."

"I love it, too," she answers and takes a sip of tea.

I drum my fingers on the table, mulling it all over. "I'm starting to understand." I bite my lip. "Patience. With not only Brandon, but myself."

"Yes." She nods. "You have both been unhappy for a while now. This is your opportunity to reinvent your marriage."

"I like the sound of that."

* * *

Again, I wake up not remembering how the night ended. I don't remember ending my conversation with Grandma or telling her goodbye. I don't remember brushing my teeth or climbing into bed. But I know in my heart that I spent the better half of the night with her.

I wake up refreshed and ready to fight for my man. But I now know that I don't need him back today. For the moment, the self-pity and desperation are gone. I'm ready to give Brandon what he needs— time. And I'm ready to give myself the same thing.

Chapter 22

We turn off Highway 20 north onto Cherokee Road. It's a gravel road and we bump along in the Range Rover. Jane holds on tight to the pecan pie.

Jane and I are on our own. Roma left yesterday for L.A. and called me excitedly when she arrived at my parents' house. That girl is so much like me. She just wants to "get out and get some of it on her," as Brandon would say. Translated, that means she wants to experience it all. She thrives on excitement and activity. When we go on trips, she goes nonstop, wanting to visit the sights, museums and restaurants. This weekend she will discover just a few exciting possibilities of where she could spend her collegiate years.

This is going to be interesting. We're going to Brandon's parents' house for our Thanksgiving feast. We will meet Brandon there. I don't know how his parents feel about our separation. Are they upset with me? Do they think it's my fault? Did Brandon tell *them* why he left me?

We pass a few scattered mailboxes labeled with last names at the beginning of long driveways. The driveways cease and we bump along for a while until we come to the end of the road. We drive through the wrought-iron gate and under the cursive "M" that welcomes us to the McCoy estate. We pass a massive oak tree that canopies a pond. Grandpa Roy often puts his little fishing boat in the pond and gives the girls rods for catching minnows.

The stately white colonial house with black shutters sits up on a little hill that overlooks the valley. Two massive columns flank the tall, black front door. To the north there is a stable that houses horses, a chicken coop, and beyond that is three hundred acres with roaming cattle and sheep. The girls have always loved spending time here. They have grown up caring for the animals and riding horses.

The front porch is adorned with bales of hay covered with orange stock pumpkins, white Cinderella pumpkins, and a variety of gourds. A huge wreath of autumn leaves decorates the door. My mother-in-law is a domestic goddess. This place looks festive and beautiful all year round.

As we step onto the front porch, I smile at Jane's adorable sense of style. She wears a denim dress, leggings that are covered in all different kinds of cats, and pink cowboy boots. "You look lovely, sweet pea."

"Thanks, Mama." Jane throws open the front door and announces our arrival. "Happy Thanksgiving, y'all!"

Brandon's mom, Leanne, rushes into the foyer to greet us. "Well, hello, sweetie!" She gives Jane a kiss.

"Hi, Grandma Lee!"

The older grandkids nicknamed her Grandma Lee. It just flows off the tongue easier for them.

"What is that you've got there?"

"The famous McCoy pecan pie." I hold it up proudly.

It's not a difficult recipe. Leanne has thrown many family recipes my way in hopes of domesticating me into a true country wife.

"Would you look at that. It looks delicious, Nina," my mother-in-law tells me warmly. If she knows that it's store-bought pie crust, she doesn't let on.

"Thank you, Leanne."

She leans in and gives me a kiss on the cheek. "Happy Thanksgiving, sweetie."

"Happy Thanksgiving."

We walk through the foyer, which has a high ceiling and a grand staircase. Brandon is no stranger to a well-to-do upbringing. His grandfather started McCoy Feed and Farm Supply in Skiatook sixty years ago. When Brandon's father, Roy, joined the family business as a teenager, they opened another store in Collinsville, just east of Skiatook. Brandon grew up working in the stores, got a degree in business from Oklahoma State University and took the family business to the next level. There are seven McCoy Feed and Farm Supply stores all over northeastern Oklahoma. The McCoys are a well-known and respected Oklahoma family.

We enter the living room into a huge commotion where Brandon's nephews, eight-year-old Titan and five-year-old Stryker, wrestle with Papa Roy. Leanne disappears into the kitchen with the pie.

Roy lies on the floor and laughs as the kids crawl on top of him. He tickles them as they shriek and stick their elbows and knees in the poor man.

Through the glass sliding door at the back of the room, I see Brandon and his brother-in-law, Jake, drinking beers next to the deep fryer on the back porch.

Roy sees us and smiles. "My girls."

"Hi, Papa!" Jane exclaims.

"Hi, beautiful!"

"Hello, Pop," I say. As soon as Brandon brought me home to Skiatook as his wife, Roy insisted that I call him Pop because I was now one of his daughters.

"How are you, honey?"

I know Roy honestly wants to know how I'm doing. But he's

lying on the floor covered with kids and the moment doesn't really lend itself to a heart-to-heart. "Fine, Pop. I'm doing fine."

"Mama, can I wrestle?"

"Yes, just don't hurt Papa Roy."

"Yes!" Jane cheers. She pulls off her boots, then runs and jumps into the dog pile. Papa Roy groans. The last I see of Jane are her cat-covered legs flailing around in the air.

I leave the rambunctious laughter and head outside through the sliding glass door. "Hello, gentlemen."

Jake leans in for a kiss on the cheek. He runs the feed store in Blackwell, which is just under two hours away. Jake is a good guy, but we bump heads occasionally. Sometimes it feels like I'm too assertive for him. "Happy Thanksgiving, Nina."

"Thank you, Jake. Good to see you."

"Hi, Nina," Brandon says to me neutrally.

I actually hate when Brandon calls me "Nina". Oddly enough, it feels so impersonal. When we got married, my name was quickly replaced with "babe". He only called me "Nina" when he was mad at me. It's all he calls me now.

He greets me with a wet noodle hug. It's so uncomfortable to have this awkward moment in front of Jake. I wish Brandon would just pretend things are normal between us for the sake of having a nice holiday. But Brandon hates to be fake. I suppose that's an admirable quality. I, on the other hand, have come to rely on the façade of our happy marriage. Now that it's out in the open, at least to our family, this is a safe place for him. He finally doesn't have to pretend. I, myself, have no idea how to act.

I hang out for another moment in the silence. I'm trying to be cool. Trying to make this easy for both Brandon and myself. Trying to take the high road. Trying to be *patient*. But he won't even throw me a bone.

"Okay," I say. "Well, I just can't keep up with all of this clever banter. I'm heading inside."

Jake smiles at my dry humor. Brandon ignores me. He slips oven mitts on his hands and grabs the tongs, ready to retrieve the turkey from the boiling, bubbling oil.

* * *

I walk into the kitchen where a domestic army bustles around in a choreographed dance. Leanne stands by the open oven door and checks on the stuffing. Jolene, Brandon's slightly younger sister, sashays past her mom and slides a cookie sheet onto the bottom oven shelf adorned with rows of white, sticky mounds of raw dough. When they emerge they will be moist and pillowy homemade rolls.

Jolene's sixteen-year-old daughter, Janessa, sprinkles a layer of mini-marshmallows onto the sweet potato pie. Ten-year-old Brinley rolls cloth napkins and places napkin rings over them.

Janessa, Brinley, Stryker and Titan. I mean, good Lord! Do these country folk make these names up? Was Jolene completely high on her epidural when she named her children? Nonetheless, I love my sweet nieces and nephews, made-up names or not.

"Happy Thanksgiving, ladies," I say.

"Nina!"

"Aunt Nina!" I am greeted with warm hugs by my sister-in-law and nieces.

You can learn a lot by watching the McCoy women at work in the kitchen. They are a talented hierarchy of domesticity, with Leanne at the top and Jolene close behind. They tend their own gardens— bountiful cornucopias overflowing with corn, squash, lettuce, cucumbers, beans, tomatoes, and strawberries, to name a few. When the family has enjoyed all of the fresh summer salads and corn on the cob that we can possibly eat, the women begin their production line of canning and jelly-making. At the end of the summer they are like chipmunks stashing away mason jars of peaches, pickled vegetables and jellies with neatly marked labels into their vast walk-in pantries for the cold months to come.

"What can I do?" I ask.

"Why don't you make the butter curls?" Jolene hands me a metal hook with a small scalloped edge.

"Yikes," I respond. "It looks like something you'd see in a horror movie." I stab at an imaginary victim.

Brinley giggles.

After Jolene demonstrates, I'm making butter curls like a pro. I should add this to my domestic résumé. *Nina Blake makes marvelous butter curls.*

"So, how are things at home?" Jolene asks.

All of the women in the kitchen, young and old, turn to me.

My face turns hot immediately. I cannot believe Jolene brought this up in front of Janessa and Brinley. But they are currently in their womanhood training so I guess in Jolene's eyes, this is appropriate. This is a privilege of being in the kitchen club— listening to gossip and dishing on relationships.

"Things are fine," I stammer, caught off guard. "There's always room for improvement, isn't there?"

I dig the tool deep into the butter. The butter curls start to get big with my sudden rush of adrenaline.

"Yes, of course," Leanne says.

Slowly, the ladies get back to work. They feel my closed-off energy.

Maybe they're trying to help. Maybe I could get some insight from Brandon's mother and sister. Hell, maybe my nieces know something I don't. But for now, it's our own business.

* * *

We sit in the dining room around an elaborately decorated table. Leanne always has the kids contribute to the décor with paper turkeys and leaves colored the warm Crayola shades of autumn. Nevertheless, it still looks elegant with flickering candles, small pumpkins and gourds.

This year Brinley and Jane convinced us all to wear pilgrim hats and Native American headbands that they made from construction paper.

After we join hands and Roy says a blessing, we begin passing serving dishes. I resisted the impulse to solicit prayer requests for my marriage. *I pray that Brandon will come back to me. We pray to the Lord. Lord, hear our prayer.*

"We certainly miss Roma today," Leanne says.

"How's her big city adventure going?" Jolene asks.

"Great," I reply. I scoop a serving of wild mushroom rice pilaf onto my plate. "My parents took her for a tour of UCLA yesterday and tomorrow they're driving down to San Diego to check out USD and UCSD."

Leanne takes a glance at Brandon, who cuts his turkey into teeny-tiny pieces. An infant couldn't choke on them.

"So what's she looking for so far away?" Jake asks. "How could she possibly not want to continue the family tradition of OSU?"

I knew this was coming.

"She wants to see what her options are," I reply. "Different schools specialize in different things. She's interested, of course, in checking out the literature and performing arts programs."

A muscle in Brandon's cheek twitches. He looks like a very angry pilgrim.

"OSU has everything anyone could want," Jake continues.

I take a large bite of candied carrots to discourage myself from responding to Jake's narrow-minded comment. I am so tired of this debate. Look, I think OSU is an awesome school. Brandon, Jolene and Jake all went to OSU. I get it. We all *looove* OSU. I'm not going to discuss this at the Thanksgiving dinner table. I want to say, "OSU is great. And Oklahoma is a beautiful state, but that doesn't mean you should never go anywhere else in your entire lifetime."

Instead I politely reply, "OSU is a wonderful school." I butter a roll and bite down on it as fast as I can.

"Nina made the butter curls," Jolene says supportively.

I smile at her, appreciative of her attempt to change the subject as her husband continues to list the attributes of OSU.

My chest feels constricted as I think about the logistics of future holidays if my marriage doesn't work out. I wonder how Jane and I can gracefully get out of here before dessert. There is, after all, a second pecan pie waiting for us at home.

I glance towards the end of the table where the kids are sitting. Jane happily eats the toasted marshmallow layer off of the sweet potato pie, laughing at the silly cousin banter. She catches my eye and her smile widens.

I nod at her and smile. We'll be staying for pie.

Chapter 23

It's a chilly morning. The thermometer on my desk that measures the outside temperature reads fifty-two degrees. I'm cozied up in the big armchair in the office with a fire crackling in the fireplace as I edit a hard copy of recent chapters of *Down and Dirty Down Under* with a red pen. Ambiance is important to a writer. It gets our creative juices flowing.

The phone rings and I groan as I climb out of my comfortable position to grab my cell phone that I left on my desk.

"Good morning, Nina." It's my editor.

"Hi, Stan. I'll bet you're enjoying a nice toasty morning in California."

"Seventy-five. A typical late November day."

"Lucky. What's up?"

"Well, I've been reading the chapters you sent."

"I'm editing them now."

"Good. I'm having a problem with Veronica. She's entirely too needy."

I frown and plop down on the chair.

"Your protagonists are usually so strong and confident. I enjoy a good, sexy damsel-in-distress situation, but needy... yuck."

"I hear you." I pout. I will have a lot of reworking to do with that character.

"Alright. Polish her up and resend the chapters."

"You got it. Thanks, Stan."

I lie back in the chair. Great. My relationship is so bad that my fictional characters are suffering from it.

My cell phone rings again. What now?

"Hello," I answer grumpily.

"Are you all right?" Becky asks.

"I'm fine. Just bad writing."

"Oh. I'm sorry. Hey, why don't you stop down at the barn and we can chat for a little while."

"What's going on?" I ask.

"Honey, it's no big deal. It's just something that I would rather you find out from me."

* * *

Another minute of questioning Becky gets me nowhere, so I drive to her shop and park on the grass. The shop is located in a field just before you head into downtown Skiatook.

This old barn was for sale about five years ago. It was a rickety old structure but Becky just loved it because it had character. She had to practically beg RJ for it because he didn't exactly see the charm that she saw.

Becky has since transformed it into a Skiatook gem. With her vision and a lot of manual labor by RJ and Brandon, the Old Barn Candle and Soap Company was born. The front section is an adorable boutique where Becky's products are displayed on wooden crates. It's very shabby chic. RJ and Brandon installed strategically placed skylights that are the size of slits to create the illusion of sunlight peeking through cracks in the roof. There are also Tiffany lamps placed around the shop to provide stylish, soft light. A giant picture window on the side of the barn looks out onto Darryl

Farnsley's pasture, which is dotted with cattle.

Becky works her magic in a workspace behind the boutique area. She has three big old-fashioned metal bathtubs where she concocts her creations. The area is in plain view so customers can watch her mixing lye with essential oils, dried lavender, oatmeal and the like, then pouring the mixture into molds to create luxurious and beautiful bars of soap. At other times you can observe Becky pouring scented melted wax into her signature mason jars and inserting and trimming the wicks. My personal favorite is the Fresh Laundry candle. If you simply leave the candle in a room without its lid on it has the effect of potpourri. You don't even have to burn it to freshen a room.

When I enter the shop I'm greeted with a waft of delicious aromas—a combination of clean citrus, sharp peppermint, spicy cinnamon, sweet vanilla. When you run into Becky out and about in Skiatook, she always smells like she's been dipped in scented candle wax.

I find her sticking labels on a batch of honeysuckle candles. "Good morning, my friend. What's up?"

Becky looks up from her work. "Hi. Well, I ran into the Kum & Go on my way to work to grab a muffin and a magazine."

I know this can't be good since she isn't making a crack about the unfortunate name of our gas station. It's a running joke in our town.

"Yeah…" I urge.

"I read about you in the *Enquirer.*"

I gasp. "What?"

"Yep. I was flipping through, waiting my turn in line, and there you were." She bites her lip and adds, "Carrie Ann read about you in *Star.* You know that's her guilty pleasure."

"Aww, man," I whine. "Where is it?"

She hands me the magazine with an apprehensive look.

I sit down on a wooden stool and thumb through it. I find what I'm looking for. "'Nina Blake Dumped by her Country Bumpkin.' Oh, shit. Where did they get a picture of Brandon in overalls?"

Becky shrugs.

"He hasn't worn them in years!"

"Well, lucky for you he probably won't ever wear them again."

I shoot her a look.

"Too soon. Sorry."

"Shit. Shit. Shit."

Becky indulges me with a few moments to vent.

"Who would've called the tabloids? Who knows?"

"Brandon lives above our garage. I'm sure our neighbors have seen him."

My phone rings. It's Veronica. I push a button to silence it.

I shake my head. The local soap-maker saw the tabloids before my publicist in L.A. I guess small-town folk are more hard up for exciting gossip. Telegram, telephone, tell-a-housewife. The latter is the fastest form of communication round these parts.

I text Veronica, *I've seen it. Call you later.*

"Oh, crap," I complain. "My mom. Brandon. The kids." I rub my temples. "What am I going to say to them?"

"You just tell them that it will pass quickly and the magazines will move onto someone else."

I know she's right, but my family is going to take this very personally.

"Aww, shoot. Dammit," I continue.

Becky brightens. "Well, do you want to hear the good news?"

"What's that?" I ask glumly.

"You really are famous!" she says.

I gaze at her.

She starts to giggle.

I narrow my eyes and stare at her, unsure of what is happening. But she looks so tickled with her realization that I have to join in. Our laughter escalates. Our guffaws fill the barn. Only Becky could find a silver lining.

Chapter 24

I go down to the feed store to present Brandon with the current issue at hand. And by "current issue," I mean the weekly issue of *Star* magazine.

I drove by Carrie Ann's house for two reasons. I knew I had to smooth her ruffled feathers. I also knew that I couldn't show Brandon the 'country bumpkin' headline. I needed a softer alternative, and I wasn't about to go to Walmart or the Kum & Go and buy it myself.

The *Star* wasn't quite as insulting, but did state that Brandon is sleeping in a friend's garage. I do not look forward to this conversation, but I know for a fact that it will be better if I tell him.

I spoke to Veronica a little while ago and she wanted to know how I want to handle the media. Do I want to make a statement? I decided to run with Becky's theory. I'll just let them speculate and ride it out until they have someone else to pester. Most people don't believe that stuff anyway. Right?

I open the door to the feed store. Lou, one of Brandon's employees, is stocking the shelves with bags of pasture seed.

"Hi, Lou. Is Brandon here?"

"In his office," he says.

"Thanks."

When I enter the office, Brandon looks up from the computer

and gives me a half smile. Good. He hasn't seen it.

"Hey," I start with trepidation.

"Hi."

"There's something I need to show you." No point in beating around the bush. "Please just know that I hate this as much as you."

He raises his eyebrows.

I put the magazine on the desk in front of him. He silently reads. "You have got to be kidding me."

"I know."

He flips through the pages and shakes his head. "I'm sleeping in a garage?"

I look down at the floor. I knew that would piss him off.

"Damn it, Nina."

I look up sharply. He continues. "My parents are going to see this. Their friends, their church, the kids."

"I didn't *do* this. I didn't call the tabloids myself! I don't want anyone to *know* about us!"

"You brought this kind of stuff to Skiatook. We didn't have national media coverage before you became the queen of romance."

I should be flattered. Danielle Steel and Johanna Lindsey are more likely contenders for that title. I'm more like the princess of romance. Or the duchess of romance. But something tells me that wasn't a compliment.

"Someone in Skiatook saw you at the Jamesons' and chose to do this," I retaliate. "Some small-town, church-going soul picked up the phone and ratted us out to the tabloids."

Frustrated, he runs his hand through his wavy hair. "You're just not like the other wives here."

"What?" I ask.

Brandon shrugs.

"That's what you have to say to me after seventeen years of

marriage? I'm not like the other wives? Are you saying that I don't belong here?"

"I didn't say that."

"But that's what you meant."

I stomp out of the office, past Lou stocking bags of feed, past the saddles, past the western wear, and into the dirt parking lot.

* * *

I drive. I drive and fume. I travel west on Highway 20 along the lake and over the occasional bridge. I don't know where I'm trying to get to, I'm just headed west. I feel like driving until I reach the Pacific Ocean. To the place where I do belong.

I drive in silence. I don't need music on— the thoughts in my head are loud enough.

You're just not like the other wives here. The first time he told me he'd never met anyone like me was the first time he told me he loved me. Now, it's a bad thing.

You know what? That is entirely unfair. I may not be from the country, but I have lived here for almost twenty years! And I do very country things. Brandon and I are financially comfortable. I don't need to get up on Saturday mornings at the crack of dawn to go to garage sales in search of steals, but Carrie Ann and Becky love it, so I bargain-hunt with them.

I may not say, "Praise Jesus!" every time something wonderful happens. I may not quilt. But I have a compost pile in my backyard. I occasionally wear cowboy boots. I Trunk or Treat, damn it.

I feel like I have really embraced country living. I love it. I have not only acclimated to this community, I've become a part of it. And that one comment takes all of those efforts and throws them into the trash. What an insult.

The crazy thing is, in six years, I'll have lived here in Oklahoma for as long as I lived in California. And Brandon is suggesting that I don't fit in? Then I never will!

My phone rings on the passenger seat and I ignore it.

Other people travel for work. If I had a corporate job and I had to go on a work trip, it would be no big deal. Brandon just resents what I do. He thinks that because my occupation is something that most people view as glamorous, it's a selfish, indulgent pastime. He acts like I'm always on book tours and signing autographs, but when I'm here, I'm here. I'm present. I'm packing lunches, helping with homework, making dinner, running 4H fundraisers, and raising our children.

Honestly, I don't need to be barefoot in the kitchen making biscuits from scratch to be a good wife. Now, let's be clear. I am not putting down country women. For God's sake, my best friend makes soap for a living. I'm also not suggesting that every other woman in Skiatook does all of these stereotypical "country" things. But when Brandon says that I'm different from the "other" wives, he is implying that there's something wrong with *me*.

When I snap out of my mental rant, I realize that I've driven past the Bull Creek Peninsula, past Black Dog Park, and over Wildhorse Creek. I've driven all the way to Hominy. I glance at the clock on the dash and see that it's already one-thirty. My morning has been consumed by the tabloid fiasco, and I realize I'm starving.

This town may have one stop light, but it has a great little burger joint. Over the menu that's posted on the wall, it says in big letters, "Home of the Big Buns." The first time Brandon brought me here, Brandon playfully asked the woman who took our order, "So, who's the one with the big buns?"

Without missing a beat, the woman responded, "The owner. But she isn't here right now." Brandon and I cracked up.

I scold myself for having a fond memory of that man.

I purchase a greasy burger with sautéed onions and sit down at one of the beat-up tables outside. I'm the only customer, so it's utterly quiet. Sometimes it's amazing to me how quiet it can be out here. It's cold and crisp outside and I set down my burger wrapped in yellow paper to button my jean jacket. The array of colorful autumn leaves have turned brown and are starting to fall off the trees. A stark season will envelop us soon.

I sigh. My cell phone rings. It's Stan. I take a deep breath and answer. "Hi."

"Hi," he says. "I feel like we need to have a conversation without any bullshit. Are you okay?"

"Yes. I guess. Things are bad, Stan."

"Why didn't you tell me?"

"It's not something I've been talking about. I've tried to sweep things under the rug for a long time. I figured as long as they were there, we wouldn't break."

"I am always here for you. You can tell me anything. I hope you know that by now."

"I do. But for my entire adult life I've made a habit of being tough so that I could make it to the next level. Be good at what I'm doing. Be strong. Keep it together. Keep going. Wear my strength like armor. But now I'm naked. My armor is gone. And without it, everything is unraveling. The whole world knows my problems. That I'm struggling. It's humiliating." My voice shakes. "I don't know what to do."

"You confide in those who love you and take strength from them."

I nod even though Stan can't see me. A few silent, hot tears roll down my face. "Thank you, Stan. From the bottom of my heart, I appreciate your friendship."

"If you need me to do anything, say the word."

We hang up. I notice that I have three missed calls, one each from Alison, Kate and Christina. I was so in my head on the drive over that I barely heard the phone ringing.

I head back to the car to make the trek home before school gets out.

* * *

The next day, I pull into the parking lot of the Sacred Heart Catholic Church. I've come to ask the good Lord for guidance. I desperately need comfort and solace.

That said, I can't bear to sit in a pew during mass, on display for so many to scrutinize. I realize how weak that sounds. I also realize how big-headed that sounds, assuming that people would be paying attention to me over God Himself. I can't justify it. I just feel too vulnerable to be around anyone besides my kids and close friends.

It's mid-morning, the girls are at school, and I walk into the quiet church. As soon as I dip my right hand in holy water and do the sign of the Cross, I feel a sense of peace.

The church is cool and completely empty. My ballet flats echo through the cavernous space of polished wood and marble as I walk down the center aisle to the front row. I genuflect to the altar then enter the pew and kneel on a cushioned kneeler. At kneeling in front of God in this holy place, my tangled web of emotions unleashes itself. My desperation to get Brandon back has converted to anger towards him. I resent him for resenting me. I'm furious at whoever called the tabloids. I'm annoyed at the people who are judging me and laughing at me. I'm embarrassed for my kids. I'm ashamed. But that one is a little foggy. I can't pinpoint what I'm ashamed about. What have I done wrong? Am I ashamed because of what Brandon had said? That I brought this trashy media into this town? Do I believe that? Am I ashamed that I have somehow ruined my marriage?

I pull out my rosary. It's Grandma's rosary, actually. The repetition of Hail Marys and Our Fathers quiet my negative feelings and comfort me.

Father Jim walks out of the sacristy. He sees me and smiles. I return his smile as he approaches me.

"May I join you, Nina?"

"Of course, Father."

He genuflects and slips into my pew. "How are you?" he asks.

"A little better now."

"I think I know why you're here."

This actually makes me smirk. "Father, have you been reading the tabloids?"

"No. But it's a small town and even I hear the scoop."

"Aah."

"I'm sorry that you and Brandon are having troubles."

"Thank you."

"And I'm sorry that those troubles are no longer private."

I groan. "I know. Thank you."

"Hang in there, my dear. This too shall pass." I look into his eyes and they crinkle in support. "You came to the right place," he adds.

I nod.

"Keep coming back and you will find strength here."

"Forgive me if you don't see me for a while. I'm trying to fly under the radar."

"It's interesting that we fear judgement from people, some acquaintances, some we don't even know. In this case, it sounds like the only other person involved is Brandon. And God, of course."

"You make a good point."

"You are a good, kind person, Nina. You just keep that up and everything will figure itself out."

"Thanks, Father. I really appreciate that."

Chapter 25

It's a frigid November evening. A wind blows down from Kansas, sending a shocking chill through the air.

I adjust a teal scarf around my neck over the collar of my black peacoat as Jane and I walk up the steps of the Skiatook High School Auditorium.

"Wooo! My bones are cold!" Jane squeals.

I squeeze her hand. "Let's get inside," I say.

The advanced drama class is performing the musical *Me and My Girl* and Roma was cast as Sally, the female lead. She's been watching Cockney dialect lessons on YouTube for the last month.

Gale Cabbot, the drama teacher, was very insightful in casting Roma. The role depicts a Cockney girl who is groomed to act like an English lady so she can stay with her boyfriend, who has just found out that he is the fourteenth Earl of Hareford. It's ironic, really. Roma is such a combination of a sophisticated lady and a down-home country girl, it's almost an inner conflict for her.

I sense stares as Jane and I walk down the center aisle. People are actually whispering to each other as they watch me. What could they be saying? That I've been fraudulently dishing out romantic advice while my own romance has gone down the tubes? That another celebrity's marriage bites the dust? That Brandon should have married a nice Oklahoma girl instead of a complicated girl from L.A.? My cheeks that were freezing a moment ago flush hot with embarrassment.

I focus on Cindi Cosgrove, a friend who's in my bunco group. She smiles at me and blows me a kiss. I return a grateful smile.

We enter the second row where Brandon sits with two empty seats. Brandon and I don't make eye contact as I pass him. We're still furious with each other from the tabloid fight. Luckily, sweet Jane sits between us. I'm relieved when the lights go down and the high school band begins the overture.

I'm always blown away when I watch Roma perform. Though she hides her true thoughts and emotions from me, she bares her soul through this character to an auditorium full of people. She uses her body as an instrument in physical comedy and moves the room with laughter. I find myself laughing and crying at the same time. Who is this girl? She is so beautiful and talented. I want to know her better. I want to be close to her and connect with her.

As Roma's flawless Cockney inflections send the audience into a fit of hysterics, I can only think how I have somehow alienated this perfect creature who was once a part of my own body. Somehow, the foundation of our family has severe cracks in it and Roma and Jane need its stability. I laugh along with the rest of the audience, but tears begin to flow down my cheeks.

Brandon glances over at me and does a double-take at my tear-streaked face. Instead of sharing a moment that says, *This is our talented child. We made her together,* his expression says, *This is a comedy. Get it together.*

Embarrassed and insulted, I discreetly wipe my face with my cashmere scarf. And then I do what everyone else in this room has done—escape.

Chapter 26

I went back and forth about this. I know Grandma said her visits were just for me, but it feels so selfish that only I have experienced the miracle of being with her again. My mom would be over the moon to see her mother and talk to her one more time.

In my emotional and drunken haze the first two times I had the miraculous cups of tea, I didn't really notice the tea bags. Before I carefully wrapped this one up in pale pink tissue paper and packed it in a small box, I cradled it in my hand and examined it. It was simple with a white string. The yellow paper tag said "manzanilla" in white letters, which means "chamomile" in Spanish. I know the likes of these tea bags. They didn't come from a beautiful decorative box from the tea section at the grocery store. Grandma used to buy her tea in the spice section at her Hispanic market in Eagle Rock. It would be hanging on a hook in a clear cellophane bag amongst pods of *tamarindo*, dried red chili peppers, and *canela* (cinnamon).

I walk out of the post office having just sent this magical parcel on a trip to sunny California. There. It's done. In two days, my mom will make herself a cup of tea and have the surprise of her life.

* * *

I'm back at home in the zone having a very productive morning of writing. Thankfully, the writing is coming more and more.

The house phone rings and I answer it. "McCoy residence."

"Ms. Blake. This is Mrs. Roundtree." Mrs. Roundtree is the principal of the elementary school. Her voice sounds exactly like she looks— stout and stern. "There was an incident involving Jane at recess this morning."

My breath catches. "Is she all right?"

"Oh, yes. This was more of a behavioral event."

"Really?" I ask. I can't believe it. Jane can be a little talkative, but she's a rule-follower. "What happened?"

"Can you come down to the school?" Mrs. Roundtree asks, giving me nothing to go on.

"I'll be right there."

* * *

I fling my purse over my shoulder and walk briskly toward the school office. Suddenly the door flies open and Brianna Wakefield bursts through it. She sees me and eyes me with fury. Brianna is a stage mom. She's had her daughter, Hartley, in pageants since she could sit upright all by herself.

"I'm furious about this, Nina. Jane should be suspended. For a week!"

"Brianna, I have no idea what has happened yet. Give me a chance to get up to speed."

"Your daughter is a bully!"

"I'm going to talk to Jane before I form a response to that." I walk past Brianna and quicken my steps. My heart beats rapidly. Oh, my goodness. What on earth has happened here this morning?

I enter the school office and the school secretary nods at me sympathetically.

"Good morning, Sue."

"Hi, Nina. Go on in."

I tentatively enter the principal's office.

A stern Mrs. Roundtree sits behind her desk. Brandon was able to get here quickly from the Feed Store and is seated next to Jane. Her eyes are red from crying.

"Good morning, Mrs. Roundtree," I greet as I sit down next to Jane.

"I'm sorry, Mama," Jane whispers and starts to cry.

I grab her hand.

"So," Mrs. Roundtree begins. "It appears that Hartley Wakefield brought this tabloid magazine to school and had it out on the playground." She holds up a *US Weekly* with a picture of me in the bottom corner. The heading says, "Where's the Romance?"

My heart sinks. Dear God. That's what this is about?

Brandon's arms are folded. He doesn't look at me.

Jane looks down at her feet, clearly upset that her mama is on that magazine.

Mrs. Roundtree continues. "Apparently, Hartley and Jane argued back and forth about the magazine, and then Jane punched Hartley in the nose."

My jaw drops. "Jane!" I scold.

"I'm sorry, Mama. She was saying awful things about you. She deserved it."

My child was defending my honor. How can I scold her for that? "Jane, I'm so sorry you had to hear those things. You shouldn't have to defend me. But it's not okay to punch someone. You've got to be able to resolve things with your words."

Brandon is pretty quiet over in his seat. But I know my husband. He's mad.

"Your mama is right," Mrs. Roundtree intervenes. "I cannot have you being violent at school any time a student is mean and upsets you."

"Yes, ma'am," Jane replies, ashamed.

"I'm going to have to suspend you for one day."

Jane inhales quickly. To a kid, suspension is like going to jail.

"Now, Jane, please go sit outside my office while I speak to your parents."

"Yes, Ma'am." Jane gets up and skulks towards the door. She turns around and looks each one of us in the eye. "I'm really sorry."

"We know you are, honey." Mrs. Roundtree softens. It's hard for anyone to stay mad at that kid, even the toughest lady in the Skiatook School District. "Close the door on your way out."

With Jane out of earshot, Mrs. Roundtree levels with us.

"Look, I can imagine how it all played out. According to the teacher on yard duty, Hartley had a group of young 'uns gathered around this magazine, cackling up a storm. She appeared to be very knowledgeable about the article inside. I can picture it well; I had her mother for a student, as well." Mrs. Roundtree gives us a sideways look, implying that the apple doesn't fall very far from the tree. "I can't punish Hartley very severely for bringing a magazine to school. But I do believe it was with malicious intent. So I gave her a detention."

"That's all?" I protest. "She planned this whole thing."

"Sounds like she got her punishment," Brandon says smugly. "Right in the nose."

Mrs. Roundtree stifles a smirk. After all, she had Brandon as a student, too.

My husband is a country boy, through and through. He's from the school of thought that getting through the day with your lunch money is half of a good public education.

"The deeper issue here is that Jane is manifesting a lot of feelings about whatever is going on at home. She needs to be able to deal with this in a healthy way. I've seen this scenario many a time when a student's parents get divorced."

I feel like I've been punched.

"With all due respect, ma'am, we're not divorced," Brandon pipes in.

I look at Brandon and I'm able to muster half of a smile.

When we exit Mrs. Roundtree's office, Jane sits hunched over in the chair outside the door. I imagine she'll remember every detail of the shoes she's wearing today for the rest of her life.

Jane looks up at us with frightened, apologetic eyes. Brandon puts his hand on her shoulder.

"Let's go, kid."

* * *

The Tastee Freeze is a small brick building with a drive-thru window. The interior contains five booths with red leather seats and the table tops have Formica surfaces with the appearance of a wood grain. The three of us sit in a booth, Jane snuggled up to Brandon on one side and me sitting across from them. Brandon and Jane bite into cheeseburgers—the secret sauce is awesome. I dip my grilled cheese with tomato into a side of house dressing. A red plastic basket of greasy onion rings sits in the middle of the table for us to share.

Jane looks like the weight of the world is on her shoulders. She lets out a pained exhale.

"Janie," I start, "I feel like we haven't done a good job of letting you talk about what's going on between Daddy and me. We want you to know that none of this is your fault."

"I just don't understand why things aren't how they're supposed to be. Daddy is supposed to live with us. We're still a family, aren't we?"

"Damn right we are," Brandon pipes in.

I'm glad Brandon speaks up. It's hard to explain what I don't understand myself.

Brandon continues. "Mama and I need this time apart to think about how we can make our relationship stronger, so we can be even better."

Blah, blah, blah. Inwardly, I roll my eyes. I hope Jane buys that, because I don't.

"People are going to keep talking about us because people like to gossip," I explain.

"Why?"

"You know, it's silly, really. People like something exciting to talk about. Some people think it's fun to talk about other people's lives. And when they do, as hard as it is, you've got to hold your head up high and ignore them. At some point, they'll start talking about someone else. It's not really fair that you have to deal with this when it's a choice that Daddy and I have made. I'm sorry about that."

"I'm in big trouble. Why are you guys being so nice to me?" Jane asks.

"Sweetie, some things in life aren't all right or all wrong," Brandon explains. "Things can get a little complicated as you get older. Having a fist fight isn't the answer. But the fact that you were standing up for your mama, that's honorable. I'm really proud of you for that."

Jane smiles and sits up a little taller in the booth. "Honorable. Thanks."

I wink at her. "So, how about a chocolate-dipped cone?"

"Mama, it's freezing outside," Jane says, surprised.

"You can't come to the Tastee Freeze without getting a cone," I say.

Jane smiles. "That's true."

Chapter 27

I'm making a batch of homemade Chex mix for Jane to take to her 4H meeting. I pull the scorching cookie sheet out of the oven and cradle the phone between my neck and my ear. My mom happily tells me about the rare rain that they've been having.

"Oh, that's good, Mom. So, did you get my package in the mail?" I ask excitedly.

"Yes, so sweet of you to send me one tea bag. Very creative. Like us having a cup of tea together."

"Did you drink it?"

"Of course! I love chamomile. It reminds me of my mom."

"I know it does. And…"

She hesitates. "And it was very soothing, honey. Thank you."

"Didn't anything happen? A special visitor?"

"No, what do you mean? Did you come to surprise me?"

"No, Mom," I say, frustrated.

"Nina, you're being very vague. What are you trying to get at?"

My heart sinks. "I can't believe it." I'm so disappointed that my mom didn't get to experience precious, impossible moments with her beloved mom. And then I realize the worst part. A visit with Grandma has been wasted. "This is very important. What did you do with the tea bag?"

"I threw it away, obviously."

I draw my breath in audibly.

"Was I supposed to save it?"

"I know this sounds strange, but will you get it out of the trash can and send it back to me?"

"Yesterday was trash day." There is a long pause. "Nina, have you been drinking?"

"No, Mother."

"You've been through a lot, and I know how you enjoy your wine."

"Forget I asked," I say, despondent.

"Honey," my mom begins. "I think you need to start therapy. You're going through a lot. And the whole tabloid thing, oy vey."

I rub my temples.

"I know how you feel," she continues. "I was just as embarrassed as you were. Your father called the *Enquirer* and yelled at them. Honey, I'm afraid you're going to crack. I'm sure there's some professional you can talk to in that little town. Or at least the next town."

I shake my head in regret. Now I have to live with the fact that I wasted a visit with Grandma. I can never get that back.

"Mom, I'm handling it the best I can. I promise, I'm not going to crack."

I don't know how my mom let me hang up the phone because even I could hear the lack of conviction in my voice.

* * *

Ever since "the other wives" argument with Brandon, I've been finding myself trying to prove him wrong. I'm capable of being a domestic goddess. So, in lieu of the Edible Arrangements that I usually send to neighbors, family and friends for Christmas cheer, I've decided to make jalapeño jelly.

I'm a pretty good cook. But I'm not a "from scratch" kind of gal. I take store-bought banana bread mix, cake mix, and brownie mix, and embellish them with my secret ingredients of Mexican vanilla extract and cinnamon. People gush with compliments.

The McCoy women, on the other hand, make their biscuits and pie crust from scratch. Who has the time? Apparently, Leanne, Jolene, and countless other ladies. Besides, I've always found the canned biscuits that you whack on the counter to be perfectly divine.

But now it's time to go against the very core of my character and conform. I will be a good country woman and make jelly from the McCoy family recipe vault. Jalapeño jelly is surprisingly delicious. It's fabulous on ham or poured over cream cheese and served with crackers. My mother-in-law will be so proud of me.

I'm kind of excited. I love the occasional D.I.Y project. I made a special trip to Walmart to buy the supplies— mason jars, three kinds of peppers, Sure-Jell, even a giant canning pot. And now I stand in my kitchen, dressed in my apron, supplies out and ready.

As I chop the chili peppers, I'm feeling pretty proud of myself. I'm excited to prove to Brandon, as well as myself, that I can do anything I set my mind to. Jelly-making, check. Being a perfect wife, check. Getting my husband back, check.

I realize my hands are starting to itch a little bit as I move onto the serranos. And burn. Okay, they're really starting to burn. Ouch! I run over to the sink and run my hands under cold water. They're as red as the lobster claws that Brandon and I ate the last time we had a date night at Duke's in Malibu. I dry my hands and shake them off. Gotta push through. I scan the recipe to see what's ahead—grind the peppers in a blender, then boil the sugar, vinegar and peppers in a large pot. I glance down to the bottom of the recipe. The very last sentence catches my eye: "NOTE: Wear rubber gloves, as peppers can burn skin."

No shit.

Damn it, Leanne. You could have led with that.

I rummage through the cupboard under the sink and find a clean pair of rubber gloves. I tug them on. It's a little late, but I still have the jalapeños to chop.

I push the butcher knife down onto a pile of jalapeños. A burst of juice squirts into my eye. I scream.

I don't feel anything yet, but the knowledge of what has just occurred is enough to make me panic. A warmth runs over my eyeball and quickly turns into an intense burning sensation.

"Shit!"

I run to the sink and stick my face under the faucet as tepid water runs over my face.

"Help!"

Chapter 28

"Will I ever see again?" I sit on the bed in the exam room as Dr. Hart, a sweet man in his early seventies, shines a penlight into my eye and examines me.

Dr. Hart laughs heartily. I'm not amused.

"Darlin', you just damaged the cornea a little. It just needs a little time to rest."

"Rest my cornea? How am I going to manage that? I can't sleep for a week."

Dr. Hart turns and opens a drawer. He pulls out an eye patch and twirls it around his finger like it's a garter belt.

"Oh, you can't be serious."

Dr. Hart stretches the elastic and puts the patch over my head. He settles the patch over my left eye.

"I look like a pirate," I complain like a kid.

"Cutest pirate I've ever seen." Dr. Hart smiles. "As for your hands, they have first-degree burns." He hands me a tube. "You need to apply this ointment liberally three times a day and keep them covered in gauze for about a week."

I scoff. "Perfect."

Dr. Hart bandages my hands. I look like I'm about to fight Mike Tyson.

I rise off the patient bed. "Thank you, Dr. Hart," I say gloomily.

"Chin up, my dear." He walks me to the reception area.

"Happy holidays," I say as I walk towards the door.

"Oh, and Nina," he calls after me.

I turn around and look at him with my good eye.

"I'd love some of that jelly."

* * *

Here they are. Thirty jars of jalapeño jelly. They didn't gel quite right, due to the fact that I had to make an emergency first-aid run during the preparation process.

I sit down at the kitchen table with a cup of coffee and a stack of adhesive labels fresh from the printer. Leanne always handwrites her labels in her beautiful swirly penmanship. "McCoy jalapeño jelly, made with love."

I can't quite claim that mine was made with love, more like made at the expense of my vision and dexterity. I adjust my eye patch and blow out an annoyed breath. Hopefully, this isn't one of those *Like Water for Chocolate* moments in which people will take on the negative feelings that I've put into this jelly. The whole neighborhood will be doomed.

I peel a label off the sheet. It sticks to my gauze mitten. I pull it off with the other hand and it sticks to that one.

"Damn it!" I shake my hands. I'm totally over this project. The only thing keeping me from throwing a jar of jelly against the wall is the knowledge that I'd have one ginormous mess to clean up.

The phone rings and I answer it.

"Hi, honey," my mom says cheerfully.

"Hi, Mom. I'm in the middle of something. Can I call you back?"

"Actually, honey, I need you to pick us up."

There is a pause.

"What? Where are you?" I inquire.

"Your father and I are at the Tulsa Airport. Surprise!"

Chapter 29

We drive in a bit of an awkward silence.

"I'm happy to see you, but what's with the surprise?" I ask.

"Well, how's that for a Christmas welcome?" my mom asks from the passenger seat.

"I prefaced it with 'I'm happy to see you.' It's just that you could have given me a chance to prepare for you," I lie through my teeth.

My dad smiles weakly from the back seat.

"Honey, I'm just going to say it," my mom says with furrowed brows. "I'm worried about you. The whole tea bag thing. It was weird."

"I'm fine. I'm doing great."

"You don't look fine *or* great."

I catch a glimpse of myself wearing an eye patch in the rear view mirror. She has a point.

My mom eyes my giant polar-bear paws that are perched at ten and two. "Can you even grip the steering wheel with those things?" she asks.

I sigh. "Yes, Mom."

We zip by the stark winter wasteland in silence. My right hand slips off the steering wheel. In the peripheral vision of my right eye, my mom shakes her head.

* * *

The first thing my mom said when I showed her to the guest bedroom was not that she loved me and was excited to spend Christmas with me or that I'm going to get through this hard time or even that she liked the new bedspread, but an inquiry about the last time I changed the sheets. She constantly keeps trying to give me marital advice. I'm not against getting some helpful hints, but her method of me winning Brandon back involves offering to take me into Tulsa to get my eyebrows and mustache waxed and reminding me to stop slouching. With my mom pointing out all of my flaws, my good eyelid is now twitching.

There is enough stress as it is with the typical Christmas madness of fitting in time to shop, decorate, wrap, school Christmas programs, and so on. I feel even more impatient with her. I honestly don't know how I'm going to get through this week.

The girls and my parents have finally gone to sleep after a marathon of decorating the house and the Christmas tree (my mom couldn't believe it wasn't done yet). So I'm about to enjoy a moment of quiet time.

I head down to the kitchen and make myself a cup of tea. The only company I want is from a sweet angel summoned by mystical chamomile.

With Mom and Dad's arrival came a light dusting of snow. Powdered sugar flurries swirl outside the window as I set a plate of Carrie Ann's gingerbread cookies on the table.

I take a tea bag from the rooster and tuck the canister safely back into the back of the cupboard.

After I prepare my flowery chamomile potion, Grandma arrives with her cup of tea in hand.

I beat her to the punch. "I know. I'm so sorry I wasted a tea bag. I wanted to share this with Mom."

"This is only for you, my love. I told you that."

"I understand that now and I will respect your wishes."

She does a once-over of me and she purses her lips sympathetically. "Oh, *mi linda*. You are having a horrible time."

I hold up my gauzed hands. "This whole ridiculous situation happened because I'm trying to be someone I'm not."

"Then don't do it, *mi linda*."

"Brandon's right, though. After all these years, sometimes I feel like I don't fit in."

"You only feel that way because of what he said."

I shrug, unsure.

"Nina, you have found yourself in foreign situations so many times and have adapted with such grace. You fit in when you sipped espresso in Parisian coffee shops. You fit in when you sang along with locals in Irish pubs. You fit in when you went scuba-diving in the Great Barrier Reef. My darling, you fit in all over the world with all sorts of people."

I'm in awe. My voice softens. "Grandma, you know about all of that?"

I was a senior in college when my grandma passed away. We never had a chance to talk about any of my travels.

"I watch you, *mi amor*."

I smile. My heart swells. I've always believed in heaven and that loved ones watch us from above. But getting confirmation of this is really comforting.

"It made me so proud to watch you experience all of those wonderful places," Grandma continues. "By the way, I know how it feels to be a fish out of water. Your grandpa moved with his family to Arizona when he was a child. He returned to Obregón one summer when he was a young man, and we met. He courted me all summer and we got married after a few short months. Then he took me back to Arizona. He already knew English, but I didn't know a word of it. I was nineteen years old and I didn't know anyone, except for my husband who I hadn't even known very long."

I frown.

"When he was at work, I would stay in the house. I was afraid to go outside and hang the wash on the line in fear that someone would try to talk to me and I wouldn't understand them. I was away from my family and friends. It was very hard for me."

"Grandma, that's so sad. I didn't know all of that."

Grandma shrugs. "I figured it out."

"How did you figure it out? How did you adapt?"

"I had my babies, your mom and uncle. And I was happy. I had them to love and talk to. I learned English, little by little, by watching television. Yes, I had to learn some new things. But I still spoke Spanish to my kids. I still cooked the recipes that my mom had taught me. I still watched my telenovelas. I was still myself."

I nod, smiling. "Wow. I'm forty years old, and I'm getting the 'be yourself' talk."

"Yes. It's the only way to be happy. It's the only way to be an example for your daughters. Besides, Brandon didn't marry a country girl who makes jelly. He married you."

I smile. "You're right, Grandma. It's so much easier that way."

"And so much more fun," Grandma adds.

I smile and nod in agreement.

"Feliz Navidad, *mi linda.*"

"Merry Christmas, Grandma." We clink our mugs together.

Chapter 30

My cart is full of holiday provisions such as wrapping paper, a few strings of Christmas lights, and toiletries for my parents. I also load up on eggnog, apple cider, and ingredients for fudge, Christmas cookies, appetizers and various meals. Last night's snow didn't stick, but I want to make sure we have everything we need in case in case weather prevents us from leaving the neighborhood.

As I load my groceries onto the conveyor belt, I notice that Pearl is my cashier. I smile at her.

"Hi, Pearl. How are you?" I ask.

"Fantastic. Thanks to your advice a while back, Merv has quit whatever he was doing and is back strong and steady with me."

"Really? My advice?" I ask, surprised. "That's wonderful! I'm so glad." Wow, maybe I'm not a total quack. Sheesh, I wish I could remember what I told her. Maybe it would help me.

Pearl scans my items.

"Forgive me, but will you remind me exactly what I told you?"

"You told me to remind him why he fell for me to begin with. And I did." She smiles. "It was my sweet temperament and my ability to calm him. I noticed he seemed a little stressed out." Pearl lowers her voice. "He was fooling around with one of those high-maintenance hussies. So in my own way, I just sweetly reminded him where home is."

"Wow. Good for you. I'm so happy for you."

"And my homemade chicken pot pies never hurt. You have a merry Christmas, ma'am." Pearl hands me my receipt cheerfully.

"Merry Christmas, Pearl."

I push the cart out into the parking lot and load the back of the Range Rover with my plethora of groceries. My mind is reeling.

I realize that I've just asked someone else for my own advice.

Pearl's words echo in my head.

Remind him why he fell for me to begin with.

Grandma and Pearl are right. It's about time I remember who Nina Blake is.

* * *

Thankfully, with all of the Skiatook holiday festivities, my mother does not have time to be focused on her quest to assess and improve my physical beauty and mental health. She has spent precious time in the kitchen with her granddaughters baking sugar cookies. They cut the dough out with Christmas cookie cutters and frosted and decorated them with festive icing and sprinkles. She also took them into Tulsa for Christmas shopping and a nice lunch.

Christmas music sung by the Rat Pack, Louis Armstrong, and other greats has been on a continuous loop in the living room, thanks to my dad, where he has been napping on the couch by the fire and playing card games with his granddaughters.

This weekend there will be Christmas caroling in the neighborhood, which always concludes with cookies, hot chocolate and hot toddies at the Atwaters' house. In addition, we will bundle ourselves up for the holiday parade that starts at the high school and heads down Highway 20 through downtown Skiatook.

Seeing Roma and Jane's joy experiencing holiday cheer with their grandma and grandpa, I understand that this is my parents' way of helping me. Mom and Dad are giving the girls their undivided love and attention, something that I admittedly have been lacking. Mom has cooked meals and has even run the vacuum without commenting how badly the carpet needed it. I'm so grateful for this help because I feel like I've been running a one-woman show. Mom was right to come. I really did need her. My parents' presence has filled the void of Brandon, and the house is permeated with laughter and holiday cheer.

One night after the girls and my dad are asleep, my mom and I watch *White Christmas* and wrap gifts. It is a rare moment of peacefulness between us. We sit on the floor and quietly tuck in the corners and tape down the folds of festive wrapping paper and curl red and green ribbon with the shears of the scissors. We sip orange spice tea and occasionally comment on the wonderful dance scenes between Bing Crosby and Vera-Ellen. We are just together.

Chapter 31

We wake up to a very white Christmas. We all slept so soundly, tucked in our warm beds, that we were oblivious to the snowfall throughout the night.

The house is quiet and I'm the first one downstairs. I find Brandon sitting at the kitchen table drinking coffee. I think it's very sweet. He didn't want to miss a moment of Christmas with his girls. We are gracious to each other, on our best behavior and feeling the spirit of the holiday. Thankfully, I'm able to lose the gauze and eye patch for the occasion.

Jane and Roma are not far behind me, and they wake my parents up to get the festivities started. They quickly find their overflowing stockings at the bottom of the stairs, and I observe the joy in my parents' eyes as they watch Jane and Roma opening their gifts from Santa. I savor every Christmas, not knowing if this is the last one that Jane believes in Santa. The sweet innocence of a child's belief allows all of us to believe in the magic of Christmas and makes the holiday that much more special.

Next, we enjoy our traditional Christmas breakfast of fruit salad, quiche Lorraine and cinnamon rolls. My mom is giving Brandon a bit of a cold shoulder. She's being polite to him, but there's a definite lack of warmth in her interaction with him. I have to admit, it's giving me a great deal of pleasure. First of all, he deserves it, and my mom can be intimidating if you're not on her good side. Secondly, it reminds me that regardless of our sometimes strained dynamic, my mom is in my corner.

After breakfast, Brandon ties two ropes to the back of the four-wheeler and ties the other ends of the ropes to two sleds. My parents stand in the driveway, waving at the girls as Brandon revs up the motor and pulls them into motion. Through the kitchen window I see them disappear from the driveway as I wash the breakfast dishes. I giggle as I hear their screams of laughter.

* * *

After a restful afternoon of watching Christmas movies and playing card games, the family convenes for Christmas dinner in our festive and fancy dining room with the addition of Leanne and Roy. They always do Christmas gifts and breakfast at Jolene and Jake's house in Blackwell and join us in the evening.

After my mom says a warm Christmas blessing, we pass around a glazed ham, seven-layered salad, scalloped potatoes, a seafoam lime Jell-O mold and rolls. Leanne opens a jar of my infamous jalapeño jelly. "This looks just lovely, Nina. I can't wait to taste it." She spoons some onto her ham. It's the consistency of water.

Brandon tries to hide a smile, but I see it.

"I had a little issue with the texture," I explain, embarrassed.

"There's a bit of a learning curve there," Leanne offers.

She passes the jelly to Roy, who doesn't bother with the spoon. He just pours it over his ham. It really looks pitiful. He sticks his finger in some jelly and tastes it. "Well, it tastes good and that's all that matters."

I smile at him.

Brandon turns to Roma and Jane. "Girls, who did you pass this stuff out to?"

"Everyone," Roma says flatly.

After a pause, Brandon bursts into laughter.

I look at him, deadpan.

Leanne looks surprised at his rudeness. The girls begin to crack up and my dad is not far behind. Little by little everyone joins in, including me.

* * *

We sit in the living room drinking eggnog and hot chocolate. Gene Autry sings *Here Comes Santa Claus* in the background.

Brandon stokes the fire in the fireplace and the aroma of smoke mixed with the cinnamon pine cones in a basket on the hearth smells like the spicy warm feeling of the holidays. It feels so cozy being nestled in our log cabin while there is a snowy winter wonderland outside.

Jane and Roma assume their jobs as the designated gift distributors. My mom and Leanne open my gifts to them— lavender mint soap and apple pie candles from the Old Barn Candle and Soap Company. They thank me and pass the candles and soap around for everyone to smell.

Leanne wove cozy socks for all of us from the very wool that she sheared from her sheep, spun into thread and dyed in various colors. She makes the absolute best winter socks.

Brandon and I exchange our gifts to each other. We knew it would be important to the girls to see us give each other something. I give him a soft, cozy navy blue chenille blanket to snuggle up to this winter. I'm sure it's cold over Becky's garage. He gives me a gift card to my favorite store, Anthropologie. A gift card is rather impersonal, but it is my favorite store. We could probably both take these gifts the wrong way, if we choose to, but we thank each other, warmly.

I watch Jane excitedly pass out gifts to my dad and Papa Roy.

Roma sips her hot chocolate and laughs with my mom. I'm so glad they could have this day. This is a typical McCoy Christmas. In this moment, we are a strong and happy family.

* * *

As the others lounge in the living room watching Roy's personal favorite, *A Christmas Story*, Dad and I sit at the kitchen table with the remnants of dessert and dirty dishes. We sip coffee spiked with Kahlua and whipped cream out of Christmas mugs. In a rare moment, I have him alone.

"So," he asks, "how are you, kiddo?"

"I'm good." My go-to answer.

He gives me a look.

"I don't know, Dad. This is hard." I extend my long legs and put my feet up on the chair next to me. "Brandon and I are just so different. We've always known it, and it used to be a good thing. I was the yin to his yang. But now it just means that we don't have anything in common."

"What are you talking about? You have plenty of things in common. The same values, the same things make you laugh…"

I nod, trying to agree as Dad tries to think of other similarities.

"Come on. How different can a Blake and a McCoy be? In the end, you both come from good Irish families."

I scoff.

It is ironic. We are two people with solid Irish names and yet our backgrounds and upbringings are so different.

"We don't agree on anything."

"It's not that you're city and he's country that makes you two different creatures, it's that you're a woman and he's a man. You just think about things differently."

This is the deepest my father and I have ever gotten on the topic of male/female relationships.

"Trust me." He nods towards the living room at my mom. "I know."

I laugh. I shouldn't underestimate my dad's relationship advice. He has lived with a complicated and demanding woman for over forty years.

"So what do I do?" I ask.

"Just stick it out," he replies matter-of-factly.

I chuckle a little and nod. Only because it sounds so simple. "*Just*," I say.

"Your mother and I have had hundreds of ups and downs over the years. And here we are."

"And you're... happy?"

My dad laughs at this. "Yes. Most days we are not a page out of a romance novel, but she is my companion through life."

"That's sweet, Dad. I think."

He laughs again.

Maybe romance isn't a top priority on my dad's list for happiness. But he does seem to be content with life. Perhaps I put too much emphasis on romance. But look who we're talking about. I'm a hopeless romantic. However, there may just be something to having a compatible partner to go through life with.

Chapter 32

The weather report tells us that an ice storm is blowing in from Kansas. Luckily my parents headed home a few days ago and avoided the logistical nightmare that bad weather can bring when traveling.

Warnings of snow and ice storms always send masses of people running to Walmart for supplies. You never know if you're going to lose power or if the roads are going to get bad, so you want to be stocked up.

On these occasions, Brandon would always make a huge pot of chili that we could eat for days, and I would make corn bread to accompany it. I can't break tradition, so sadly I will have to make the chili myself. The girls have an entire line-up of movies that we plan on watching in our jammies.

As I unload the provisions from the blue reusable Walmart bags onto the island, the phone rings and I answer it.

"Hey." It's Brandon's deep voice. "I want to make sure you girls have everything you're going to need for the storm."

I'm touched at his concern.

"We'll be fine. But we're down one chili chef. I don't know how we're going to manage."

Brandon doesn't respond, but I think he's smiling.

I decide to take the bull by the horns. "Do you... want to come and be with us?"

He hesitates and I know that he's tempted. "No. Thank you. But call me if you need me." My heart sinks. "Batten down the hatches," he says, his signature phrase when a storm is coming.

"Okay. We will. We'll… be thinking of you."

There is a pause.

"I know."

We're like a repressed boy and girl in high school who want to say so much to each other but don't have the nerve to speak the words. However, despite our inability to articulate, it somehow feels like progress.

* * *

It's always a huge deal when we get a new establishment in town. When we got the Walmart Supercenter several years ago, there was a protest with about fifteen picketers marching around the parking lot with signs that said "To Hell with Big Business." The congregation of the Baptist church was up in arms about the inappropriate signage. But the rest of the Skiatook population, including me, was thrilled to get a decent grocery store. On the day of the ribbon-cutting, a small brass band played at the entrance with great fanfare, and we flooded the store in a frenzy.

In the same spirit, another momentous occasion has arrived. McDonald's is coming to Skiatook. This is huge. We already have the Tastee Freeze, so this will be the second fast-food chain here in town. Most of us are just beside ourselves, yet there are citizens opposed to its addition. They think it will provide too much competition for local eateries such as Mac's BBQ and Fern's Frozen Custard and Coneys.

The big day comes on Saturday, January twenty-three, and the first fifty customers will eat free. As a result, the event has brought on outright pandemonium. Many people plan on spending the night in order to get a good spot in line. Among the suckers is my eldest daughter. She begged me to let her join her friends in "participating in a moment of local history." I only agreed when Brandon said he would chaperone the girls.

It is the dumbest thing anyone has decided to do in this town, and trust me, there have been a few runners-up for that title. It is, after all, winter. This sort of town event would be better suited for spring. I would be all for it then.

The eve of the big event has arrived and Jane and I are going to visit the squatters. The temperature for tonight is predicted to be a very crisp thirty degrees. Jane and I park on Highway 20, since the parking lot is jam-packed with tents.

"There it is!" Jane has spotted our hunter-green tent and runs towards it.

I arrive at the tent as teenage voices ring out, "What's the password?"

"Hot chocolate," I answer.

"Thank God," one of the voices says.

The door unzips.

"Get in! Get in!" Voices encourage us to hurry to prevent the frigid air from rushing into the tent.

Roma, her two best girlfriends, Hailey and Stacey, and Brandon are bundled in coats, scarves and winter hats. Only their little faces can be seen through the one place that is absent of bulky winter clothing. They are lounging on sleeping bags and their laps are covered with blankets. Messy piles of playing cards are scattered in the center of their circle. Brandon smiles sheepishly from the back of the tent. Shoot, I won't be able to sit by him without climbing over everybody else.

"How are you guys doing?" I ask.

"The hand warmers you gave us are lifesavers," Roma gushes.

I made sure each one of them had one for each jacket pocket to keep their hands toasty.

"I'm so glad they work. It looks like there are a lot more than fifty people here," I report as I pour hot chocolate into styrofoam cups. Jane passes out slices of homemade chocolate-chip banana bread to her daddy and the girls, who thankfully accept.

"We're counting on people leaving in the middle of the night," Hailey informs me.

"Don't worry, Mama. We're in position," Roma says.

"Thank goodness," I reply. "You would not want to sleep here all night only to pay for your own breakfast."

Brandon grins. "I have money, just in case."

Jane and I stay for three games of Michigan rummy. "Well, guys, Jane and I should be getting home."

"Yeah, let's go, Mama. It's freezing!" Jane shivers.

"Jane!" Stacey cries.

Brandon and I laugh.

"Don't worry. We'll turn off the heat when we get home just so we can sympathize with you."

"We will?" Jane sounds disappointed.

"No," I whisper to her. Everyone laughs. "Sleep tight, everyone." I unzip the tent.

"Nina, thanks," Brandon smiles warmly at me. Our eyes lock. It's a good, sincere smile, and it makes me blush.

"Thanks, Mom."

"Thanks, Ms. Blake!"

"You're welcome." I smile back. And I'm actually disappointed to be leaving this cramped tent in the McDonald's parking lot on this frigid winter night.

Chapter 33

Valentine's Day is crisp and windy. I'm making it a wonderful day. I bundled myself up and went for a nice hilly walk around the neighborhood. I don't have expectations that Brandon will bring me flowers. It's just another day. I'm not giving it any weight or power.

In college, my roommates and I would host a singles party on Valentine's Day. We viewed it as badass and liberating when we were single and free. We would make trays of red jello shots and have a dance party in the middle of our tiny living room and everyone would end up with someone to kiss by the end of the night.

I unload a few groceries, provisions for my Valentine's party of one that will take place later. It doesn't feel badass and liberating this time, but I'm pretending it is. As I put away various cheeses, wine and coffee ice cream, Jane and Delilah burst through the front door.

"Hi, girls!" I call.

"Hi!" they answer.

Ooh, maybe Becky will have a glass of wine with me now. "Delilah, is your mom still out front?" I ask.

"No, she had to go."

"Oh." I frown. Valentine's Day party of one.

"Mama, Roma got flowers from a boooy," Jane teases right as Roma walks through the door carrying a bouquet of pink carnations.

"Shut up, Jane," Roma snaps.

"Roma," I scold.

"Roma's in love. Roma's in love," Jane and Delilah sing as they run up the stairs to Jane's room.

Roma growls, annoyed, as she walks into the kitchen.

"Knock it off, girls," I call. I turn my attention to Roma. "Oh my gosh! Who are those from?"

She exhales and lays the flowers on the counter. "I don't want to tell you."

"Why?"

"I don't want to talk about it," she says, elusive.

I'm a little confused at how getting flowers on Valentine's Day could be so upsetting to a sixteen-year-old girl. Roma sees my perplexed expression.

"Because he's not for me, all right?"

I furrow my brow. "All right." I pick up the bouquet. "What do you want me to do with them?"

"They're so pretty. Put them in your room so I don't have to see them."

"Okay."

Roma begins to walk out of the kitchen.

"Sweetheart, I'm always here for you if you want to talk about something."

"Thanks. I'm fine. I'm going to do my homework."

* * *

Brandon is due any minute to pick up the girls and take them out for a little Valentine's Day dinner. Jane and I empty the dishwasher.

"Mama, I feel bad that you're going to be all alone on Valentine's Day."

"Sweet pea, you and Roma are my Valentines. I couldn't ask for anything more."

"I know, but…"

"While you're out with Daddy, I'm going to take a hot bubble bath, put on my jammies, snack on some of my favorite goodies, and catch up on my recorded shows. And when you get home, you can climb into bed with me. It'll be perfect."

Jane smiles. "Okay." The doorbell rings.

"Go get it, sweet pea," I tell her. I stay in the kitchen as she runs to the door.

As soon as she opens it, Brandon steps inside and scoops her up.

"There's my Valentine! Are you ready for our date?" he asks her as he puts her down.

"Yes!" She beams. "Where are we going?"

"I was thinking coneys. It's all-you-can-eat night and I'm really hungry."

"Me, too," Roma says as she skips down the stairs and kisses Brandon on the cheek. "Happy Valentine's Day, Daddy."

Roma gives her dad a long hug. It makes me sad that she was upset and clearly needs some comfort. Why won't she let me give it to her?

Brandon helps Roma and Jane into their coats.

"Have fun," I call from the kitchen.

"Thanks," Brandon returns.

"You know," Jane starts. "Mama really loves coneys. Can we invite her?"

That's my girl.

There is a noticeable pause in the conversation.

I loudly put a plate into the cupboard so it doesn't sound like I'm eavesdropping.

"Of course," Brandon says.

Jane shouts to me, "Mama, do you want to come?"

I step out of the kitchen. "I'd love to."

Chapter 34

Fern's Frozen Custard and Coneys is a long-standing Skiatook establishment that sells homemade ice cream and Coney Island style hot dogs. Fern Crain owned it when Brandon was a kid and when she got old and feeble, she passed it onto her daughter, Fern Galloway. Conveniently, they didn't have to change the name.

The restaurant is a tiny room with two red booths and two tables and chairs of the same hue. The floor is covered with big red and white checked linoleum. On the wall there is a Coca-Cola clock and a wooden cut-out in the shape of the state of Oklahoma. A few shelves hold empty glass vintage Coca-Cola bottles.

Fern is a tall, wiry lady in her fifties. She has a short bleach-blonde pixie cut and the voice of a chainsmoker. She busily wraps a Coney in foil behind the counter.

The four of us are stuffed into a booth, with our coats piled high next to the wall. We munch on our hot dogs adorned with meat sauce, mustard, relish, and chopped onions. Jane is humming, something she does when she's really enjoying a meal. Brandon is on his fourth dog. They're pretty small.

Fern walks around the counter and hand-delivers Brandon's fifth. "You know, Brandon, I only make a profit if you eat three or less," she says as she returns to her post.

Brandon gives us a funny look. Jane giggles.

"Your sign advertises all-you-can-eat coneys, Fern." He takes a bite of his dog.

"The average person only eats two or three," Fern answers from behind the register. "I lose money on people like you who want to make a contest out of it."

"I was planning on having two more," he says.

We all snicker.

"I'll get two more and give them to you," I say and I wink at him.

"Thanks, babe." As soon as he says it, he catches himself.

Roma glances at me and smiles.

Jane happily takes a huge bite of her hot dog and returns to her humming.

* * *

After we've had our fill of coneys, which we self-consciously limited for Fern's profit, we head home. As Brandon pulls his pick-up truck into the driveway, I feel a pang of disappointment that the night is ending, and I sense that we're all feeling the same way.

"Jane and I made peanut butter cookies yesterday. Would you like to come in for dessert?" I ask. I know he's a sucker for the Hershey's kiss in the middle.

"You did?" he inquires to Jane. "You know I love those."

"We could make hot chocolate, too," Roma offers.

My heart sinks. Roma clearly misses her father. She's so grown up and elusive that I sometimes forget to think about how all of this is affecting her.

"Sounds too good to pass up," Brandon says.

"Yes!" Jane cheers.

Roma smiles.

So we head inside and demolish the entire batch of cookies, as well as a pot of Mexican hot chocolate complete with cinnamon and orange zest, just like my mom used to make for me.

The girls head up to their rooms and Roma climbs into bed and sticks her head in a book. Brandon tucks Jane in and reads her a chapter of *Charlotte's Web*.

I put a load of whites into the washing machine. My heart is singing. Tonight felt so fulfilling, as a family outing should.

As I pour detergent into the washer and press start, Brandon appears in the doorway of the laundry room. He puts his arm up on the door frame and leans against it.

"That was really fun," he says.

I turn towards him to agree and I can't help but notice how his manly build fills up the entire door. In that moment, I can't think of a single thing to say. His gaze holds mine.

He grabs me and kisses me hard. I reciprocate hungrily. Yes! It's been so long. Brandon's hands grasp my shoulders and he pulls me to his body. I wrap my arms around him and find my way under his shirt. I relish the feeling of his warm strong back. How does his skin feel so amazing?

His hands slip under my shirt and find my breasts. I gasp with pleasure. We unbutton each other's jeans and push them to the floor.

"The door!" I pant.

Brandon closes the laundry room door and smirks. He lifts me up and sits me on the washing machine. He pulls me close and I wrap my legs around him and pull him closer to me. He gives himself to me and our moans of desire are muffled by the swishing of the wash cycle. It's hot and passionate. It's amazing for us to have no walls up, just honest, pent-up desire.

We both get there quickly and I start to get loud. Brandon shushes me and we start to giggle. We hug and breathe hard.

I hop down from the washing machine and step into my jeans. As

I get myself back together, Brandon leaves the laundry room.

I come into the kitchen and Brandon is turned towards the island with his hands planted on the counter. I come up behind him and wrap my arms around him.

"Nina," he says. "We shouldn't have done that."

I pull away. "What are you talking about? That was amazing."

"Yes, it was," he says as if it's a bad thing.

"I'm your wife. If it's that good, we should do it every day! Or one point five times a week like the average married couple."

"I can't think straight after we make love," he says, troubled.

"Uh… okay. That's a good thing. Honey, we just had a breakthrough!" I reach for him and he escapes my grasp.

"Nothing has been resolved here. We still have a lot of things to work on. We can't do that again."

He heads out the front door.

"Let's talk then," I call out.

The door shuts.

I am left leaning against the kitchen counter in a daze. I'm trying to process what has just happened. My expression morphs from confused to flabbergasted, and I throw my arms up in the air in dismay.

And then I think about the sex. It was good. After all this time, we've still got it. A sly grin spreads across my face.

Chapter 35

It's early in the afternoon and I still can't wipe the smile off my face. Last night was phenomenal! I've had a fantastic morning of writing. I'm back! And as a result, so is my main character, Veronica. She's no longer needy. She's a sassy little minx. It's amazing how a little romance can get the creative juices flowing.

For the moment, I'm actually feeling like my life isn't going to fall apart. Making love to Brandon expelled so much bottled-up sexual frustration and negativity that I feel light and airy, refreshed and empowered.

Our marriage is by no means fixed, but our chemistry exists. He still wants me. And until last night, that had been a big question mark in my life. Yes, he ran out of the kitchen as fast he could afterwards, but for now, I'm going to focus on the progress.

I'm feeling so high that I want to see her. I realize that I have only summoned Grandma during the middle of crises. There have been so many lately. But that's despicable. I've longed for her company for so many years and now that I've been presented with this miracle, all I do is cry and complain and beg her for an answer. I've been selfish.

So now I am going to share a moment of presence. I am going to just be with Grandma and revel in the miracle of her company.

I prepare my cup of tea and a plate of pan dulce. A few days ago

I drove to the south end of Tulsa to a little Mexican store to find these nostalgic delights. The seashell-shaped sweet bread is topped with bright pink sugar. They were always my favorite.

I carry the tray upstairs to the sitting area in my bedroom. There is a fireplace in the corner of the room and two cozy chairs that overlook the backyard and the lake. I light a fire and wait eagerly for my guest.

The fact that I can have lucid, quality conversations with Grandma is truly remarkable. She suffered from Alzheimer's for about eight years. At first, she would forget little details here and there. Then she forgot names, including my own. Next, her English went and she only spoke in Spanish. In the last few years of her life the disease progressed and conversations ceased altogether. She was silent.

Some days when I visited her in the nursing home she would stare into nowhere. It was painful when there was no flicker of recognition for me. On good days there would be a crinkle of happiness in her eyes that I was there. Seldomly, I would get a squeeze from her hand and that would send me over the moon.

But when she comes to me now, she is exactly how I remember her— full of vitality, positivity and love. In her nighttime visits she wears a zip-up rose-colored velour robe with pink isotoner slippers.

Today, she wears a lovely coral-colored short-sleeve crocheted top that she made herself. Two shell necklaces, one coral and one white, are twisted into one and hooked at the back of her neck. Small pearls decorate her ears, and she wears a light shade of pink lipstick.

"Hi, Grandma." I smile. "Oh, you look so pretty."

"Thank you, *mi linda*. So I understand congratulations are in order."

I laugh. "They absolutely are. But you know what? We don't need to talk about it. For the first time since you've been visiting me, let's not focus on my drama. I just want to us to visit."

"Okay. That sounds nice."

"First of all, what the heck am I missing in my pancakes?"

Grandma laughs. "You forgot about the baking powder. Just a teaspoon."

My jaw drops. "Oh, my gosh. That's right."

"It just adds a little something."

"Thank you! That's been driving me crazy for years. Okay, let's talk about you for a change. Tell me something I don't know about you."

"Ahhh…" Grandma sits back, cradles her mug in her hands and thinks. "Did I ever tell you about the time I went to Hawaii without Grandpa?"

"No," I say in disbelief. "When did you do that?"

"Our senior citizens group was going and Julio didn't want to go. I did." She shrugs like it wasn't a big deal. "I made a pan of enchiladas and some refried beans to last him all week. And I went."

Grandma looks proud of herself.

"It was wonderful. Dolores, Adele and I all went without our husbands, and boy, did we have fun! We went on a tour of an active volcano and to a luau. The coconut cake was so good. I mostly enjoyed seeing the colorful native flowers. I picked so many plumerias up off the ground, our hotel room smelled amazing!"

"Wow, Grandma. I'm so glad that you were able to do that. I don't remember Mom telling me about that."

"You were little when I went," she explains. "I had always wanted to go. It was the trip of a lifetime." Grandma smiles and takes a deep breath as she remembers her trip, as if she can smell the plumerias.

"I'm so in awe. I just never pictured you and Grandpa apart like that."

Grandma nods her head. "It was a rare occasion. At first I felt a little bad that I was there without him. And I realized I was spoiling my trip. I was never going to be back there again, so why waste it? I took him some guava jelly and macadamia nuts."

I laugh, knowing that those were the perfect gifts for Grandpa.

"I always put your grandpa first. But, *mi linda*, as long as you are meeting your husband's needs, you've got to do your thing, too. And sometimes, you should put yourself first."

* * *

I pull into the pickup line. It's ten till three and parents are lingering around their cars socializing until the kids come out. As I check a few e-mails on my phone, I happen to look up and do a double-take. Brandon and Marlena Morrison are chatting. No big deal— they did grow up together, after all.

Marlena picks something off of Brandon's shirt and then pats his chest. I roll my eyes. I can see her smile as she stares up into his eyes. She's trying to hypnotize him. He totally lost his virginity to her. We never talked about it, but I know it in this moment. He lost it to her.

I turn off the engine and get out of the car. Crap. Before my tea break with Grandma, I'd been holed up in my office all day writing, so I didn't put a lot into my appearance. That's the great thing about the pickup line. You don't have to get out of your car.

I'm wearing yoga pants, Ugg boots, an LMU sweatshirt and my hair is pulled back into a stumpy little ponytail. The only thing I applied to my face today was chapstick. I look like a college student who has been cramming for finals. This is not the appearance I had planned on having when I saw Brandon after our hot sexual encounter.

I approach Brandon and Marlena and they turn around when they sense my presence.

"Happy Friday!" I attempt to say casually, but it comes out a little too enthusiastic. I feel like a dork.

"Well, hi!" Marlena says in her sugary-sweet Southern drawl. It sounds like nails on a chalkboard to me.

Marlena glows, both in cheerfulness and skintone. I don't trust a woman with a golden tan in February. She wears snug white jeans that accentuate her tiny little thighs. A skintight long-sleeved pink t-shirt that says "Skiatook Bakery" in swirly black letters hugs her petite and perky upper body, boasting to all that she's a double threat— an infamous baker with kick-ass boobs.

"Hello, Nina," Brandon says as he eyes my appearance.

"Don't you look *cute*," Marlena croons. The way she says "cute" is comparable to how you would compliment a new parent on their ugly baby. "I just love how you pull off casual and indifferent."

I raise my eyebrows at her back-handed compliment. I'm tempted to flick her in the forehead.

"What's up?" Brandon asks me like I'm interrupting them.

Are you kidding me? I had intercourse with the man less than twenty-four hours ago and he acts like I'm the third wheel here. I feel foolish for replaying the incident so many times in my head.

"I didn't know I was going to see you," I tell him.

"I left a message that I would pick the girls up and take them over to my parents' house for dinner."

"Oh, sorry. I was writing. I must've been in the zone."

Either that or I was having tea with my dead grandma.

"Well, y'all, I see Kayla," Marlena interjects. "I'll let you two talk shop."

She insinuates that the only thing we have to talk about is logistics with picking up our kids. Bitch.

"Nice catching up with you, Brandon," she says sweetly. She smiles only at him and walks away.

There it is. He totally just looked at her butt. It was very quick, but it happened. I'm not even going to say anything. I'm not going to state the obvious and sound like a naggy, suspicious wife.

"Nina, we were just making small talk," Brandon explains.

"I didn't say a word," I say.

"Right."

I decide it's best to change the subject. "Will you talk to Roma? She's so distant. I'm worried there's something going on, you know, other than us."

"She seems fine to me."

"Well, that's because you don't see her every day."

"I see her plenty," he says defensively.

"But you only see her during uncomplicated fun times, like taking her out to dinner and camping out in the McDonald's parking lot."

"And you think I want it to be that way?"

I frown. "That's an interesting question."

As I listen to us bicker in an unproductive loop, the faux sex therapist in me points out to myself that in this case, sex was just sex. It didn't strengthen our connection or bring us closer. We are still a very broken and unhappy couple.

"Daddy!" Jane cries as she and Roma walk up to us.

"What are you doing here?" Roma asks.

"Well, I was going to take some grain over to Grandma Lee and Papa Roy's house. They have a ewe that's pregnant and she needs to eat well."

Jane breathes in excitedly.

"Can we come?" Roma asks.

"I thought you might want to," Brandon says.

I smile. "Have fun."

Chapter 36

I set a laundry basket filled with folded clothes on Roma's bed for her to put away. I pick up a paintbrush that has fallen off of the easel in the corner of the room and admire her latest painting of what looks to me like a Malibu beach, no doubt inspired by her Thanksgiving trip to Grandma and Grandpa's house.

I glance out the window at the bald leafless trees and sigh. Winter needs to end. I'm tired of the cold, gray and barren scenery. Perhaps because I feel cold, gray and barren inside. My disappointing interaction with Brandon kind of took the wind out of my sails from my previous high.

I grab a petticoat that Roma wore in *Me and My Girl* that is long overdue to return to the attic. As I walk out of her room, my gaze falls on her diary on her desk. I ignore it and walk into the hallway.

I would never be that type of parent. I respect Roma's privacy.

However, I could really use some insight as to what's going on with her. She just won't talk to me lately. But Roma's a good girl. It's not like she's out doing drugs or having sex. Kids are having sex so early these days. A mother needs to know these things.

I cringe and walk back into Roma's room.

I grab the diary, open to the last page, and peruse her beautiful, swirly penmanship. My eyes land on the word "dysfunctional" referring to mine and Brandon's marriage. That's sad. She can't really mean that, can she? I mean, yes, our marriage lacks many things, but "dysfunctional" implies so much conflict and misbehavior. Surely Roma is exaggerating because she's upset. However, it's obvious that Brandon and I weren't as successful at covering up our marital misgivings in our own home as we thought.

I read from there. "Mom has the nerve to tell people how to fix their relationships. It's beyond embarrassing. She's such a hypocrite."

I draw in a sharp breath and continue to read.

"She doesn't even know how to fix her own marriage. She's just so depressed and doesn't even try to do anything to get Dad back. I don't know if he will ever come back."

My heart sinks. I sit down on the edge of the bed. Roma's words make my throat burn. I swallow hard. My own daughter thinks I'm pathetic. She thinks the problems between Brandon and I are my fault.

* * *

I mope around my bedroom putting my own laundry away. I just can't believe Roma is thinking so poorly of me. It breaks my heart. She doesn't have faith in me to win her dad back. I'm failing her.

I think about how I've been carrying myself for the last few years. I've been in survival mode in my relationship. Roma's right. I haven't been my usual charismatic self. I've been a watered-down version. I haven't been cracking jokes or belting out in song in Brandon's presence. Until recently, I hadn't been challenging him when I didn't agree. I was trying to keep the peace.

Clearly I'm not setting a very good example for my daughters.

What kind of women do I want them to grow up to be? Needy? No. Insecure? Absolutely not. Someone who tries to be someone they're not? Hell, no. *Nina Blake, where the hell are you? Get back here and raise your daughters to be happy, confident and strong women!*

I grab Roma's petticoat and head into the hallway. I yank down the ladder that leads up to the attic and I climb up the rungs with sluggish legs and a heavy heart.

I put the petticoat into the costume trunk, close the lid and take a seat. It's quiet up here. And chilly. I can see white plumes of my breath as I exhale.

I'm surrounded by boxes. Boxes full of holiday decorations, souvenirs from my travels that didn't make it downstairs into my house decor, stuff from my Marina del Rey apartment that I couldn't part with.

I start opening boxes and reminiscing. I thumb through a college photo album. There are pictures of my friends and I at the beach. A houseboat trip when we went to Lake Havasu on spring break. There's a shot of Alison, Kate, Christina and me at Sharkeez drinking their signature shark attack out of a bucket with a lot of straws and a rubber shark. We wear tube tops and halter tops.

I laugh.

Memories flash through my mind. Shooting Alabama slammers at Patrick Molloy's on the Hermosa Pier. Dancing with guys on a jam-packed dance floor. I think about my cute little apartment in Marina del Rey where I lived alone. How free I felt when I ran by myself on the bike path in Playa del Rey with the ocean at my side. A time in my life when things were very uncomplicated. I lived by my own rules and exuded confidence. I would have laughed at the thought of trying to win someone back. I would've just walked away. I loved life and who I was. I seized the day. Obviously, I have responsibilities now that caused me to evolve as a mom and a wife, but I miss that version of myself.

When you're in your twenties you should throw a little caution to the wind. It's wise to have the occasional naughty memory in your arsenal to recall when you're in your thirties, wearing giant maternity pants, changing diapers, and driving carpool. You'll need to remember that you were once very cool and sexy. These flashbacks will serve their purpose when you're forty, your husband has left you, and you're sitting on a trunk in the attic wondering where you've been.

You know what? Brandon is having a gay old time flirting with divorcées in the pick-up line at school and Lord knows where else. I have granted him with space and, apparently, the freedom to act like a bachelor. It's about time *I* have some fun.

* * *

I call my mother-in-law and ask if the girls can stay the night, and of course she is happy to oblige. It happens to be a rare weekend that we don't have activities to shuttle around to so the girls can have a relaxing time with Grandma Lee and Papa Roy.

Mama needs a night off.

Becky picks up after three rings.

"Can RJ watch Delilah tonight?" I ask without so much as a greeting.

"Of course. Is everything okay?" Becky asks, concerned.

"With your help, I just know there will be some improvement."

"Say the word, my friend."

"We're going out."

Chapter 37

The Handlebar Bar is located on Highway 20 right before you make the turn onto Lake Road. It's a seedy little biker bar and the parking lot contains a cement statue of an oversized hog with handlebars on it. If it's a good night, someone will end up "riding the pig".

Becky, Carrie Ann, and I saunter into the bar, a little embarrassed because we know we're out of place. In the beginning days of my marriage, as well as my friendship with these dear pals, we used to end up at the Handlebar Bar just about every weekend. Brandon, myself, Becky, RJ, Carrie Ann, and Todd would generally start out drinking a few beers sitting by Becky and RJ's firepit in their backyard. After we ran out of stories to tell, we would end up at the Handlebar. We would often drive up on our four-wheeler, all of us somehow fitting on it, piled onto each other's laps. Brandon once tried to drive the four-wheeler into the bar. We were asked to leave that night. Probably a good thing.

We haven't been here in years. Nowadays, if we have a girls' night out, we head into Tulsa for a nice dinner. But tonight I suggested that we go back to our stomping ground from the past.

We sit down at a table in the back by the pool table. Becky gets the first round— overly sweet margaritas, clearly not the specialty of the Handlebar Bar.

Two good-looking cowboys walk in. After grabbing a few bottled beers, they head towards us and park it at the pool table. One of them pulls a few cue sticks off the wall and hands one to his buddy, who racks the balls.

"They're cute," Becky remarks.

I nod in agreement.

"Becky!" Carrie Ann lectures. "You are a married woman."

"Well, they are." Becky guiltily hangs her head and latches onto her margarita.

"I'm totally uncomfortable and self-conscious," Carrie Ann announces.

"Drink your margarita." I pat Carrie Ann's hand.

"I guess I don't know what the protocol is for a girls' night out when you're married. I don't think I've ever been to a bar as a married woman without Todd."

Becky opens her mouth to speak and promptly closes it. "I was about to say how pathetic that is, but I just realized I don't think I have either. A night out has always just been bunco at one of the girls' houses. Why has this taken so long?"

"I'm happy I could help," I say dryly. I lick the salt off the rim of my glass.

Becky smirks at me.

"I'm unsure how to act," Carrie Ann continues nervously. "When someone looks at me, I smile at them. It's just how I was raised. But, if I make eye contact with a man and I smile at him, he's going to think that I'm signaling him to come and talk to me. And then I'm going to have to rudely reject him. I don't wanna be a cocktease."

Becky chokes on her drink.

She and I start to laugh hysterically. "It is a predicament," I agree through my chortling.

Becky sighs, satisfied. "Man. I was sure I was going to go through life without hearing the word 'cock' come out of Carrie Ann's sweet mouth. Things are looking up."

Her laughter escalates and I cackle in agreement.

"You see?" Carrie Ann says. "I'm already behaving badly. This is wrong. No good can come from this. We are married women."

"Well, I am a separated woman," I announce.

"Hear, hear!" A crusty old man at the bar lifts his glass to me.

I nod at him politely and continue. "The protocol is that you have fun with your separated friend. And your separated friend needs to get her mind off things. Good God, I'm speaking in third person."

"Does that mean you're going to start dating again?" Carrie Ann asks.

The question catches me off guard. "Whoa. That's a question I never thought I would be asked again in my entire life. I don't know. No. Of course not."

"Do you think Brandon will?" Carrie Ann asks.

I feel like I've been punched. I turn to Becky. "Why did we invite her? This is not the girl talk I had anticipated."

"I'm sorry," Carrie Ann says. "But it's a valid question. You and Brandon are separated. Are you guys allowed to get involved with other people?"

I take a moment to think about it. "I have no fucking idea."

"Nina!" Carrie Ann looks appalled at me.

"Sorry. You just asked me about my husband seeing other women. I think the f-word is appropriate in this conversation."

"We're also in an establishment that never takes its Christmas lights down," Becky says. "The f-word's definitely allowed. Look at that." She lifts her empty glass. "Carrie Ann, it's your turn."

Carrie Ann gets up. "I'll get us some beers."

"Mixing liquor and beer already. That's a great strategy," I comment grumpily.

Carrie Ann heads to the bar.

"You okay?" Becky asks.

I shrug. "It is a valid question. It just never crossed my mind."

One of the pool-playing cowboys appears in front of us. "Ms. Blake?"

I look up at the guy, searching his handsome face for familiarity. After a moment, I find it. "Ethan Parker?"

"Yes, ma'am."

"What are you up to?" I smile. It's been ages.

"Well, ma'am, I finished up at OSU last spring and now I'm helping my daddy with his farm."

"Does he still raise rodeo bulls?"

"Yes, ma'am. He does."

"Ethan, do you know Becky Jameson?"

He shakes Becky's hand warmly. "Nice to meet you, ma'am."

"Likewise," Becky replies.

"Ethan used to cut our grass when he was a wee little Boy Scout," I explain with a chuckle.

"Well, that was a long time ago." Ethan runs his hand through his golden blond hair. He smiles at me. "It's so good to see you, Ms. Blake."

"Goodness. Call me Nina."

"Okay, Nina. Well, it's my turn"—he gestures towards the pool table—"but I'd love to catch up with you more later."

"We'll do that."

Ethan nods at Becky politely. He walks away, picks up a pool stick and bends over the pool table to shoot. Becky and I find ourselves looking at the back of his Wranglers.

Becky gives me a lopsided grin. "Ethan likes."

"Oh, come on. I used to give him lemonade and cookies."

"I just watched you check out his ass."

"You did first."

Becky breaks. "I totally did."

We crack up.

"This is fun!" she says, liberated.

"Yes, why has it taken us so long to flirt with underage men?" I tease.

"He graduated OSU. He's well beyond the legal age."

"Why do I feel like you're encouraging me to be inappropriate?" I ask.

"I'll bet you've never been called 'ma'am' so many times in a bar before."

"No, ma'am, I haven't."

"Who was that guy?" Carrie Ann asks, putting three Bud Lights on the table.

"He used to mow Nina's lawn," Becky replies with a smirk.

* * *

As we make the transition from liquor to beer, it doesn't take long for us all to feel buzzed and carefree. Carrie Ann, my sweet choir-singing mother of four, starts to loosen up and giggle at naughty conversation and it is a beautiful thing to behold.

The night becomes a blur once we leave our seats and head to the five-by-five-foot linoleum dance floor. By then the bar is beginning to fill up, meaning there are about fifteen other people here. It's then that I perform a confident rendition of Shania Twain's *Man! I Feel Like a Woman* on the karaoke machine. I receive a very good reaction from the crowd.

Someone thinks it's a good idea to get a round of Long Island iced teas. More dancing ensues on the very crowded and small dance floor and it's then that Becky and I teach Carrie Ann how to do the Roger Rabbit.

Carrie Ann has her moment in the spotlight and belts out *I'm Here For the Party* by Gretchen Wilson. She does a beautiful job, but I have a feeling she'll regret it in the morning. When she wants to follow it up with an encore performance of Hank Williams' *Family Tradition* and starts to climb onto the bar with the microphone, Becky grabs Carrie Ann's foot.

"Shweetie," she slurs, "I want you to be able to show your face in sshhurch on Sunday. S'time to go home."

Carrie Ann jumps onto my back in order to get down off the bar gracefully, and I give her a piggy-back ride out to the parking lot where Ethan Parker kindly offers to drive us home. There's only one thing left to do to cap off this memorable evening before we clamber into Ethan's pick-up. The three of us straddle the pig and take a selfie.

* * *

When I open my eyes, I feel my swollen brain pulsating inside my head. I groan. Didn't I learn this lesson about a million times in my twenties? With my kids at my in-laws' house, I'm free to move like a sloth.

I need something greasy, so I pull my hair up into a ponytail and sluggishly slide into jeans and a long-sleeved thermal pink camouflage John Deere shirt, care of McCoy Feed and Farm Supply. I drive into town and go through the Tastee Freeze drive-thru and order some extra-large coffees and breakfast sandwiches.

Good friend that I am, I deliver some fast food to Becky, who is also feeling quite sluggish.

With mascara-smeared eyes, she hugs me gratefully. "It was so difficult to deal with my child this morning. RJ wanted to let me sleep in, but Delilah climbed into my bed and attacked me. She was so loud and obnoxious."

I chuckle.

"Or maybe she's always like that and my brain is just extra-sensitive." She laughs and grabs her head.

"You poor thing."

"You know, there's a reason we don't do that anymore," she says as she unwraps her bacon, egg and cheese croissant.

"What? Our age? Bite your tongue. I feel more alive than I have in years. I will need a nap later, though. And a second dose of ibuprofen."

"Exactly. But it was good for the soul." She elbows me. "And it was great to see you have a good time."

"Thanks. I needed it. I feel like I unleashed a little bit of the old me."

"Ooh! Watch out, Skiatook!" We giggle.

"Okay," I say as I chew my last bite and dust croissant flakes off my jeans, "I've got to pick up the girls. Have a lovely weekend."

"You, too," Becky says as we hug.

As I exit her kitchen door, I glance up at the room over the garage. Brandon watches me through the window. I smile at him and I just keep walking.

Chapter 38

March came and went. It began with my baby turning seven. Jane chose to have a horseback riding party. She invited her cousins and best friends from school. We went to Darryl and Belinda Farnsley's farm and the girls groomed and rode the horses.

Jane has always had a heart of gold. As she grows older, I love her even more. She's an optimist. She's a caregiver to those around her, regardless of age, regardless of human or animal species. Jane has taught me a lot this year. With so much sadness and struggle this year for all of us, she constantly shines her beacon of hope and positivity.

Roma had another opportunity to do what she loves as her drama class performed a show of individual scenes from plays. She portrayed Shelby in a scene from *Steel Magnolias*. As usual, she threw herself into her character. I loved the sentimental moment that she and her ensemble cast created, showcasing the power of female friendship.

I made another notable discovery in the last days of winter. I saw it while I was brushing my teeth— a gray hair. I frantically weeded through my hair and found another. I blame Brandon.

* * *

I stand in my walk-in closet staring at my dresses, deciding what to wear to my book signings over the next few days. Dallas is a quick forty-five-minute flight from Tulsa. I can power-pack some publicity into one weekend in our neighboring state of Texas.

My cell phone rings and I answer cheerfully. "Hello?"

"Hi, Nina. It's Jolene," my sister-in-law says.

"Hi! How are you?"

"I'm good…" she says.

"You don't sound good. What's up, hon?"

"Well, I stopped by Brandon's… room," she says, unsure of what to call his living quarters. "I just wanted to make sure he was taking care of himself. He wasn't there, but I dropped off a tuna noodle casserole and tidied up a little."

"That was sweet of you," I say.

"Uh-huh… well, when I was there, Marlena Morrison dropped by… with a pie."

"A pie?"

"Yes. A pie, Nina. French apple. The crumb topping looked amazing. That hussie wants your husband."

I exhale. "I knew it."

"Look, Nina. I know her. I went to high school with her. She gets whatever she wants. The only thing she didn't get was Brandon. You need to fight for your man."

"I *am* fighting for my man," I say defensively. "I'm fighting for him by leaving him alone. Because that's what he wants me to do."

She scoffs.

"So what happened next?" I ask.

"I took the pie from her and I told her to scram. And then I told Jake that I made him a pie."

I chuckle.

"This isn't funny!" Jolene scolds me.

I stop laughing. "I know. Believe me. Well, should I confront Brandon about it?"

"No!" Jolene cries. "He'll just think you're jealous. It won't go well."

I nod. "No, it won't. What do you think I should I do?"

"Just... you've got to lure him back."

I sigh. "Okay. Thanks. I really do appreciate it." We hang up.

I sit down on the bed. The plot thickens. I know in my heart that I can't come on strong with Brandon. It will just push him away further. Honestly, what can I do that I'm not already doing?

My cell phone rings again and I jump. It's my mom.

"Hi, Mom. How are you?" I ask as I envision Marlena making homemade pie crust in her cheerleading uniform that she wore on Halloween.

"I'm fine," she says, annoyed. She always knows when I'm not totally paying attention to her. "I wanted to see how things are going over there."

The way she says "over there" sounds like we live on the moon.

"We're all great," I say, sing-songy. I raise my eyebrows at myself. "I'm just packing my suitcase to do a book signing in Dallas this weekend."

"You're going away? Who's going to watch the girls?"

"Uhh... their father..."

"Where are they going to stay?" Why my mother needs to know all of the logistics is beyond me.

"Our house. Brandon's staying here for the weekend. It's just easier that way, and it is his house, too."

"When he wants it to be."

"Mother!" I exclaim, but she's right.

"I just don't know what's taking him so long."

"Well, I don't know either. But I can't go there right now."

"Nina, is this really the best time to get away?"

Valid point. "I'm not going on vacation. I'm going to work."

My mother exhales. "It's just that things are so up in the air."

"Mom, I can't put things on hold until Brandon gets his shit together."

"Well, no need for foul language," she huffs.

"I really need to pack before I pick Jane up from 4H and head to the airport."

"Okay, honey. Have a safe flight."

"I love you, Mom. Bye." I press "end" on the phone and toss it onto my bed. "Ugh," I say out loud to an empty room.

I cannot win with that woman. I cannot please her. I'm her only child and she has naturally always wanted so much for me. She wanted me to be successful and was always proud of my tenacious work ethic and international ventures as a journalist. She is proud of my success as a novelist. But I'm a different mother than she was. A different wife. It's like she wants more for me, but she also wants me to be exactly the same as her. And she's still upset with me for moving away from home.

The outcome is always the same. She disapproves of my actions and I get off the phone angry.

If Brandon begged me not to leave him this weekend, Mom would be pissed off that he was holding me back. If I canceled my book tour because "things are so up in the air" she would accuse me of sulking and waiting around for my indecisive husband. I always feel like I'm damned if I do and damned if I don't.

I should know how to channel this energy. By now, I should have a strategy to let the effect of Pilar Blake roll off my shoulders. But still, after forty years, I don't. Oh, how that woman unglues me!

I stew.

My mother... Brandon... Marlena...

I stomp out of my bedroom and down the stairs with purpose. When I arrive at the bottom, I realize that I have no idea what I'm doing downstairs.

"Roma!" I shout upstairs.

After a moment, I hear, "Yeah?"

"Grab the keys. You're driving!"

There is silence. And then I hear footsteps running towards the stairs.

* * *

As we make our way out of Beverly Hills and Roma pulls onto Lake Road, I am still in my head about my conversation with my mom. Would it kill her to be supportive? *Have a great book tour! You'll do great, my talented daughter! Everything will work out with Brandon!* Instead, she contributes to my stress.

I'm not being a very good driving instructor. I haven't said a word to Roma since we put on our seat belts. I'm not even sure if she adjusted her mirrors before starting the engine.

As we drive over the dam along the rocky shore, I happen to glance at Roma's face. She's beaming.

Lucky for her, Mama needed some air, so she got an obviously much desired driving lesson. It seems to be so hard for her to ask me for things lately. She would rather chew off her arm than ask me for help. But since I instigated this excursion, she jumped at it.

The dam is, in my opinion, one of the coolest spots in Skiatook. On one side you overlook the green grassy valley covered in endless treetops, and on the other side you overlook flat black water. Here we are on the road that divides it all.

Roma looks luminous with the lake as her backdrop as she glances in the rear view mirror.

My cautious girl. Deliberate and safe.

It is awesome to see her smile. I cannot take my eyes off of her enormous grin as she is literally in the driver's seat.

I relax into my seat.

Alabama sings on the radio. I start to sing along. "'I'm in a hurry to get things done. Oh, I rush and rush until life's no fun. All I really gotta do is live and die, but I'm in a hurry and don't know why.'"

I turn the music up. As I channel my frustrated energy into the music, I really start to get into it. I attempt to harmonize with Alabama, but fail.

Roma glances over at me. "Oh my God, Mom."

I roll the window down, stick my head out the window into the cool air and howl like a coyote.

The look on my daughter's face is priceless. She is equally startled, embarrassed, and intrigued.

I break into laughter. Roma's eyebrows are furrowed like, *Oh, shit. My mom has lost it.*

And then she starts to laugh. Our laughter syncs up together and we roar with guffaws as I wipe tears from my eyes.

As our giggles die down, Roma rolls her window down. She sticks her left arm out the window and lets her fingers carve into the oncoming air stream. We make eye contact and smile.

Chapter 39

I just took a shower and put on my pajamas and fuzzy socks. I stand at the window and gaze at the sparkling Dallas skyline.

I already unpacked my suitcase and put all of my clothes into drawers and toiletries on the sink. Even though I'm only going to be here for three days, I had to nest in order to feel comfortable in my temporary home. It's my way.

I use the mini-coffee maker to heat up some water for a cup of tea. I brought a special bag of chamomile from the rooster as I knew I would have some quiet time in my hotel room to visit with a special companion.

I inhale the steam of the herbaceous elixir and exhale, completely relaxed. I set the mug on the nightstand and prop myself up on the pillows on the bed to get comfortable. In a blink, Grandma is next to me leaning against the pillows in her robe and isotoners.

"Hi, Grandma," I say with a smile.

"This is just like one of our sleepovers, *mi linda*."

"It sure is."

When I used to spend the night at Grandma and Grandpa's house as a child, Grandpa would pull the heavy pull-out bed out of the couch in the living room. Grandpa would kiss us both good night and go back to their room, and Grandma would stay on the pull-out and sleep with me. It seemed as though we talked all night. We would snuggle and giggle, and it was just so special.

"How nice that I get to join you on one of your trips."

The way she says "trips" isn't insulting at all. It's just the opposite, like it's something really special.

"Grandma, why have things always been so easy with you and so difficult with Mom? Either she says everything the wrong way or I take it the wrong way."

Grandma looks thoughtful. "As you know, motherhood is not simple. All mothers want the best for their children. They want their children to be safe, successful and happy. Sometimes it's hard to want all of those things without them conflicting a little bit."

I nod. "That makes sense. I get that part."

"Your mother has always wanted you to go to the moon and back. But, in that, she loses control. She can't keep you safe. She can't navigate any part of your life anymore. She probably feels like you don't need her anymore."

"Grandma, I left home at eighteen when I went to college. I traveled to a different country every month when I worked for the *Times*. And then I moved halfway across the country when I was twenty-three. Shouldn't she have those feelings figured out by now?"

"It's harder for some mothers. Your mom likes to be in charge. This is one of the few things your mother feels like she can't control. Cut her some slack. Can you imagine how you're going to feel when Roma goes off to college? And Jane?"

"I like to think I'll be really excited for them. I'll miss them, of course." I nod, honestly. "I'll worry about them."

"Universal feelings of motherhood."

"I really hope that Roma, Jane and I can be friends when they're adults. My connection with Mom makes me scared that Roma and I are drifting apart and won't find our way back." I shake my head, frustrated. "I'm an adult and my mother is still telling me how to do things. And when I don't do things her way, she judges me. I wish she would stop trying to mother me and just be my friend."

"Don't give up on her. Everything she does for you comes from a good place. She may have a difficult time expressing herself to you, but her intentions for you are always from the utmost love."

"It's not going to be easy, Grandma, but I'm going to really try to see that."

We sip our tea.

"So, how about this whole Marlena thing?" I raise my eyebrows, annoyed. "As if Brandon and I need another obstacle in our way."

"That's just it. An obstacle. I think you should just focus on what we've talked about. Doing your own soul-searching, listening to Brandon's point of view. Don't let her derail your path."

"She has a lot of nerve."

"Yes, she does," Grandma agrees. "But so do you. And I mean that as a compliment."

* * *

I call my mom first thing in the morning before my first book signing of the weekend. "Mom, I need you to be a little spontaneous today."

"What do you mean?"

"I booked you a flight to Dallas at noon. We have dinner reservations this evening, a book signing in the morning and then a spa appointment. Just tell me you'll be here."

There is a pause on the other end. "What will your father eat if I leave?"

I exhale. "Leave the Thai delivery number on the fridge." I'm only half kidding. Jeez.

There is another silent pause.

"I'll be there."

Chapter 40

Mom arrives in Dallas wearing her best Chico's pantsuit and matching jewelry. She looks great and appears proud of herself for throwing a little caution to the wind.

We're dining at the best steak house in Dallas. It sits on top of a tall business building and has a fantastic view of the city lights. We raise our glasses of sauvignon blanc.

"To us, Mom."

"Yes, to us." We clink our glasses together and taste the crisp wine. "Nina, this was such a wonderful surprise. What's the occasion?"

I'm thoughtful for a moment. "Mom, I mean this with the best intentions— I want us to work on our relationship."

She furrows her eyebrows.

"I didn't say that to hurt your feelings. I feel like we both need to adapt to this phase of our relationship. I want us to enjoy each other's company. I want us to be better friends."

"I enjoy your company," my mom says, offended.

"Mom, you're misunderstanding me. I don't want you to feel the need to always parent me. I'm forty years old. I just want us to be able to be together and just be."

Mom crinkles her nose and shakes her head. "I don't understand what that means. Parenting isn't something you can turn on and off.

Do you plan on seeing your daughters in less than desirable situations and just biting your tongue? Well, I can't do that." Okay, she's turning the tables on me. Hypothetically.

I try to respond reasonably. "Perhaps when they are adults and they're in those situations, I will just be there for support and listen. I hope to let them make their own decisions and not judge them for it. And in the good times I will congratulate them and be happy for them."

"Are you insinuating that I'm not a good parent?"

"Of course not. I'm insinuating... I mean, I'm not trying to insinuate anything. I don't know. I have thoroughly confused myself. The point is, I want us to have fun together."

"This is fun. I'm having fun. Pour me another glass of wine."

I'm not sure I'm getting anywhere but I refill her glass anyway.

* * *

After a delicious dinner and mediocre conversation, Mom and I return to our hotel room. We take our showers, put on our pajamas, pull back the blankets and recline on the bed side by side. We watch a repeat of *Grey's Anatomy*.

I'm a little sad. I want more than this with her. This is an opportunity to bond and share moments together, and I feel like we're blowing it. My mom and I don't see each other every day. How many opportunities like this are left for us?

Somehow we've alienated each other. I have put geographical distance between us and she has put emotional distance between us. We just don't connect. I don't feel like I've done anything to her to deserve this aloofness. It hurts my feelings. Maybe my mom doesn't understand that we could have more. Maybe she thinks our relationship is fine. It is *fine*. But who wants fine?

Why do I always have conflict with my mom and now Roma? Am

I that difficult to get along with? Or is this just a universal mother-daughter thing?

"I better get some rest, Mom."

"Okay, honey. Me, too." She points the remote at the TV and the room goes dark and quiet.

Incredibly quiet.

"I love you, Mom."

"I love you, too." We go to sleep.

* * *

We sit across from each other over our complimentary breakfast in the dining area of the hotel. Mom pokes at her oatmeal.

"Nina, our conversation last night at dinner hurt my feelings a little."

"I'm sorry, Mom. That's the exact opposite of what I was trying to accomplish. I could just keep those thoughts to myself, but I want it to get better."

"How exactly do I need to change?"

"Mom. I don't want *you* to change. I want our dynamic to change."

"Well, that's very vague. How do we do that?"

"Okay, here's what I would like you to work on and then you can tell me what I should work on."

Mom half-heartedly nods.

"I am your daughter. However, we're different in many ways."

"Obviously," she says.

I pause. "Okay, the way you say that insinuates that my characteristics that are different from yours are wrong. That your way is the right way. I feel like you're always judging me. I always feel like you disapprove of me and it hurts my feelings."

"Well, it hurts my feelings that you always have to be so different than me. You try to do everything your way to spite me."

I roll my eyes. "I knew you thought that. You take everything I do personally. I'm just living my life. I'm just being myself. It's unfortunate that you don't like who I am."

I shake my head and angrily saw into my Belgium waffle with my knife and fork.

My mother huffs. "How can you say that after all the support I have given you over the years?"

"I know you have." I shake my head. "Actually, I feel like you used to support me. When I was in college and when I worked for the *Times* and I had exciting stories to tell, I felt like you were really proud of me. Oddly enough, ever since I became a mother, I don't feel it. The bond of motherhood should help us to relate to each other, but it doesn't. And professionally, I'm more successful than I've ever been and I'm not really sure if you're proud of me."

"I adore my grandchildren and I've read every book you've ever written. How can you say I'm not proud of you?"

I shake my head. I really don't know.

"I want to ask you something, Nina."

"Okay."

"How would you feel if one of your daughters got married and didn't invite you to the wedding?"

I feel like I've been punched. "Mom," I say very carefully. "Our wedding was completely spontaneous. We didn't have time to invite anyone."

"Just answer the question, Nina. How would you feel if Roma called you and told you she was married?"

My eyes well up with tears.

I look up and see Veronica Knight walking through the automatic sliding door in the lobby.

"Crap," I say under my breath. "I've got to run upstairs and brush my teeth."

Chapter 41

We ride to the bookstore in a limo. I used to think it was silly and extravagant, but Veronica insisted. "You can't drive yourself to your own book signing in a rental car," she said.

The energy between my mom and I is strained and uncomfortable, but Veronica is able to defuse it a little with a story about the quirky man who sat next to her on her flight over who had a parrot as a comfort pet.

There's a big crowd when we pull up to the bookstore. I smile and shake some hands and chat with readers as we walk in.

Veronica introduces me to Pam Daily, the manager of the bookstore, who leads us near the podium where I will speak. Mom sits down in a chair in the first row. Pam introduces me, and the crowd applauds.

"Good morning." I smile. "Thank you so much for coming. It warms my heart to meet you all. I'm going to read you an excerpt of what I'm currently working on, *Down and Dirty Down Under*. It's a raw and sexy jaunt through the Australian outback with a hunky guide who we would all love to be stuck with."

They giggle.

I read an excerpt of the book and it is welcomed with enthusiastic approval.

Veronica steps forward. "And now we will open it up to any questions you may have for Ms. Blake."

"Hi, Ms. Blake. I love your books. I've read every one."

"Thank you. What's your name?"

"Jane."

"That's my daughter's name!" The audience laughs. "Thanks for your support, Jane. What's your question?"

"Well, I adore South Africa. Do you think you'll ever write a novel that takes place there?"

"I've never been to Africa. But travel is one of my loves. And I recognize that not everyone has the time or means to jet-set all over the world, so one of my constant goals is to bring different settings to my readers as vividly as I can. I was really, really lucky. Before I was a novelist, I had a dream job at the *L.A. Times* that actually paid me to explore beautiful international cities and write about them."

The audience "aahs".

"I know. I don't know why they hired me. I didn't know what I was doing."

The audience laughs.

"But I figured it out quickly because I was not going to lose *that* gig! However, I've not seen Africa. Jane, if you say South Africa is fabulous, then I'm going to have to put it on my list. Will you make sure that you e-mail me and tell me what you love about South Africa and exactly what I need to do there when I make it?"

"Absolutely!" Jane replies excitedly.

"Thank you." I choose another guest.

"Hi. I'm Susan."

"Hello, Susan."

"I was wondering... how you are. Is your marriage okay?"

My mother whips her head around to see who has asked her daughter such a personal question. Pam Daily looks like she is going to personally escort this guest out of the bookstore.

I realize that my mouth is hanging open. I take a deep breath. This was one of my biggest fears— my dirty laundry being aired out in front of my fans, in front of Skiatook, in front of anyone in America who was interested in hearing gossip about me. And here I am with nowhere to run because I've been put on the spot in front of a crowd of people looking at me expectantly. Most of them are as shocked as I am.

Oddly enough, I realize that I'm not freaking out. These people came down here early on a Saturday morning to wait in line for hours to spend some of their time with me.

I find myself making eye contact with a woman in the third row. She's about my age. She has light brown hair and soft blue eyes. She has a hardback of *Irish Fog* on her lap. She nods at me in encouragement. As my eyes are locked on to hers, I make a decision. I turn my attention back to Susan.

"You know what, Susan?" I begin.

My mom has her hands clapped over her mouth in fear because she thinks I'm about to tell Susan to stick her newly purchased Nina Blake paperback where the sun don't shine.

"Despite a whole lotta talk about it, not many people have asked me that to my face."

I start to chuckle. A few nervous chuckles follow suit.

"First of all, thank you for your concern. I'm okay. We're working on it."

"Next question," Veronica says quickly with a forced smile.

I shake my head because I realize that like Brandon, I, too, am tired of putting on a charade. "Wait." Veronica looks at me.

I continue. "We're not really working on it, and I think that's how we're working on it. It's been extremely difficult. Some days I could barely get out of bed."

The room is absolutely silent. My poor publicist looks like she's about to pass out. Women in the audience wear blank and surprised expressions. Clearly my mother is wondering if this is the moment that I actually lose it.

"But that's the thing. You have to get out of bed. And brush your teeth, and take your kids to school, and get some work done. And little by little you become yourself again."

The lady in the third row smiles and nods. In fact, I see many supportive faces nodding at me in assurance.

"I'm doing a lot of soul-searching and I'm learning a lot about myself," I continue. "My daughters and my girlfriends are getting me through it. They make everything manageable. When it comes to my husband and a working marriage, when it comes to real-life romance and how to prioritize that, I'm still working on cracking those codes."

I get a few laughs. I see some smiles. I see some nods. And then silence. They're waiting for more.

"Perhaps in my books that follow, I can spare you some of the trouble and share my newfound insight. Lord knows we shouldn't all have to figure it out."

A few people begin to clap. Collectively, the rest of the audience join in and some wholeheartedly whoop. What they're applauding for— my books, my honesty, the fact that I don't have everything figured out—I'm not exactly sure. Women start to get on their feet as they applaud. My mom stands up and wipes a tear from her eye. Veronica mouths the words *Good job*. I shrug. I'm exposed. This is me. And I'm not apologizing for it.

Chapter 42

I've just had an aromatherapy facial and a full-body citrus sugar scrub. I'm oily, moisturized and dewy, and I'm all wrapped up in a fluffy white robe and white slippers. I'm alone in the quiet room of one of Dallas' most popular spas and I'm sipping a cup of lemon ginger tea.

Being honest with my readers was liberating. All this time, I've forced Brandon and myself to put on a façade to keep a certain image with them. Really, all I felt today was support. Of course there will always be haters, but you just can't please everyone. And why should you? I can't hide from the tabloids, even living in small-town USA. I've got to be me, unapologetically. And Brandon and I should be a united front in our marriage. I shouldn't have forced him to be what he wasn't or what we weren't. I should tell him that.

The door opens and Mom enters the room with a cup of hot tea in hand. Her face is shiny and glowing. She looks relaxed and happy.

"How was your massage, Mom?"

"Amazing," she purrs. "I'm so glad you told them to add on a lavender hot oil scalp massage. It felt so good I almost passed out."

I laugh.

Mom sits down next to me.

"Good. I think spas should be our thing."

"What do you mean?"

"Well, it's something we love to do together. We always hit the Korean spa together when I'm home. Maybe we should see how many different spas we can visit together in the United States."

"That sounds like a fabulous idea."

It's quiet for a while. Since we are momentarily in a mother-daughter happy place, we could just sweep our earlier conversation under the rug. It's what we usually do, we fight and then we don't address it. But once it's swept under the rug, it doesn't disappear. It always crawls back out again.

"Mom, I'd like to answer your question from this morning."

Mom stays quiet.

"If Roma or Jane eloped, I would feel like I had really missed out on once-in-a-lifetime moments. I would be hurt. Maybe even offended. Probably heartbroken." I exhale. "Mom."

My mom looks up. Our eyes lock.

"I'm really sorry. Until you brought it up today, I never thought about it from the perspective of a mother. I wasn't a mom when I eloped. I was twenty-three. Brandon and I weren't thinking about anyone else when we were in Rome. As far as we were concerned, we were the only two people who existed. And I guess that's your point— that we didn't think about anyone else. But, I promise you, we didn't intend to hurt anyone's feelings."

Mom nods, looking down at her cup of tea as she dunks her tea bag up and down.

"Now that I think about it from your perspective, I can see how hurt you must've felt."

She nods sadly. "You left me, Nina. My mom died and then my daughter left. Talk about heartbreak."

I literally grab my heart. "Mom." My voice cracks. My mom dabs at her own. "I didn't know you felt that way."

"I know you thought it was so romantic to run off with Brandon. But I felt like you abandoned me. Whether it was right or wrong to feel that way, I felt hurt for a long time. Maybe even still."

I grab my mom's hand. "I'm sorry. And I take some blame for that, but you've got to let me live my life. You can't hold a grudge against me for doing what makes me happy."

My mom wipes her eyes and looks down at her lap.

"Mom."

She looks up at me with vulnerable eyes. "What?"

"Please forgive me."

She grabs my hand and squeezes. "I do."

"Can we move on?"

She nods. "Yes. It's time."

"Okay."

"I love you very much, Nina. And I was really proud of you today."

"Oh, Mom. Thanks. I love you, too. I really had good intentions for us this weekend. I wasn't trying to be hurtful. I just know we can do better."

"I agree. So, tell me. How can I do that?"

"You've done a great job raising me. I am who I am today because of you and Dad. But now I could really just use a great friend."

It's quiet for a moment and I wonder if she is taking this the wrong way.

"So could I," she replies in an uncharacteristically vulnerable tone.

I think about all of the times I've rolled my eyes at my mother's comments and rushed her off the phone. I, too, have effort to put into this relationship.

"Then you've got one." I stand up and take my mom's hand to help her out of her chair. I wrap my mom up in a huge hug. "Oh, mom. I love you with all my heart."

"I love you, too, Nina." She squeezes me back.

"Now, let's go have some fun."

* * *

We're both flying out tonight at eight-thirty, so we decide to pack in as much as we can. We have sushi for lunch and then visit the Dallas World Aquarium. Mom buys Jane a stuffed sea turtle and Roma a beautifully photographed Smithsonian book about the ocean.

It's almost as if by dealing with some of our disagreements, we have pulled a cork out of what has kept things bottled up for years. Conversations are flowing freely like we're old friends who haven't seen each other for a long time. It's like when I was in college and my mom would drive down to have dinner with me. We would go to the Cheesecake Factory in Marina del Rey and have lemon drop martinis, share a plate of chicken marsala, have a slice of cheesecake, and talk excitedly about what was going on in our lives.

As we walk around and look at the jellyfish, I tell Mom that I'm sad that we don't celebrate our heritage anymore. We don't speak in Spanish and we don't cook Grandma's food. We agree to do a better job of incorporating those things back into our lives.

There's a light, fun energy between us. We are simply enjoying each other. It makes my heart so happy. I guess sometimes things have to get worse before they can get better.

Chapter 43

On my flight home, I don't crack open a magazine or book. I look out the window into the black night sky. *Down and Dirty Down Under* is just another formulaic and fluffy romance novel. After being emotionally naked in front of my mom and the guests at my book signing, I feel like I owe the rest of my readers the same thing. I owe my characters in the book the same honesty.

When I arrive home, the girls are asleep. I offer for Brandon to stay the night, but he kindly refuses and leaves. I kiss Roma and Jane in their beds and head back downstairs.

Though it's late and I've had a full few days, I'm charged with creative energy. I make a cup of green tea and settle into the chair at my desk. I fire up my laptop and I write. I start making some big changes. When I'm writing, real time isn't relevant. In the world that my characters exist in, I am there in a scene that lasts a few minutes and look up from my laptop to find that hours have passed.

When I notice soft light outside my office window, I pad into the kitchen and put on a pot of strong coffee. I yawn and decide that it's break time, knowing that Roma and Jane will be up and getting ready for school soon. I start cutting cantaloupe and strawberries and put raisin bread into the toaster.

After a sweet reunion with my daughters, I drive them to school and rush back home. It is foolish to break my momentum, but I have to take a two-hour nap to recharge. I set an alarm to wake me.

* * *

After two more days of burning the midnight oil and taking short naps when necessary, I have rewritten the entire draft of *Down and Dirty Down Under*. What started as a light and sexy romp through the outback with an American woman and a hunky Australian has transformed into a strained and uncomfortable trip between an American husband and wife in the outback. Their vacation begins as a forced celebration of their fifteenth wedding anniversary, but the truth comes out that they have both been cheating on each other. When their guide drives off with their wallets, they have no choice but to hash things out on their own in the wild.

I decided that they would both have been unfaithful so they would equally shoulder blame in the breakdown of their marriage. They both have a lot of anger and bitterness towards each other. With nothing but obstacles and time on their hands, the husband and wife are forced to confront each other, see each other's side, and take responsibility for their own actions. In the end, they discover that not only can they not survive without each other, but they can't live without each other either.

At dawn on the third day, I e-mail the new draft to Stan. I could almost collapse from exhaustion. Over the last few days, I have cried, felt anger, disappointment and longing towards the characters. But I am so pleased with the honest portrayal of this man and this woman. It's a different kind of writing than I've ever done and I'm very satisfied with myself.

After I send the email, I collapse on my bed from physical, mental, and emotional exhaustion. I sleep a peaceful sleep all day until Becky brings the girls home from school.

* * *

That night, when I see Stan's name on the caller ID, my stomach has a pit in it. It's that Jerry Maguire moment in which I've poured my heart out and have completely exposed myself, and I suddenly wonder if maybe my passion and impulse got the best of me.

"Hi, Stan," I say neutrally.

"Well, I've got to know. What prompted *that*?"

"Stan. It was the craziest thing. One of my readers at the Dallas book signing asked me point blank about my marriage and I had no choice but to be honest. I admitted that I didn't have all of the answers, which I always thought was the worst thing I could do, but it felt incredible."

"Wow," Stan says.

"And even better than that, they were supportive. They applauded me for it! They gave me the courage to write from an honest and bare place instead of the light-hearted bullshit that I usually write."

There is silence.

Oh, no. I went overboard. Stan has always championed my light-hearted bullshit.

"Well, I love it."

I didn't realize I was holding my breath until I let out an exhale that comes from my toes.

Stan hears it and lets out a bellow of a laugh.

"Sweetheart, I actually adore your bullshit, but this novel will be a breath of fresh air and I think your readers are going to be caught off guard. In a good way."

"Thank you," I gush. "I'm so glad you like it."

"You're welcome. Kudos to you for digging so deep. The results are beautiful. Quite honestly, it's your best work ever."

I inhale. "Really? Thank you!" I let out a whoop.

Stan laughs. "Honey, you sound pooped. And a little delirious, if I'm honest. Get some rest and I'll send some little notes for a polish."

"Okay. Good night."

When we hang up, I can feel the blush on my cheeks from smiling and my heart is pounding. I fist-pump the air in celebration and then I fall backwards onto my bed. I climb under the covers and fall into another peaceful and exhausted sleep.

* * *

With my Texas book tour behind me, it's time to decide what I'm going to work on. I'm in such a good place with my writing. Maybe because I'm getting to be in a better place with myself. I'm thrilled that the energy between my mom and I has been so positive. Roma and I have been okay. I've been taking my focus off of my relationship with Brandon and putting it towards other things. And, as a result, I'm feeling happy.

I have a solid draft of *Down and Dirty Down Under* that I'm really quite proud of. Naturally the book will require revision, but before the editing process begins I always like to take some time away from the project so that when I return, my perspective can be fresh and objective.

I don't have any new storylines that I'm chomping at the bit to explore. I think I'd like to think outside the box some more. But I'm so depleted from the characters of the Outback that I need a break from my stories and to focus on someone else's.

I have an idea on how I can do just that and help the next generation of writers.

I make a phone call to Sheila Alcorn, the high-school principal, and inquire if they need anyone to help the juniors with their writing skills for the college essays they'll be focusing on in the fall. I propose a twofold plan. This spring I'll come into their English classes to strengthen basic writing skills and motivate creativity. In the fall I will guide the seniors as they compose their essays for college entrance in after-school workshops. Sheila loves the idea.

Chapter 44

The landscape seems to transform overnight. The bulbs that we planted during a previous autumn burst through the thawing soil like alarm clocks signaling that spring is here! Daffodils and tulips cover our yards, and ivory Queen Ann's lace blankets the countryside. Dogwood trees flowered with fuchsia blooms remind me of the whimsical trees in a Dr. Seuss book. The mornings and evenings are still cool, but the days warm up enough to dig up our t-shirts and flip-flops. With spring comes a feeling of opportunity, possibilities, and rebirth.

I receive a package from my mom. It is heavy and I lay it carefully onto the island in the kitchen. I slide a knife across the packing tape and open it to reveal a layer of bubble wrap and layers of lavender tissue paper. I smile, my curiosity piqued.

Inside is a wooden box, which I lift out, and flip open the lid. It's full of recipe cards, and the first one is for arroz con leche. My heart skips a beat. The recipe for rice pudding is written in Grandma Isabel's familiar slanted handwriting. I flip through the cards, their edges worn with use. They are all here— chile rellenos, Mexican rice, and chicken mole (my grandpa's favorite).

My Grandpa Julio's orange Julius and vanilla raspados recipes are here, written by Grandpa himself. He used to crush ice for the raspados using a hand crank that was attached to the side of the kitchen cabinet over their sink. He would make a simple syrup by simmering sugar, water and Mexican vanilla. It was such a simple recipe but it made the best snow cones I'd ever had as a child. It conjures up memories of running through the sprinklers in my underwear in Grandma and Grandpa's backyard. This recipe box is a treasure chest, a time machine, a portal into my childhood and my heritage.

There is another tissue-wrapped item in the packing box. It's a cast-iron tortilla press, one that belonged to my mom. She used to let me press Play-Doh into little tortillas sitting at my child-sized wooden table while she bustled around me doing housework.

I wonder if my mom knows what a gift she has bestowed upon me. I call her and thank her profusely. We chat some more and make plans for her and dad to visit for the Fourth of July. I hear the joy in mom's voice as a result of her gift bringing me so much happiness.

* * *

With the arrival of spring comes another surprise. Coldplay blasts through the living room as I dust shelves with a Pledge-drenched rag.

The phone rings. It's Alison.

"Al!" I screech. "How are you?"

"I'm good, but I miss you. I was thinking how great it would be if we could spend the weekend together."

"Oh. That sounds amazing. Let's plan that. When are you free?"

"I'm free now."

I pause to process. "What do you mean?"

"I'm on the curb outside of the baggage claim."

"What?" I exclaim.

She giggles and hangs up.

I run to the car and drive the twenty miles to the Tulsa Airport as fast as I can.

When I pull up to the baggage claim and park along the curb, Alison, Kate and Christina jump up and down. I scream as I throw the car door open. "What are you doing here?"

"We thought you could use some familiar faces," Kate answers.

"You were right." I throw my arms around all three of them in a group hug.

When I pull away, I grab Alison's hands and assess her. She's wearing a purple plaid blouse, Wranglers, and cowgirl boots. "Wow, you look festive."

"I went to Bootbarn yesterday. I wanted to fit in."

"Yeah." My voice involuntarily rises an octave.

"What is it?"

"Sweetie, I don't think I've ever worn a plaid shirt here, but I love your enthusiasm."

"Do I look like a dork?"

"You look great," Christina, Kate and I chime in.

"Right," Alison says.

Kate chose to dress on the other side of the spectrum. She wears a snug gray designer power suit and black stilettos.

"I went to the airport straight from work," she explains as she reads my mind.

Christina is dressed in relaxed jeans, a gray t-shirt with a gauzy scarf draped around her neck and Ugg boots. "I'm the Goldilocks of outsiders," she says. "I dressed juuust right."

Chapter 45

We bustle around the kitchen island setting out cheeses, dried fruits and olives for a cheese board. Christina opens a bottle of pinot grigio.

"Woohoo!" she cries as she pulls the cork out.

Once we catch each other up on our initial news, the elephant in the room cannot be ignored.

"So, how's it going? Really," Kate says.

Alison puts her arm around me as I explain what a hellish six months it has been with Brandon's absence and his lack of participation in repairing our marriage. But I also elaborate about how I've given myself permission to enjoy myself and not care as much about what people think of me. I tell them about my recent breakthrough with *Down and Dirty Down Under* and we see this as an opportunity to toast. We clink our wine glasses with resounding whoops and cheers.

"Mom?" Roma calls.

Jane and Roma walk in tentatively, not knowing what and who they are going to find.

Their jaws drop when they see who the boisterous voices belong to. Although my friends have each visited a few times since I've lived here, it's been years since their last visit so this truly is a big surprise.

"Aunties!" Jane squeals.

My girlfriends scoop up my daughters and smother them with hugs and kisses.

Jane and Roma take Alison and Christina to saddle up the horses for a double horseback ride around the lake, so Kate and I decide to run into town for emergency provisions.

* * *

I give Kate a tour of our Walmart Superstore and she is in awe of its sheer magnitude. It's a one-stop shop. You can buy a yoga mat, knitting needles, a Skiatook Bulldogs sweatshirt, plants and soil, or a hunting rifle. You can get a fishing permit, refill your prescription, and have your tires rotated.

But for now, we load up the cart with anything and everything edible. We are proving the age-old adage that you shouldn't shop for groceries while you're hungry.

Still dressed in her work attire, Kate click-clacks in her stilettos as we turn the cart down the beverage aisle. There stands Marlena wearing skin-tight capri jeans, a snug fuzzy white sweater that begs to be petted, and open-toed pink kitten heels. Her lustrous, cascading hair glistens under the fluorescent lighting. "Well, slap butter on me and call me a biscuit!"

Kate's eyes are wide with curiosity. She is equally confused by this stranger and her greeting.

"Hi, Marlena," I say flatly. I despise fake nice. She's just rubbing it in my face that she deflowered my husband so many years ago.

She eyes Kate.

"This is my friend, Kate."

"Oh. My. God! Aren't you the cutest? You are so *L.A.*," she says stressing both the "L" and the "A". "You look like you're about to conquer the world!"

"Nice to meet you," Kate says. She doesn't even know the

backstory and she's skeptical of Marlena.

Marlena grabs two bottles of Boone's Farm Strawberry Hill off the shelf.

"That's a good year," I say, dryly.

"Oh, you!" Marlena giggles. "Well, y'all, I've gotta run. I've got a hot date!"

Good. Take someone else your pies of seduction.

"You look cute," I say. I just made fun of her taste in wine in front of someone she just met, so I feel the need to say something nice. My mother raised me better than that. "You look like Ann Margaret in *Bye, Bye, Birdie.*"

"Oh, I love that! Thank you!"

"Have fun," Kate says.

"I plan on it," she says with a little shoulder shimmy.

We watch as Marlena sashays her little butt down the aisle and disappears.

"Wow. How much wine did I drink?" Kate asks. "I just hallucinated meeting Skiatook Barbie."

I throw my head back and laugh.

"Seriously, who was that?"

"That," I say, "was Brandon's high-school girlfriend."

"No!" Kate punches me in the arm.

"I wouldn't lie to ya."

"I haven't drunk Strawberry Hill since our junior prom."

I cackle and nod as I grab a few bottles of tonic water off the shelf.

Chapter 46

Seeing an opportunity to open Grandma's recipe box, we have embarked upon cooking up a Mexican feast. The house is filled with the delicious savory aromas of smoky chipotle peppers and onions.

Kate and Christina are on team mole. Christina stirs a pot with onions, garlic, cumin, coriander and dried chilis in it. Kate chops a disk of Ibarra chocolate that will be added to the sauce. Later, chicken thighs and drumsticks will bathe in the sweet and savory sauce. A luxurious sauce made out of chocolate— the Mexicans were really onto something there.

I sprinkle a handful of cilantro into my grandma's rice. Now, this one I didn't need a recipe for. My mom made this rice so often that I caught on just by watching her simmer rice with garlic, tomato sauce, onions, green bell peppers, and cilantro.

Roma, Jane and Alison sit at the kitchen table in a tortilla assembly line. Alison mixes masa and water together with her hands, Roma rolls it into balls and hands them to Jane, who flattens them in the tortilla press. Alison tells my daughters an animated story and they giggle as they work.

My grandma would have loved this sight. The room is filled with so much activity, steam and joyful noise. Glasses of limey gin and tonics are scattered around our work spaces. Christina tips some into

Kate's mouth since her hands are covered in chocolate. Kate tries not to laugh as she takes a sip. My heart is so full, it could just burst.

* * *

In an attempt to digest our abundant meal, we lie on patio furniture down on the big deck, unable to move. The evening air is chilly and we wear various sweatshirts that we sent Jane up to the house to gather for us.

Roma sits with Christina and Kate at the table and is in the middle of a heart-to-heart. Alison and Janie snuggle up on a chaise longue and gaze at the stars.

Eventually, Roma and Jane reluctantly head off to bed. It is Thursday, a school night, after all.

Kate turns to Alison and Christina. "I forgot to tell you. When we were at the grocery store, I met Brandon's high-school girlfriend!"

"What?" Christina wails.

"You have to see your husband's ex-girlfriend on a regular basis?" asks Alison. "That must be awful."

"It's fine. More like a nuisance. She's like a pesky fly buzzing around my head with an incredibly high voice."

The ladies giggle.

"She's very in your face," I continue. "Apparently, she baked him a pie and dropped by his place the other day."

"What the hell?" Christina asks.

"That's kind of unacceptable," Alison says.

Kate's face whips around to mine. "Do you think she was implying that her hot date was with Brandon?"

I stare at Kate. I bolt upright on the chaise longue and whip my cell phone out of my pocket.

"Come on, would she really tell you if she had a date with your own husband?" Alison asks skeptically.

219

I dial with purpose.

"'Bout to find out." Becky answers on the second ring. "Is Brandon's truck there?" I inquire without any small talk. The night is utterly silent while Becky goes to glance out her kitchen window. In the dark I can feel six eyes on me.

"Thanks. I'll talk to you later." I press "end" and glare at my girlfriends.

"Let's go," Christina says.

Chapter 47

We haven't done a stakeout like this since high school when Kate thought her boyfriend was cheating on her with a girl from another school. I've had a lot of full-circle moments with these ladies, but I have a feeling it will take me years to appreciate this one, if ever.

Marlena lives in a subdivision just south of town.

"It's up here on the right," I say in a stern voice.

We drive down Buffalo Boulevard and there it is in plain view to me and all of Skiatook— Brandon's truck. It's parked on the street right in front of the bimbo's cute little red-brick home.

My mouth is open, but I don't say anything.

"That asshole," Kate says.

"That bitch," Christina says.

"I'm not sure who I'm angrier at," Alison replies.

I stay quiet because my girlfriends are articulating my thoughts for me and my throat feels too constricted to say anything. I keep driving.

"Wait a second. Why aren't we going in there?" Christina asks.

"She's devising her plan," Kate says.

When we turn out of Marlena's neighborhood and onto Highway 20, I break my silence. "How could he?" I ask.

My girlfriends are silent.

"I mean, really." My volume suddenly changes to shouting. "How could he?"

They know that I am not expecting a response.

"After the life that we have created together— our children, our home— he is at *her* house? On a date with a woman who doesn't come close to measuring up to me?"

"That's right."

"That's for sure."

"Not even close." My cheerleaders beckon in the background.

"That bitch! I complimented her on her outfit before she seduced my husband!" I hit the steering wheel.

"What are you going to do?" Alison asks.

I contemplate for a moment. "I guess I'm going to ask him how it's going."

"I'll dial," Kate offers from the passenger seat. "Putting it on speaker."

She hands me my cell phone. After a few rings, he picks up.

"Are you enjoying your cheap wine?" I ask.

There is a pause.

"What do you mean?"

"What do you think I mean?"

"Nina," Brandon attempts calmly, "this is not a date."

"Your truck is outside of Marlena's house!" I squeal. "You're alone with her in her house!"

He takes a breath. "She offered to make me dinner. We're just old friends."

"Really? So, should I be calling up 'old friends' and offering to cook for them?"

"Calm down."

"I think I'm being pretty calm, actually," I sneer. "You'd know it if I wasn't calm."

"Nothing is going on here."

"Well, don't let me interrupt. I'm sure she has something really *special* planned for dessert." I hang up and toss the cell phone in Kate's lap. She jumps. "I imagine it has something to do with that fuzzy white sweater. Or the absence of it."

I raise my eyebrows at Christina in the rear view mirror. She shakes her head.

"I really think you should go back there and get him," Alison offers.

"I refuse to take him by the hand and lead him out of there like a child. He's got to decide on his own to do the right thing."

The Range Rover crosses over the dam. The black water of Skiatook Lake is perfectly still and the moon's reflection illuminates a bright path down the middle. Its serenity contrasts with the craziness that I feel inside.

We drive up the steep road that takes us into the hills above the lake. I abruptly pull the car over to the shoulder and throw it into park.

"I have to walk," I say as I hurl the car door open.

"Oh," Alison says, unsure. "Do you want company?"

"No."

"Let her go," Christina says.

"Okay, sweetie." Alison says, her skeptical tone asking me to be careful.

The passenger door opens and Kate emerges, jogs over to the driver's side and climbs in behind the wheel. I take off, walking fast down Lake Road in my flip-flops. The Range Rover passes me. Its tail lights get smaller and disappear around a curve in the road. I pump my arms and it feels good to exert the furious energy that is coursing through my entire body.

"Aaaahhh!" My voice cuts through the silence into the night and it sounds strange, like it's not mine.

I break into a jog and build into a sprint. My feet begin to burn from the lack of support in my inadequate footwear. I bend over and put my hands on my knees, panting, mostly from my overwhelming emotions. I take a deep breath, stand up and walk down the road.

* * *

I open my front door and walk through an empty house. Warm light flickering through the kitchen windows draws me outside. I step outside to the kitchen patio and Alison and Christina have settled into the Adirondack chairs. They have dragged three kitchen chairs onto the small brick patio and Kate and Becky sit on two of them. The chiminea is lit and the fire throws incandescent shadows onto the wall. The ladies each hold a glass of red wine and there is one waiting for me on the little red wooden table.

"Hey!" they say supportively, glad that I'm home.

"Look who we found here when we got back," Kate says and smiles at Becky.

"It was clear that something was up," Becky says. "I just can't believe it."

My walk has calmed me down considerably and I feel as though I can think clearly now.

"So, is this it?" I collect my glass of wine and sit in a chair. "The end? He's moving on already?"

"I don't know," Alison answers softly.

"I don't think so," Christina replies. "He's just acting out. He's certainly not moving on with this Marlena. He's just experimenting. I really do think he will come to his senses."

"I do, too," Kate agrees.

"I think we all know Brandon well enough to believe that he wouldn't be unfaithful," Becky says.

"I'm not sure I really know Brandon all that well anymore," I say. The girls shake their heads in disbelief.

"I mean, I get it. She's… softer than I am. She's uncomplicated. And she's everything that I'm not."

"And you're everything that she's not," Becky says.

"I don't know. Sometimes I think Brandon and I are like a square peg and round hole. I'm the square, and Marlena is round. Perfectly tiny and round."

"I don't think this has anything to do with Marlena," Kate says. "I think this is Brandon wanting a distraction."

"How distracted do you suppose he is allowing himself to be?" I ask. I put my face in my hands.

We hear the crunching of gravel around the side of the house and we momentarily freeze. Brandon emerges from the dark.

He seems taken aback when he sees me surrounded by my posse.

"Oh. Wow. You're all here."

I can tell that he wants to give each of them a hug. Brandon loves my friends, but the situation is heavy with tension.

"Hi," he says awkwardly.

My girlfriends would normally gush over Brandon, but out of loyalty to me, they don't move a muscle.

"Hello, Brandon," Christina says, pointedly.

Brandon is taken back by her tone. "Nina, can I speak to you, please?"

"Yes."

I stand up and follow Brandon into the kitchen. He leads the way into the office.

He closes the door behind him and looks at me. He's waiting for me to initiate.

"Yes?" I say.

"I want to explain about tonight. It really isn't a big deal."

225

I shrug like I don't care.

"Marlena and I are friends. She went through a rough divorce and knows what I'm going through." As soon as Brandon says it, he's sorry.

"Divorce? Am I missing something?"

"That's not what I meant."

I point my finger at him. "I do not want you talking about me or our marriage to Marlena Morrison."

"It was absolutely nothing, Nina."

"Then why are you here? If you're so innocent, why are you here defending yourself?"

Brandon looks confused. "Because I know you're mad."

"And what does that matter? Of course I'm mad. I'm furious! I'm not happy with any of this." I gesture with wide arms to encompass the entire situation. "But since when do you care what I think? Or how I feel?"

"Of course I care," Brandon says defensively.

"None of it matters." My voice is loud and out of control. "You have the upper hand. Apparently you can do whatever you please. I am here waiting for you, raising our children, and on my best behavior until you decide that you're ready to come back to me— if that is indeed what you decide."

I walk out of the room.

I walk into the dark kitchen. I plant my hands onto the island and lean my head down. A sob escapes my mouth.

"No," I scold myself.

Moments later I hear heavy footsteps and the front door open and close.

I summon the energy to stand up straight. I pull two more bottles of wine out of the cupboard and head back outside.

* * *

When we wake the next morning, we congregate in the kitchen around the coffee pot. We had a late night gathered around the fire talking shit about Brandon McCoy.

"Let's get one thing straight," I say as we all sip our coffee. "I am not going to waste a precious visit with all of you bitching about Brandon the entire time."

"But sweetie, it's why we're here," Alison says, "to make sure you're okay."

"Then what I need from you is quality time. Just us being us."

We've decided that Jane and Roma most definitely have to play hooky. So, after I call the girls' schools, we pack a cooler of sandwiches, sodas and a few of our old favorites like salt and vinegar potato chips and bottles of Killian's Red beer. We throw a few fishing rods into the back of my rig and pile in. We drive down Lake Road, cross Highway 20, and park on an isolated cross street.

We hop out, grab our poles and head down a rough trail which takes us to Polecat Creek. We abandon our sandals, roll up our jeans, and the air fills with screams as we wade into the frigid water. The weather may be nice, but it will be another month or two before the streams and lakes are bearable.

As we wait patiently with our lines in the water, occasionally recasting, Alison, Kate, Christina and I sing songs from a summer camp that we attended on Catalina Island when we were in junior high.

Roma and Jane crack up that we remember all of the words. To them, we're acting like a bunch of kids. I hope that they will have lifelong friends who will show up for them whenever they need it. Friends who will stick together through both fun and tough times in their lives. Because what a treasure it is.

Chapter 48

I'm happy that my girlfriends picked a beautiful weekend to visit Skiatook. At about eighty degrees, the air feels like bath water. Jane and I drive with the windows down, our hair flapping in the warm wind. We just dropped the aunties off at the airport. Roma chose to stay behind at home to catch up on the work that she missed from playing hooky. It's been a fantastic few days, despite a certain chain of events, and my soul feels happy and cleansed from the company of my very best friends. They reminded me that no matter what curve balls life throws at me, everything will be all right.

We head north on 75 and make the left turn onto Highway 20 that will take us home to Skiatook. As we drive along the fence line of a farm, we approach a guy riding a tractor. I squint and notice that it's Ethan Parker. "I know that guy."

"You do?" Jane asks, surprised.

"Daddy used to hire him to help with yard work when he was a kid." I pull the car over and stop.

"He doesn't look like a kid anymore," Jane replies. I laugh.

We get out of the car and walk over to the fence. I wave at Ethan and he slows the tractor down as he approaches us.

"Hi, Nina," he calls.

Ethan's sweaty six-pack glistens and contracts as he jumps off the tractor. He wears very worn blue jeans that ride low on his hips, revealing that defined moment where lower abs and hips come together that Jane is probably too young to see. I glance at her and see that her eyebrows are raised. In fact, I'm not sure who is blushing more, me or my seven-year-old daughter.

Ethan grins as he approaches us.

"Hi, Ethan. This is my daughter, Jane."

"Hi," she says, sheepishly.

"Pleased to meet you." He tips his cowboy hat to her.

My stomach jolts. I'm experiencing a very distinct sensation of déjà vu. Oh right. The moment in *Legends of the Fall* when Brad Pitt tipped his cowboy hat to that poor, doomed Susannah character. She was a goner. That scene was when I first realized I had hormones.

"You must love this beautiful weather," I say, steering us to more wholesome territory.

"Yes, ma'am. It's days like this that I'm thankful to work outside." His blue-green eyes squint as he glances into the sun behind us.

"That must be fun to drive a tractor around." Jane says.

"It is. Would you like to go for a ride?"

"Can I, Mama?" she asks excitedly.

"Sure."

Ethan's biceps clench as he lifts Jane over the fence. I remember hearing that he was the second-string quarterback at OSU. He definitely has the arms of someone who has been throwing a football around.

"Hold on tight," I instruct.

"I will, Mama," Jane says.

As they pull away on the tractor, Jane giggling, I shake my head in disbelief. I'm not sure if Ethan is further out of Jane's age range or mine, but she didn't waste any time getting a moment alone with him. It almost makes me proud.

* * *

The very next day, there is a knock at the door and Jane runs to answer it. "Mama! Ethan's here!" she shouts.

"Invite him in." I walk to the entry.

"Come on in." Jane ushers Ethan in.

"Hi, Ethan. Nice to see you again."

He awkwardly holds up a Tupperware to me. This is not the confident twenty-two-year-old who was showing off his abs yesterday. "My mama made some deer jerky and I thought you'd like some."

"Sounds delicious." I reach out and accept his gift. "That is so sweet that you thought of us."

"My pleasure." Ethan nods, like he's unsure what to say next.

"If you don't have anywhere to be, we're making cookies for Jane's 4H bake sale. We're making a lot, so we can eat some," I say conspiratorially.

Ethan smiles at me. "I would love to help."

He follows me into the kitchen where Jane hops up on a stool and continues stirring a bowl of cookie batter.

"I was in 4H when I was a kid," Ethan says.

"I just turned seven," she says, offended.

"Oh. Sorry." Ethan glances at me and I stifle a laugh. "Jane," Ethan continues, "can you remind me what the four H's stand for?"

I smile at him. He's so great with her.

"Head, heart, hands, and health."

"That's awesome," Ethan says.

Jane blushes. "Wanna help me stir?" she asks.

I wink at him.

Chapter 49

I've said it before, our downtown is a bit lackluster, but it has great potential. The old brick buildings have deteriorated over time, but the bones are still there. There are beautiful details like swags and raised words on the bricks. The buildings house antique stores that no one really frequents, a dingy bar that some do frequent, a barber shop, and many vacant spaces. I've always had high hopes for a new and improved, charming Downtown Skiatook.

Which is why tonight is so exciting. It's the grand opening of a new sports bar called The Bank Shot. It's actually a clever name since it used to be the old bank and a "bank shot" is a pool term. I'm thrilled that there's going to be a cool new spot in town to dine or grab a drink, and it's a big step towards sprucing up downtown.

I sit on the edge of my bed and slip on my black stilettos. I'm wearing snug dressy dark blue jeans, a black silk tank top and a taupe linen blazer. I put on a long gold necklace and gold hoops.

I thought about offering to pick up Becky and RJ, but I realized that Brandon would naturally be driving with them since he lives on their property, so I'll just take myself. It's going to be awkward enough in a party setting being in the same room with Brandon, yet not "being" with Brandon. I'm sure people will be watching how we are interacting and how we are handling the situation.

To be honest, I'm kind of over worrying about what everyone else is thinking about us. At the moment, I just care about what I think. And quite frankly, I'm almost coming to a place of... peace? Complacency? I'm not sure which sentiment it is. I recognize that although I'm coming to a healthier place with myself, my complacency at being separated is probably not good for the destiny of my marriage. Is this how it will happen? Will we just get used to being apart and then eventually decide to make it official? I shrug off this morbid thought and pledge to myself to have fun tonight.

I park on the street and approach The Bank Shot, which is on the corner. The word "BANK" is in its original brickwork. It's so cool. There's a chalkboard sign on the sidewalk that says "Grand Opening" and states that appetizers and draft beers are half off.

There is light, music, and chatter pouring out of the place and it's filled with patrons already having a good time. Good. I want this place to succeed.

I walk in and with a quick perusal of the room, I see that Becky, RJ, and Brandon haven't arrived yet. I say some hellos and head straight to the bar. I quickly become friends with the bartender (always make friends with the bartender) and I order an amber ale from a micro-brewery in Tulsa.

Marlena shoots me a fake smile from across the room and I shake my head and return her dumb grin with the stink eye. I'm done being friendly to that husband-stealing hussie. Her smile fades and she turns away, knowing that her agenda is now transparent.

Keith Andrews rubs up next to me at the bar, pretending his close proximity is due to the establishment being crowded. I sigh.

Keith Andrews is a prick. I met him my first summer in Skiatook. A bunch of us were at the lake and we tied our boats up together in a cove and had a huge party. We were having a great time lying out and drinking beers. Brandon had gone out with a group of people on RJ's boat to wakeboard and I opted to stay back and hang out with Becky and a few other girls. I was still just getting to know some of them and I was excited to make new friends.

I was lying on my stomach on the front of Bob Hopkin's boat. Keith Andrews scooted right up next to me, introduced himself, warned me about the brutal Oklahoma sun and took it upon himself to grab a bottle of sunscreen and squirt some on my back.

Before I had a chance to object, RJ pulled his boat into the cove and Brandon saw Keith lubing up his wife with Coppertone. Brandon leaped from one boat to the other and told Andrews to get his hands off me. Keith's poor wife, Stephanie, who had also gone on RJ's boat to waterski, started to cry. The drama ruined the energy of the day and we all went home shortly after.

Over the years, he's been no stranger to offensive shenanigans. Needless to say, we have never liked Keith Andrews. And by the way, he's been divorced twice.

"Hello, Keith," I say, reminiscent of how Seinfeld used to greet his annoying and scheming neighbor, Newman.

"Nina. How are *things?*" His tone implies, *I know things suck right now. Want me to help you feel better?*

Just then, Brandon walks in to The Bank Shot with RJ and Becky. He sees me standing with Keith Andrews and his brow creases. I can read my husband's conflicted expression. He wants to rescue me but isn't sure if he should reclaim me as his woman just yet. We also haven't spoken since the aftermath of the Marlena dinner date.

Keith tries to snake back in and continue our conversation. "So, how are you?" he asks flirtatiously.

Brandon's eyes remain locked on me. I roll my eyes, annoyed with my fair-weather husband.

I turn to Keith. "Better than you'd think." I grab my beer and walk the other direction, away from Keith and away from Brandon.

* * *

I finish off a pale ale and order a hefeweizen, both from Tulsa micro-breweries. I am a proud Okie. I am supporting the Tulsa economy. I'm having a good ol' time at The Bank Shot. This place rocks!

The bartender hands me my hefeweizen, garnished with a lemon wedge. I turn around and Brianna Wakefield, the awful woman who supplied her daughter with the *US Weekly* magazine, is canoodling with Keith Andrews at the bar.

I laugh heartily. They look at me.

"Perfect. You guys make a *great* couple." I give them an enthusiastic two thumbs up.

Brianna glares at me and I chuckle as I walk away.

I find Dr. Hart and throw my arm around him. I thank him profusely for saving my eye last December. He thinks I'm hilarious.

Judge McClintock sidles up next to me. He's in his early sixties and is very distinguished. He reminds me of a young James Garner. "Nina. I've just written a novel."

"You have? That's wonderful!" I cheer. "You've got to let me read it."

"Well, I was hoping you'd say that. I'd love some advice."

"I'd be happy to help. Now, do you want to me to boost your confidence or take a red pen to it?"

Judge McClintock laughs. "Uh-oh. Now I'm afraid," he jokes.

"Don't worry, I'll give you constructive criticism, but I'll also draw stars next to the things that I like."

"Sounds good. Why don't you stop by my houseboat tomorrow and we'll have a cocktail on the lake and then I'll give you the manuscript?"

"It's a date," I say cheerfully.

"Good. Bring your red pen."

* * *

I stand with Becky and Carrie Ann. Becky tells us about some new soaps she's working with, like coconut lime and lemon rosemary. We convey our enthusiastic interest in trying them out. Carrie Ann expresses her gratefulness for having Robbie in preschool this year. After twenty-two years of being a mother, she's finally back to having a few mornings to herself. God bless her.

I've really had a fabulous time tonight, but it's time to head home. The girls will long have been asleep, but I'll have to be up early to get them to school. I did not plan on drinking so much and am in no condition to drive, so Carrie Ann offers to drive me home and Todd will follow in my car.

I haven't talked to Brandon at all this evening. He knows that I'm mad about his dinner with Marlena, and as a result he's made an obvious attempt to stay away from her this evening. Should I read his distance from her as effort towards us or a confirmation of his guilt?

Chapter 50

It's less than half a mile from our house to the marina. It's a beautiful day, about seventy-five degrees, so I walk. One thing about Oklahoma weather is that it fluctuates, so we'll likely have more pleasant days of weather before the heat of summer sets in.

I walk down the ramp to the boat slips and pass by speedboats and pontoon boats. I continue to the last row and follow it to the very end where there is one lone houseboat.

The Judge is notorious for being the only one who actually lives here on the lake. As I approach the houseboat, he sees me from the top deck and waves. He's wearing a Hawaiian shirt with the top few buttons open and khaki shorts. It's really cute, actually. He was a very successful man during the life of his career and he now seems to be a happy bachelor, living a retired life of leisure.

"Good afternoon, Judge!" I call.

He disappears momentarily and greets me at the entrance. "Hello, Nina. Please, call me Bruce."

I've been an acquaintance of the Judge for about ten years. It's a little strange to start calling him Bruce all of a sudden, but I acquiesce. "Okay, thanks, Bruce." He offers his hand and helps me aboard. "I'm excited to see your home."

"This is my little piece of heaven." He leads me into a medium-sized living room area with an open kitchen. The serene expanse of lake is visible through the many windows.

"I can see why. You must enjoy the sunsets."

"Can I offer you an afternoon cocktail?"

"Whatever you're having."

He shakes up a few dirty martinis, gives me a tour of the boat and we end up on the upper deck.

We sit at a small table where his manuscript waits. Resting on top of the manuscript is a red pen tied up in a metallic gold bow.

I laugh. "That's good, because I thought it would be rude to actually bring my own."

"I'm lucky to have a bestselling author read and critique my first novel."

"Your first. So, do you have plans for more?"

"Nina, I'm retired. What would be better than to sit up here with a martini in hand and write about some of my life experiences?"

"Honestly, Judge… Bruce," I correct myself, "I can hardly think of a better plan." I look around. "Wow, I didn't think there was a better view than the one from my backyard."

"Yep. I'm a lucky man."

"Seems like time for a toast, then." I lift my glass and the Judge follows suit. "To life on the lake and to your first novel."

"Cheers. Thank you, Nina." He drains his glass. "Another martini?"

I've only just taken a sip of the one that I have, but I'm having a lovely time and I nod. "Seeing as how I walked, I really don't have an excuse to refuse."

"Perfect. I'll bring you a fresh glass so you can finish that one. Excuse me."

The Judge disappears inside and I open his manuscript. The introduction is good. He has a strong voice— it sounds just like the Judge is narrating the story himself.

The boat bobs calmly from the lukewarm breeze. I exhale a contented breath and take a sip of my cocktail. The Judge returns carrying two fresh martinis. He wears only black silk boxers.

I choke on my drink and it sloshes over the glass onto my lap. "What are you doing?" I ask, shocked.

The Judge sets the martinis on the table and looks at me with an intense, fiery glare. "How about you come over here and bring your little red pen. I'll draw stars next to all the things I like about you, starting with those long legs."

"Are you kidding me?" I squeak. My gaze focuses on his ample, curly brown and gray chest hair and I shudder.

"You're a firecracker. You're different than any woman I've ever met. You make me feel exhilarated!"

The Judge leaps toward me and I shriek. I jump out of my chair and dodge him. His manuscript falls to the floor.

"This is not happening!" I'm saying this to the Judge to let him know that nothing sexual is ever going to happen between us, and also to myself because I cannot believe this is happening.

"I see that you're a little caught off guard."

"Uh, yeah. I'm leaving!" I grab the manuscript frantically from the floor. "I will read your manuscript because I said I would. But that's it!"

"Awww, don't go." The Judge attempts a coy frown.

I run through the houseboat, and slip while rushing down the spiral staircase. I fall hard on my butt. "Ow!" There will surely be a bruise to remind me of this grotesque and frightening moment.

"Are you okay?" he asks from the top of the stairs. "Should we put some ice on it?"

"No!" I grab my purse in the kitchen where I left it.

"Nina, don't fight this. We'd be great together! I'll show you how a woman should be loved. We'll make waves together on this love boat!"

"Ugh!" I convulse in disgust as I jump back onto the dock.

The Judge leans over the balcony from the upper deck in his silky boxers. "Just know that every night, I'll be gazing up at you on your pedestal, *thinking* about you." He grins.

How could someone make the word "thinking" sound so dirty? I run past the other boat slips and up the ramp towards the marina boat shop. A few crusty fishermen sit on the patio drinking some cold beers. They snicker as I escape from the direction of the Judge's houseboat. It's evident that they heard the Judge's promises of seduction.

I lunge up the steep hill out of the marina and do the walk of shame. Even though I didn't participate in anything inappropriate, I feel so dirty and so ashamed.

Later that night, I glance out at the lake. Against my better judgment, my eyes swivel towards the marina. A small light flickers from one of the bobbing boats. It can only be the Judge's houseboat. I experience a full-body shudder at the possibility that he's fantasizing about me in his silky black boxers. I jump away from the window in the unlikely event that he can see me.

Chapter 51

It's been a few weeks since I started teaching the high-school writing class. The first few sessions have focused on the students writing about themselves. I wanted to encourage them to write from the heart and to allow the writing to flow out of them. For many early writers, getting the content out can be difficult. I'm teaching them that writing is not set in stone. That's what erasers, whiteout and the backspace key are for. Write first, edit later.

To practice this methodology, the students are working on a piece we are calling "My Ultimate Life". I encouraged them to entertain the idea of where they would want to be in ten years. I told them that anything can happen! What dream job would they have obtained? What kind of house would they live in? Would they be married? Would they have children? Would they travel?

Some of them explored the idea of being pilots and video game programmers who live in Hawaii and go on safaris in Africa, while others wrote about staying close to home and joining the family business. Some talked about the large families that they would have and the cool things they would do with their kids.

The students seem to be enjoying the assignment and the ideas are pouring out of them, which was my goal. Next, I will use these pieces to teach the editing process. I love witnessing the students in their creative process, and it's allowing me to get to know many of them better.

I notice the boy I now know as Brock Anderson reading his piece. This is the boy I suspect gave Roma the flowers on Valentine's Day.

Brock is the mysterious, silent type. He's tall, lean, and is the Bulldogs' running back. His sandy-blond hair falls across his honey-brown eyes when he leans down to read his paper. He's super cute.

I squat down next to his desk and ask him if he'll read what he's got down so far.

"In ten years, I'll be vice-president of Osage Bank." He looks up at me. "My dad will still be president," he explains.

"I love your ambition, Brock. Go on," I encourage.

Out of the corner of my eye, I can see Roma glance our way from the front of the class.

"My wife and I will live in a big brick house on fifty acres of land with a creek where we'll fish. I'll play football in the yard with my two sons and my two daughters." He looks up at me again. "Girls should know how to throw a football."

I smile at Brock. "I totally agree."

* * *

I'm editing the Judge's manuscript. A promise is a promise. The story is actually pretty good, but I've jotted down notes that will help make some of the characters more dynamic. I only have a few chapters left and then I plan on dropping the manuscript off to RJ to drop off to the Judge. I know it's a total wimp move, but I cannot bring myself to revisit the scene of the proposition.

The doorbell rings. I open the door to reveal Ethan Parker.

"Hi, Ethan," I say cheerfully. "What can I do for you?"

"Well, lately I can't get a certain Shania Twain song out of my head."

I hang my head in embarrassment. "Great. I had managed to suppress that memory."

He laughs. "You shouldn't. It was awesome."

"I've wanted to thank you for driving us home that night, but I didn't want to say anything in front of Jane."

"That's okay. It was my pleasure." This guy is adorable. It's too bad he's too old for Roma.

"Are Roma and Jane here?"

"Oh, you're so sweet. No, they're with their dad at the feed store."

"Finally." He grabs me, pulls me to his body, and plants a hard and intense kiss on my lips. His tongue slips into my mouth.

Oy vey.

My eyes bulge out in utter shock and I push Ethan away. "What are you doing?" I try to catch my breath.

"I'm sorry, ma'am. I've been dying to do that. You being back on the market and all. You're so accomplished and sexy." Ethan goes in for another kiss.

I put my hands up to stop him. I'm so floored by the situation, it takes me a moment to find words. "Ethan, I'm beyond flattered. Sheesh, am I flattered. But I am not on the market."

"That's not what I heard. My friend Billy's dad was at The Bank Shot the other night and he said that you were the hottest woman there. He said that all the men were after you and that your husband just ignored you. He also said that you visited Judge McClintock's houseboat the next day and that Mr. McCoy and Marlena Morrison are a thing."

My head swoons. "That's a lot to process." I lean against the front door. "Well, you can tell your friend Billy's dad that I am very much married. It's possible that my husband needs to be reminded of that, but it is still the case. Secondly, I am way too old for you, however I love the fact that you think otherwise. And, finally, Ethan, never kiss a girl and call her ma'am."

Chapter 52

The next day, Jane is quiet the entire ride home from school. I can't drag a single word out of her.

"Sweetie, if there's something bothering you I'd like to help you."

We pull up to the house. Jane jumps out with her backpack and slams the car door. I follow her into the house ten steps behind her. She tosses her backpack inside the living room, opens the sliding glass door, and runs into the backyard. Moment later I can see her jumping on the trampoline.

I head into the kitchen, concerned about Jane, but granting her space. I begin to make her a snack.

I hear the sliding door open and close and she appears in the kitchen, panting.

"I'm not sure what I'm more mad about," Jane starts.

I look up from slicing apples and cheese.

"The fact that you kissed a guy who isn't Daddy or the fact that you kissed the one guy I have a crush on!"

Oh, no. Not Jane. The one person who is never mad at me. And now she's having romantic feelings for grown men? I can hardly handle this.

My mouth opens. I hesitate because I'm not sure where to even start. "Honey, are we talking about Ethan?"

"Obviously!" she shouts. "Sheesh, are there others?"

"No!" I wave my hands around in dispute. "And I didn't kiss him."

"That's not what people are saying."

"Dear Lord." I drop my head back, annoyed. "Is there no one else to talk about on the playground?" I shout to the heavens. "Jane, do you have any idea how tired I am of people gossiping about me? And they put their own spin on things that completely changes the truth."

"What happened, then?"

"Ethan stopped by the house and *he* kissed *me*. And I put a stop to it."

Jane's intense brown eyes morph from anger to sadness.

"Oh, Jane." I go to her and put my arms around her. "Let's sit."

I pull out a kitchen chair, take a seat and motion for her to join me. She climbs onto my lap.

"First of all, I am not looking for anybody other than Daddy. He is the one I love and I want him to come home."

Jane nods. "Why did Ethan kiss you?"

I shrug. "I guess he just thought since I was being nice to him that maybe I like him in a different way. For some reason, I am stirring up all sorts of things in this town. I'm definitely not doing it on purpose. I'm sorry. I know all of this is frustrating for you, too. And probably really embarrassing."

"I know. It is. But I get it." Jane puts both of her hands on my face. "Everyone knows that you're special."

My breath catches. "Jane. That's a really sweet thing to say."

"It's true," she says matter-of-factly.

I smile. "Do you want to tell me about your feelings for Ethan?"

Jane exhales hopelessly. "What's the point? He's too old for me. And that makes me sad. But he makes me feel really good about myself when I'm with him."

"And that is exactly how a boy should make you feel."

"It's a tragedy that we're not the same age."

I manage to stifle a smile. "Jane, do you know how many boys there are in this world?"

"No," she answers, interested.

"Well, I don't entirely know. But let's guess that there are roughly three hundred million people who live in the United States alone."

"Wow."

"And let's guess that about half of them are boys."

"Okay." Jane is on board with this theory.

"As cute and nice as Ethan Parker is, he is not the only fish in the sea."

Jane smiles and nods in agreement. "I gotcha."

* * *

Brookside is a cute little area in Tulsa along the Arkansas River where there are boutiques, antique shops, art galleries and restaurants. Carrie Ann and Becky spent the morning getting manicures and antiquing.

I, however, had to finish reading the high school "Ultimate Life" papers so I could return them to the kids at second period. They did a beautiful job. I didn't take a red pen to the papers because I didn't want to stifle the students' creativity, I wanted to applaud it. I assessed their strengths and weaknesses so I could establish what subsequent workshops should focus on.

Now that that's taken care of, I'm meeting Carrie Ann and Becky at the Brook for lunch. I enter the restaurant and see them at a corner booth in the back.

Carrie Ann looks up from her menu as I approach the table. "Well, hey there, Mrs. Robinson!" Carrie Ann catcalls.

My jaw drops. "Becky! You have such a big mouth." I look

around self-consciously and scoot into the booth.

"How do you know *I* told her?" Becky protests. "The rumor mill of Skiatook doesn't need my help."

I put my head in my hands. "I know. I can't keep up with my own rumors. I went from depressed and pathetic to being propositioned for sex by a dirty old man, and now apparently I'm a cougar."

Becky and Carrie Ann cackle like witches.

"It's not funny," I whine. They laugh harder.

I crack a smile. "Okay, if it was happening to someone else I would think it was funny."

They nod and guffaw. I start to chuckle along with them.

"Well, how was the kiss?" Becky asks, catching her breath.

"It was sort of an out-of-body experience," I explain. "The last time a twenty-two-year-old guy kissed me, I was standing outside of a bar in Hermosa Beach wearing a tube top."

The laughter ensues.

"Honey, you're the hottest ticket in town," Becky says.

"Seriously, what is going on?" I giggle.

"You are available and the men can smell it on you," Carrie Ann explains.

"But I'm not really available." I shrug.

"There are not many eligible women in this town," she continues. "Single men of all ages are having a feeding frenzy. You could be ugly and they'd still be all over you."

"Okay..." I say, because this is definitely not sounding like a compliment.

"And you just happen to be a catch, so it's getting beyond crazy," Carrie Ann adds.

"Well, thanks," I reply.

"Speaking of the feeding frenzy, Brandon paid a visit to the Judge," Becky tells me.

"What?" I implore.

"When he found out that you asked RJ to drop the manuscript off for you, he insisted that he go instead."

"Really?" Carrie Ann croons.

"What did he say?" I ask.

"That's all I know." Becky puts her hands up in the air. "But it sure is fun to imagine how things went down."

I mull over the image of Brandon showing up at the Judge's houseboat in my place. "Well, that's sweet," I say. "It's nice to imagine that he would want to protect me."

"Of course he would," Becky says. "He does love you."

I nod, non-committal.

"Interesting," Carrie Ann says coyly.

I eye Carrie Ann. "Okay, what is with you?" I ask her.

Carrie Ann furrows her brows. "What do you mean?"

"You are especially perky and playful today." I cock my head to the side as I inspect her. "You're glowing, actually."

Carrie Ann smiles. "I do have something I want to share with y'all."

Becky and I look at each other. "Are you pregnant?" Becky asks.

"Good Lord, no. I've decided to go back to school and finish my degree."

Becky claps her hands together.

"That's fabulous!" I cheer.

"You know, I got pregnant with Justin at the end of my junior year of college, so I got most of my credits. I just never finished. It's time."

Becky and I nod.

"I've looked into it. I'm going to take online classes through University of Tulsa and every now and then I'll have some weekend classes in the city."

"Good for you," I say supportively.

"Let us know if we can help," Becky offers. "I can watch Evelyn and Robbie when you need to go to class."

"And if you ever need someone to edit your papers, I'm your girl."

"Thanks, pals. Your support means a lot." Carrie Ann smiles warmly. She glances at me. "To be honest, it's because of you."

"What do you mean?" I ask.

"You know, I've noticed that lately you're doing things that make you happy. Like the writing class for the high school kids, and changing your book to reflect your experiences this year. And just being yourself and enjoying it. I want to be that way."

I'm so touched by her words that I clutch my heart. "Carrie Ann, that's the nicest thing anyone has said to me for a long time."

Chapter 53

The girls are having a cousin sleep-over at Jolene and Jake's house and I'm about to watch my all-time favorite chick flick, *You've Got Mail.* I put a bag of popcorn into the microwave.

I jump when someone starts pounding on the door. It's definitely angry knocking.

I run over to the front door and peek through the peep hole. It's Brandon. Who else?

I fling the door open with my hands on my hips. "What?" I say, ready to defend myself.

"Really? You have no idea why I'm here?"

"Brandon, you're always mad at me. I can't keep up."

He purses his lips. "I'm here to express my displeasure about all of your questionable relationships with other men."

I laugh out loud. "I don't have relationships with any men but you. And that's pretty dubious at the moment."

"Don't be coy with me. Everyone knows about the Judge."

I laugh again. "Oh, yeah, I really want a man who could be my father to strip for me on his "love boat"- his words. Do you have any idea how freaked out I was? I did not ask for that."

"Okay, how about Ethan Parker? The boy who could be your son?"

I roll my eyes.

"I hear he's been spending some time over here."

"Who are you getting your information from? He dropped off some deer jerky! At the time, I didn't realize that gifts of smoked meat indicated that I was being pursued. But, hindsight is twenty-twenty. He probably shot that deer just for me as an offering of his love. And then his mom smoked it with me in mind, hoping that a forty-year-old separated woman with two kids would show her son how to be a proper lover."

"All right, Nina. Cut it out." Brandon starts to chuckle.

"Trust me, I am not enjoying this. Although, perhaps I should be. It's kind of nice to get some attention from *men*." I practically spit out the last word. "You put me in this situation, you know."

Brandon nods.

"I can't help it if all of the single men in Skiatook, young and old, can smell my pheromones."

Brandon looks at me with an amused twinkle in his eye. "What?"

"Men keep telling me how sexy and desirable I am," I say with attitude.

Brandon's smile fades. "Well, they're right."

I give Brandon a funny look. Is he joking? Was that a compliment?

Brandon pushes past the threshold, grabs me and kisses me. "You are sexy." He slips his hand under my t-shirt and finds my breast.

What? I did not expect this. I didn't even shave my armpits.

"Brandon. You are so confusing," I breathe.

Why am I protesting?

"Kiss me, woman," he says fiercely.

Oh. He's in caveman mode. This is going to be good.

I grab his face and kiss him hard.

Brandon scoops me up and throws me over his shoulder like a bale of hay. I yelp in surprise. He kicks the door closed with his foot.

Fueled by sheer strength and pent-up desire, he carries me up the stairs and into our bedroom.

Brandon tosses me onto the bed. He peels his t-shirt off and tosses it across the room, then crawls across the bed like a grizzly bear and climbs on top of me. He kisses my neck. I pull my t-shirt over my head and he helps me. He continues kissing my neck and moves down to my breasts. I squeal with pleasure.

It must be eleven o'clock because my sound machine turns on. The sound of waves crashing and seagulls cawing fills the room. I pull Brandon back up to me and kiss his lips. I reach down to unbutton his jeans.

"I can't do this," Brandon says.

"Hmm?" I continue to kiss him.

"I can't do it with these damn seagulls in my ear," he says, annoyed.

"Okay, I'll turn it off."

I reach over and push a button, and our bedroom no longer sounds like we're floating on a raft in the middle of the Pacific Ocean.

I turn back to Brandon and find his lips. His entire body has become stiff. I feel his closed-off energy.

"You always want to be somewhere else."

I sit up. "What are you talking about? Trust me. There is no place I'd rather be."

"When we sleep, we're at the beach. When we're eating breakfast, we're in Italy. When we're taking a shit, we're in Bali!"

"Okay…" I reply, confused. "Is this really about my decorating?"

"Can't we just ever be here?" Brandon continues. "Even when you're not on some trip, you've got to surround yourself with reminders of your trips. Every time you walk into a different room in our house, you're in a different damn country. It drives me crazy!"

I sit up, dumbfounded. We seriously stopped making out because of the décor of our house? And to be fair, when you walk through our front door, the first thing you see is a framed American flag that I found at an estate sale in Collinsville.

"Brandon," I say slowly. "I am a worldly person. People decorate their houses to represent their interests. I also moved into a log cabin in the middle of nowhere. It's called compromise."

"Oh, so now you don't like our house?" he spars.

"I love our house! Why are you picking a fight with me?"

He doesn't answer. What is happening? I honestly can't keep up with the moods of this man.

"You know what?" I blurt out. "I feel like I have really tried to meet you halfway, and I'm fine with that. But clearly you're not. Clearly, my compromises don't mean anything to you. This is me. I love to travel, I love other cultures, and I want to share that with my family. This is who you married. And you're nitpicking the hell out of me!"

"You always want to leave. And now you want Roma to leave. What are you trying to do to me?"

I'm quiet for a moment. "This is about Roma looking at colleges?" I shake my head in disbelief. "Why are you trying to hold her back?"

"Because I don't want my daughter to leave. People who leave small towns like this don't come back."

Oh.

"Honey. I'm not trying to get Roma to leave. I'm trying to give her the opportunities that I was given. I want to give her the exposure and the means to choose where she wants to go."

"You know," Brandon says, "there are people who live in small towns their entire lives and they are happy and they are proud and they never leave."

"Well, that is a shame."

Brandon narrows his eyes at me. "You think you're better than everyone because you've seen the world." Brandon stands up.

"I do not! You are blaming me for *your* insecurities. You want to keep your wife and kids locked up in a box!"

"I don't need to listen to this. I'm leaving." Brandon strides out of the bedroom.

"When you get to the bottom of the stairs and enter the USA, show yourself out!"

I plop back on the bed furious. I realize that Brandon's shirt is wadded up in a corner on the floor. He's too proud to come back for it. I imagine him storming into his room over Becky's garage, shirtless. That should give the neighbors something to talk about.

Chapter 54

Okay, now we're getting somewhere. At least Brandon has finally given me some insight into the Roma college battle. He's worried she's going to leave him forever. On one hand, my heart goes out to him. On the other hand, come on! You can't live your life being afraid of something that might happen sometime in the future. Where did this come from?

Aah... Yes. It's my fault. Brandon is afraid of his daughter's talent taking her far away. It reminds him of me. Yet it's a ridiculous notion because here I stay. Can I please just simply *be* without offending someone or causing a problem? Lately, I feel like if anyone is displeased with anything, I am somehow to blame.

Yet clearly Roma fleeing Skiatook without return is a true fear of Brandon's, so we need to discuss it.

So here I am at Mac's BBQ picking up a peace offering.

Mac's wife, Kay, smiles as she hands me my change. The dreamcatcher earrings nestled in her wispy, gray, layered hair and her high cheekbones are just a few indications of her Cherokee heritage. She emanates free-spirited positive energy. Her bangle bracelets jingle as she stuffs a handful of napkins into the paper bag.

"Thanks, Kay."

"Sure, honey. You know," she smiles, "Brandon has loved this barbeque sauce since he was a baby. His mama used to give him some of our ribs to gnaw on when he was teething. Dab a little bit behind your ears and you'll have to beat him off with a stick." She hands me an extra container of sauce and winks.

* * *

I knock on Brandon's open office door. He glances up. I hold up a paper bag from Mac's. "I thought you could use a pulled-pork sandwich."

Brandon smiles with his mouth, but not his eyes. It's a start. "Thanks."

I take that as an invitation, and I enter his office and sit down in the chair across from his desk. I hand him a sandwich wrapped in beige paper and take one out for myself.

"I've been thinking about our discussion last night. I'm glad you gave me some insight about why you're not excited about Roma looking out of state."

Brandon takes a bite of his sandwich.

I look at him seriously. "I don't want Roma to leave and never come back either. But she wouldn't do that. This is home, and Roma and Jane love it here. We're raising our daughters to know where they came from. But I also feel like we're raising them to be their own people, make their own decisions and go after what they want."

It's a good thing that Brandon is staying quiet because I have a lot to say.

"I don't know where Roma wants to go to school. If she decides on an Oklahoma school because it's the best place for her, I will be happy for her."

"Then why doesn't it seem like you're encouraging that?"

"Brandon, she has visited the OSU campus for football games since she was an infant. She's even been in your old dorm rooms. When OSU has had away games elsewhere in Oklahoma, we've been to those schools. You haven't been at all interested in the college search except to express displeasure about it. If there are colleges you want to help Roma take a better look at, let's do it. We'll all go together."

Brandon nods. "Okay."

"I'm sorry if this is scary for you. As it gets closer, I may feel the same way. Right now, I'm just excited for Roma. She's excited about it."

Brandon nods as he eats his sandwich. Believe me, this is going well. Nodding quietly is a good thing. It means he doesn't totally disagree.

I add, "You know, Roma could go to OSU for four years, fall in love with a student from Seattle and move there after college. We have no idea what is going to happen. Or she could want to move home the day after graduation because she misses her mom."

Brandon stops chewing and smiles. "Those are possibilities. Did you bring any pickles?"

I scoff. "Don't you know me at all?" I toss him the bag and he rummages around for pickles.

Again, the heating pad is tucked behind Brandon's back. I feel bad that my guy is in pain. Presumably from carrying me up the stairs last night.

I smirk.

"What?" Brandon asks.

"It's unfortunate that you left last night when you did."

Brandon raises his eyebrows, surprised that I brought it up.

"Maybe we should try it again sometime," I suggest coyly.

He puts his sandwich down on his desk.

"I think we should," he answers.

I feel a burning sensation between my legs. Holy cow. Is this about to go down right now?

Brandon's eyes burn into mine. He rises from his desk.

There's a knock on the open office door that makes me jump.

"Oh, sorry to startle you, Nina," Lou, the store manager, says. "Brandon, the gates and fencing is here that Darryl Farnsley ordered."

My heart is pounding from the anticipation and the interruption.

Brandon exhales. "It was supposed to be delivered to his ranch."

"They tried, but I guess he doesn't want it yet."

"That doesn't make sense," Brandon grumbles.

"Well, the truck is here wanting to know what to do with it."

Brandon looks at me. "I'm sorry. I need to deal with this."

I smile regretfully. "It's okay. Maybe we can talk later."

Brandon nods, smiling. "I think we should. Thanks for lunch."

Chapter 55

I have a crush on my husband. I've been sitting at my desk, not typing anything because I am so distracted by how giddy I'm feeling.

The doorbell rings. Oh, my. That was fast. I run to the door and smooth my hair.

When I open the door, I realize that the old adage is true— when it rains, it pours.

Josh Decker stands on my doorstep.

I laugh, surprised. "What on earth? What are you doing here?"

"I was in the neighborhood covering a baseball game at OSU. I couldn't pass up seeing you."

"OSU is two hours away."

"Nina, you're the only soul I know in Oklahoma. I took a detour."

I stand in silence with my mouth literally hanging open.

Josh laughs. "Are you going to invite me in?"

"Of course!" I wave him in. "I'm sorry, I'm just in shock."

Josh steps inside and I reach out and hug him. There it is, that intoxicating smell. I squeeze him tight.

Josh lingers there for a moment and gives me a kiss on the cheek. Electricity courses through our bodies. I immediately get flushed.

"Can I get you something to drink?"

"Sure. I'll take a beer. Thanks."

I head to the kitchen with Josh on my heels. An empty house, an old flame, and the palpable chemistry that Josh and I have always had between us. Bringing alcohol into the mix seems like adding gasoline to a pile of hay. Surely the match isn't far off.

We take our beers out back and make ourselves comfortable in the cushioned patio furniture on the back porch. Josh sits down on the couch so I choose the chair to ensure some distance between us.

"How are you, Nina?"

"I'm great. How are you? How was the game?" I wonder how long I can get away with small talk.

Josh gives me a look that says, *Cut the crap.*

My stomach drops. For a moment, I completely forgot that the whole world knows about my rocky marriage. It was always my safe place in a conversation with Josh. I could stand strong and unreachable behind my marriage. *Don't go there. I'm happily married.* That was the vibe I radiated when I ran into him over the years.

I sneak a glance at him over on the couch. Josh Decker from my previous life is in my backyard in Skiatook. What a far-fetched scenario. God, he looks amazing. He always has a mischievous look in his eyes. It's really sexy. And, boy, can the man wear pants.

Focus, Nina!

I realize that between last night and this afternoon, Brandon has primed me for sex. Of all the people in the entire world to be here right now, this is not ideal. My self-control is about to be tested. I purposely look at the lake instead of at Josh's eyes.

"I'm sorry about you and Brandon," Josh starts.

"No, you're not." I smirk at him.

He laughs. "Okay. I'm not. I was being polite." He smiles at me with that twinkle in his eye. "I never did understand why you ran off with a guy like that, so different than everything you stand for."

"What do I stand for?" I ask.

"Adventure. Sophistication. Drive."

"Brandon is extremely successful and driven."

"Of course he is. What does he do again?"

"He expanded his family's feed and farm supply store across the entire state of Oklahoma." I can feel my face and neck turning red as I get worked up.

Josh nods.

"Did you come here to insult my husband? The life that I chose?"

"No." Josh leans forward with his arms folded on his knees. "I came here because for twenty years I've regretted us not working out, so I jumped at the opportunity to turn your husband's foolishness into my future."

I gasp out loud. The wind has been knocked out of me. I can't respond. Here is someone who values all of the things about me that my own husband dislikes. Someone who yearns for a life with me while my own husband has barely been able to tolerate it.

Everyone can pinpoint crossroads in their lives. Taking Brandon to Italy was mine. There was no turning back from there. We were in too deep. And suddenly here I am, at another one.

I put my head in my hands.

"This is our chance, Nina."

I don't say a peep. I'm actually thinking about it. There is no question that Josh would love and appreciate me. Despite all of his casual dating and flirtatious comments, he and I have a deep connection and history. There's something about having history with someone that can always leave a thread of involvement and attraction. I was the one who got away and he and I have always known it.

"Josh, my world is so turned upside down right now. I'm not the confident, put-together woman you used to know."

"Nina, that's not the only part of you that I love."

My eyebrows involuntarily twitch. Josh and I never actually said, "I love you." It was clear and unspoken that we always felt very strongly for each other, but we always kept our relationship light to suit our career situations.

"Come over here," Josh says intensely.

"I don't think I should."

Josh grins. "All right."

"Josh, I don't want to lead you on. I won't lie. It would be so easy to run off with you and pick up where we left off. I'm sure it would be amazing. We would probably be really happy."

"I know we would."

"I am dangerously tempted and that is why I'm staying planted in this chair. If I sit next to you on that couch, my marriage is over."

"Come here, then." His eyes burn into mine.

"Let me be honest with you. I'm devastated that my marriage is crumbling. It's possible that I'm fighting a losing battle. But there are hopeful moments between Brandon and I. We had one today. I'm not done fighting for him. I'm not ready to give up on holding my family together."

"I will love your girls like my own." A look of intensity crosses Josh's face that I've never seen before.

The fact that he's bringing up the girls brings this to a whole other level. This year has been absolute hell. Suddenly a very attractive door is opening.

"I'm about to jump off a cliff here. I am begging you to stop talking," I plead. I blow out a deep breath, trying to get my breathing under control. I put my face in my hands until I'm thinking logically. Finally, I sit up.

"Josh, I love you for driving eighty miles of back roads to see me." I think for a moment. "And I do love you. There. I finally said that.

I loved you then and for that reason, a part of me will always love you."

His smile softens.

"You've given me a lot to think about. And I will. But I think it's time for you to go."

He looks hesitant. "How about I stay at the local motel while you think about it?"

"Honey, I wouldn't put up my worst enemy at the Skiatook Motel." We laugh.

Just then, the sliding glass door opens. Brandon steps outside and the look on his face is one of fury.

"What's going on here?" he asks calmly, but angrily.

"Brandon." I feel like I've been caught and then I remember that I've been a very good girl. Despite the fact that I just told my ex-boyfriend that I love him. Repeatedly. "You remember Josh Decker from the *L.A. Times*."

But Brandon knows we were once more than colleagues. He never liked Josh. He knew we had "dated a little". My words.

"Right. What are you doing in Skiatook?" Brandon interrogates.

"I was covering the OSU baseball game."

"That's in Stillwater. I asked what you're doing in Skiatook."

"Brandon!"

"Visiting a friend," Josh answers. "It appears that she needs one."

My jaw drops. Oh, crap. This could get ugly.

Brandon's chest puffs up. "You're going to say that to me at my house?"

I stand up before a cock fight ensues. "Okay, calm down. I was just about to walk Josh to his car."

"I'm sure he knows the way," Brandon says.

I shoot Brandon a look. "I'll be right back. Come on, Josh."

Josh stands up. "If you're going to act all territorial about your woman, you should at least keep her happy."

My eyes bulge out.

Brandon lunges at Josh and lands his fist on Josh's cheek.

"Brandon!" I shriek.

Josh swings and just barely catches Brandon's chin.

"Josh!" I shout. Now I'm scolding the other one.

Brandon tackles Josh to the ground. Never mess with a country boy.

"Brandon! Josh! That's enough!" I squeal.

My demands go completely ignored. Suddenly, they're off the back porch and on the grass. I cannot believe I am watching my estranged husband and the ex-boyfriend of my youth wrestle on the lawn. There's a lot of pride, testosterone, and years of jealousy in that heap of men. But I'm not about to watch them tear each other apart.

I run to the hose, turn it on, and spray those grown men down like they're raccoons I found rummaging through my trash cans. They look at me, utterly shocked, two grown men sitting on the grass, furious, soaked and dripping. They look ridiculous.

"Enough," I demand. "Josh, I will meet you at your car. Brandon, stay here. I'm going to get some damn towels."

* * *

Drenched, Josh leans against his rented silver Toyota Camry.

I throw my hands up in the air as I approach him with a towel. "Really? Was that necessary?"

Josh shrugs.

"How's your cheek?" I reach up and touch it gently.

"It's fine." Josh stares at me. "I don't know what you're doing here."

I fold my arms and bite my lip. "I can't give up yet."

He grabs my hands. "We'd get it right this time. I promise. Think about it and call me."

I look into his vulnerable, intense blue eyes, knowing that I definitely will think about it, over and over and over. "It means a lot that you came all the way out here to see me. We both know you don't typically cover college games."

We smirk at each other.

Josh opens the car door.

"Wait," I say.

Josh turns back to me quickly.

"There have been many moments these last few months that I needed an old friend. Someone who gets me. You have no idea how much I appreciate that you want me for who I am."

Josh looks at me like I've just said the stupidest thing in the world. "Are you kidding me? Nina Blake, you're the best woman I ever met."

Josh reaches out and pulls me towards him. His clothes are wet, but his face and breath are warm against my cheek. I melt into him and let myself enjoy a long embrace. I let out an audible sigh.

I pull away and look at him sadly. "Goodbye, Josh."

He smiles and shakes his head.

I watch him pull out of the driveway and wave as he drives away. There he goes. Physically, symbolically, and every other kind of way. I take a deep breath and head for the gate on the side of the house.

My heart is heavy at the knowledge of what I've just turned away, but by the time I reach the backyard, I'm fuming. Talk about my emotions taking a one-eighty-degree turn for Brandon today. He is sitting on the patio couch where Josh just proposed that I run away with him. He's staring at the lake, deep in thought.

"What was *that*?" I exclaim.

"You tell me." He eyes my damp clothes.

"He showed up at our front door. I had to invite him in."

"When I walked out here, it was obvious that I was interrupting something."

"We weren't even sitting next to each other. You shouldn't have treated Josh that way."

"Don't speak his name to me. I have never trusted that guy. When we used to see him at parties, he would always stare at you like I wasn't even there."

"I'm sorry about that. But why don't you trust *me*? Why do you think *I'm* going to cheat on you?"

"Because I don't believe in us!" Brandon says in a raised voice.

A gasp escapes my mouth. I cover my mouth with my hands. I stay like that for a moment until I can muster up the courage to respond.

"Why is that?" I ask.

He lowers his voice. "I don't know."

I let out a long, frustrated sigh and massage my temples. A headache is spreading across my entire scalp. "Brandon," I say quietly. "At some point you're going to have to tell me why you've lost faith in me."

He doesn't look at me. He takes a few steps away from me and looks at the lake.

"You left me, remember?" I shout. My voice begins to shake. "I'm holding onto this marriage with my fingernails. You're keeping me on your hook by paying attention to me once every few months. But I want to be with someone for the long haul. At some point, I may choose to look at my other options."

Brandon turns and looks at me. His expression is very grave.

"I'm not done fighting for us," I continue, "but I'm really getting tired."

Chapter 56

I'm emotionally exhausted from the events of the day. I sit with a steaming mug in my hands, a pouch of magical floral chamomile bobbing inside. My hands shake as I cradle the mug.

I smile sheepishly when she appears next to me.

"Well, this is going to be a doozy," Grandma begins.

"Yep." We hug.

"Oh, *mi linda*, you are trembling."

"A lot went down today."

Grandma nods. "Did you enjoy being fought over by two men?"

I shake my head. "Grandma, it's so complicated I couldn't even enjoy it. Knowing how much those two hate each other kind of took the fun out of it."

"How do you feel about Josh's proposition?"

"It's hard not to entertain the idea. To be with someone who admires the kind of woman I am, someone who wants me. And there's some intense history there."

Grandma nods.

"I was on such a high after leaving Brandon's office today. We connected. I knew it was still there. But I'm getting impatient with him. What is he waiting for? He's not valuing me. And I know that Josh would. But Brandon is a once-in-a-lifetime kind of guy. Even though I've seen the worst of him recently, if I could get back the Brandon I used to know, I know he's worth the wait."

I rub my temples. "But then he dropped the bomb that he doesn't believe in us? That may be the worst thing anyone has ever said to me." I shake my head. "Maybe we're through. Believing in a relationship is kind of essential, don't you think?"

"You can't do all the work," Grandma says. "You both have to want this."

I nod, so frustrated with Brandon.

"Tell me about Josh."

I feel my stress level drop slightly at my thoughts turning from Brandon to Josh. I smile. "He's a great man. Our connection is easy, and boy, is that a draw. I know that given the opportunity, we would pick up where we left off so many years ago and evolve. I realized today that we could have an amazing relationship."

Grandma looks at me, surprised.

"I have to admit it, Grandma. I hadn't been alone with Josh in almost two decades and sitting with him in the backyard reminded me how it feels to be loved by Josh Decker."

"And how does that feel?"

I let out a low whistle. "Like you're the only woman in the world."

Grandma smirks. "How many men did you and Jane guess live in America?"

I smile. "What are you getting at, Grandma?"

"Just that if Brandon doesn't love you how you should be loved, maybe he's not the only fish in the sea."

My eyes widen.

"I'm not saying that Brandon is not the one for you. I'm just saying that it's something for you to think about. I don't want you thinking that you are lost without him. You are worth much more than that."

I furrow my eyebrows, so confused. "Josh Decker. There's a lot there."
"Like I said," Grandma continues. "*Hay muchos pescados.*"
Lotsa fish.

* * *

I didn't sleep a wink. Even though I'm tired, I'm so tense. My jaw, neck and shoulders are stiff and sore. When I'm harboring troubled feelings, that's where they manifest.

Despite my exhaustion, my legs move one after the other on the rocky trail around the lake. Even though I told Josh goodbye, I can't get him out of my mind. I had a realization in the middle of the night. Josh and I have unfinished business. We never saw our relationship through to its ultimate potential. Nothing ever went wrong between us, I just ran off with Brandon. The chemistry between Josh and me is incredible. Feeling that yesterday showed me that element is missing in my life. I could have it. We could share a life of passion and similar interests. We have so much in common.

What would a relationship with Josh look like now? Would he live here? No. He'd hate it. Would the girls and I up and move to California? We could have an amazing life with him there. A new adventure. Josh and I could be so in love.

But how could I uproot my children for my love life? That wouldn't be fair. I can't risk their happiness for my own. I'm a grownup and I made a decision seventeen years ago. Brandon and I planted deep roots for them. Their happiness is more important than mine. I believe that. But don't I deserve to be happy, too? Or do I need to be stoic and forever put their needs first?

I don't want to be divorced. I don't want to start over. I don't want my kids to go through that. But I want *more.* Until Josh's visit, I never considered the alternative to staying with Brandon. I hear Grandma's words.

Hay muchos pescados.

Josh isn't the only other one either. Presumably, there are many other men in this world I could connect with and have a fulfilling life with. Is that something I want to explore? This is the hardest and most unexpected thing I've ever contemplated.

Chapter 57

I'm in the zone during a productive moment of editing. I've been away from *Down and Dirty Down Under* long enough to see the story clearly again. I'm now able to take Stan's notes and fix some of his concerns in a way that I'm creatively happy with. And it's really nice to immerse myself in someone else's drama. I've given it a new and improved title- *What We Discover Down Under*.

My office is filled with the voice of Damian Rice. The depressing tune is setting the mood for my struggling married couple. I sip a glass of sweet tea and over Damian's emoting, I hear the doorbell.

I save my document and walk through the hallway to the foyer feeling very satisfied, which I always do after a productive session of work.

I open the door to find my mother-in-law holding a tray of cinnamon rolls. She smiles warmly.

"I thought you might be ready for a snack break."

* * *

It's a lovely spring day so we sit in the backyard. We've carried out a few plates and forks and a few heavenly homemade pecan cinnamon rolls dripping with sugary-sweet icing.

I pour sweet tea into two glasses of ice and hand one to Leanne.

"Thank you, dear."

I smile at her. She's obviously up to something.

She returns my smile.

I take a sip of my sweet tea.

"He's being an ass."

I cough on my tea, surprised.

"I've made a great effort to stay out of your business this past year, but I need to say a few things before it's too late."

I sit up, interested in any perspective my husband's mother can shed on the situation.

"Brandon is stubborn and he's acting foolishly. I'm aware that men around town have been showing interest in you."

I blush. Oh, this is kind of embarrassing. "There have been a few misunderstandings."

"They should be. You're a sensational catch— as beautiful inside as you are outside."

I cock my head, touched by her kind words.

"You're kind, loyal, talented, ambitious. The list goes on." Leanne waves her hand. "I'm asking you to be just one more thing."

My eyebrows furrow, unsure of what she is going to say next.

"Patient."

I frown. "I have been," I say. "Quite honestly, I don't know how much longer I can be. How much longer do I have to be strong?" My voice cracks on the last word.

Leanne nods. "Sweetheart, I've had a chat with Brandon." I look at her intently. "Now, you know I don't like to meddle, but I am his mother and it was high time that I said something. I told him to wake up from dreamland before it's too late. His father has been hearing him out along the way and has been encouraging him to go back to you."

I clasp my heart and tears spring to my eyes. I can't get the words out of my mouth so I just shake my head back and forth.

Leanne grabs my hand.

"I didn't know," I say through sobs. "I didn't know how you both felt about it." I blow out a breath of relief. "I thought you might be upset with me. I thought maybe you wished he married someone else. Someone less different than him."

Leanne scoffs. "Honey. You are a daughter to us and we love you. You are good for Brandon, and he is good for you, contrary to how he's been acting."

I smile, thankful for Leanne's declaration of support.

"So, I'm asking you this, no matter how many men are dropping at your feet, please wait for Brandon to come around."

"I've never been more confused. He's not trying to work on things. I'm not even sure if he wants me."

Leanne's face falls. "If he doesn't, he's a damn fool."

"Damn" and "ass" are as close to cussing as Leanne gets. Clearly, she's feeling passionate about this. It's very endearing.

"Honey, there is something that I know Brandon hasn't told you, but I feel like you should know."

I lean forward. "What is it?"

"He's been going to therapy."

My eyes widen in surprise. "For how long?"

"He started right after Christmas."

My jaw drops. "I had no idea."

"I know. And I know he hasn't given you anything to go by…"

"Nothing," I emphasize.

"… but he has been working on things."

"What things?"

Leanne breathes out. "I don't really know. Things about himself that he's not happy with."

My brow furrows in confusion.

"I believe Brandon is trying to work his way back to you. Just hold on."

I exhale and smile at my mother-in-law. "Thank you for coming by today. It means the world."

"It's my pleasure. And you can freeze some of the cinnamon rolls."

I laugh. "You really do think highly of me."

Chapter 58

Carrie Ann is hosting bunco at her house tonight. Bunco is a game of chance played at three tables of four players. It involves rolling dice and keeping track of points. It's simple and mindless enough that it allows for simultaneous conversation and there is always an amazing spread of refreshments and cocktails.

I have found excuses not to attend for the last several months because I was avoiding putting myself in the position of talking about my situation. Since I've been trying to get out of the rumor mill of Skiatook, I didn't want to go straight to the center of a gabfest with eleven other gossiping women who would be asking me questions and observing how I was "holding up". But my absence has not gone unnoticed and Carrie Ann will not allow me to miss bunco at her house.

I arrived a little early to help Carrie Ann set up the card tables and chairs. I feel a little awkward, mostly because here I am after missing the previous five bunco gatherings.

"You're going to be fine," Carrie Ann says, reading my mind.

As the ladies arrive, they greet me with warm outstretched arms and "Where have you been?" and "We've missed you!" They are warm and sincere and I can't help but feel like I may have underestimated them.

Tonight's spread does not disappoint. Becky brought a lovely cheese platter to accompany the many bottles of wine we will drink. The island in the middle of Carrie Ann's kitchen is adorned with bruschetta, a red Jell-O mold, pigs in blankets, and meatballs bathing in a crock pot of barbeque sauce. For dessert there are chocolate-chip cookies still warm from the oven and a homemade pineapple pie.

We are crammed in the kitchen as we fill our plates and our wine glasses. The room echoes with chatter and laughter. We all put our ten dollars in the jar, which will result in prizes later for a few lucky gals— the one with the most points, the one with the fewest points, and the one with the most buncos.

We head to our tables, pair off in our teams of two and start rolling the dice. Nobody asks me any uncomfortable questions, just how I am and what Roma and Jane are up to. We all have children to talk about, husbands to joke about, but nobody asks about my estranged husband. Alice Atwater thanks me for graciously teaching the writers' workshop at the high school.

In between rounds as we reload our plates and head to the next table, Cindi Cosgrove puts her arm around me. "Nina, I feel like I owe you an apology."

"For what?" I ask.

"I never checked in on you. It wasn't because I wasn't thinking of you. I thought about it. But I figured you were tired of talking about certain things. I figured you were getting support from many places. But, as soon as I saw you tonight, I knew that was a bad choice on my end."

Okay, obviously friendship is a two-way street. Many of these ladies could have called me during my crisis. But would I have opened up to them? Was I approachable? It is I who didn't show up to bunco, month after month. It is I who chose not to attend Mass at Sacred Heart Church. It is I who hid in my bed on many days, crying. It took me an entire month of being separated before I would even open up to Becky. Perhaps I felt like an island because I chose to.

I squeeze Cindi's hand. "For a while, I didn't allow anyone to be there for me. But I'll never forget that warm smile you gave me at the fall play when I really needed it."

Cindi returns my squeeze. "Anytime, my friend."

Tonight these women have solidified that Brandon McCoy or no Brandon McCoy, I am relevant here. This is my town, too. This is where I brought my children home from the hospital. This is where I started my writing career. This is where I find refuge, running on the trails around the lake. Where I've made some of my closest friends. I've completely underestimated myself. I don't belong here *because* of Brandon. I belong here because I'm me.

Chapter 59

I'm worried about Roma. She seems very stressed out and emotional and despite my continuous inquiry, she will not give me any clues as to what is bothering her. She's getting excellent grades. There aren't any more plays this year, so that's not a factor. It could certainly be about Brandon and me, but nothing new or crazy has happened there recently. She says it's not about a boy or friends, but who knows? Is the college search stressing her out?

I've just finished my most recent line of questioning and haven't gotten any closer to any clarification.

"I'm going to ride Valentine," Roma says, frustrated from my meddling.

As soon as I hear the side door close, I sprint up to her bedroom. I see no other choice but to check for answers in her diary. I don't immediately see it, so I have to do a little bit of searching. Not in her desk. Not in her dresser drawers. Yes, I do feel badly about this, but I've got to know what's going on.

After lifting up her pillows, I find what I'm looking for. I sit down on the edge of her bed and page through to the last entry. My heart is pounding. I'm worried about my little girl. What could be bothering her?

"Mom."

I jump.

She stands in the doorway in her blue jeans and riding boots and an expression of astonishment. "I forgot my sunglasses. What are you *doing?*"

"I, I'm sorry. I just wanted to know what's going on with you."

"So, you're reading my diary?"

"Yes, I'm so sorry."

"Do you *do* that?" she asks, shocked.

"I, I," I stammer. "I've read it once before," I admit.

Roma walks up and tears the diary out of my hand. "I can't believe you. How dare you! Do you think I'm doing something wrong?"

"No, Roma. You're a good girl. I love you. I'm worried about you and you don't share anything with me."

"And I'm not going to! You've totally invaded my privacy!"

"I'm sorry. You're totally right. I shouldn't have done that."

"Get out of my room. And leave me alone!"

I cover my mouth with my hands. Mortified, I rush out and close the door.

Roma leaves and rides Valentine for an hour. When she returns, she doesn't talk to me. When I call the girls for dinner, she comes into the kitchen, takes her plate and glass of milk and goes up to her room. Ordinarily, I wouldn't allow that, but I am totally in the wrong here.

For days, our interactions are strained. I feel terrible. I've admitted my blame. I've apologized profusely. Somehow, I have to fix this.

* * *

"I've really done it now, haven't I?" I ask as Grandma appears in her pink velour robe.

Grandma nods. "You have." I throw my head back in defeat. "Aww, it's going to be okay," she says. "All of us mothers make mistakes."

"I doubt you made any. I can't imagine Mom being mad at you."

Grandma tilts her head to the side, thinking. "She was usually mad at her father." Grandma chuckles.

I shake my head. "I shouldn't have done it. Roma has every right to be furious with me."

"She does. But in your defense, you read her diary because at the time you thought it was in her best interest. Knowing it would upset her, you went ahead and did it for her protection."

I shrug, unsure if my behavior really was justified.

"It reminds me of the time you were going to visit your friend Sharon in Santa Barbara and your mother canceled the trip."

My mouth drops open as I remember. "Oh, my gosh," I say. "I had just learned how to drive stick-shift, but Mom and Dad didn't think I had mastered it enough to drive the Jeep all the way up there by myself. So, they didn't let me go. I was furious. It was going to be my first time visiting Sharon at UCSB and we were going to have an amazing weekend full of frat parties and lying on the beach."

"Would you let Roma drive stick shift right now all the way to Oklahoma City to visit a friend in college?"

"No way! I see your point, but I am still so in the wrong here."

Grandma and I sit in silence for a while.

I chuckle. "I completely forgot about that," I say, referring to the Santa Barbara incident.

"Exactly," Grandma says as she takes a sip of her tea.

I smile at her. "Oh, Grandma. So this is why people go to therapy. You're so good at this. You've always known how to keep me talking or have had the perfect analogy to help me understand."

Grandma winks and points to her temple, as if she knows all the answers.

I laugh. "Okay, so in a few decades Roma will forget about this. But what am I going to do to get her to forgive me in the near future?"

Grandma taps her mug with her forefinger as she thinks. "You need to admit that you were wrong."

"I did."

"I'm sure she didn't hear it at the moment," Grandma points out.

"Right," I concede.

"Even if you don't understand her, she needs to *feel* understood. She needs to know she has a safe place to fall."

"It makes me sad to think that she doesn't already know that."

Grandma shrugs. "You need to bond."

Chapter 60

I'm headed to New York City this weekend for a book signing. I'm ecstatic with excitement.

Grandma is absolutely right. Roma and I need to bond. Maybe we don't need to talk about what's going on with her. Maybe we just need to spend time together and connect. And sometimes, it's easier to do that when the problems seem far away.

So, I'm taking Roma with me to New York. She's never been and I just know my worldly girl will love it. We'll also have the opportunity to check out at a few colleges while we're there.

Brandon has given me his blessing, as his attitude about the topic has lightened up since we had our conversation about checking out both local and out-of-state colleges. Last week, he took Roma on a weekend visit to Sherman, Texas to check out Austin College. He also recognizes that Roma and I really need quality time to sort things out.

So, this trip will accomplish many things. Yay, book signing! New York is beautiful in the spring. And we'll have fun. Mother-daughter bonding time! Now, if only Roma would have some enthusiasm about it.

* * *

Roma continued to give me the cold shoulder on the plane, but I could sense her excitement. Her face was glued to the window of the taxi that we took from the airport.

When we arrived at our hotel, she looked up at it in admiration and rushed through the revolving front doors. When I opened the door to our suite, she ran to the window and gushed about the view of the bustling street seventeen floors below.

After dressing for dinner, we took a taxi to Little Italy where we ate at a quaint trattoria that the concierge recommended. Roma blushed when the cute waiter with thick black hair and bold brown eyes flirted with her as he took her order. He was excited to meet a girl named after his great-grandmother's hometown. We ate antipasta salad, an amazing thin-crust margherita pizza and to-die-for tiramisu.

As she relishes her first night in New York City, her anger begins to dissipate.

"Roma," I say gently. "I know that invading your privacy was very wrong. Sheesh, now that I mention it, there have been so many moments this past year when I wanted people to respect *my* privacy. And it felt just awful to feel violated like that." Roma nods. "I know that I have to earn your trust back."

"I forgive you, Mom."

"You do?" I ask, surprised.

"Yes," she says. "You've had a hard year, and I know I haven't made it easy on you."

I'm so happy I could almost cry. "Thank you," I breathe. I reach across the table and squeeze her hand. She puts her other hand on top of mine. "Now, I suggest we get you your first cappuccino. You're going to need to stay awake during your first Broadway show!"

* * *

Upon waking in our luxurious bed under a sumptuous pillowy white duvet, we order room service for breakfast. Pancakes, bacon, fresh-squeezed orange juice and my very own French press of hot, bold coffee fuels us for our day.

We lie around for a while and read; Roma buries herself in *Rebecca* and I peruse the *New York Post*. We take our time getting ready. We bathe leisurely in the huge shower that has three shower heads and little shampoos, conditioners and bath gels that smell beautifully of lemon verbena.

I have a book signing at a little bookstore in Greenwich Village. Veronica joins us for lunch beforehand. Roma loves Veronica and I can see why. Veronica has such a youthful and contagious energy. Her drive excites Roma.

Later, we head to the bookstore and I speak to a fun and eclectic crowd. The energy in the room is alive and inspiring. It's amazing to me that so many different types of people read my books. What a blessing that my writing connects me to so many walks of life. I make eye contact with Roma and it's almost like she's thinking the same thing. She looks radiant.

Chapter 61

Roma and I walk around Liberty Island. Lady Liberty stands strong above us. We lean over a rail and gaze out at the water. I'm on a high from my book-signing event, but with it behind me, thoughts of my life back home begin to poke their way in. I think about Brandon. I've never done so much soul-searching in my entire life. But I have come to a conclusion. I need to see my marriage through. I need to find out if Brandon and I are going to make it. I'm not going to fantasize or speculate about relationships with other men, namely Josh, unless there is nothing left between Brandon and me.

The water is calm. The cityscape of New York City is incredible. There's a weight and energy behind it.

"Oh, I love it here." I breathe. "It's been a fun trip, hasn't it?"

Roma nods. "It's good to be away," she says a little sadly.

"It's always fun to go somewhere new and exciting."

"No, I mean it's good to be away from Skiatook."

I look at her. "Sweetie, what's going on?" I ask.

Roma looks hesitant.

"I can be a really good listener," I say.

She nods. "There's someone I like. A boy."

"That's great," I say optimistically. Boy troubles. We can handle this.

"No. It's not." She turns around and walks over to a bench, sits down and slumps.

I follow her. "Tell me about it." I'm dying to know details.

"It's Brock Anderson."

Knew it. "Does he like you back?"

"Yes."

"What's the problem?"

She exhales painfully. "He's always going to live in Oklahoma."

"Okay. Has he told you that?"

"No, but he's the type. He's always talking about how he's going to play football at OU."

"Uh oh," I interrupt. "He's a Montague and you're a Capulet. Don't tell Daddy."

"Mom."

"Sorry. Go on."

"Then I'm sure he'll work at his family's bank."

Now is not the time to confirm her suspicions. "That sounds like an ambitious plan."

"*Forever*," Roma adds.

I laugh.

"Mama, it's not funny."

"I know, I know. I'm sorry. It's just that you make settling down in Oklahoma sound like torture."

Roma looks around. "This trip only confirms that there is so much that I want to experience. If I get involved with Brock and things work out, I'm trapped." Roma looks at me intently. "You know what I mean?"

My heart sinks. "Oh, my gosh, honey. Do you think that's how I feel?"

"Well... yeah. You have an amazing career. You're a superstar. You could live somewhere exciting, like here." She gestures towards the New York City skyline. "But you don't. Because of us."

I almost need to grab my heart. "Are you kidding me? Roma Grace McCoy. I live in Skiatook because it's my home. You, Jane and Daddy *are* my home and I would never be happy anywhere without you." Why do the people I love think I feel stifled?

"Honey, do I give the impression that I'm unhappy with my life?" I ask, worried for the answer.

"Well, besides the whole Daddy thing, I guess not. Maybe it's just because I want to get away. I'm dying to", she struggles to find the words, "break out and see what I can do."

I nod. "It's easy for someone to say, 'I understand,' but I do. I always wanted people to know my name. I wanted to go as many places as possible. I get it. But you can't wish your life away. You can't push away a boy you really like now because in five years you plan on living in L.A. or New York with the perfect job and the perfect boyfriend. You need to experience what's happening in your life in this moment. Yes, plan ahead. Know what you want in the future. But be present. If you really like Brock, you have to go for it."

Roma nods. She looks so conflicted. "He asked me to prom and I said no."

"OMG! You've got to tell him yes!"

Roma cracks up. "Mom, please don't say 'OMG.'"

"Yeah, I heard that." I shrug. "New York City makes me feel young."

We giggle.

We stare out at the water with a feeling of satisfaction for our own reasons. The weight of the world seems to have lifted from Roma's shoulders. And I have really connected with my daughter for the first time in ages. With the honesty of this one conversation, we feel close again.

"So, you really think I'm a superstar?" I joke.

"Yes, I do." Roma leans against me and puts her head on my shoulder.

* * *

Roma and I take a tour of NYU, which hosts a variety of drama, musical theater, dramatic writing and theater history programs. As we view the campus, Roma glows. I try to picture her walking between classes wearing an NYU sweatshirt, a ponytail and her reading glasses, and the image comes easily. The thought makes me emotional. Excited and nostalgic for my growing lady.

After eating lunch on the NYU campus, we head to Lincoln Center for the Performing Arts for a tour of the very prestigious Juilliard. For a thespian like Roma, this is like the ultimate collegiate dream. Juilliard has a playwrights' program, which is extremely small and coveted. Playwrights can attend drama classes and have their work read by the Juilliard acting students. The school is a hub of creativity and inspiration.

I can sense Roma's nerves. Juilliard accepts only about seven percent of their applicants. But as we walk around the classrooms and rehearsal rooms, Roma lights up. I feel her excitement and hopeful energy. She's imagining what it would be like to be a part of this program. It's an amazing thing to be on this ride with her. I know this girl is going places, and I get to be her mom.

* * *

On the plane ride home, all of our activities have caught up with us and we're pooped. Roma fluffs a travel pillow against my shoulder, leans against me and closes her eyes. "Thanks for bringing me, Mom. I feel rejuvenated."

I grin. "I know exactly what you mean."

And I do. Because like her, my heart is bursting with energy, culture, the promise of a world to explore and the swell that I got to share that with her.

* * *

Jane flings open the front door when she hears us drive up. "Mama! Roma!" She runs to us.

Once we are inside, Roma distributes souvenirs. She gives Jane a rock and crystal collection that we bought for her from FAO Schwartz and an "I ♥ New York" t-shirt that she will proudly flaunt at school.

She gives Brandon some barbecue rub from Bobby Flay's restaurant.

Brandon gives her a funny look. "Barbecue rub from New York City?"

I laugh.

"It's supposed to be really good, Daddy. Bobby Flay is a master barbecuer," Roma says.

"Oh, well, thank you very much." He feigns snobbishness.

"Daddy!" Roma pushes him, playfully.

He pulls her into a bear hug. "I'm just kidding. Thanks for thinking of me." He kisses her on the top of her head. "So, have I forever lost my firstborn to New York City?"

"I *love* Juilliard, but it's super hard to get into," Roma answers. "But NYU would be awesome, too. They both have amazing theater and writing programs. I would just die to go to either one of them."

She stops talking when she sees the look on Brandon's face.

"Daddy. Skiatook will always be my home no matter where I go to college. I promise."

Brandon smiles at her so sweetly. He looks simultaneously proud, pleased, and in awe. "Honey, I'm just happy to see you so excited."

Brandon's gaze catches mine and I smile. I'm pretty sure we're both thinking the same thing— it's nice to have a happy and animated teenager in this house again.

Chapter 62

Grandma and I are snuggled up on the couch in the living room with our cups of tea in hand. Although she saw every minute of my trip with Roma, we have both just relished in my play-by-play description of every New York City landmark, meal and Broadway show.

"*Mi linda*, I'm so pleased that you and Roma are on the same page again. That trip was really special bonding time. I'm so glad that you and Roma can enjoy each other now, just as you and your mom have discovered how to do that."

"I know. I'm so thankful that each of us is learning how to better communicate with each other. It's amazing that three women at completely different places in our lives all needed to figure that out."

"It is. Now, don't be lazy about it." Grandma tucks a curl of salt-and-pepper hair behind her ear. "You will need to be conscientious of how to keep those channels open. Take it upon yourself to not let any of you slide back into your old ways."

I nod. "I will. Thank you, Grandma. I never could have gotten through this year without you. Just look at all you helped me resolve. And even though Brandon and I aren't there yet, I at least have learned how to navigate through this situation. You've taught me that no matter what happens, everything will be okay."

"Yes, it will. And, Nina, it was you who did all of the work. Just remember to step back and observe, be patient, and believe in yourself."

"I will, Grandma."

The way she is giving me a pep talk makes it feel like we're starting to wrap things up. My throat constricts at the very thought of it. I pick up my tea cup and inhale the flowery concoction. Here I am having tea with my sweet Grandma Isabel. I do my best to really experience the moment.

"I'm getting nervous about the last tea bag." My voice falters at the end of the sentence. "We only have one visit together after this." A tear runs down my face.

Grandma reaches up and caresses my face. I close my eyes and savor her touch.

"I know," she says. "I know." She pats my cheek.

"I've been such a fool. Why have I gone through them so quickly? I should have rationed them and used only one tea bag each year. I've been frivolous and extravagant."

"No, *mi linda*. You have not. I came to you because you needed me now. I will always be with you. I'll be smiling over you during happy times and I'll be your strength through hard times. Remember that. Please know that even though you won't be seeing me, I will be here. Talk to me and I will be listening. And promise me that you won't be too sad."

I frown involuntarily.

"I want you to realize in the moments that you feel like you need guidance or support from me that you have many others in your life who can fill that void. Haven't you discovered that this year?"

I think about it. "Yes."

"Tell me," Grandma says. "Who has been there for you?"

I look away for a moment to ponder that thought. "Jane. The first person who pops into my mind is Jane. Punching someone in the nose for me." I laugh. "I shouldn't be laughing, but she had my back."

"Yes, she did." Grandma laughs. "Who else?"

"Roma. As strained as we were, I know she was worried about me. I'll never forget the look of concern in her eyes the morning after Brandon left. In her own way, she carried that burden for me." I take a sip of tea. "Alison, Kate and Christina. Becky. Carrie Ann. I always know I can count on them."

Grandma nods. "You're so blessed to have those friendships. The list goes on, Nina. Your mom and dad, Stan, Father Jim, Leanne and Roy. Your readers. And many you didn't realize here in Skiatook."

"I see that now." I put my tea down and grab both of Grandma's hands. "Grandma, there are so many things that I still want to say to you."

"I know. And when you think of those things, I will hear you, my love." Grandma's eyes crinkle as she smiles at me.

"I love you so much, Grandma. You've always understood me and you've always cheered for me. You're the best friend I've ever had."

"And you are mine, my sweet girl."

I put my arms around Grandma and wrap her small frame in my love. "I love you so much, Grandma."

"Te quiero mucho, mi linda. Mi niña."

I rest my head on her shoulder like a little girl. I close my eyes and take in her sweet vanilla scent.

* * *

I'm folding laundry on the couch as I watch the Pioneer Woman on the Food Network make her own pizza dough. With her wit and charm, my fellow Okie, Ree Drummond, demonstrates how to make a simple dough and let it rise for an hour. It looks easy. I think I can do it! Maybe I don't need to drive into town the next time we want pizza.

Ree's going to put goat cheese on her pizza. I wonder where she gets goat cheese in Pawhuska. She probably makes it.

"Mom," Roma calls out from upstairs.

"What is it, sweetheart?" I call back.

She bounds down the stairs with a smile on her face. She's wearing jeans and a white tank top with the word "PROM?" that she has puffy-painted on in fluorescent colors. Her hair is thrown up in a high ponytail and her face is fresh, rosy and beaming.

"Can we go for a drive?"

I grin back at her. "Absolutely."

* * *

Across the street from Brock's house, I sit in the passenger seat of the car and wait. I've got a great vantage point to see how this all plays out. Roma knocks on the door and turns to me. She silently screams out of excitement. I laugh.

I realize that my heart is pounding for her. How lucky am I? How many parents get to witness this magic?

The door opens and Brock stands there, surprised and delighted to see Roma standing on his doorstep. It takes him a mere second to notice her shirt and he smiles from ear to ear. He picks her up and spins her around. Roma giggles.

I'm giggling right along with her, so much that my eyes are filled with tears.

Chapter 63

The air is beginning to thicken with sultry moisture. It's amazing how lush and green the landscape is in Oklahoma in the spring and summer. Pretty soon we'll be swimming through the heavy air.

When I said "I do" to Brandon so many years ago, before setting foot on Oklahoma soil, I imagined the dust bowl in *The Grapes of Wrath*. I loved that man so much I was willing to move from my sunny ocean paradise to the dusty, barren plains that I envisioned. I was so surprised to find a beautiful state with green foliage, rolling hills, and crisp lakes. There is more mileage of lakeshore in Oklahoma than the coastlines of the east and west coasts of the United States combined.

Frogs are beginning to hop up from the lake and set the scene to music. The cicadas are emerging from their hiding places underground and joining in on the ambient soundtrack of the season.

The blackberry bushes along Lake Road are now bursting with berries, and Jane skips down the road carrying her bucket, eager to collect them and bring them home to share with us. They'll be scrumptious in yogurt parfaits and on top of Bluebell vanilla ice cream.

Summer also promises fun on the lake with friends— swimming, wake-boarding and fishing in quiet coves. Although we are all chomping at the bit for summer vacation to begin, there are two more weeks of school, and with that is the highly anticipated Junior-Senior Prom.

Roma and I head into Tulsa for a day of shopping. With her late prom proposal to Brock, we only have one week to find the perfect dress. This is crunch time.

We look at the Tulsa Mall, and she has fun trying on many lovely gowns, but there just aren't any that are screaming at us.

I turn to her seriously. "It's time to pull out the big guns."

She grins in response.

I take her to Saks Fifth Avenue at Utica Square, an upscale outdoor center that has boutique stores, high-end department stores, hair salons and restaurants.

As soon as she puts on a strapless floral gown, I gasp. "Roma. It's beautiful, playful and sophisticated all at once." She beams with pink cheeks.

The gown is blue, fuchsia and green floral with a rouched sweetheart neckline. It's floor-length and flowy.

"Look, Mama. Pockets." She slips her hands into invisible side pockets and sways back and forth. She giggles.

"Well, this is obviously the dress."

Roma can't wipe the smile off her face, and for that reason, I pay way too much for this prom dress. Brandon would have a fit. But my kids have been through a lot this year and they've handled things like champs, so I think showering them with gifts is completely justifiable.

"As you may be aware, your mom has a fantastic shoe collection that doesn't see the light of day in Skiatook."

"I'm aware. You probably aren't aware that Jane and I try them on sometimes."

"Oh! The truth comes out!"

Roma laughs.

"I have a pair of strappy gold heels that I think would look fabulous with this dress. And a matching purse."

"I know the pair," she says guiltily. "I'd love to wear them. Thank you!" Roma tackles me with a hug.

"Oh, man," I tease. "I'm going to have to spoil you more often. Now, I think we'd better buy something for your sister and decide on a place for lunch."

Roma grins. "I have a better idea."

Chapter 64

Jane sleeps with a huge smile on her face. A gray striped tabby is curled up on her feet.

Knowing her sister well, Roma steered us to the Tulsa Humane Society. She chose a sad adult cat with only one eye who looked like he'd lived a hard life. Roma knew Jane would want to give that sweet little guy a home and take good care of him. I didn't even know Jane could scream as loud as she did when she saw her furry surprise. She named him Pirate.

I peek in on Roma, as well. She sleeps with an open book face down on her chest. I gently remove her reading glasses and the book and place them on her nightstand. I pull the sheet up over her long legs and caress her cheek. My heart is so satisfied that she is feeling happy once again.

I grab the almost empty mug off of her nightstand and close her door. I head down to the kitchen, looking forward to tidying up and turning in myself. Roma and I shopped until we dropped today.

I pour out the contents of the mug, and as it sloshes into the sink, I smell the familiar fragrance of chamomile. A soggy tea bag with the familiar yellow "manzanilla" tag plops into the sink.

A frenzy of fear surges through me.

I rush to the cabinet, find the terracotta rooster and take off the lid. My heart plunges to my feet. It's empty. There aren't any left. Roma used the last one. The tea bags are all gone!

Emotions wash over me. I'm scared. What am I going to do? I'm devastated. I feel loss. I feel panic.

I begin to rummage through the cupboard to see if I can find the tea bag, but it isn't there. I pointlessly continue to rummage, the contents of the cupboard falling out onto the counter, even though I know exactly where the last tea bag is. I just tossed it in the sink with the remains of Roma's tea.

I retrieve it from the sink and put it back into Roma's mug, fill it with water from the faucet and jam it into the microwave.

"Please, please, please…" I chant, as I wait for the water to heat and revive the last of the magical leaves.

After a minute of praying and begging, I pull the mug out and hold it to my chest. I breathe in the faint smell of chamomile, waiting for her.

"Please come. Please come." I attempt a few yoga breaths, but the tears start to fall. "No," I whisper. "How do I reach you?" My throat constricts.

"Grandma!" I shout. "Come here. I need you!" I begin to weep. The loss of her is fresh again. It burns in my chest. The hollow emptiness makes me feel like a child. My throat is tight and the hot salty tears continue to stream down my face. I taste them in my mouth.

I suddenly feel like I can't draw oxygen into my lungs. There is no air in this house. I run outside, but it's no better. The air is thick and warm.

I sprint down to the deck and lean over the wooden rail as if being closer to the water will bring more oxygen. I sit down on a lounge chair and bring my legs to my chest. My body heaves with sobs.

I was going to save that. I was going to save that last tea bag for years to come, so that I would always know that I could see Grandma one last time.

I grab my chest. It feels as though my heart might break in two.

This feeling is very familiar. It's heartbreak. I felt it when Brandon said we should separate and I've felt it many times since. How strange that loss and heartbreak feel exactly the same. In both circumstances you are grieving for someone, you are longing for them. There is the knowledge that you don't have them anymore, that a piece of you is now missing, and that you'll miss them forever. It's unbearable.

After crying for what must be hours with my entire body, I lie back on the lounge chair, depleted. The sound of the cicadas is deafening. They are all I can hear. The cadence repeats over and over again and I begin to breathe along with the rhythm. Thousands of stars twinkle above me and though my nose is completely stuffed up and I can't inhale a sniff of air through my nostrils, I swear I smell vanilla powder.

* * *

My alarm is going off and the radio is blaring *Fancy* by Reba McEntire. I swear, they play so much Reba here.

I groan and hit the power button.

I vaguely remember waking up on the lounge chair in the middle of the night and going to my bed. I scratch a patch of mosquito bites on my calf. They must've had a field day feasting on me last night.

I rise. I wash my face and brush my teeth. I begin to cry again.

No. I need to pull myself together. I've got to wake Jane. I just feel so numb. And exhausted. I walk down the hallway to Jane's room.

She is turned around haphazardly with her head at the foot of the bed by the cat. Covers have been thrown off and her face is still and sweet.

"Wake up, sweet pea." I plant kisses on her face.

She opens her eyes with a smile, but her expression turns to concern when she sees my face.

I go to her window and pull up the shades. Sunshine floods her room with bright, warm light. "I'll see you in the kitchen," I muster, attempting to pretend that everything is normal.

I go back to my room to get dressed. As I pull on jeans and a t-shirt, I hear Jane run down the hall to Roma's room. I hear her muffled voice.

"Roma. Mama's sad again."

I sit down on my bed and cry. She's right. I am sad. What am I supposed to tell them? I can't give them a logical explanation for this pain. That I've lost my sweet Grandma Isabel again. That one more visit with her is gone forever. I can't tell anyone about my unbelievable secret. I'm alone. I can't be mad at Roma for using the last tea bag. She didn't know.

Here I am again. A horrible mom who lets her children see her sadness.

* * *

I walk into the kitchen and my good girls are taking care of business. Jane slathers peanut butter onto bread for their school lunches and Roma measures out a cup of flour and dumps it into a mixing bowl. Roma looks up at me and smiles warmly.

"Good morning, Mama." She pours a cup of coffee and brings it to me. She gives me a kiss and pulls out a chair for me to sit. "We thought we'd make pancakes since they're your favorite."

I clear my throat. "Aren't you sweet?" I kiss her on the cheek and sit down.

Jane grabs an apple out of the fruit bowl on the island and takes a bite out of the top of it. "Here, Mama." She hands it to me. There at the top of the apple is a heart bitten out of it. "See it?"

I grab her chin and give it a loving squeeze. "You're the best."

"We love you, Mom," Roma says.

Roma and Jane hover with their worried faces. They wrap their arms around me and give me a group hug.

I know for a fact that right now Grandma is nudging me in her own way, pointing out that I have all the love that I need right here.

"And I love you," I tell them. I reach up, grab them both, and squeeze them. "Let's try adding a teaspoon of baking powder. Something tells me it'll make the pancakes just perfect."

Chapter 65

I walk out to the mailbox. Amongst the pile of bills is a *National Geographic Kids* magazine for Jane with a fox on the cover. She'll be thrilled. There's also a package from Malibu.

Curious, I sit on the front porch swing and open it. Sitting on folded layers of tissue is a note in my mom's handwriting. It says, "I know it isn't cold outside, but I was going through some cupboards and I found this. Love, Mom."

I open the folds of tissue and find a crocheted blanket. It's brown with many colorful squares. My breathing catches. My mom knew that this blanket needed no explanation. I remember it vividly. My grandma crocheted it and kept it in a cupboard under the window seat in her living room. She used to pull it out and cover me with it when I would watch *The Smurfs* and *Scooby-Doo* in Grandpa's recliner.

I pull the blanket out of the box and squeeze it to my chest. Mom is right— it's a hot summer day in Oklahoma, but I wrap the blanket around myself anyway. I wrap myself up in Grandma's love. A tear runs down my cheek, but one of nostalgia, not sadness. It's amazing how mothers know, with uncanny timing, what their children need.

* * *

Becky and RJ generously host a pre-prom party at their house. Their dining room table is set with appetizers, champagne glasses and chilled bottles of sparkling apple cider. The parents nibble on cheese and crackers as the high-school kids excitedly mingle with their dates.

Roma looks lovely in her billowy strapless floral gown. Her hair hangs in long and loose beachy waves down her back. She wears simple gold jewelry and my strappy gold heels. But her grandest accessory is her smile. She and Brock remain side by side, her arm through his. They are adorable. His cummerbund and bow tie are royal blue to match the blue tones of her dress.

I take candid pictures as Brock slips a corsage of fuchsia rosebuds and baby's breath onto Roma's wrist. Roma blushes as she fumbles with Brock's boutonnière.

The couples line up outside on the lawn and the parents take group photos of them.

"It's almost five, everyone. You don't want to miss dinner!" Becky says in a sing-songy voice.

The location of the prom this year is at the Hilton in Tulsa. We head to the front yard and a black limo waits in the driveway. The teenagers cheer.

As the couples pile into the limo, Brock takes Roma's hand to assist her as she lifts the hem of her long dress. Roma turns to us before she climbs in and waves. Brandon and I stand next to each other and wave back to her.

As the limo drives away, an overwhelming wave of emotion rushes over me. Now I get it. I understand why Brandon has been freaking out about Roma looking at colleges. We only have one more year of Roma living at home with us.

I burst into tears.

"Hey," Brandon says gently. He pulls me into a bear hug.

"She's a woman," I say through hot tears. "When did this happen?"

I feel Brandon's warm breath on my cheek. Knowing this is just a rhetorical question, he simply whispers, "I know."

Chapter 66

The next evening, Papa Roy called Roma and Jane to tell them that the ewe was having her babies. I dropped them off at the McCoy estate immediately. Knowing that I would not be able to take them away from the ewe and her babies in a timely manner, the girls packed an overnight bag with school clothes.

Having an unexpected evening to myself, I did something that I rarely get to do. I drove clear into Tulsa to pick up Thai food. When I got home, I ate pad thai noodles and yellow curry out of the takeout containers on the couch and watched *Breakfast at Tiffany's*. I cuddled up in my bed early and fell fast asleep.

In my book, that's a recipe for a nearly perfect evening.

Around eleven-thirty, I awake with a start to the phone ringing. I answer to the sound of Jane crying. I turn on the lamp and listen. In broken speech and sobs, Jane explains to me that one of the lambs didn't make it.

Leanne takes the phone from Jane. "I'm sorry, Nina. I just can't get her to calm down."

"It's okay, Leanne. I'll be right there."

I pull on jeans and a t-shirt and head to the McCoy estate. When I arrive, I find Leanne, Roy, Roma, Jane and Brandon in the barn with the ewe and her lambs. Jane sits on the floor holding the lifeless animal in her lap and pets him as she cries. The sight fills my eyes with tears.

When Brandon manages to take the lamb from Jane, she runs to me crying. "It's not fair, Mama! She never had a chance."

I kneel down and hug her hard. "I'm so sorry, sweetie. It really is sad."

Brandon looks at me with hurt in his eyes. We're heartsick to watch our little girl learning such a hard life lesson so soon.

I take the girls home and put them to bed. They had a late, hard evening. Roma was exhausted and down, but not to the same extent as Jane. I let Jane sleep in my bed with me, and long after she fell asleep, her breathing shuddered with the aftereffects of a hard cry.

* * *

I keep them out of school the next day. We head back to Grandma Lee's and Grandpa Roy's, and pick some flowers from the field behind their house. Brandon and Papa Roy bury the lamb in the yard under a maple tree.

As Jane lays wild flowers on the fresh mound of dirt, she says, "I named her Daisy."

"When did you do that?" Brandon asked.

"This morning. I thought she should have a name," she says.

"It's a sweet name for her, honey," Papa Roy says.

After a quiet moment, Leanne says, "I think I should make us all some lunch."

"I'll help you, Grandma Lee," Roma offers.

As Leanne, Roma, Roy and Brandon head toward the house, I grab Jane's hand. "Shall we sit on the porch for a little while?" I ask her.

She nods.

I sit down on a big white wicker chair and pull Jane onto my lap.

"Sometimes, life has a strange way of doing things. Things can happen that seem cruel, and you just don't know why it had to be that way."

"You're right, Mama," Jane leans her head against my chest. "I just don't understand it."

"I can't really say anything to make it better, but I can tell you that I understand how you feel."

"You do?"

"Absolutely. When I was in college, I lost my very best friend in the whole world."

"Your grandma?"

"Yep, Grandma Isabel. When she died, I missed her so much and I cried a lot."

"How did you feel better?"

"I will always be sad that she's gone, but I honor her by thinking about my happy times with her."

"But I didn't have any happy times with Daisy." Jane begins to cry again.

I frown. "I know. I'm sorry." I exhale, thinking. "Maybe you can honor her by caring for her brothers and sisters. That would make her happy, don't you think?"

Jane nods. "Yeah."

"You know what else helps? I know that I can talk to my grandma Isabel whenever I want to and she will hear me."

"Okay." Jane musters up a small smile. "That sounds nice." We sit in that wicker chair together for a while without talking. Suddenly, the trees start to rustle as a wind begins to rush across the plains, as it often does before a good Oklahoma storm. The summer wind is warm and strong like the Santa Anas, just like the day I poured chamomile tea on Grandma Isabel's grave.

Chapter 67

The Bluegrass Festival is Skiatook's celebration that marks the beginning of summer vacation. It's always the Saturday night of Memorial Day weekend, the day after the last day of school, so everyone is pumped and ready to celebrate.

The white doily-like flowers of Queen Anne's lace line the sides of the roads in billowy bushes. The sticky Oklahoma summer air has taken over the plains and all we can do is surrender to it. The escalating heat has brought out scorpions, tarantulas, centipedes and all the other culprits that I've had to learn to coexist with during my time here. The lightning bugs are back to illuminate our evenings.

I can't believe the school year is over. I'm now officially the mother of a high school senior and a second grader.

And so, this evening we head to the Skiatook Fairgrounds to kick off our summer vacation with great music from a long line-up of bluegrass bands and all of the typical southern carnival food and rides you could ever hope for.

* * *

I bite into my deep-fried pickle as Roma and Jane get whipped around on the Scrambler. I glance around the crowd for Brandon, who is meeting us here.

"Mama!" Jane yells as she flies by.

I wave.

Roma and Jane squeal hysterically. Their joy makes me laugh out loud. I've got my Roma for one more year at home. And Jane is still a little girl. Thank God. I lean against the metal gate surrounding the ride and take in the sounds of the festival—the bells and whistles of the rides and games, screams and laughter. The decadent scent of fried funnel cakes permeates the air. I close my eyes and revel in the moment.

"Nina," a distinguished voice calls behind me.

The hair sticks up on the back of my neck. I turn around and the Judge pushes past a few people to reach me.

"Hello, Judge." I won't be calling him Bruce anymore.

"Nina, I owe you a heartfelt apology. You did a very nice thing for me by reading my manuscript and I repaid you by putting you in an awkward situation. I'm really sorry about that."

"Thank you, sir. I appreciate that."

"You're calling me 'sir.' That can't be good."

I shrug and make a face that he's right.

"I hope you can think of my advances as a form of flattery."

I imagine him lunging towards me in his black silk boxers. "I'll try," I say flatly. I decide to change the subject. "I really did enjoy your book. If you need help getting in touch with publishers, I can give you some suggestions."

"I'd be very grateful. Thanks for all of your help."

"Have a good evening." I nod and turn back to watching my kids. He may give me the heebee-jeebies, but he's a fellow Skiatookan and we've got to take care of our own.

Roma and Jane flutter over in a fit of giggles and chatter about how fast the ride was. As we rush off to the Ferris wheel, I search the crowd for Brandon. This night has always been a fun tradition for us so I don't want him to miss out on our family fun.

As we stand in line for the Ferris wheel, Brock intercepts Roma, which leaves Jane and I alone to snuggle up together on the ride as it swoops us up around and around.

It is dusk and the sky is beginning to swirl into soft shades of yellow and pink.

"Look, Mama, we can almost see our house," Jane says as the Ferris wheel carries us up into the sky.

I glance towards the lake. We can see the length of road that stretches across the dam, and our house is just on the other side of the hill that leads to the marina. "Yep. It's just over that hill."

We can see the glint of water as we look towards the lake. I turn and look at the blur of grassy countryside as the ride whips us around again.

"Isn't our town beautiful?" Jane says with wonder.

"Yes, it is," I agree.

Jane has traveled to several states and has put her feet in both the Pacific and Atlantic Oceans, but this little piece of country right in the middle is her favorite spot.

Chapter 68

I've got to say, one of my favorite things about any fair in the south, besides the deep-fried pickles, is the armadillo races. I don't think there is anything that makes me laugh harder. You watch these adorable little armored creatures that look like they're from prehistoric times waddling frantically in the race of their lives.

After Roma, Jane, and I check out the competition, we place our bets at the Historical Society booth. All this year's money raised is going to revamping the Skiatook Senior Citizens' Center. Loving the cause, I make a pretty sizeable bet on the one called "A Boy Named Sue".

The armadillos are on the starting line. People from the crowd volunteer to be the armadillo blowers. And here is the hilarious part. They kneel down on the ground behind the armadillos, and when the whistle sounds, they blow on the armadillos'… well, for lack of a better word, buttholes. This is what makes the armadillos run like hell.

The race begins and the volunteers crouch down and start encouraging the armadillos to run. The little guys start running every which way. The crowd roots for their favorites, shouting out the armadillos' ridiculous names. It's like the redneck Kentucky Derby.

I howl with laughter. My little guy is dilly-dallying toward the back. "'A Boy Named Sue', pick up the pace," I shout.

I'm laughing so hard that I am wiping tears from my eyes. Jane and Roma laugh because of how loudly I am guffawing. Probably not my most graceful moment, but I just can't help it.

I glance up and happen to look squarely into Brandon's eyes. He is standing on the other side of the race. He has a grin on his face that I haven't seen in a long time.

The look in his eye makes me stop laughing. It makes me feel self-conscious and shy, like he really sees who I am for the first time in years. I shrug and smile back at him.

"Mom, your armadillo didn't win," Jane tells me. "One named Ichabod won."

"Oh, well," I say. "There's always next year."

Brandon makes his way through the crowd to us.

"Daddy!" Jane hugs Brandon.

"Hi, sweetheart!" He hugs her back.

"Hi, Dad," Roma says, still giggling. "Oh my gosh, Dad. Mama is crazy when she watches the armadillo race."

"I know," Brandon says and smiles at me. "Hi," he says just to me.

"Hi," I say back. A warmth spreads across my chest.

"Hey, I've been looking for you girls."

"We've done *everything*," Jane says dramatically. "I'm almost getting tired. *Almost.*"

"I'm sorry I missed it," Brandon says, a little left out.

"Well, we haven't done any carnival games yet," I offer.

He smiles at me. "Let's do it. I've got some tickets burning a hole in my pocket."

* * *

After tossing rings around Coca-Cola bottles, throwing basketballs in hoops, and throwing baseballs at the target of the dunk tank, Jane is covered in glow-stick jewelry, her choice of prizes, and she is lighting up the now dark night. I savor a frosty root beer float.

Teachers from the elementary and high schools graciously offered to be the victims in the dunk tank to raise money for the school district. Kids love seeing their teachers make spectacles of themselves. Mrs. Hawthorne's long wet skirt clings to her legs, proof that she doesn't, in fact, have a wooden leg. Mr. Frizzly waits next to the dunk tank, ready to take his turn.

"Daddy, we have to ride the swings."

Brandon makes a face. "No way. Not the swings."

"Come on, Daddy," Jane cries. "Buck up."

A mouthful of root beer involuntarily sprays out of my mouth.

"Mama!" Roma shouts.

Brandon, Jane and Roma break out into laughter.

"She did that the first night I met her."

"What?" Jane inquires.

"She did. Pretty much my first image of your mama was her drink shooting out of her mouth."

"No, Mama," Roma says.

"It's true. I'm sorry," I mutter as I wipe my mouth and chuckle. "Janie caught me off guard." I turn to Jane. "You just put Daddy in his place."

Jane's shoulders rise up as she giggles at me.

"Buck up?" Brandon challenges.

"Daddy, you never ride the swings," she pushes.

He grabs his head. "Honey, I can't. My brain sloshes around when I ride the swings. I can't do it."

"Oh, jeez," Jane replies.

Brandon picks Jane up. "You're tougher than I am. I'm okay with that." He gives her a kiss on the cheek and puts her down.

She smiles. "Okay, your loss!" Jane says and takes off towards the line for the swings. Roma follows at a slower pace.

"I see Darryl Farnsley and I need to talk to him."

"Okay. See you in a bit."

I chuckle as I walk toward the swings. It amuses me that a big ol' cowboy who can maneuver large farm equipment can't handle a ride on the swings.

* * *

After a few rides on the swings, I look around and don't see Brandon.

"I guess Daddy will find us," I say, and the girls and I head to stage to watch some of the performers.

The section below the stage is a dance floor, and behind that are picnic blankets where people eat carnival food and hang out.

"Let's dance, Mama!" Jane squeals.

"You got it!" I answer.

Jane, Roma, and I swing along to the happy twang of the banjo. We all hold hands and groove together and giggle. Even Roma is having fun with her little sister and her mom. This last month has done wonders for her. This is heaven.

The song ends and a slow song begins. People move off the dance floor as couples move on. Brock rushes up to Roma and asks her to dance. She smiles shyly, accepts, and Brock pulls her close. His hands clasp low on the small of her back. Now I'm the one who's blushing.

Jane grabs my hands and begins to sway with me. She attempts to twirl me and we giggle as I squat to lean under her arm.

On the other side of the dance floor, Brandon leads Marlena by the hand and pulls her in for a dance.

On this hot night, a wave of chill covers my body in goosebumps.

Brandon lifts Marlena's hand and twirls her. She laughs.

I feel like I've been punched in the stomach. We've got to get out of here. I turn to Brock quickly. "I'm so sorry to interrupt, but we

313

need to go." I become very flustered as I try to talk them off the dance floor. "Girls, wait for me at the car and we'll go get ice cream at the Tastee Freeze."

"They have ice cream here," Jane replies, confused. "Besides, I want cotton candy."

"Let's go, Jane," Roma says firmly. The tone of her voice tells me that she sees exactly what I see. "Sorry, Brock," she says. "We'll talk tomorrow." Brock looks stunned and confused.

I look at Roma apologetically. She nods at me and steers Jane off the dance floor.

I fish a few dollars out of my pocket and walk through the dance floor on a mission. When I approach the dancing lovebirds, Brandon's face falls and Marlena gives me a guilty smile. I'm not sure what I'd like to do first, slap Marlena's face or punch my husband in the nose. Instead, I grab Marlena's hand and press the dollar bills into it.

"Marlena, why don't you go buy yourself a deep-fried twinkie. I need to talk to my husband."

Marlena scoffs. "I think I'd rather stay here and dance with this handsome gentleman."

"Well, a twinkie isn't going to pull out a handful of your pretty hair," I answer.

Her jaw drops. I am, after all, a wild card from the mean streets of L.A.

Fury burns from my eyes into hers.

"Nina," Brandon says.

"I'll go," she squeaks.

As she leaves, my steely gaze turns to Brandon. "A slow dance? Really?"

"Don't overreact. She asked me to dance. It was the gentlemanly thing to do."

"No, the gentlemanly thing to do was not to dance with the woman who is rumored to be your mistress in front of the whole town. Including your *children*," I sneer.

People are starting to watch. I don't care. Screw it. This may be the most important moment in my entire marriage. I'm finally standing up for myself. I'm finally putting my foot down and saying, "Enough."

"Do you even care?" I continue. "You've been jerking me around for months. One minute you're ignoring me, the next you're cutting me down, then you're flirting with me. You give me just a little reassurance and then take even more away from me. Do you even want me anymore?"

"Keep your voice down," Brandon insists. "I'm not doing this here."

"Oh, yes, you are. You started this. You brought that floozy out on the dance floor in front of me."

"Come on." He grabs my hand and struggles to pull me off the dance floor.

"No. We're *all* dying to know what your plans are for once and for all."

"Damn it, Nina," Brandon growls.

"Forget it. I'm *done*." I practically spit the last word in his face. I break free from his grasp and stride off the dance floor.

As soon as I leave him, I realize I'm shaking. Hot tears stream down my face. I wipe them away quickly and walk through the crowd of shocked onlookers. Out of the corner of my eye I see Becky and Carrie Ann standing with RJ and Todd, looking shaken and concerned.

I don't make eye contact with a soul. I only have a minute to pull myself together before I get to the car, and I still have to take the girls to the Tastee Freeze.

Chapter 69

When we pull into the driveway, Brandon's truck is there. He's sitting on the front porch waiting for us.

"Hi, Daddy," Jane says tentatively. By now, she knows something big is going down.

"Come on, Jane. I'll tuck you in," Roma says.

"Okay," she says, unsure, as she glances at both Brandon and I.

"It's okay. Go to sleep." I kiss her on the head as she walks by.

"I love you both," Brandon says to them.

Without a glance at Brandon, Roma leads Jane into the house and closes the front door. Brandon exhales, hurt from being rejected by his daughters and the knowledge that he has really messed up.

I look at Brandon.

"Nina, I'm sorry," he says.

"About what exactly?"

"I'm sorry about tonight. You were right. I shouldn't have danced with Marlena."

I laugh bitterly. "After everything we've been through, that's what you're apologizing for? I'm glad it happened. It brought me some clarity. I meant what I said. I'm done. I'm not putting up with any of this anymore."

Brandon gapes at me.

"I don't want you to be done," he says.

"You have a funny way of showing it," I say.

He takes a few strides to get to me, grabs my hands and looks into my eyes. "I don't want us to be done," he says.

"What *do* you want?" I ask, although I'm not sure that I care anymore what Brandon McCoy wants.

"I want us to figure this out. I want us to end up together."

I scoff. "That's a revelation," I say, heavy with sarcasm.

"Babe, please," he pleads.

"Oh, I'm 'babe' again? Wow. She hasn't been around for ages."

Brandon looks down.

I take a deep breath and shake my head. "Brandon," I say calmly. "I am mentally, physically and emotionally exhausted. And after I announced to the entire town of Skiatook that we are through, I had to keep it together while I sat across from our daughters and ate a dipped cone at the Tastee Freeze. I know this much. Nothing is going to be resolved tonight. Come back in the morning."

He watches me intently.

"Okay," he says.

With that, I walk inside the house.

* * *

It's kind of funny. I managed to get a really good night's sleep. I fell into bed and slept like a log. The release of so much emotion last night took so much out of me. Maybe I could finally rest because I had been holding onto almost a year of desperation. In fact, giving up hope last night, deciding to cut my losses, took the weight of the world off my shoulders. I had already lost so I had nothing to lose.

When I awoke, I was starving. I made a pot of oatmeal and a fruit salad. I feel strong, like I'm ready to go into battle. After the girls and I ate breakfast I sent them on a horseback ride, knowing that

Brandon would come over to talk.

I sit on the front porch swing with my cup of coffee, waiting for him. I feel oddly indifferent. It's like I'm having an out-of-body experience. I have stepped back and am ready to make an objective decision about my future.

I see Brandon's truck approaching and my stomach is suddenly hit with nerves. Am I really about to tell him that I want a divorce? The moment of truth is just moments away and I feel myself starting to chicken out. I wasn't bluffing at the Bluegrass Festival when I said that I'm done. How can I forgive Brandon for what he has put me through? I don't even know if he's been faithful. It's quite possible that he's been having a full-blown affair with Marlena. I'm not a fool. I highly doubt that they've just been having great conversations. What I do know is that I will not stay in this situation any longer. There is either a committed plan to work towards being dedicated to each other or I'm out.

Brandon pulls into the driveway and his serious eyes lock onto mine.

Buck up, Nina, I tell myself.

Brandon approaches me and sits next to me on the swing.

We have sat here so many times, my legs in his lap, looking over the canopy of trees towards town, having easy conversation. This is the very spot that I told Brandon that I was pregnant with Jane. We now sit stiffly, with both feet on the ground as the swing sways slowly.

"I have to know one thing," I begin. "Did you have sex with her?"

"Absolutely not," he answers. His eyes are dead serious.

"Do you swear to me?"

"Yes, I do, Nina. I swear."

Okay. I believe him. I have known this man for seventeen years and if I can't believe him, I can't believe anyone.

"You were right. It was wrong of me to spend time with her. She wanted more and I knew it all along. It felt good to be wanted by her. It felt good to have someone give me so much attention."

I feel sick. I'm surprised that he is elaborating, but he knows that I need to hear this. His answer is a relief, but it still hurts.

"I have a lot to explain to you," Brandon continues.

I've been yearning for answers for a long time, though my perspective has changed over the last year. I'm not as needy as I was ten months ago. I know my worth and what I want from a partner.

"I'm listening," I reply, guarded.

"When you moved here almost twenty years ago I couldn't believe that I had landed a woman like you. We were so devoted to each other."

"Up until last night, I've been completely devoted to you," I interject.

He stops me. "Nina, I know I deserve that, but I have a lot to say. Please let me."

I nod and look at my lap.

"You were still working for the *Times*, taking our baby girl all over the world on your jobs. Now, that was a lot for me, but I allowed it since you came here for me. And when Roma started kindergarten and you decided it was time to stay home, I was so relieved. I thought you would finally settle down. I thought you would stay with me here forever."

I bite my tongue and let him continue.

"Things were really great for a few years, but I watched as you started to get fidgety. Then you started writing your books, which obviously brought you satisfaction, and I was really happy for you. Practically overnight, you found success. And the exciting traveling began again. I started to get nervous. I thought, 'I can't compete with book tours and autographs.'"

"Brandon," I say, trying to interject.

"Writing gave you wings. I knew that. I was sure it was just a matter of time before those wings flew you right out of here for good. For most of our marriage I've felt guilty about keeping you caged up in Skiatook."

I can't believe what I'm hearing. I've never kept it a secret that Brandon is the love of my life. How could he really think that I would leave him?

"Why didn't you ever tell me this?" I ask, dumbfounded.

"I haven't been proud of these feelings, Nina. In fact, I haven't liked myself for a while because of it. This past year, I've gone through some sort of crisis, and I've punished you as a result."

I take a moment to process these thoughts. "I'm so sorry you've felt this way. It's true that I'm a city girl. I love action, I thrive on it. And that's why I can't understand how you don't get it. I always come back. As much as I need to feel that energy run through my veins, I love you more. To me, that compromise feels like a sign of my devotion to you."

Brandon digests this.

"I choose to have my life here with you, Roma and Jane," I continue. "The three of you are my home."

"And you're mine." Brandon grabs my face, looks at me intently and kisses me. He wraps his arms around me and holds me tight.

I smile as I hold him. This outcome is not what I anticipated of this morning. This communication and affection is what I have really longed for. But I feel a nagging little pit in my stomach. There's just something missing here, something that still doesn't feel resolved. For two people who could not communicate for the last few years, this is just too easy a conversation. I don't feel satisfied and complete about this resolution.

I pull away. "Hmm."

"What is it?" Brandon asks.

"I just… There's something…" I shake my head.

Brandon raises his eyebrows. He knows it's not a good thing when I can't put a complete sentence together.

"… I don't feel good about." I take a deep breath and I begin slowly and quietly.

"No. It can't be. You have put me through all of this because you're…insecure? Our kids have been without a father in the house for ten months. I have searched my soul wondering what I've been lacking, what I've done wrong. I have asked myself, 'Why won't my own husband make love to me? Why can't we connect in conversation?' I have questioned every part of myself. I have watched as this canyon has developed between us and had no idea why. All because you are insecure?"

I yell that last word. Oh, my fire is lit. I stand up and pace back and forth in front of him.

"I write because I love it. It's always been my way to shine since I was a little girl. I write to show our daughters that anything is possible, that if they work hard and believe in themselves, they can accomplish whatever they want to, go wherever they want to go. But I also write to make you proud of me. Because the man I fell in love with loved me because of the fire inside me. Instead, you have resented me for my success, for the fact that I too want to provide for our family."

My arms wave all over the place. Brandon sits, quietly, like a three-year-old getting reprimanded. My volume has escalated to yelling.

"If you had just communicated with me years ago, I could have squashed this ridiculous insecurity before any damage was done. But instead, you have made me miserable. You have humiliated me and the girls. You have put me through hell!"

"Nina…"

"I always knew it was about my career," I say bitterly. "But against my better judgement I would tell myself, 'No. Brandon is not that small-minded, that chauvinistic!'"

"Nina."

I cut him off. "No. You know what? I think you need to crawl back to your little bachelor pad for a while longer. Because guess what, Brandon? *I* need space!"

I storm into the house.

Chapter 70

I've been cleaning the house in an insane frenzy attempting to blow off steam since Brandon left an hour and a half ago. I need another outlet because a) I think I may have a heart attack, and b) I think the girls are a little scared of me right now.

As much as I adore my father-in-law, I don't think I've ever picked up the phone and called him for a favor. So, when I call him now, he is pleasantly surprised.

"Nina! How are you, sweetie?"

His enthusiasm makes me feel very bad that I've been such an MIA daughter-in-law. "Okay, Pop. How are you?"

"I'm great, but I miss my girls. And that includes you."

My heart swells at his affection. "Well, how about we fix that? I need to shoot something."

* * *

"Pull."

A clay disc soars through the air. I raise my gun and pull the trigger. The clay disc disintegrates into fragments.

"Mama, you're good," Roma says, impressed.

"Thanks, sweetie," I reply.

I'm focused and I'm pissed off. Apparently, a perfect combination when it comes to skeet shooting.

Roy, Roma, Jane and I stand in the empty field behind my in-laws' house. We take turns, and as I find my rhythm, I'm starting to feel a little better. It feels fantastic to blow something into smithereens. The girls are having a blast. Roy gets behind Jane when it's her turn and helps her aim.

Brandon and I used to do this together. We would come here and have brunch with his parents when we were newlyweds and then shoot some skeet with Roy. We started Roma and Jane off by lining cans up on a fence and having them use a BB gun. I pause and think about how this is yet another activity that we used to do together. When did our time together start to dwindle away?

Chapter 71

It's Tuesday night and there's a knock on the door. Becky and Delilah are coming over to hang out, since we'll be living a life of leisure for the next few months of summer. They're about an hour early, though.

I fling the door open. "You're early." I smile.

Brandon stands on the stoop holding a pizza box.

"Oh," I say, surprised.

"Hi." Brandon smiles. His eyes crinkle. "I thought you might like a night off from cooking."

"Brandon..." I wrinkle my forehead, annoyed. "I'm furious with you. I don't want to see you for a while. You can take the kids tomorrow, but we have plans tonight."

He touches the spot between my eyebrows that is creased with displeasure and rubs it with his forefinger. "I know you're mad. I'm really sorry."

I back away. "Becky and the kids are coming over and we're going to watch the new *Star Wars*."

"Oh. Well, here you go." He hands me the pizza.

"Thank you," I huff.

"I'd like to take you out to dinner this week."

I look at him, deadpan.

"We can head up to Bartlesville and go to the Copper Restaurant."

I put my hand on my hip. "That's below the belt."

Brandon smirks.

The Copper Restaurant and Bar sits atop Price Tower, a nineteen-story building built in 1956, designed by the great Frank Lloyd Wright. It's the only completed skyscraper that was designed by Wright, and it exists in Bartlesville, Oklahoma, about twenty minutes north of us. It's such a gem in a very unexpected location. Brandon took me there on our first anniversary with baby Roma in tow. It has remained one of our favorite dining spots in Oklahoma.

"Maybe another time, Brandon."

He tilts his head in disappointment. "Enjoy your night," he says.

"We will," I say firmly.

* * *

The kids gather excitedly on the couches as they prepare for our movie night. I wrangle several cold cans of root beer and Coke from the kitchen.

"Cool," Jane says as she pulls back the lid of the pizza box on the coffee table.

"Nina, you've got to look at this," Becky says.

I set the sodas down on the coffee table and glance at the pizza. There, smack dab in the middle of it, is a heart constructed entirely out of bacon bits.

Becky gives me a knowing look. "You said Brandon dropped this pizza off?" she asks.

"Uh-huh," I reply.

Becky nods and smiles. She hands me a slice, smugly. "Here ya go."

Chapter 72

After pizza night, Brandon leaves me alone for a grand total of three days. Then he comes to me daily with little courting gifts. He brings flowers, soap made by Becky, and gourmet coffee from a coffee house in Tulsa.

At first I'm aggravated. He needed nine months of distance and time to contemplate our marriage, yet he's not granting me the same request. I gave him offerings of Halloween cookies and chicken-fried steak and he was irritated that I was suffocating him and burdening him with my presence. But he is starting to wear me down after a mere few days and that makes me resent him even more.

So here he is again tonight on my front porch with a slice of chocolate cake from the Skiatook Bakery. It's a risky move considering who owns the place, but Brandon knows me well and is aware that a good chocolate cake trumps all. I may loathe Marlena for her intentions, but no one makes chocolate buttercream better than her.

"Hello, Ms. Blake. How are you tonight?"

I shake my head with aggravation. "I'm doing just fine, Brandon. How are you?"

"Spec-tacular. I'm happy to see your lovely face."

I scoff. "Brandon. Are you going to just let me be for a while?"

"I'm going to come to you every day until you take me back. And when you do, I'm going to remind you constantly that I love you and that you're the woman of my dreams."

I laugh.

He turns serious. "I'm not joking, Nina."

"Why the sudden change? You're like a different man all of a sudden. The man I used to know."

"Good. I'm different because I know what it feels like to almost lose you for good. I see that I was foolish and cruel."

"Brandon, there are things we need to talk about. If you want to get back together, there are issues that we need to resolve."

"Okay, let's do it. What do you need me to do?"

"For one thing, I need you to be supportive of me. I'm not going to choose between you and my career. It's not that I wouldn't choose you. But I won't be with you if you make me choose."

He nods. "You know, most men wouldn't follow your confusing and wordy rhetoric. I get you."

I roll my eyes.

He turns serious. "I'm not going to make you choose. I think you're brilliant."

"Do you really mean that?"

"Of course I do. Okay, what next?"

I laugh. "You're so impatient."

Brandon grabs both of my hands. "Nina, I don't want to waste any more time."

"You know, I could have said that in October, but you wouldn't have listened to me."

Brandon furrows his eyebrows. "Are you trying to drag this out so you can punish me?"

I sigh. "Maybe I am," I answer honestly. "You deserve it." I surprise us both with this admission. "It's your turn to feel helpless and desperate to do anything to save us."

"Wow," Brandon says. He lets go of my hands.

"Look. I gave you the luxury of time and freedom. Something you definitely took advantage of. It's a little unfair that you're rushing me back into things. You punished me for your insecurities. You told me that you didn't believe in us. After what you've put me through, I would say I'm taking it pretty easy on you. And yes, I think I'd like you to suffer a little bit. Maybe a lot."

Brandon looks hurt. "I'm sorry I put you through so much," he responds. "I have to live with that. I'll give you all the time you need. But I hope you don't take too long."

* * *

Today is a big day. Roma McCoy passed her driver's test and has been given her driver's license! She's been studying for the written test since school got out. I'm sure she would've passed ages ago, but that girl is a perfectionist.

We pick Brandon up.

"Congratulations, sweetheart!" Brandon gives Roma an enthusiastic high-five through the driver side window and nods hello to me in the passenger seat. I respond with a return nod. He slides into the back seat with Jane.

We decide that we need to go on a celebratory adventure, one that involves a medium-length drive. We settle on heading north to Bartlesville to a little hamburger joint that makes their own sasparilla.

As Roma excitedly recounts the play-by-play of her driver's test and the perils of parallel parking, I feel Brandon's eyes on me from the back seat. I try to ignore him, but I am so torn. I have been dying for attention from him for so long, but now that I'm getting it, I'm reminded of how far he had to push things to conclude that he still wants me around. The ball is in my court. I do want him back, but he's right, I am punishing him. I want him to know how I felt this year. I feel like that's fair. I've had quite a journey and I'm wearing it like a badge of strength. I'm much stronger now than I was last fall. I feel like it would be disrespectful to myself to take Brandon back at his first whim.

But I recognize that I am holding myself back from what I really do want. I know that if I want us to move forward, I have to forgive him. But I'm not there yet.

Lately, I've been thinking about the blessing of having Grandma Isabel's guidance this year and I've been reflecting on her advice. One thing that has been sticking out is that Grandma told me to think about what I wanted from my marriage.

Think about why things were good with Brandon back when they really were good.

So, I've been writing those things down. First of all, I want a partner I can count on. I can't be in a marriage that is delicate. At the very least I have to know that no matter what, we will get through things together. No more running away. No more turning away from problems.

I want fun. Okay, so we're not in our twenties anymore and we've changed a little, but I want the relationship we started with. Our relationship started as an adventure and we still need to view life as such.

I need romance. Yes, it's really that important to me. I'm a hopeless romantic, and I always have been. My expectations have had to change a little to be more realistic, but if I'm never going to flirt again or feel a spark for the rest of my life, I might as well crawl into a hole and die.

I need mutual respect. Brandon and I need to respect where both of us came from and where we want to go. And in that, there has to be respect for my career. I need him to be happy for me.

* * *

When Roma drives us home from our excursion, Brandon walks us inside.

"Congratulations, sweet girl." Brandon pulls Roma in for a bear hug and kisses the top of her head. "I'm so proud of you."

"Thanks, Dad," Roma replies proudly. "See you soon." She gives him a kiss on the cheek and heads to the living room. She plops down on the couch and cracks open a paperback copy of *Jane Eyre*.

"Driving is hard work," Brandon jokes.

I smile.

"Daddy, do you want to hang out with us for a while?" Jane asks.

"I need to go into the store for a little while and get some work done," he replies.

Jane nods, disappointed.

"I could use a helper, though." He looks at me. "If it's all right with you."

"Of course." Jane claps her hands together.

"Great! Let me just go upstairs and grab a few things." She runs upstairs.

"I actually have something I'd like to give you before you leave," I tell him.

"Oh," he says, surprised. "Okay."

"Be right back." I jog off to my office. I grab my list of marriage goals off the desk and run back to him. "As you know, writing is the best way I get my feelings out. Here."

I hand Brandon the piece of paper. This is crucial. I am telling him how I want the rest of our marriage to go.

"Thank you." Brandon's eyes search mine and he gives me a solemn smile.

Jane runs down the stairs. She slings a tote bag over her shoulder. "I packed a work bag. A calculator in case you need me to add a whole bunch of prices up and some pens and a note pad for writing down *invenstory*." Brandon and I glance at each other and smile. "I have a lot of work to do, too. I am going to run the place some day."

Chapter 73

Jolene, Jake, and their kids picked Roma and Jane up this morning to go swimming and tubing on Skiatook Lake. I sit at my desk and contemplate what to write about next. I have a file of ideas that I've started developing here and there over the last few years. Which story am I ready to delve into right now? Which characters do I want to commit to? I rub my eyes and spin around in my desk chair. My eyes fall on our leather-bound photo albums on the bookshelves behind my desk. I grab the very first one and lean back in my chair. It contains the first pictures of Brandon and I— metaphorically, our first chapter together.

I open and run my finger along the pictures— Brandon and I in Italy, our first summer here on Skiatook Lake, Christmas at his parents' house, Roma's baby pictures, the three of us happily together, pictures of me at the airport with Roma strapped to my chest in a baby carrier. There are pictures of baby Roma and I in London and Ireland, my last few pieces with the *Times*. I close the album, return it to its place on the bookshelf and grab the next one and then the next.

I arrive at the place in our lives when my literary career took off. There are pictures of me at my very first book signing in Los Angeles. And then one in Las Vegas. They are pictures just of me. Me with my readers. Me with Stan. Me with Veronica. I look exuberant. But what is so apparent to me is the absence of Brandon in these pictures.

Suddenly, I'm struck with Grandma's words about when she went to Hawaii without Grandpa.

As long as you're making sure his needs are met, you shouldn't feel bad about doing your thing.

Did I make sure Brandon's needs were met? I took Roma with me on those last *L.A. Times* assignments. Her needs were met. But I may in fact be responsible for planting a seed in Brandon that I didn't need him or that *we* didn't need him. When the literary world embraced me, I took off running to pursue my dreams and I may have left Brandon in the dust. I didn't do it intentionally. But perhaps I did, in fact, do it. Maybe he felt like I would be fine with or without him. It isn't true. That's never how I felt, but when I started to fly, I left him with his feet planted firmly on Skiatook soil to watch.

I close the photo album and hug it to my chest. I'm dumbstruck by the sudden perspective. My heavy introspection is interrupted by the sound of the doorbell.

When I trudge though the living room and open the front door, I am greeted by Rosalee Potter, the owner of Petals, the flower shop in town. She holds a humongous bouquet of orange roses. I love orange roses. Rosalee smiles from ear to ear.

"Oh, my goodness! How gorgeous!"

"Good afternoon, Nina."

"Hi, Rosalee. How are you?"

"Great." She glances at the roses and winks at me. "I've been praying for you and Brandon all year. Looks like it's starting to pay off. Praise Jesus!"

"Thank you. That's really kind of you."

Rosalee smiles and nods. She hands me the bouquet.

I smile. "They really are beautiful. Thanks."

"Don't thank me." She winks again. "Bye now." I close the door and smell the roses. I know he loves me.

Nestled in the blooms is an envelope. I open the envelope and pull out a folded paper covered in his words. I know it's his response to my letter. My breath catches.

I rush to the phone in the kitchen and dial Brandon's office at the feed store.

"McCoy Feed and Farm Supply," he answers cheerfully.

"Hi," I say. I feel the blush on my cheeks. With my recent revelation I feel a little ashamed.

"Hi," he answers with promise.

"I haven't read the note yet, but before I do, I just want to say thank you for the roses. They're stunning."

"You're welcome, babe."

I feel the impact of being called 'babe' yet again.

"You're going to get tired of all of my romantic gestures," he says. "Just wait until I start with the poetry."

I laugh. "I anticipate a lot of 'Roses are red. Violets are blue,'" I tease.

"No, no. I've been working on my material."

I smile though he can't see it. All right, he gets my message about being romantic. He's showing me that he hears me. "Brandon?"

There's a pause. "Yes?"

"I'm anxious to read your note. A little nervous, but anxious."

"Nothing to be nervous about, darling."

"I'm really thinking some things through. Can we meet in a few days to talk about it?"

"Tell me when you're ready."

* * *

The next morning the girls and I enjoy a lazy Saturday morning. Jane has fixed herself a bowl of Froot Loops downstairs and Roma is sleeping in.

It's a beautiful morning and I decide that a nice jog on the lake trail is in order. I need my legs to move me around the lake on autopilot so my mind can navigate through all of my thoughts about Brandon.

I pull a running tank top over my head and grab some socks out of my drawer. I pull Brandon's letter out of my pocket and unfold it. It isn't a long laundry list of demands.

I read it again.

"I read what you need from me. Yes. I will work on giving you all of those things. I just ask for one thing from you. I need to be confident that you and I are strong enough to withstand all of the things that are brighter and shinier than Skiatook. A lot of that falls on me and my own confidence, but some of that needs to come from you. It may seem silly to you that I need that reassurance, but you, Roma and Jane are everything to me. I don't need you to be anything that you aren't. I just need you to be mine. I'm still in love with the girl from the swings at Manhattan Beach. I told you then that I never want to tell you goodbye."

I clutch the romantic sentiments to my chest. *My* Brandon is back. And now I know where he went. I'm so ready to rush to him and tell him that I'll cherish him forever, but I just want to get my thoughts and words together for a humble way to apologize and ask him to come back to me.

"Mom! Can you come here?" Jane calls to me from downstairs.

"I'm coming," I call back softly as to not wake Roma.

I make my way to the kitchen. Jane and Brandon sit at the kitchen table.

I look at him, startled. He looks uneasy.

"What's going on?" I ask.

"Janie called me," Brandon starts.

"I asked Daddy to come here. I need to tell you guys something," Jane says seriously.

Brandon and I look at each other, concerned.

My mind races around, creating scenarios of what this is about. "What is it, sweetie?" I ask. I pull out a chair next to her and sit down.

"I don't know if either of you have noticed, but the character sign for June has been up *for weeks,*" she says.

"Okay," Brandon says gently to encourage her to finish.

"The character trait is forgiveness." Jane looks back and forth between the two of us. "Don't you think it's time?"

There's a long pause. She looks at Brandon with intent, then me.

I suddenly feel very selfish for indulging myself with my month-long revenge upon Brandon.

"Yes," I say. I turn to Brandon. "I do."

Brandon searches me with his eyes. I smile and nod at him.

We stand up and rush to each other. We hold each other tight.

Jane begins to jumps up and down, causing us to laugh. Brandon picks Jane up and kisses her.

"Thank goodness!" she cries. "I thought you'd never come to your senses."

I chuckle. "Thank you for the final nudge, sweet pea."

"Anytime," she responds.

"Jane, would you mind if I took Mama for a drive?" Brandon asks.

"Be my guest," Jane says.

"Okay, you're in charge," he says.

"*I'm* in charge?" Jane squeals.

"Yep."

"Yes!"

Brandon puts her down. She smiles at me victoriously then turns and runs out of the room, presumably to wake Roma up and boss her around.

Brandon offers me his hand. "Can I take you somewhere?" His eyes glimmer with excitement.

"Sure."

I take his hand and he leads me to the garage. He opens the garage door and I walk straight to the Range Rover.

"Over here," he says with a grin. He stops next to the four-wheeler.

Chapter 74

We fly down the street on the quad and I scream with excitement. My arms are wrapped around Brandon's waist. We turn right onto Crosstimbers Drive and head down to the marina. My arms squeeze tighter as we accelerate down the hill.

When we get down near the boat slips, Brandon slows down through the parking lot and continues onto the trail that wraps around the entire lake. The four-wheeler charges up and down the steep bumpy hills. I squeal when we pick up speed. Sunlight flickers through the trees. It's been a long time since I've ridden on the four-wheeler and I feel exhilarated. I lean my head against his back and think about myself as a twenty-four-year-old clinging to Brandon.

We slow down when we approach the bottom of a hill close to the water. Brandon cuts the ignition and takes my hand as I climb off. I observe as he unties his work boots and takes off his boots and socks. He rolls up his jeans.

"Come on," he says.

I slip off my sandals and follow him down to the water. He grabs my hand. As I step into a few inches of the clear, cold water, it's an unexpected shock to my body. It feels like it's about to give us new life.

Without warning, tears spring to my eyes.

"Whoa. Why are you crying?" Brandon asks, surprised.

I shake my head. "Because we're almost done with this. For the first time in a long time, I actually believe we're going to be okay." I let out a huge sigh, letting go of doubt, letting go of fear.

Brandon squeezes my hand. "Of course we're going to be okay."

"You say that like it's a given, but things have been pretty bleak here for a while."

"I know," he says tenderly. "But we *are* okay." Brandon pulls me close. "I'm so sorry," he says in my ear.

I let out a huge breath and a burst of hot tears escape down my face. "I'm so sorry, too," I whisper back in my husky, emotional voice. I pull away so that I can see his face. "I recognize that I haven't put you first for a long time. The girls and my writing are always in the forefront, and I can see how that must have felt for you. I'm really sorry about that." I shake my head. "I'm not just saying it. I *really* am sorry about that." Brandon purses his lips together and nods. I look into his eyes. "I vow to take better care of you."

Brandon smiles. "And I vow to take better care of you," he reciprocates.

We stand there, hugging and wading in the cool water. It's absolving us, it's restoring us, it's purifying us. There is much more work to be done. There is much more to discuss. But for now, it's all we need to say.

* * *

An hour later, we move Brandon's things out of the room over Becky and RJ's garage. Becky is absolutely thrilled when she walks out her kitchen door with a trash bag and finds us loading Brandon's truck.

Jane and Roma are over the moon. Once we are home, Brandon fires up the grill and we celebrate with hamburgers, watermelon and corn salad, one of our quintessential summer dinners. We eat on the deck overlooking the lake. I am filled with a sense of contentment and anticipation, like it's Christmas Eve and there is so much happiness to come.

With our marital and family problems symbolically over, Brandon is exhausted. His long, strong body is stretched out on the couch in the living room and he watches *Deadliest Catch* in his spot. I head in there to give him a kiss and find that he has fallen asleep. My heart sings.

With everything feeling as it should, I think about Grandma Isabel. Because of her, I was able to survive this journey. She must be so happy for us. I'm so grateful for the inexplicable and impossible miracle of having spent more time with her.

I heat a kettle of water on the stove. Jane puts a chamomile tea bag in each mug. The kettle starts to whistle and Roma pours the boiling water into each cup. Jane stirs clover honey into the tea and the three of us gather around the kitchen table.

It is time that I share this ritual with my daughters. I decide to tell them a story about their Great-Grandma Isabel. I tell Jane that she has Grandma's sweet nurturing nature, how she is always taking care of her family, friends and animals. I tell Roma that the round apples of her cheeks are just like Grandma's and that I see Grandma every time she smiles. I tell them some of the many memories of Grandma that are forever in my heart. And just like Grandma told me, even though there is nothing magical about these tea bags, I know that she is here.

Chapter 75

Summer parties in the marina are always top-notch, but the Fourth of July celebration takes the cake. When we arrive, a five-person band is playing *Calling Baton Rouge* by Garth Brooks. If history repeats itself, and it always does around here, we will be hearing lots of cover songs by Reba, Brooks and Dunn, Blake Shelton, Carrie Underwood, Miranda Lambert, Vince Gill and Toby Keith— all famous fellow Okies.

The Fourth at the marina is potluck, and we make our best picnic dishes for all to share. Potato salad, coleslaw, baked beans, homemade mac and cheese and triangles of watermelon cover long folding tables that are dressed with patriotic plastic tablecloths.

Pans of pound cake frosted with whipped cream and decorated with strawberries and blueberries as the stars and stripes of the American Flag, lemon squares, brownies and fluffy banana pudding make an impressive dessert table. I see that Carrie Ann brought her famous peach cobbler. As always, she will serve it with a scoop of Bluebell vanilla ice cream and it will be a fight to get a serving. Coolers are stocked with soft drinks, cold beer, pitchers of mojitos and margaritas, and Otter Pops and juice boxes for the kids.

Brandon and my dad each grab a beer and join RJ, Todd, and a few other men at the industrial-size grill. The air is filled with the scent of charcoal, smoke, and savory meat as they cook up steaks, chicken breasts, hot dogs, hamburgers and corn on the cob.

Later, when the fireworks shoot up and explode into the dark sky, the speakers will blare patriotic favorites like Neil Diamond's *America*, and songs by Toby Keith about America kicking ass. As usual, the finale will bring me to tears with Lee Greenwood's *I'm Proud to be an American*.

The Fourth of July is the absolute best day to be an American and, furthermore, the best day to live in Skiatook, Oklahoma.

Roma and Brock sit on the dock and dangle their feet in the water. He has said something to make her laugh and she leans against him cracking up. Hailey and Stacey walk up and sit down next to Roma. They hear the tail end of the joke and join in on the laughter.

Jane and her school friends run around writing their names in the air with sparklers. Mom and I are settled into chairs next to Becky and Carrie Ann with minty mojitos in our hands. I'm so lucky to have them. "Ladies, I want to tell you something."

"Uh-oh," Carrie Ann says.

"No, it's good." I laugh.

They look at me expectantly.

"I want to thank you all. I don't know what I would've done without you this past year. I always knew I had your love and support, and I can never thank you enough for that."

"Of course, pal," Becky says, smiling.

"You're our girl," Carrie Ann says.

"And you're mine. And that includes you, Mama."

My mom pats my hand. The four of us smile at each other.

I lean back in my seat, close my eyes and listen to the music. I feel the heat of the summer air. There's an excitement in my belly. This is the first holiday this year that I've actually been excited about. I'm so happy that life has worked itself out for us. I realize I'm smiling from ear to ear.

I glance over at Brandon at the grill.

Things between us feel so different. There are still things we disagree on occasionally, but we approach each other differently. We give each other the benefit of the doubt before getting annoyed or upset. We didn't use to do that. We treat each other with kindness. I'm also happy to report that I love David Gray again. Can't get enough of him.

Brandon catches my eye and winks. He hands his spatula to RJ and walks toward me. "Ladies."

"Well, hello, Mr. McCoy," Carrie Ann flirts.

"Happy Fourth of Joo-ly," Becky says.

"Happy Fourth. I was wondering if I might borrow my lovely wife."

"You can have her for a little while," Becky teases. "We're gonna to want her back when the dancin' starts."

"It's a deal."

"Of course," Carrie Ann answers.

I stand up and Brandon takes my hand.

"Kiss her!" RJ yells from the grill.

Brandon catches me off guard, dips me back and kisses me.

There are whistles and shouts. Father Jim raises his glass of red wine and smiles at me. Rosalee Potter throws her arms upto the heavens in thanks. Everyone loves a happy ending.

"Aww, quit it," Brandon mocks.

I know I'm blushing and I laugh. My mom is blushing, too.

The commotion caught the attention of the kids on the dock. Roma smiles at us. Carrie Ann winks at me as we walk off.

Brandon leads me down the ramp to the boat dock.

"What are we doing?"

"Do you always have to know what's coming?" Brandon asks.

"No, I don't." I motion that I'm zipping my lips.

We walk down the first row to our slip.

Brandon climbs into our boat, takes my hand and helps me aboard. I pull the bumpers in. Even though it seems like ages since we've been out on this lake together, I know what my duties are as first mate.

Brandon backs the boat out of the slip and we drive slowly until we get past the break. And then we take off. The force pushes me back into my seat. The sun is setting and the Oklahoma sky is painted with a magnificent swirl of pastels. The wind whips through my hair and sings a muffled song in my ears. I throw my arms up into the air as we zip through the sultry evening. We make eye contact and laugh. The weight that has been removed from this relationship has taken years off of us both.

Brandon slows the boat down when we get to the island. On any given day in the summer, the water around the island is packed with pontoon boats and speedboats. People float around on rafts and jump off the rope swing that hangs from a huge tree near the water's edge. There isn't a soul around now. Everyone is at the marina. Brandon cuts the engine and I throw the anchor in.

"What are we going to do now?" I grin.

It's so quiet out here, except for the cicadas and frogs that we hear chirping on the island. In the distance we can hear the muffled sound of the band. The air is still and warm.

Brandon's smile disappears. "Come here."

I do as I'm told.

It's been a really long time since I've been on a first date. But I remember the excitement at the beginning of a date that I could tell was going to be great. I feel that anticipation now, being alone out here with Brandon.

He grabs me by my shoulders. "I love you. You're never going to doubt that again," he says strongly.

"Okay."

He pulls me toward him into a kiss. Slowly at first, then hungrily. His hands are all over me. My hands are in his hair, all over his back. He pulls my tank top over my head and drops it on the seat. My bra is not far behind. I pull his t-shirt off and suddenly our skin is pressed against each other.

Brandon walks backwards and guides me to the back bench. He unbuttons my shorts and pulls them and my panties off in one swift move. I follow suit with his shorts and boxer briefs. He sits down and pulls me down to straddle him.

I look into his eyes and we become one. We hold each other tight and move out of love and desire. This just might be the best place in the world. Better than Rome, better than Australia, better than Malibu. This spot on Skiatook Lake with my one true love is beyond compare.

When we finish, we laugh at how good it was.

"I've officially made a resolution," he says with a twinkle in his eye.

"What's that?" I ask.

"We're going to do a lot more of that."

I raise my right hand and feign seriousness. "And I resolve to support your resolution."

Brandon stands up, climbs onto the back of the boat and does a cannonball into the lake like a teenage boy. The last thing I see is his pale bare bottom breaking through the black water. I stand on the back of the boat and my hearty laugh cuts through the still air of the darkening night.

It's so odd. These last few years with Brandon not watching me undress made me self-conscious. I used to assume that he didn't want to see my body, so I would undress in my walk-in closet. Here I am standing stark naked in the moonlight as Brandon treads water in the lake below me. I feel liberated. Comfortable. Sexy.

"You're beautiful," he says to me.

I smile. And then I scream and dive into the brisk water.

We laugh and hug and kiss, as much as we can without pulling each other under.

"The stars are amazing!" I shout. I turn to Brandon. "It really is beautiful here. It's home to me, you know."

"Good."

The first firework of the night disrupts the calm sky in an explosion of red, white and blue. Brandon and I are breathless at its beauty. It looks as though we are right underneath the fireworks, and as they trickle down the sky, the colors reflect on the water and seem to dance all around us.

We enjoy the sight from our remarkable vantage point for a moment longer and then we scramble up the boat ladder.

Brandon offers his hand as I step into the boat. He holds up a towel. "Come here, babe." He wraps the towel around me and squeezes me tight. The look in his eyes tells me that our bad times are behind us. I nod back at him and we kiss. Our kiss communicates apologies, forgiveness, and promises. We smile at each other.

"Let's go find our kids," he says.

We dress quickly, then Brandon sits in the passenger seat, leans back and interlaces his fingers behind his neck. "You drive."

I hop in the driver's seat. "Hold on," I say coyly.

I gun the engine and Brandon laughs as he grabs the side of his seat to steady himself while we jet across the water.

As we race back to the marina so we can catch some of the fireworks, and hopefully some of Carrie Ann's peach cobbler, I feel like the stars are winking at me. I smile right back at them.

Grandma always loved a good fireworks show.

Grandma Isabel and Grandpa Julio's Recipes

Mexican Rice

Ingredients
1 cup uncooked long-grain white rice
About 1 tablespoon of vegetable oil
About 1 clove chopped garlic
1 small diced white or yellow onion
1/2 chopped green bell pepper
8 ounce can tomato sauce
14 ounces chicken broth
About 4 tablespoons chopped cilantro

Instructions
In a saucepan, lightly brown the rice in the vegetable oil along with the garlic, onion and bell pepper. Add tomato sauce until a light orange, about 1/2-3/4 of the can. Add the chicken broth and cilantro. Stir. Cover and simmer on low for 20-30 minutes or until the broth has been absorbed. Do not stir while cooking.

(You can use broken pieces of vermicelli instead of rice to make Fideo.)

Serves 3-4

Vanilla Raspados (Snow Cones)

Ingredients
2 cups sugar
2 cups water
2 tablespoons Mexican vanilla extract
Crushed ice

Instructions
Bring sugar and water to a boil in a pot, whisking once or twice, and then lower to a simmer until the sugar has dissolved. The mixture should be clear, not cloudy. Mix in the vanilla extract. Let the mixture cool and then pour over crushed ice. Store the leftover vanilla syrup covered in the refrigerator for about two weeks.

Arroz con Leche (Rice Pudding)

Ingredients
1/2 cup white rice
1 1/2 cups water
1 cinnamon stick
1 strip lemon peel
4 cups milk
1 cup sugar (or less if you don't want it too sweet)
1/4 teaspoon salt
1 teaspoon Mexican vanilla extract
Ground cinnamon

Instructions
Rinse the rice in a saucepan and drain it. Add fresh measured water, lemon peel and cinnamon stick and cook on the stove over medium heat until it is soft. Add the milk, salt and sugar, and cook over low heat for approximately one hour or until it gets thick. Stir the rice mixture occasionally to prevent from sticking. Remove from heat, add Mexican vanilla extract and mix. Sprinkle with ground cinnamon. Serve the arroz con leche warm or cold.

Acknowledgments

Writing *Tea with Isabel* has been a dream come true. Countless thanks to my husband, John, for his patience and support of my dream even in the moments when it felt like it would never actually happen. He's the one who introduced this city girl to the beauty of Oklahoma and brought out the country girl in me. I'd like to thank my kids, Isabel and Brady, for being proud of me and cheering me on with statements like *You're my favorite author!* and *You're going to be famous someday!* I'd like to thank my parents, Esther and Terry Sneed, for providing me with so many opportunities that paved the way to this moment and my mom, specifically, for always wanting me to pursue my writing goals.

Thank you to Helena Danni, Missy Horner, Romina Pailey and Dimple Pradhan, my dear friends and the very first readers of *Tea with Isabel*. Their notes of encouragement and constructive criticism drove me forward. Thank you to Jennifer L. Hayes, author and friend, for endless publishing guidance over coffee, texts and emails. I truly couldn't have navigated it without her. I'm so thankful to my editor RJ Locksley for helping me fine-tune many moments, large and small, in the story. Thank you to Deranged Doctor Design for my beautiful book cover. They took my vision and made it even more beautiful than I had imagined it. Thank you to Marina and Jason

Anderson at Polgarus Studio for taking my manuscript and making it look like a book!

I'm grateful to my Skiatook friends for making our time there so fun and special the first time around. I'm so excited that we get to do it again!

Most of all, I send my utmost gratitude and love to my guardian angel, Maria Isabel Apodaca Diaz, my sweet Grandma Isabel, whose love and friendship inspired this all. Even though I probably won't share another cup of chamomile tea with her anytime soon, I know she's always with me.

Julie Sneed Womack is a Los Angeles native who lives in Oklahoma with her husband, two children and cat, Valentine. *Tea with Isabel* is her first novel.

You can find Julie on Instagram (juliesneedwomack) and Facebook (Julie Sneed Womack).